The Ghost of
Monsieur Scarron

by Janet Lewis

THE GHOST OF MONSIEUR SCARRON

THE TRIAL OF SOREN QVIST

GOODBYE, SON AND OTHER STORIES

AGAINST A DARKENING SKY

THE WIFE OF MARTIN GUERRE

THE INVASION

POEMS 1924-1944

POEMS OLD AND NEW, 1918-1978

The Ghost of
Monsieur Scarron

by Janet Lewis

SWALLOW PRESS
Chicago

*With the exception of
actual historical personages,
the characters are entirely
the product of the author's imagination
and have no relation to any person
in real life.*

First published 1959 by Doubleday and Company
Alan Swallow and Swallow Paperbooks edition 1965
Library of Congress Catalog Card Number: 65-16520
ISBN 0-8040-0133-2

Reprinted in 1981 by
OHIO UNIVERSITY PRESS

Swallow Press Books
are published by
OHIO UNIVERSITY PRESS
ATHENS, OHIO

I wish to thank once more
the John Simon Guggenheim Memorial Foundation
for a Fellowship granted me in 1950
which made it possible
for me to revisit France.

Janet Lewis

This book is for Dan

Chapter One

*J*EAN LARCHER, BOOKBINDER, was at supper with his wife and son. The day was Easter Sunday, which in that year of Grace, 1694, the fifty-first year of the reign of Louis XIV, fell upon the eleventh of April. They sat about a table spread with white linen in one of the four rooms which he rented in an old building in the rue des Lions, in Paris, a building which was old even then. The room served as kitchen, living room, and sales-room, and it was very small. It had a certain elegance, however, in spite of the stone floor and huge old-fashioned hearth, the elegance of the past generation. The proportions were good.

Beyond the window, still unshuttered, the spring twilight held the air, fading slowly from the cloudy sky. In the kitchen the air darkened imperceptibly, while the Larcher family broke their bread and ate their soup. Jean, laying down his spoon at last by his empty bowl, leaned back in his chair and observed with surprise that the faces of his companions, although near to him, had grown indistinct. The corners of the kitchen were dark. Even the glow of coals on the hearth had faded to a dull red. But through the barred, unshuttered window he could see the street still luminous in comparison with the interior and, being so reminded of the lengthening of the days, felt a sense of reassurance. Spring had returned; winter lay behind them.

It had been a winter more difficult than most, with deprivations and disasters far beyond the ordinary. The Seine had frozen, the cold had been so great. The city, provisioned largely by the river traffic, had been for days as if in a state of siege, and this extreme deprivation, coming at a time when there had already been for long a lack of grain and bread, had caused great suffering for the general populace. When the cold relaxed and the ice began to break up, boats and barges were flung together, or forced by the rush of water against the piers of the bridges, and so were broken and sunk. Jean Larcher had seen this havoc. The rue des Lions was near the river. The streets had been full of the homeless, the sick and the hungry, all winter long. There had been violence in the markets where bread was sold; and though the rich seemed to live as well as ever, marrying their daughters with feasting and display, business such as his own had not been good. The King economized, and it had become the fashion to economize, if not in weddings, at least in the collection of well-bound books. Nevertheless, the winter was over, and the Larcher family had survived.

They had even survived with a small profit. They had "made their Easter," as the saying went. They had been shriven, and had taken communion, and further, in honor of the day, they had eaten well. There was a white cloth on the table, and there had also been white bread, and a boiled fowl and leeks, and for dessert, walnuts and raisins.

He was a devout man, this Jean Larcher. He made his springtime penitence soberly and thoroughly, as he audited his business, and feeling that all was in order, he took his hour of contentment quietly, and still in the fear of God. Physically, he was well built, broad-shouldered, with a face more square than round, with blunt but pleasant features, his hair grey about the temples, a few deep lines about the mouth. He filled his chair completely. As for the small profit from the business, it was in the form of two pistoles, in one of the pockets of his long vest. He reassured himself from time to time of its existence with the tip of a forefinger.

His wife, seated across from him, had laid both arms on the table, and her head, in its white linen coif, drooped toward them. She clasped both elbows in her hands for warmth, and for warmth also leaned her bosom against her arms. The deep ruffles of her Sunday blouse fell over her hands like a muff, and all this whiteness of her cap and her sleeves showed much more clearly than her face. A fluted, fan-shaped ruffle on her cap tilted forward as her head drooped.

Jean did not need to see her face to know her features, the round chin, the heavy-lidded, heavily lashed grey eyes, the lips which had always showed, since he had first seen her, a delicate pink in the even pallor of her face. He knew this face by touch also, smooth, firm, and cool. The skin had never been marred by any illness.

The face of his son nearer to him, more nearly visible through the twilight, was more difficult to decipher. He knew the mask well enough, the features so like his own, the young, downy skin, the single pock mark between the smooth thick brows—he knew it was there although he could not see it. He knew it was there because he had sat for hours beside the bed of a little boy, a feverish little boy, holding his hands, trying to keep him from scratching himself. But of what went on now behind that mask, what itching ideas, urging the young man to actions of which his father could not approve, he had a less clear knowledge. The boy seemed half a stranger to him now. He could not place the change, but his awareness of it dated, most naturally, from the day of the boy's return from his apprenticeship. The boy worked now as a full-fledged journeyman in his father's shop, but without the contentment which his father had anticipated. Jean had apprenticed his son in one of the best shops in the city, not only that the boy might learn to become a better craftsman than his father, but that he might learn under a discipline more strict than his father in his affection would know how to enforce. He had not explained the second reason to the boy, nor had he spoken of it to his wife, being unwilling to acknowledge such a weakness.

The boy, intent upon cracking a nut, frowned slightly. His father saw the frown and was aware that it had nothing to do with the nut. It brought a return of his uneasiness regarding Nicolas, and to dispel this feeling which had plagued him too often of late, he drew a deep breath and said:

"Life is good."

He said it firmly, as if the firmness helped to make it true. His wife looked up and gave him a quick smile.

"Life is hard," she corrected him. "The soup was good."

"Well," he agreed, "the soup was not bad."

"I do no more than give you back your own saying, Jean. Life is hard. But I would not mind being praised for the soup."

"I praise you for the soup, Maman," said Nicolas.

Marianne smiled at her son, and Jean said nothing, thinking that he had praised her sufficiently over the years for her cooking, her thrift, and for other good qualities. It would have been a waste of words to tell her what she knew quite well. Instead, he drew from his vest pocket the two pistoles. A passer-by in the street stopped at the window as he still held them in his closed hand, and stood a moment to look at the display of books arranged there, to attract custom to the shop. When he turned away Jean waited still until it was quite clear that he did not mean to enter the shop. Then he laid his coins on the table, covering them still with his hand.

"What have you there?" said Marianne. "Silver?"

"Gold," said Jean, and lifted his hand. "Are you pleased?"

"Naturally, I am pleased."

"Take them," said Jean. "Sew them into the rouleau in blue silk."

"But the rent?" said Marianne.

"Paid."

"And the account for leather, at Pincourt?"

"Paid also." He permitted himself a slow smile. "It's a pleasure to be able to put away a little money now and then."

Nicolas remarked abruptly, "It would be a pleasure to spend it, too."

"Nicolas!" exclaimed his mother in quick reproach. His father, astonished, rebuffed, nevertheless said reasonably:

"But we do not need to spend it. Is there pleasure in spending money one does not need to spend?"

"Yes," said Nicolas defiantly, and then, to modify the bluntness of his defiance, and making matters worse, added, "At least I think there might be. I have never had the experience."

"It's an experience you can well do without," said Jean. "Another experience," he continued, "which you have not known is that of needing money when there was none to spend."

Nicolas stared sullenly into his empty bowl. Jean looked from his son to his wife, who bent her head again and considered her ruffles. No help from her. He swept a few scattered nutshells from the cloth with his broad hand, rather clumsily, and tossed them into his own bowl. The two golden pistoles lay on the white cloth, untouched. He studied them, trying to recapture the satisfaction with which he had laid them there. He said, with a change of tone:

"My little Colas, what would you do with two pistoles?"

"I would travel. You know that I would travel."

"You could not travel far on two pistoles."

"I could get to Lyon. Or to Rouen. Then I could work. I could learn a great deal."

"And what could you learn in Rouen that you could not learn better in Paris?"

Nicolas did not reply. He looked at his mother, who met his

glance, smiled slightly, and shook her head. Jean, excluded, knew that the discussion was over. There should not have been a discussion in the first place. He stretched out his hand toward the coins, thought better of it, folded his big linen napkin and laid it by his place, his motions deliberate, careful, slightly fumbling, and rose to his feet. The contentment was drained from his evening. He walked to the fireplace, groped in the semi-darkness for his tobacco and his pipe, dropped them into his coat pocket, and then, passing behind his wife, took his hat from its peg near the door. Hand on the latch, he looked back at the two people seated at the table. Neither of them had stirred, and neither looked up. They knew where he was going.

In the quiet which followed his departure some coals in the dying fire clicked as they broke and fell apart, and a small tongue of flame sprang into being and burned gaily for a minute or two. Marianne began slowly to clear the supper table. The two pistoles she slipped into the pocket of her skirt beneath her apron. When she had removed the cloth, and folded it, and put it away, she brought an iron candlestick furnished with a tallow dip and set it in the center of the table, and lighted it from the hearth with a paper spill. The flame on the hearth died away. The sooty yellow flame of the candle took over the duty of illuminating the room.

Marianne closed the wooden shutters and saw through the glass where her figure blocked the reflection of the flame that a wind was rising. Dust flew along the street, and bits of straw. The sky was darker. She thought, "It will rain soon." She returned to her place, leaning her arms upon the table, her bosom upon her arms, as before. To the handsome sullen young face beside her she said:

"You spoiled his pleasure."

"He is like the miser in the play," said Nicolas.

"No, the miser is unreasonable. Your father is not unreasonable. He knows"—she paused, searching for a phrase—"the reality of want."

"I believe you are on his side."

"No," she replied again. "But I am not happy at the thought of your leaving us."

"You agreed once that I should go."

"And you agreed to wait a little."

"Waiting is hard. When I was a prentice I thought how fine it would be to get my papers, and be a free man. Now I'm a journeyman, and I'm no more my own master than when I was bound out."

"A child is naturally bound to his father."

"I'm not a child."

"You agreed to let me choose my own time to speak to him."

"The money set me off," he said. "I forgot. Perhaps he is not like the miser in the play, but when he speaks of money it's as if there were nothing in the world so important."

"He has a great fear of illness, of age."

The young man interrupted her impatiently.

"I know, I know. He's always talking of disaster, of illness, of his old age. Illness in him is unimaginable. He's as solid as an oak."

"Nevertheless, he's no longer young."

"He's not old."

"He's the same age as the King. The King, I think, is old."

"The King is fifty-five," said Nicolas precisely.

The wick of the tallow dip had burned to a long black crook which drooped against the side of the candle and made the flame uneven. The boy took a knife from his pocket, unsheathed it, and with it straightened and trimmed the wick. His face, as he employed himself in this small business, lost much of its resentment. It became softer, so that his mother ventured:

"You might try to understand him."

"Why?" said the boy calmly. "He doesn't try to understand me."

"You don't know."

"Was he ever young?"

Marianne did not reply at once. She looked into the soft round yellow flame for a long moment, and then she said with a sigh, "He was a man grown when I first met him."

"He is older than you?" said the boy curiously.

"Much older. I was your age when I married."

"And yet you think me too young to leave Paris by myself."

"That's not the question," said Marianne. "He's looked forward a long time to having you with him in the shop. He's doing for you what his father could never do for him, and he thinks you don't appreciate it. That's what he can't understand."

Nicolas laid down his knife, having cleaned the blade with his fingers, and began to play with it, rolling it gently this way and that. It was a curious knife, meant for paring leather, with a very fine blade and a handle of ivory or bone, carved in the shape of a crocodile, the snout closed over the haft of the blade, tail curled under the belly, so that the entire animal became a good shape to fit the palm of the hand. His mother, observing, said:

"He gave you his best knife. He loves you."

"He prefers a curved blade," said the boy ungraciously.

"His father gave him nothing that I know of."

"Oh, I know he loves me," Nicolas said, but with exasperation. "I don't say he's not good to me. I only say I need to get away from here for a while, a very little while—six months at the most. I could learn so much, working in other places—perhaps not always about books. What do I know of the world? The Quartier St.-Jacques and the Quartier St.-Paul, the rue des Lions, this building."

He stopped abruptly, checked by the impossibility of explaining or even expressing the full force of the unrest within him. The wind had dropped for the moment. The street was quiet as the room in which they sat. Marianne, as if to change the subject, began:

"Do you remember when you were little, before you were

apprenticed, your brother, your grandparents, all of us living together?"

Nicolas wrinkled his forehead. "I remember a lot of funerals. Why?"

She shrugged her shoulders. "I thought it might help you understand." It was the wrong approach. She should have known better than to mention his childhood at this time. Besides, she thought, even if he were willing to remember, what memory could he have that would resemble his father's memories of those years, or mine?

The boy said, "I understand quite enough. He's taught me my trade—or had me taught. Now I'm to work with him—whether as apprentice or journeyman, it makes no difference, because he will always be the master."

"In the end, you will be the master. All his work is for you, in the end."

"I don't wish to hurry him to his end," said the young man.

He stood up, walked to the hearth and back, unable in the vehemence of his feeling to remain still. Finally he stopped beside his mother. "I see the good of his plan," he said, his voice controlled and reasonable. "I'm willing to help him. But don't you see, if I'm to do this, spend all the rest of my life here in the shop, I must first move around a little on my own? Why can't he give me his blessing and let me go? I would be home the sooner."

"He says he needs your help."

"Let him hire an assistant."

"He wants a son."

"If he had no son he'd hire an assistant, and that would be an end to it. But he's got a son. Oh yes. He's too stingy to hire an assistant." The words were spoken with such scorn and violence that Marianne was suddenly as angry as was the boy.

"You have no right to speak like that!" she cried, rising to her feet so that he could no longer look down on her.

"It seems I have no rights at all while I'm at home," he returned, as passionately. "Well, I can go. I don't need to ask his leave. In that case, I won't come back."

His face had flushed, and she saw that there were tears in his eyes, tears of rage, but still tears in the eyes of this great lad who was as tall if not as heavy as his father. Then all at once they were neither of them angry. "I'll find him an assistant. That should be easy. Then will he let me go?"

"I can ask him," said Marianne.

"All I want is six little months of liberty," said the boy, and then, unable, as earlier in the evening, to explain why he wanted that liberty so desperately, he turned away and, like his father, with almost the same gesture, took his hat from the peg on the wall. His mother made no attempt to stop him. When he opened the door upon the porte-cochère a great gust of fresh, damp air invaded the kitchen, but there was no sound of rain. Nicolas stood a moment in the shadow of the tunnel, long enough to turn up the collar of his coat. Then he thrust his hands into his pockets, and stepped into the street. He was out of sight at once. His mother, looking after him, thought, "It could be a relief to have him out of the shop if he's going to behave like this," and then, "It's extraordinary that he can look so like his father, and behave so unlike him."

Jean had gone to the Golden Harrow. It was an inn much favored by the country folk who brought their produce to sell in the city markets, either by road or by the river. It was situated at the corner of the great rue St.-Antoine in the shadow of the Bastille, and of the rue du Petit-Musc, which led from St.-Antoine to the river. Jean had but to turn from the rue des Lions into the rue du Petit-Musc to find himself almost at the Harrow.

He had his favorite seat there, in the tavern of the inn. He could buy a dram of brandy and, for a sol, rent a copy of one of the gazettes which printed, under *privilège du Roi*, something of the news from abroad and a great deal of news about the court. He could read, and smoke his pipe in peace. And although he paid more for the brandy than when he drank it at home, the renting of the gazette was an economy.

The sign of the Golden Harrow creaked in the rising wind as he passed under it and entered the courtyard. He thought, as his wife had thought, that the wind presaged a rain, and this would be a good thing. The country badly needed a thorough drenching. He found his place in the corner and ordered his brandy. The host brought him the *Gazette de France*, without his needing to call for it, and he opened the brochure at once, even before he filled his pipe. It was a way of signifying to his host and to those at the table beside him that he did not care to converse.

He read, as he drew his twist of tobacco from his pocket and cut a few slices, that in Hungary the Turks were massing an army of a hundred thousand men, without counting the Tartars. There had been disastrous floods in Austria. He ground the tobacco in the palm of his hand with his broad thumb, turned a page or so and read that in England new and severe taxes had been imposed upon salt, soap, and leather. The herring fishers had protested the tax on salt. He filled his pipe and lighted it, and when it was drawing smoothly, read further in the news from England that the Prince of Orange would soon be on his way to Flanders, and that the English were arming a fleet with extreme diligence. Furthermore, to man their fleet they were impressing boatmen from the Thames. The war, which had been quiescent during the winter, would soon begin again with force on all the fronts, in Flanders, in Catalonia, in Savoy, and on the seas. The English, he reflected, must be as tired of the war as were the French.

He could not imagine the King descending to the impressment of boatmen from the Seine. However, he remembered having heard talk of a conscription for the King's army from among the peasants, and in the cities, from the young artisans and the healthy unemployed. He thought of Nicolas wandering through the provinces without work; he would be among the first to be conscripted. Or if the boy were without funds, he might be tempted by the salary and the thought of adventure, and enlist of his own free will. Nicolas had no idea of what it meant to fight as a foot soldier. His father had little faith that he would be able to find continued employment outside Paris. The times were not fortunate. The sense of depression deepened in Jean. The taste of tobacco was no longer sweet. He reached for his brandy, which he usually made last him for the entire evening, and emptied the glass in one swallow.

He could not reconcile himself to the boy's attitude. The boy had no sense of reality. He did not know the meaning of danger nor even, as his father had tried to tell him at the supper table, the meaning of want.

He thought of his own childhood, now so remote. He had not talked of it, not even to Marianne during the first days of their marriage. It had been something to forget. His father had not been a bookbinder, nothing so fine. His father had been a cobbler, and an honest man. There was no good reason why he should not have made a decent living. People always need shoes. Perhaps it was as his mother said: his father's shop was two flights up from the street—the best he could manage—but who, she had asked, is going to climb two flights of stairs to have his shoes mended when he could have the same work done and for the same price without climbing any stairs at all?

When his father had died, his mother had spent all that she owned to bury him. She had sold all but the clothes off their backs. Then she had bound her son to a master in the rue St.-Jacques, to make certain that he should know a better trade than his father's. He thought sometimes that it was a mistake, that he would have been better as a cobbler than as a book-binder; but that had become his métier, and his son's métier, and they did not do too badly with it.

It had been a hard life, however, for a little boy. Since his mother could pay less than the usual fee for an apprentice, more was demanded of him and less was given to him than to the other boys in the shop. He slept in the attic under the slates on a straw pallet, winter and summer. He was always up before daylight to sweep out the shop. He saw his mother seldom. She did her best, poor soul. She worked long hours to keep him where he could be taught, and she starved herself. Then one day, not being very quick on her feet from fatigue, or perhaps dizzy from lack of food, she was struck down by the wheel of a cart and then caught under the wheel. Jean was taken to see her before they buried her. He had been less than ten years old.

In time he earned his papers and was employed by Bourdon as a journeyman. Bourdon, not then Beadle of the Corporation of Binders and Gilders as he was now, had proved to be a kind employer. Jean had worked, and when he had one sol that he did not need to spend, he had put it away. Eventually the day came when the parents of Marianne offered him a dowry for their daughter which was equal to the sum he needed to purchase his master's papers and open a shop of his own. It had been a great honor. In turn, he had done justly by them. He had lodged them in their old age; Marianne had nursed them through their last illness; and he had buried them with decency. It was a fair exchange, and such as they had wished for. As for Marianne, he had loved her, and still did. She had brought to the business not only her dowry, but her presence in the shop, a gay and easy way of meeting people in the salesroom, and she had given him the warmth of a home.

They had sorrows. Nicolas was the only child to survive, Nicolas who did not appreciate all that had been done for him. A deep sense of injury grew in Jean along with a great fear of what might befall his son away from home in these unsettled days. He should not need to forbid his son to leave him. His son should wish to stay. He called for another brandy and refilled his pipe.

Sometime later he caught his name spoken and looked up.

The voice of the hostess, nasal and high, carried easily above the rumble of the general conversation.

"I met your son the other day, Mademoiselle Larcher. I hardly recognized him. If he had not spoken first I would have passed him like a stranger. We see each other too seldom, for such near neighbors. As for me, I am a grandmother for the second time, did you not know? Ah, it's the children make us feel our age."

Jean saw his wife beyond the shoulder of the hostess in its bright green bodice, a small trim figure clothed in dull blue and brown, unwinding the shawl about her head and shoulders. Her attention was on the hostess.

"Is it raining yet?" continued the innwife.

"A few drops only."

"Likely it will blow over. There's a pity. The folk who come here talk of nothing but the need of rain. Your good man is in his corner."

Marianne looked toward Jean. He dropped his eyes and would not watch her as she approached. When she sat down beside him, her garments smelling of the evening air, he glanced at her briefly in recognition of her presence, and went on with his reading. He knew why she had come. He was resolved not to open the conversation.

He felt her lean against him slightly, and then withdraw. He saw her hand stretched forward to the table. He did not need to lift his eyes from his reading to see it. The hand flicked a few crumbs of tobacco with the thumb and forefinger, the thumb releasing the finger like a spring. The hand gathered the crumbs together and pressed them into a pill, and let it fall, then took possession of his glass of brandy, not lifting it from the table, but turning it by its stem, first clockwise, then counterclockwise. At last the hand withdrew from his range of vision, and presently his wife murmured:

"You heard what she said? How they change!"

Larcher turned a page and pressed down the central fold.

The hum of voices surrounded them. They could not have been more private in their own kitchen. The privacy left him without protection from her. Then she said, as he had half expected her to:

"Could we afford an assistant for a few months?"

"You should know," he answered without looking up. "You keep the books."

"I say we could."

"I should not like it." He had employed an assistant before, on more than one occasion, and things had never gone well. She should remember that. She said:

"I'm afraid to have him go without your consent." He heard the fear in her voice, although she tried to speak lightly, and it echoed the fear which he himself had felt. However, he answered without sympathy.

"He would go?"

"Not——" She hesitated. "Not with a plan. He would just suddenly find himself on the road. And then he would be afraid to come back. Or too proud."

"In that case, he would be a fool."

"Yes. But that would not prevent him from going."

She had said what she had come to say. He wished she would leave him now. He needed to think, and he could not think freely while she sat beside him, no matter how quiet she kept. And she kept very quiet for several minutes. Then she said, with the emphasis on her third word:

"Would you consider hiring an assistant?"

"I would consider," he said, repeating the emphasis, but he knew he was defeated.

Marianne stood up. Then she stooped quickly, and lifted Jean's thimbleful of brandy, and finished it. He saw the hand as she set down the glass precisely; he had never once lifted his eyes to her face during the conversation. As she left him, he watched her, still without lifting his head, from under his lowered brows. Her step was springy, and the motion of her waist, as she threaded her way between the crowded tables, was supple and quick.

He stayed on alone long after his usual hour for quitting the Harrow. When he left the inn he was still filled with gloom. He still considered his son's choice of action imprudent, irresponsible, and his attitude ungrateful. He felt betrayed also by his wife. However, his gloom was infused with tenderness for his son and for his wife. He thought that if any one of the three of them was to be made unhappy by the boy's unreasonable desire it might as well be himself. It had best be himself, in fact, for was he not the father?

The wind had fallen. He trudged the familiar way in darkness. It was past curfew. Not a gleam of light showed through any shutter. Only the street light, hanging above the intersection of the rue des Lions and the rue du Petit-Musc, was haloed with mist. Jean walked with his head bowed, his hands in the pockets of his long-skirted coat, and heard only the beat of his shoes upon the cobbles. The mist intruded coldly beneath the brim of his hat, beneath the collar of his coat.

The great doors to the porte-cochère were closed. He halted to unlock them and lock them again, and went on into the courtyard of the building where he rented two rooms on the ground floor for kitchen and workroom, and two on the first floor directly above them. Feeling very tired, very solitary, he mounted the stairway, his hand upon the cold narrow iron of the railing. He knew the slow lift and curve of the steps by heart. At the first landing there was another door to be unlocked. Nicolas slept here, and here were stored materials for the shop. The windows, from which by daylight one could look down into the court, were duly closed and shuttered. The room was as dark as the inside of his pocket. He passed through the room to the door to his own bedroom, where he paused, his hand on the latch, and listened. He thought he heard a quiet breathing. He waited until a deeper breath assured him that he did not imagine what he heard. Nicolas was at home this night, he thanked God, and went on into the next room.

He removed his shoes and his cloth stockings, and hung his coat, damp with the river fog, on the back of a chair. The window of this room, which, like that of the kitchen below, opened upon the street, was shuttered also. He was in complete darkness, but he did not need to see. He knew where everything stood and exactly how it looked. Beneath his feet were the smooth uncarpeted boards of the parquet, laid in a herringbone pattern, for the house had been built, and well built, in the lifetime of the last generation. In three steps he could reach the bed. The curtains were of serge, once a deep red, now faded on the outer folds to the color of dried blood. Across from the bed was a fireplace with a high mantel, the opening closed now by a neatly painted wooden cover. Beside the fireplace was an oak chest with a good stout lock, covered with a piece of tapestry, faded like verdigris, and above the chest, encircling a white porcelain shell filled with holy water, was a rosary of dark beads, each as big as a rose haw. Above the shell was a sprig of fresh green, blessed a week ago that day and fastened there by his own hand. In the chest was his money, sewn into rolls in scraps of silk, of old brocade, of heavy white canvas. The key to this chest he himself carried. All this was security, for this life and for the life beyond. The porcelain shell and the rosary stood between him and the pangs of hell, and so did the square scapular which his fingers touched as he changed his shirt for his night-shirt; but the golden pistoles, the écus, even the humble livres, stood between him and the lazarhouse. He tied his nightcap under his chin, parted the serge curtains, and climbed into bed, stretching himself cautiously between the cold rough linen sheets, beneath the heavy woolen covers, and turned his head upon his pillow toward that of his wife.

Marianne was there; he heard her breathing, measured and light, as if she were asleep. If she slept he would not waken her, but he hoped that she was still awake. He lay for a while, staring into the darkness, waiting for some motion from his wife, but she did not stir. By and by he turned on his side and reached a hand carefully toward her head. He found her cap, crisp with starch. He moved his hand gently down to her face and encircled it, gently, and then ran his forefinger beneath her chin, between the moist, smooth skin and the harsh twist of the bonnet strings. If she felt the caress, she gave no sign. He withdrew his hand regretfully, and turned away to sleep. His last thought, as consciousness faded, was of the two pistoles which he had laid on the supper table, and he felt a rush of alarm. What had become of them? Then he remembered that Marianne would doubtless have taken charge of them, and he relaxed, and fell asleep.

Chapter Two

THAT SAME EVENING a little before sundown Paul
Damas came upon the great Place des Victoires. He had not
been searching for it; he had, in fact, been lost. But, working his
way through a tangle of narrow and evil-smelling little streets,
he emerged suddenly upon the clarity and spacious symmetry
of the Place, and knew at once where he was. He had heard of
the Place des Victoires even in Auxerre, from which he had
lately come, and for the first time, to Paris.

There stood the great hôtels, the mansions of the rich or of
the noble, encircling with their identical and elegant façades
the Place itself, and there in the center of the Place stood the
reason for its existence, the statue of the King and of his Winged
Victory. The two figures surmounted a high pedestal of white
marble veined with blue. They were life size, and they were
covered with gold from top to toe. The Victory, poised behind
the King's shoulder, held over his head a golden laurel wreath.
A flight of swallows veered about them, as Paul stared, and
then wheeled away.

The Place was busy with early evening traffic; it was holiday traffic. There were no market carts, but there were plenty of peddlers of food and drink, and hawkers of holiday trifles. A few horsemen, a few coaches, some with six horses, moved right or left about the statue as they pleased. The level sunlight shone on bright harness, on the coach windows, the arms emblazoned on the carriage doors, and on the gilded statue. A woman, wrapped in old shawls, with an apron tied over the wrappings, with a wicker tray held level before her by a sling about her neck, stopped before Paul, inquiring in the sharp voice which he had already learned to recognize as the voice of the Parisian, "Buy a ribbon for your sweetheart?" Her tray was loaded with loveknots and laces, as bright as a trayful of flowers. Her shrewd eyes swept his face, and she moved on without waiting for an answer. He was not a prospect.

The sun withdrew behind a mass of dove-colored clouds, leaving the edges golden. A breeze sprang up, as if evoked by the wheeling of the swallows, a sweet breeze, smelling of rain. Paul drew a deep breath to clear his lungs of the stench of the streets through which he had passed, and eased in a habitual gesture the pressure of the strap upon his shoulder, the strap which held the leather sack in which he carried everything he owned.

He was a bookbinder. In his pouch were the tools of his trade, such tools as a man could carry, and a clean shirt, and a little money—a very little money. He avoided, for the moment, the thought of how little, and regaled himself with the famous spectacle before him.

He had come to Paris with no preparation, leaving Auxerre suddenly one morning, between bed and breakfast, under pressure of circumstances which he was willing to forget for the moment, even more willing than he was to forget his precarious financial situation. He had seduced—and far too easily, he thought, when he had time to reconsider the whole adventure— he had seduced the wife of his employer, and she, for reasons of her own, after a few weeks of pleasure, had betrayed him to his master. Upon consideration he was convinced that she had planned it all from the beginning. It was a great wound to his vanity. On the other hand, it freed him, largely, from the guilt of having betrayed a man who had been, in the long run, kind to him, and this seemed to him, in his reaction against the woman's action, the more serious defection. She had seduced him. The conclusion permitted him to enjoy the sunny days, as he journeyed by water coach to Paris, the gentle landscape touched with fresh green, the blue horizon pricked here and there by small dark spires like thorns, the scent of water; and it had not prevented him from exchanging kisses with a pretty country girl, with a baby in her arms, who was coming to the city to be a wet-nurse. The landscape slid by, hour after hour, day after day, to the sound of water rippling under the barge, as the barge floated with the current, and Paul Damas told himself that he had always wanted to come to Paris, that he possessed talent as a craftsman which had not been fully appreciated in the provinces, and that he would do better for himself in Paris than he had ever done in Auxerre. Things had happened for the best.

However, when he began to look for work up and down the rue St.-Jacques, which was the stronghold of the book trade, he found it not easy to become appreciated in Paris. For one thing, he brought with him no letter of recommendation from his master. His other papers were in order, but there were plenty of journeymen trained in the rue St.-Jacques to fill the positions which the bad times left open. Moreover, after his first twenty-four hours in the city he was ill of a flux of the bowels. No one had told him not to drink the river water, or indeed that he had any choice in the matter. Most of the fountains of the city were supplied by the river. The Parisians who had not died in infancy of drinking it had built up an immunity to it.

He had a proper provincial fear of being robbed or gulled, and, where women were concerned, of being infected. The street corners were placarded with advertisements for venereal cures; a man might be cured without any necessity of being confined to his chambers. Each cure was warranted to be inexpensive, easy, and certain, and each, far from reassuring Damas, made him resolve to be more cautious. The fear of being questioned too closely on the circumstances of his leaving his former employment made him present himself awkwardly. For these reasons he struck up no chance acquaintanceships and entered into few chance conversations. The nearest he had come to beginning a friendship was to have a longish talk with a young printer who, because he came from Lyon, seemed almost a compatriot. The mistress of the shop was out, and the printer, a kindly fellow with a phenomenally gaunt and ugly face, happy to meet a young man from Auxerre, stopped his work and gave to Paul Damas the sort of advice which one stranger in town can give another. For the rest, Paul had kept to himself, and on this holiday when the streets were full of people rejoicing in the end of Lent, he felt his loneliness.

He watched the woman with the trayful of laces and love-knots disappear into the crowd, and from the crowd, where she disappeared, he saw emerge an old man carrying a ladder. He was not a workman. He wore a perruque and a plumed hat, and his coat was elaborately decorated with lace-braid and buttons. It was the incongruity of this lean and shaky figure, bending to balance the weight of the ladder, and yet proceeding with a decorum as sober as if he were performing a religious rite, that caught Paul's attention. Then, idly, he followed the old man with his eyes, wondering where he was going.

The old man set down his ladder before a marble column at the edge of the Place. It was a triple column, hung with bronze medallions and surmounted by a lantern. The old man gave his ladder a shake to test its steadiness, and then climbed it slowly. He was, Paul noted, less steady on his legs than was his ladder. He reached the top safely, however, and, having opened the lantern, drew out the guttered stubs of candles, which he dropped in a pocket of his coat. He replaced them with fresh candles, which he lighted, and then, closing the lantern with infinite precaution, prepared to descend. No one paid any attention to him. The lantern bloomed with a soft yellow light, and the old man, having reached the pavement safely, folded his ladder and disappeared into the crowd.

There were, Paul now observed, four such lanterns, spaced widely about the Place; the other three were still unlighted. When they should all be lit the statue of the King would be illuminated from all sides. When the windows of the great hôtels should be illuminated also, there would be a wreath of lights about the whole Place. This would be splendor of a fine sort, he considered, and, his interest in the statue being enhanced by this preliminary lighting up, like the lighting up of candles before a play, he stepped out into the shifting traffic and presently found himself before the grille which surrounded the pedestal. Within the six-foot grille the marble pavement lay smooth and shining; without, the stone paving was stained with ordure of every sort, littered with trash and torn papers, which the wind lifted and flung against the grille, where they clung for a space and then dropped, as the wind dropped. Around the grille was a line of buffer stones which kept away the wheeled traffic, so that Damas found himself in a zone of safety; he could contemplate the statue without fear of being struck down. No one else had approached the statue. He had the very center of the Place des Victoires to himself, a private audience with the golden King.

A slightly built young man in a snuff-colored suit, he lifted his chin and leaned back a little to see the figures so far above his head. His coat was unbuttoned because he had grown warm during his walk. It let show a rust-colored vest as long as his coat. He wore no wig, and no feathers on his brown felt hat. His thumb, under the strap of his bag, eased the pressure on his shoulder. Above the clatter of the traffic which now enclosed him on all sides he heard the twittering of swallows. A band swept once again around the statue and away. The dove-colored clouds which he saw now as a background for the statue had grown darker and were moving toward the west. The dual motion of the clouds and the birds made the statue seem to move also.

The King was portrayed as a young man, no older, possibly, than the young artisan who looked up to him. He wore his coronation robes; his gaze was level and his air serene, untroubled by the presence of the Victory at his shoulder. But this was not all. There were other figures which were a part of the monument besides those of the King and his Victory. At the corners of the pedestal, on the marble pavement, crouched four figures in bronze, larger than life, chained, and bowed in attitudes of submission and grief. They made of the entire work a pyramid of which they were the base and the golden laurel wreath the apex.

There was an inscription incised and gilded in the marble. There were also plaques and medallions of bronze in low-relief, and a multitude of details which Damas did not understand but which interested him. The whole monument was an extravagant exercise of the imagination on the part of the sculptor, as well as a folly of extravagance on the part of the donor. It would be something extraordinary to talk of when he returned to Auxerre.

But he knew that he would never return to Auxerre. He would starve first. The decision brought him back coldly to an awareness of his own predicament, and although he continued to stare at the monument, his attention deserted it completely. He lost track of time in his unhappy revery. He was startled when a voice said in his ear:

"Well, you admire it?"

Dusk had settled upon the Place. The light by which Paul saw the statue now came chiefly from the four lanterns on the marble columns. He turned, and found by his elbow the old man of the lanterns. The old man had disposed of his ladder. He stood with his hands sunk in his pockets, his chin tucked into the collar of his coat, his head tilted sideways, peering from beneath the shadow of his plumed hat like a bright-eyed old bird. He was a figure both sad and ridiculous. Paul was impressed again by the singularity of his appearance. He felt sorry for the old man, and he welcomed a distraction from his own thoughts. He answered very pleasantly:

"Why not? It is a noble piece of work."

"As you say," returned the old man with a sigh. "A noble piece of work and a noble subject. And yet, my friend, of all the people in the Place tonight, you and I are the only ones who have eyes for it."

He spoke as if they had been long acquainted and had long shared a common loyalty and a common grief. Paul's admiration had been less than the old man assumed, but the young man saw no reason for saying so. He observed that though the coat the old man wore had once been splendid it had been much abused by the passing seasons. His wig was of a fashion ten years old. The black curls lay harshly against his faded skin, pointedly artificial against the greyed stubble of his cheeks. The wig was not even set straight on his head, but let show a few strands of his grey hair above one temple. His hat also had seen better days, its buckle tarnished, its plume ragged, its style antique as the wig; yet with all this, the costume still showed some magnificence. It was not haphazard. It was a livery which had been designed by someone with an eye for splendor to indicate the splendor of the unknown patron or employer.

The old man bore the scrutiny of the young man without uneasiness, finding nothing but sympathy in it. He asked with deference, but without servility:

"You are perhaps a student of the arts? Or a scholar?"

"I am a bookbinder," said Paul Damas.

"Then you can doubtless read," said the old man. "You are a stranger in Paris?" Paul acknowledged the fact. "You are

French, and from Vézelay, perhaps, or nearby? I hear it in your voice. But of course there are no foreigners in Paris of late years, not since the war. There was a time when one might find men of all nations standing before this statue. To whom I was sometimes useful. I should consider it a kindness, since you can read, if you would read the inscription for me."

Paul, flattered, turned toward the pedestal. The light was clear enough upon the gilded lettering. He read obligingly:

" '*Viro Immortali*,' that is to say, 'To the Immortal Man.' "

"Yes, yes, to the Immortal Man," repeated the old stranger, taking Paul by the elbow and moving a little closer. "Pray, go on."

" 'Louis the Great,' " continued Paul. " 'The Father and Leader of his Army. The Ever Fortunate.' " The old man did not interrupt again, but gave a little squeeze to the young man's elbow as he read forth each line. " 'For a Perpetual Memory,' " said Paul, completing the translation. The old man gave a sigh of satisfaction.

"That's it," he said, releasing the elbow and giving Paul a pat of commendation on the shoulder. "What a fine inscription! And I know that you have read it correctly, because it is all done into French on the other side. Not that I can read that, myself, either, but I have it all by heart. Nevertheless it sounds better in Latin, do you not agree? A greater sonority. More grandeur. I never tire of hearing it. And you have a fine voice for the Latin, a well-modulated voice, my friend. Indeed, I think you may call yourself a scholar. Now the scenes in bas-relief, you have observed them? You recognize them? There are four of them, one on each side of the pedestal, well worth noting. There is the crossing of the Rhine—that needs no explanation. There is likewise the conquest of Franche-Comté . . . the triumph we had over the Spanish . . . and then the signing of the famous treaty at Nimeguen. All marvelously executed. You see that the King is standing on a three-headed dog? That Cerberus is the Triple Alliance. The King—or shall we say Monsieur Desjardins—has dealt properly with the Alliance. The statue is by Monsieur Desjardins, as you may know, cast in his atelier here in Paris."

He paused for breath, and Paul prompted him:

"The slaves—what do they represent?"

"Ah, the chained captives. They are nameless, but every Frenchman, and we are French, you and I, must recognize them without difficulty. They are of course the nations which bowed to the King's power in the last war—Austria, Prussia, Spain, Holland. Taken all together, this monument, is it not fine indeed?"

"Very fine," said Paul. He had an uneasy feeling that the old man would expect a few coins in return for all this information, and that he himself should not be accepting what he had no intention of paying for—he was asking for a moment of embarrassment—but such a glow had kindled in the old man's face that it would have been uncharitable not to listen.

"I could tell you more," said the old man, "if you have the time to spare. I could tell you the significance of the bronze medallions on the columns which support the lanterns, and perhaps, since you are newly come to Paris, that would not bore you." He lifted his chin, a narrow chin upon a stringy neck, both chin and neck coated with grizzled stubble, and gestured with his head toward the surrounding crowd. "They come here to amuse themselves, but who comes now to observe the King, their host? Only a stranger like yourself, and an old man, like me. They abuse the Place with gambling and thieving and singing of improper songs, and they ignore the King. Yet I was here on the day when incense burned before the monument, the very same incense they burn in the churches to Our Lady and to Her Son"—he crossed himself rapidly—"burned before the King's statue as if he were a god, which indeed, in a measure, he is. And the King himself, my friend, I saw him seated over there, on a little platform under a canopy, in an armchair as if he were at home, with his big plumed hat on his head, and his leg thrust out before him, so. Nothing of all this was built then." He swept an arm toward the enclosing façades. "They had not much more than pulled down the old hôtels, the Hôtel d'Eméré, the Hôtel de la Senecterre. They had set up, mind you, where the new hôtels had not yet been built, to make the circle complete, façades of canvas painted to look like the finished buildings. Like a casket for a jewel, and the jewel, ah, that was the statue, new as the newest louis d'or."

He broke off with a sharp little laugh. "That is a joke, my friend, a golden Louis. And there were the lanterns. I had not the honor to light them on that day, eight years ago, but ever since, lacking one month, I have lighted them every night." He again took Paul by the elbow. "Do you know who pays for all the candles?" he demanded. "The Marquis de la Feuillade, who paid for the statue also. He is dead now these three years, and he still pays. But it is I, my friend, who watch over them, never to let one gutter, but that I see it replaced. Yes, I replace them with my own hands. These candles burn all night, did you know that? From sunset to sunrise, the four lanterns burn. I light them, and the Marquis pays the bill."

Against his shoulder Paul felt the old man tremble with cold or with pride. His hand tightened on Paul's elbow. He went on:

"I cannot read the inscription, true, but you can be sure I know what it means because I was here on that day, the day of the dedication. On that day—music, incense, a great procession, fireworks before the Hôtel de Ville, and dancing in every street. Don't you find it a magnificent idea, never to leave the image of the King in darkness? The Sun King. The Marquis said that the Roi Soleil must never be left in darkness, and everyone applauded. Now they make jokes about it, and the lackeys of the Great who live here tell me that their masters will have the light put out, because they draw the riffraff of the city, who make too much noise under the windows of the Great. Ah, I resent all this riffraff as much as they do. Why does not

Monsieur de La Reynie, who is so powerful, who is the King's own man, sweep them from the Place, as he has his men sweep the rest of the trash, hah, the droppings of the horses and the other rubbish? What are they? Are they any better? They tell me that I shall soon be out of a job. Well . . . So . . . I can suffer for myself, that is my affair, but must I also weep because of the insult to the King?"

His indignation had given strength to his voice. He paused abruptly, overcome by the contemplation of such an outrage, and when he spoke again his voice had changed.

"Do you think," he said anxiously, "that they could do such a thing? It is written plainly in the last will and testament of the Marquis that the candles shall burn every night, and that a fixed sum shall be paid for the tending of them. There is law in France still, is there not? They cannot change the will of the Marquis, can they?"

Paul knew nothing of law, but he replied out of pity that once the will had been accepted by the Parlement it surely could not be broken, and since Paul could read both Latin and French, the old man believed him. He relaxed his grip on Paul's elbow, but his hand remained there, in friendship. In response to this easy weight upon his arm, Paul thanked the old man for his discourse, adding that he felt very fortunate to have met a man who had actually been present at the dedication.

"You are very kind," said the lantern lighter gently. "Very kind. It was this time of year, a cold spring day, like this, but the sun shone, the statue glittered; the gold and jewels in the costumes of those who took part in the ceremonies would have dazzled you." His voice trailed into silence, nostalgic and sad. Then with an antique courtesy he said, "But I detain you," and lifted his hand from Paul's arm.

The moment for parting had come and there had been no mention of a fee. The old man, retreating a step or two, waited to be abandoned.

"You don't detain me," said Paul. "I'm on my way nowhere."

"Ah," said the old man, "a young fellow like you—you should be on your way to a good supper, a pretty friend, and a warm bed. As for me, my day's work is all at night. It is breakfast time for me now, although I have not breakfasted."

He smiled faintly. He was not asking alms; his dignity was intact. But Paul, out of his loneliness, and in gratitude for confidences offered in friendship, said:

"Let me buy you a breakfast."

He spoke on impulse, without taking thought for the state of his finances. Once he had spoken, he made a rapid calculation; he was certain that he had at least enough cash to afford the old man a hot drink of some sort. The wind blew more strongly, bringing with it a few drops of rain, and the old man turned up the collar of his coat. He said:

"You are generous. But it's not necessary. Not necessary at all."

"It would be my pleasure," said Paul.

The old man hesitated the fraction of a moment longer, and then, with no loss of dignity, but with the promptness of a cat pouncing upon a mouse, replied:

"Since you urge me, sir, I accept."

There was a vendor of hot coffee not far off. Paul could see him moving slowly through the crowd, with his urn on his shoulder and cups hanging from hooks upon his belt. Paul made a motion to attract his attention, but the old man said, "No, not coffee."

"Soup, then?"

"No, nothing here. Whatever you buy on the street is bound to be infected. For me, it's no matter, but for you, who are unaccustomed to the city, it would make you ill. Come with me."

He seized Paul by the hand and darted into the crowd.

No one seemed to notice the few scattering drops. They had all but ceased entirely when Paul and the old man reached the edge of the Place. The shower was blowing over. Then

Paul heard a low roll of thunder which seemed to issue from the very street which they were about to enter. People were running from the street into the Place. Paul felt a final tug upon his hand as the old man turned aside with the fugitives from the street. Then the old man's hand slipped from his; he lost sight of his friend, and, standing stupidly in the middle of the street, he saw bearing down upon him two lackeys with torches. Directly behind these link-bearers came the first two horses of a coach and six. He leaped aside, and with great luck managed to reach the corner of the building which fronted on the Place, and, climbing on the stone which rounded and protected the sharp angle of the building, managed to cling there like a monkey while the rest of the horses and the coach itself passed by him. Even so, the coach swung so close to him that the high rear wheel, rising out of the gutter, sprayed him with mire upon cheek and shoulder.

He descended from his perch, his knees shaking, and wiped his cheek on the sleeve of his coat. He straightened his hat, adjusted the strap of his bag upon his shoulder, and looked about him for the old man. The pedestrians who had been cleared from the street so thoroughly returned to it, unconcerned, as if they had not all just escaped from sudden death, and Paul felt a touch upon his elbow.

"This way," said the voice of the old man.

They went on. The way became darker, the number of passers-by diminished. Paul found himself treading on broken glass. The voice of the old man said in his ear, cautiously but with indignation:

"The dirty beasts! They throw rocks at the street lanterns so that they may rob in the dark. Every street in this quarter should be called Vide-Gousset. Keep your hand on your bag when you're in this quarter."

The wind blew; the shop signs swung and screeched overhead. The rain had ceased, but the wind was cold. Paul lost sense of direction. He did not know what ways they took or where they were when the old man stopped and pushed open a door. He had been so long in the darkness that, entering the warm, close room, he was half blinded by the glare of half a dozen tallow dips.

The warmth was most welcome. He was presently seated across from the old man at a long table, bare of any cloth, but so rubbed and polished by use that each individual flame had its wavering reflection on the wood. It was a humble sort of tavern, crowded and cheerful, the air thick with smoke and steam; Paul, looking down the table, saw the faces of his fellow diners through a golden haze. He felt unaccountably warmed and reassured. His neighbor gave him a look of appraisal, neither friendly nor unfriendly, and went on eating his soup. A bowl was set before Paul, and another before the old man, the soup of the day. They were not asked what they would have. The servant, young and thin but with a firm high bosom, stooped to serve the old man and stayed a moment to speak with him. Where had he been all this time? Had he been ill?

"Never ill," said the old man, taking up his spoon with trembling fingers.

Paul's neighbor said between mouthfuls, "Nothing ails him that food won't cure."

The girl smiled, looking at Paul, and Paul, returning the look, forgot to smile, being fatigued, but continued to look, finding her charming, until she gave a little shrug and moved away.

The soup was wholesome, very hot and thick. There was meat in it. This was the first time since he had come to Paris that Paul had sat down to a meal under a roof. The soup and the enclosing sense of comfort were invigorating. He began to feel less of a lost cat, and congratulated himself upon his extravagance. The old man also looked more brisk. He laid down his spoon and with a new assurance called for bread.

"No bread tonight, Father Lanterns," said the young servant.

"My friend makes me his guest," said the old man, gesturing toward Paul.

"Still, no bread," said the girl. "We had bread at noon, but it's gone."

"Who asks for bread in Paris?" said a deep voice behind Paul. "He must be a fool, or a stranger."

"Certainly he is a stranger," said the old man. "For that, he should receive a better welcome. I know my credit is a little threadbare, but my friend will pay cash."

"It's not a question of your credit, Father Lanterns. It's that there's no more bread."

"No matter," said Paul to the old man. "Who needs bread when the soup is good?"

"Who indeed?" said the resonant voice behind him. "We must remember, Father Lanterns, that man does not live by bread alone." The voice then rose in song. It was husky, but remarkably rich and flexible. The air was familiar to Paul, but the words were new. The singer brought them out with relish.

> *"White bread's too dear to eat;*
> *Good wine is seldom found:*
> *Hard cash is in retreat,*
> *Safe-buried underground.*
>
> *"It's costly still to die—*
> *We always pay the priest.*
> *Of women—we've a good supply,*
> *But that's what we need least."*

The old man continued to eat his soup in profound disapproval of the performance. The song ended in a roar of laughter and applause, and shouts for another. Paul joined in the applause. The old man shot him a reproachful glance. The singer hushed the uproar with three raps of his spoon upon the table, and

began again. When he reached the chorus, nearly everyone
in the room joined him.

> *"The Maintenon, that pious whore,*
> *Still sends our Louis forth to war.*
>
> *"She regulates His Majesty*
> *And keeps us all in poverty.*
>
> *"Diradon and diradon,*
> *That famous whore, the Maintenon."*

"La Maintenon," cried a voice as the song ended, "I heaved a
rock at her coach myself one day."

"You dream. She never comes to Paris. She fears Paris."

"Ah, but it was her coach."

"Then it was empty."

"She was in it, believe me. The blinds were drawn."

"All this singing," said the young servant brightly, "deserves
wine. Who will have wine? Father Lanterns, will you have wine
tonight?"

The old man looked up from his bowl at that, and answered
reproachfully, "He is irreligious and you encourage him." There
was a single laugh followed by a general amused murmur. The
old man was not to be silenced so easily. "He becomes ever
more free with his tongue, this peddler of ballads, and so do
his friends. One of these days he will bring the police down
upon the house, and you will regret it. On that day you will
not consider me so silly."

"No one calls you silly," said the girl. "As for the police—
these are all friends."

"Not silly," said the Ballad Singer. "No, just the least trifle
crazy. He is unreasonable, my friends. He wants to do me out
of my profession. How shall I live if I do not sing? Do I protest
his lanterns? There is something silly for you, if you like, his

lanterns. This old man thinks that four lanterns are as good as the sun."

"Let him follow an honest trade," said the old man firmly. "Let him practice an honest trade and cease to be irreligious, and I will say nothing more against him, although he insults me personally, as well as the King, and a great lady who deserves respect."

"Irreligious," said the Ballad Singer, and demanded of the room at large, "I am irreligious with a little song? I have not yet begun to be—as he calls it—irreligious." He did not raise his voice, but it rumbled about the room; it rolled softly beneath the tables and penetrated even to the corners. Paul twisted about for a look at this man who spoke so freely and sang so well.

Hatless, wigless, thick-set, ill-shaven, his skull surrounded by uncombed white hair as thick and wiry as a horse's mane, both fists set squarely on the table before him, he met Paul's look with open mirth, and Paul returned his look with horror because of the appalling disfiguration which confronted him. One eye was completely obliterated by a red and running sore which drew the upper part of the cheek as with a puckering string.

"Four lanterns for the sun," repeated the Ballad Singer, fixing Paul with his good eye. "It is time to change the title. The sun does not shine as brightly as of old. Le Roi Soleil becomes le Roi à Quatre Lanternes." His voice changed. His manner became cajoling. "So the King's wars keep us in poverty? My songs keep us in good humor. We must have merriment in order to bear our misery. I keep us gay. Therefore I am a great patriot." He looked about him for confirmation, his wide mouth stretched in a smile. No one spoke. He banged his pewter mug upon the table. His face changed again, all the mirth draining from it, leaving only one fine spark in his good eye. His voice darkened; it became like velvet, like the tongue of a dog, and then, changing again, like the tongue of a cat, rasping and rough. He intoned like a priest before the altar, and Paul, listening, felt the chills run up and down his back.

"Our father who art at Marly," said the Ballad Singer, "thy name is no longer glorious. Thy reign is towards its end. Thy will is no longer done, neither on earth nor on the sea. We do not ask this day our daily bread, but forgive us our offenses, as thou forgivest the offenses of thy great generals. And lead us not into revolt, but deliver us from evil. Amen."

The room remained quiet. Not a spoon clinked, no one coughed, nor stirred a foot, but in the quiet, as the Ballad Singer ended his *paternoster*, could be heard a long, shuddering, indrawn breath as the old man began to weep. A voice in a far corner said, "Amen." Then the voice of the young servant cut in sharply.

"You are unkind. He's an old man—he does you no harm."

"He's an old relic," said the Ballad Singer in his natural voice. "Let him come out of the past. Let him cease to converse with ghosts—only excepting the ghost of Monsieur Scarron." He gave a great laugh, and was joined by a number of people who seemed to be in on the secret. The lantern lighter had produced a not very clean handkerchief and was wiping his eyes and his nose with dignity.

"Monsieur Scarron?" said the girl. "And who, pray, was he?"

"Illiterate daughter of the people," said the Ballad Singer, "he was one of us. In spite of his noble kinfolk, one of us. A bum. A dead-broke. A Frondeur, and a torment to the late Cardinal. How time passes! Here you are, a creature old enough for love, and yet too young to know the meaning of a Mazarinade! You make me feel my years. And I have made you blush! A triumph! A delight!"

"But Monsieur Scarron?" persisted the girl, embarrassed.

"Ah yes. Scarron. A poor devil of a cripple, bent like the letter Z. A great wit, already, it seems, forgotten. The author of the *Roman Comique*, and of comedies from which Molière learned his trade. And the husband, while he lived, of her who is the Widow Scarron, now that he is dead."

"Oh, now I know," said the girl, and sang a scrap of song: "*La Veuve Scarron, la Sainte Maintenon.*" Then she realized that she too was bedeviling the old man, and broke off.

"On second thought," said the Ballad Singer, "I do not think that the ghost of Monsieur Scarron would be fit company for Father Lanterns. The King could not approve of him, and therefore neither would Father Lanterns."

The old man made no attempt to reply to all this. To do so would have been like trying to halt a wave from mid-ocean by spitting at it. He sat with head bowed, and the girl said to the Ballad Singer, with pity, "Can't you let him be now? You've had your fun."

"And very good fun," said the Ballad Singer genially. "I will buy him a glass of wine, him and his young friend here."

"I will not drink his wine," said the old man, without lifting his head.

"Serve him nevertheless," said the Ballad Singer.

"I will pay for his wine," said Paul, though when the slate was brought, he found that he had to turn his pocket inside out to settle the score.

He took the situtation cheerfully, more cheerfully than he felt in fact; he remarked that he would spend the rest of the night with the beggars in the porch of St.-Eustache.

"The stones of St.-Eustache are cold," said the Ballad Singer.

"But I shall have company," said Paul.

"Bad company. You have a tender heart, my pretty. Will you not offer the young man a warm bed?"

Before the girl could answer, the old man said to Paul quietly, "You shall sleep in my bed. I shan't want it before daylight. The lodging is humble, but the bed is clean. The sheets are changed once a month."

"A reckless offer, Father Lanterns," said the Ballad Singer. "I wondered what stank. Now I see it is your young friend.

Will you let such a stinking man inhabit your clean bed?" The old man flushed, but the Ballad Singer went on, to Paul: "You have been baptized by the famous mud of Paris. The coaches of the Great fling the mud very high. It is even on your shoulder." Then unaccountably he abandoned all his nonsense and, lighting his pipe, began to question Paul about his work, his lack of funds, and his plans. Paul answered with discretion. The Ballad Singer listened while the smoke curled up past his nose, so that from time to time he needs must close his good eye and move his head from side to side, like a baited bull. In the end he summed up his advice.

"Paris swarms with bookstores. Don't waste your time by poking your nose into every little shop. Go to the Beadle of your guild and make him responsible for you."

"Bourdon is out of town," said someone.

"Then go to Mademoiselle Bourdon, who is for your purpose as good a man as her husband. With your hat in your hand, and a compliment. If you have a clean shirt, put it on. You're an honest fellow, and not bad-looking, either. She'll find something for you. One more word of advice, since you're an honest fellow. Steer clear of the police, even if you should find your wallet missing. The police!" He lifted his mug. "I give you the police, a necessary evil." He drank and set down his mug, and smiled at Paul, his good eye snapping with mischief. Then his face sagged. He was tired. He turned to the man who sat at his elbow and said, "What are you gaping about, with your mouth open like a dead fish?"

It was late when Paul and the lantern lighter left the cabaret. The old man tucked his hand in the crook of Paul's arm as before, and as before led him through the darkness, up one street and down another, and through another door into a pitch-black vestibule.

"Do not move," said the old man.

Paul felt the damp plaster of a wall on one side. On the other, the old man went through a series of strange motions. He was only searching his pockets for his tinderbox and a candle end. The lean hands, the lined and shrunken face emerged suddenly from the darkness, the mouth pursed to blow upon the flame, the hands trembling. In spite of the tremor of his hands, the old man was very deft, nor did he flinch when a trickle of hot wax ran over his fingers. He said proudly, peering at Paul through the dazzle of the flame:

"This is the true spermaceti, such as is used at Versailles. Wax, not tallow. Candles fit for a King. Mount the stairs before me, I pray you. You will see better; the light will not be in your eyes."

The stairway rose steep and narrow. Paul mounted obediently, the old man following. The yellow glow wavered upon the walls, upon steps hollowed by wear save where the hard wood of knots had resisted and remained like bosses. The steps slanted irregularly, the stained walls seemed to lean together, and Paul's shadow fell broken upon the steps, struggling upward before him.

The stairway turned, reversing its direction, and then turned again, and at each turning there was a closed door, but no platform. Their footsteps echoed on the hollow wood, between the bare walls, and after they had passed the first turning Paul heard behind him the forced breathing of the old man. The plaster walls sweated with damp. After a while Paul lost count of the turnings. He felt himself mounting into a region of lost souls, an ascent rather than a descent into a cold purgatory, far from all living things, so clammy was the air, so absolute the shadow into which the small flame pushed its way. The warm, bright room of the cabaret, the sound of voices, the taste of food and wine grew momently more distant. Apprehension crept into his mind, and grew into panic. He wanted to turn, to plunge downward and escape from this stairway to hell, but he could not turn without throwing himself against the old man. And the old man climbed ever more slowly, stopping often to catch his breath, and then resuming his effort, too breathless for conversation. Paul himself became fatigued and out of breath. The stairway ended finally before a closed door. It might have been a seventh story, or perhaps only a fifth, but it was as high as they could go. The old man said, when he could speak:

"Enter. It is not locked."

He passed by the young man to a table where he dribbled a little wax, enough to fix his candle upright, and Paul saw that they were beneath the peak of the roof. For furniture there was the table, a three-legged stool, and a bed without posters. Above the bed, and hung from a hook in the slanting rafter, was a piece of stuff which could be spread about the bed like a tent. A sour and musty smell, the odor of the old man, exhaled from the draperies of the bed. Nothing else was to be seen. The taper, spermaceti though it was, did not illuminate the corners.

The old man made Paul free of this apartment with a gesture, and turned to go. From the doorway he said: "Do not be concerned for me. I have not slept at night for many years, and the constitution becomes adapted to the regime one keeps. It is a pleasure, also, to see the dawn. There are the birds, the first light on the King's laurel wreath." He smiled very sweetly, touched his hat in farewell to Paul, and made as if to leave. But he had still something to say which the eloquence of the Ballad Singer had prevented him from giving words to earlier in the evening. He turned about once more.

"I have a post of honor. It is humble, but it is, though somewhat indirectly, in the service of the King. They do wrong who mock the King. You must pay no attention to these songs and these sayings. Paris is full of them, as full as the gutters are of mud in rainy weather, and they are just as foul. The King"—he drew a deep breath and his voice strengthend—"is a sacred person. He is a priest of the Church, also, and has been anointed with a sacred oil, a miraculous oil. Who else is there alive today whose touch can cure the sick? You must think of that.

Those who mock him sin greatly, and heaven will punish them.
As for Madame de Maintenon, perhaps she is, as they say, the
King's mistress, but even in their dirty songs they acknowledge
that she has reformed the King."

Chapter Three

"Our Father who art at Marly," went the paternoster of the Ballad Singer. But the King was not at Marly on that Easter night, nor at any of the other châteaux where he sometimes went for relaxation. He was at Versailles. He had returned there at the beginning of Holy Week to perform his part in the ceremonies of the church. He had passed an exhausting week. He had prayed, he had repented, he had washed the feet of the poor and given alms, he had touched for the King's evil, and he had also suffered extreme anxiety because of the illness of his youngest daughter. It was a mysterious illness to which the King's physician had been unable to give a name, and it was an illness which the King could not cure by the laying on of hands, as he cured the scrofula. The fever had broken, the crisis passed before Easter, the girl was convalescent, but no one knew what had saved her, any more than was known what had caused the illness, unless she was saved by the prayers of Madame de Maintenon and of the King.

The good Bontemps, Premier Valet du Roi, moving about in the King's bedchamber on the morning after Easter, making ready for the King's *lever*, considered these things with a gentle detachment. He thought of the King's anxiety with a fatherly pity, and of his stoicism with admiration. He had himself helped to force the King's swollen foot into its shoe. He knew that it was a penance for the King to stand upon it, and even more of a penance to walk in procession from the village church of Versailles to the Orangery of the château, where the healing of the sick took place. The weight of the robe which the King wore for the ceremonial was an added penance, that robe of blue velvet lined with ermine, the velvet embroidered all over with little golden fleur-de-lis; and there was also the weight of the golden collar of the Order of the Holy Spirit. In the burden of this regalia, suffering the constant pain of his gouty foot, the King had passed among the sick, and repeated the ritualistic words: *Le Roi te touche; Dieu te guérisse.* He had repeated them over two thousand times in the course of the ceremony, and he had confided to Bontemps afterward that he was drained of energy. He had felt the virtue go out of him, like the Saviour in whose memory he acted. As for his anxiety over the Duchesse de Chartres, he had not spoken of it. Bontemps had suspected that, as on all other occasions where one of his children by Madame de Montespan was concerned, the King had blamed himself, feeling the child's illness a punishment upon him for the sin of its conception.

Bontemps had spent the night, as always, on a small pallet at the foot of the King's bed of state. The pallet had been removed. A fire had been kindled on the marble hearth, and burned briskly with a faint crackling. Bontemps parted the curtains at the long window, and folded back the painted shutters. A cold light entered the room. The courtyard below was full of mist.

The King's bed, on a dais behind a gilded wooden balustrade, was a box of red damask, the curtains smoothly drawn, the corners surmounted by white ostrich plumes and egret feathers. The egret feathers rose like stiff jets of water, the ostrich plumes bending below them like breaking waves. The curtains hung straight and unmoving. The room was in order. Bontemps listened a moment and heard a subdued murmur of voices beyond the door to the King's antechamber, but no voice called to him from behind the damask curtains. He opened a door directly opposite the door to the antechamber, and passed into the Grand Salon where the greater part of the *lever* would take place.

There were fires burning here also, one on each side of the room. They hardly took the chill off the air, but this did not trouble Bontemps. The crowd which would enter with the fifth and final Entrée of the *lever* would heat it to the point of suffocation. He crossed the room, his feet making no sound on the gold and white Savonnerie carpet, and paused, between the two fires, to move the King's chaise percée a foot nearer the center of the salon. He thus brought it exactly in line with the central window, and, coincidentally, into the exact geometrical center of the whole château. He did this to please himself as well as to please the King. He had absorbed over the years something of the King's passion for symmetry. He then went on to the cabinets on the farther side of the salon to exchange a few words with the gentlemen of the wardrobe and the King's barber, and, being satisfied that all was in order in that direction, he returned to the salon and took his stand before the central window, which opened upon the Cour de Marbre and the narrow balcony which overlooked it. It lacked some minutes yet before the hour when he should wake the King.

First Valet of the King and Governor of the village and of the castle of Versailles, he met his responsibilities seriously but with calm. He had his own recipe for coping with them. He allowed himself plenty of time. He allowed for emergencies which never occurred because he had always taken every precaution to allow for them. And so, never feeling harassed, he was able to

maintain at all times—and the times were often very trying—
an inner tranquillity which enabled him to exercise his natural
kindliness. Standing there, his hands behind his back, looking
down into the mist which veiled the scene below, he reflected
that too many people under pressure of circumstances seemed to
lose control of their words and actions, and to do and to say
the most regrettable things; and this was a great pity. There was
enough intentional malice at work in the court; there was no
need for unintentional malice.

He knew that he was called the good Bontemps. No doubt
the play upon words had first inspired the title, *le bon* Bontemps,
but he flattered himself that it would not have continued in use
if he had not deserved it. He felt that he had no enemy at court
in spite of his long years of service and his nearness to the King,
which had exposed him to every intrigue. He had been the
King's witness at his secret marriage to Madame de Maintenon,
and that event was all of ten years ago. For more than ten years
he had met the malice of the court with tact and with charity.
He was an old man now, he took pride in the fact, and he
wished to keep his record clear to the end. He foresaw the end,
as one foresees a sunset on a fine summer afternoon, something
neither to be dreaded nor avoided. And when he was tempted to
speak out with bitterness against certain abuses of favor, or other
matters which disturbed him, a temptation which beset him
more and more frequently of late, he reminded himself that his
days were not eternal. The fact that he had not too many years
longer to put up with what annoyed him was, oddly, perhaps,
more comforting than depressing. Yes, he thought, looking
down into the mist, the malice of the court, like the poor, he had
always with him, and further, he reflected with a smile which
was strangely grim for such a kindly man, it was the members
of the King's own family who displayed the most malice.

Meanwhile the Duc d'Orléans, the King's brother, styled at
court Monsieur, proceeded from his apartments in the Orléans
wing of the château toward the Hall of the King's Guards. At

the head of the Queen's Stairway he was jostled by the tide of servants, courtiers, and nondescripts mounting and descending the marble steps. There were no back stairways at Versailles; wood, water, salvers of food, trash and slops were carried up and down the broad steps, while personages bound for the King's *lever* made their way slowly and cautiously between the hurrying lackeys.

Where the press was greatest, Monsieur was halted for a time. He saw no one to whom he wished to speak, and several whom he wished to avoid. He yawned and stared remotely over the heads of those nearest to him. Resentment at having to rise so early to attend his brother's *lever* had long since faded into habit. He would have felt a lack if he had suddenly been excused from the obligation. But he had been up late the night before, and he had not had his sleep out. His wits were still numb. His face still bore rouge and powder of the previous day, and his person exhaled strongly the odor of a violet pomade which had lost all its freshness. He was passionately fond of perfume, of jewels, of music, and of young men, whom he adored as most men adore women. He was in his early fifties, a potbellied little man who wore very high heels, and who balanced himself adroitly, even when he was half asleep.

He had been handsome in his youth, more handsome than his brother. There were still traces of this young comeliness in his debauched countenance. He had also been very popular. His popularity had been such that the King had taken measures to check it, measures well disguised in the form of favors. They left Monsieur with leisure on his hands, too much leisure. He was bored, and it was useless to protest his boredom to the King. The days when they slept together, romped together in the King's bed, with its torn sheets, flung pillows at each other and even in their excitement pissed upon each other, to the dismay of old La Porte, those happy days were too remote to be of any use to him now.

He stood near the head of the stairway, between two closed

doors. On his left was the door to the Salle des Gardes, on his right the door to the apartments of Madame de Maintenon, a door through which he passed but rarely. His friendship with the lady was purely formal. He had not yet forgiven her, nor had Madame, his wife, for her part in the marriage of the Duc de Chartres to the King's youngest bastard. Nor had he forgiven the King. It was not that either Monsieur or Madame suffered for the unhappiness of their son; it was the insult to the Orléans branch, the sullying of the Orléans blood with the blood of a girl begotten in a double adultery, which united them in indignation. It was by now the only issue in which they were united. Monsieur turned his back upon the door to his right. He looked at the stairway and saw, climbing the steps, with his head bowed, the King's only completely royal son, Monseigneur, the Grand Dauphin. Behind him followed close the Little Dauphin, the Duc de Bourgogne.

The crowd parted for these two as it had not parted for Monsieur. He took advantage of the action, as they passed him, to follow in their wake. He followed them through the Salle des Gardes and into the Salle du Grand Couvert, where the King dined when he dined in public.

Here, on a table midway in the room, stood a small vessel curiously fashioned of silver "bathed," as the term was, in gold, a vessel of vermeil. It was formed like the hull of a ship, and it contained the King's napkin. Just as the ritual of the court demanded that everyone passing the King's bed, whether the bed was occupied or not, should bow to it, so everyone who passed the *nef du Roi* was obliged to salute it also. This obligation was particularly in force for members of the King's family. Monsieur waited, therefore, while Monseigneur paused, removed his plumed hat, and bowed low before the gleaming little vessel and his father's napkin.

The young Duc de Bourgogne, following Monseigneur, also thrust forward his left leg, as he had been taught, bent his right knee, and brought his hat in a careful semicircle from his head to his stomach. The performance was awkward. The boy needed more work with the foils. Monsieur, smiling faintly, permitted the boy to follow his father from the room, and then approached the nef and made, with nonchalance, an obeisance of perfect grace. Recovering his full height, he let his glance rest a moment longer than was necessary upon the golden ship and then upon the Swiss in blue and red who guarded it, before he replaced his hat upon his periwig and continued his progress.

The final antechamber was the smallest, the dimmest, the most crowded of the three. There was no flicker of firelight. The only illumination came from an oval window set high in the wall and giving upon a small dim inner court. In this small, chill, viewless room the most eminent gentlemen of France waited to greet the King.

Monsieur entered jauntily. He had come awake in the course of his obeisance to the nef. He looked about him with a distinct sense of anticipation, observed the King's Almoner, Monsieur de Mailly, reading his breviary beneath the high window, saluted, with a practiced blending of graciousness and reserve, the King's Physician and the King's First Secretary of State, who paused in their conversation upon his entrance, and so moved down the room to take his place beside Monseigneur and the young Dauphin. The Swiss still blocked the panels of the King's doorway. Monseigneur, standing with his hands in his muff, his hat tucked under his arm, in readiness to greet his father, acknowledged with a nod the presence of Monsieur, and sank his plump chin in the lace of his cravat. The young Dauphin looked at the floor.

The King also, behind the curtains of his great bed, waited for the hour of eight. He woke that morning after Easter a tired man, inordinately depressed in spirit. He woke in darkness, and from force of habit. He had made habit his servant, and it assured him of the hour, although he opened his eyes on nothing visible. Nor scent nor sound of the spring morning reached him where he lay, nor any hint of the activity in his vast château. He was aware of his body, sticky with sweat beneath the pile of feather quilts. He lay on his back, his head propped by a huge feather bolster, and when he moved a leg, the pain in his gouty foot started to life. He remembered then the past week, and began to think of his plans for the present. He knew that in a little while Bontemps would come to wake him. He closed his eyes upon the stale immobile darkness and faced his problem; his own physical exhaustion and the poverty of France. They were, in his mind, one and the same.

France is become a vast desolate almshouse. The words sounded in his head. He had read them in a letter. No one had dared pronounce them to him, nor had he as yet repeated them to anyone, nor shown the letter to anyone, not even to Madame de Maintenon. They phrased too sharply what he was well aware of, and they had been accompanied by reproaches, by accusations, and by advice.

The letter itself had been handed to him by a man he valued, the Duc de Beauvilliers, but it had not been composed by the duke, the King was certain. He believed also that Beauvilliers could have no exact knowledge of what it contained. The letter had been unsigned, but the writer had made no attempt, obviously, to disguise either his hand or his style. The written words spoke quite as clearly in the voice of their author as if the man himself had been in the room. He was undoubtedly the young abbé Fénelon, the tutor of the little Dauphin, the King's grandson.

The letter wounded him in that it ignored his own deep concern for his kingdom, his pity for his people. It insulted him in that it presumed to inform him of matters in which he was well informed. It offered him advice on how to rule his kingdom, a métier at which he worked twenty-four hours a day. All this was intolerable. It suggested further that he should ask advice of Madame de Maintenon, as if he did not already know what her advice would be, and as if he were incapable of ruling wisely without her.

She prayed for peace. And had he not carried on, all winter long, negotiations for peace? That the negotiations had proved fruitless had caused him quite as much grief as it had caused Madame de Maintenon.

Lying there in the close darkness, he felt the bitterness of his resentment fill his mouth, more bitter than on the occasion of his first reading the letter—when had that been? weeks, months, earlier?—because he had been unable to forget it. He had put the letter away among his privy papers, but the words had haunted him. He had met also at his *levers*, as often as he was at Versailles, the intensely luminous eyes of the young priest, inquiring and self-confident. There shone in those extraordinary eyes, the King thought, not only a challenge, but a desire for martyrdom, as if Fénelon waited to be unmasked, accused and punished for his temerity. But the King had no intention of bringing the offense into the open. He had appointed the abbé tutor to the prince at the request of Madame de Maintenon. If Fénelon were to be disgraced, she would feel herself disgraced also; and then there would be tears, and headaches, those terrible, prostrating headaches of hers, and an end to all her pleasant conferences with the abbé. Furthermore, his work with the young Dauphin had begun to show good results. The King was not yet willing to interrupt the education of his grandson. Fénelon was safe for the present. The King had no choice but to swallow his resentment. A maxim which he had been set to copy as a child, when he was learning to write, recurred to him with irony. *Le pouvoir des rois est absolu; ils font ce qu'ils veulent.* He had copied it twenty times. He had learned. Kings do not do as they wish, but as they must.

Bontemps, looking down from the central window of the King's drawing room, saw through the mist a carriage enter the Cour Royale, where but few carriages were permitted. It disappeared from his view beyond the angle of the building to his right, and when it reappeared it held two women. One of these was mantled and hooded in black velvet. He could not see her face but he knew very well who she was. Madame de Maintenon and her attendant were departing for St.-Cyr. The mist engulfed the carriage before it reached the outer gate. Shortly after, Bontemps heard behind him the first silvery strokes of a clock. He proceeded with unhurried step into the King's bedroom, and on the stroke of eight drew back the curtains of the King's bed.

The face on the high pillow, shadowed by the canopy and framed by the white *bonnet de nuit*, was grey with the stubble of a day's beard, the skin pock-marked and deeply lined, the nose long, the jowls heavy, the mouth, with its full Bourbon underlip, impassive, but the dark eyes were very much alive. They met those of Bontemps unsmiling, but attentive.

"Sire, I hope you slept well."

The King replied to the usual question with the usual answer, his voice resonant and grave. "I thank you. And you, my good Bontemps?" The day had begun.

The King sat up in bed and lifted his arms to permit Bontemps to remove his sweaty nightshirt. Bontemps rubbed down the King's body with a warm dry towel, helped him into a clean nightshirt, removed his nightcap and replaced it with the small wig of the First Entrée of the *lever*. The King experienced a slight dizziness as he sat up, but it passed as Bontemps rubbed his shoulders, and he did not mention it. The *lever* began with the Entrée Familiale, the gentlemen of the King's family. At rest once more against his pillows, he offered his hand to his son, who kissed it, murmured a few words, and retired beyond the balustrade. The Duc de Bourgogne approached. He was pale and slight; he had the poor carriage of a child who has grown too fast. He made his bow, and pressed his lips to the knuckles of his grandfather's hand, and would have retreated, but the King retained the child's hand in his own.

"Monsieur Fénelon has given me a good report of you," said the King gravely.

The child blushed, and wished to withdraw his hand, but

feared to. The King felt the momentary tug, and let him go, saddened by the instinctive gesture.

"Tell me, are you content with Monsieur Fénelon, as he is with you?"

"Oh, yes, Sire," said the child fervently.

"Then tell him from me that you must not neglect your exercises for your books."

Monsieur greeted his brother, the Duc du Maine kissed the hand of his father, the members of the King's household made their Entrée.

The Grand Chamberlain folded back the King's bedcovers, the King swung his bare legs over the side of the bed, and the Grand Chamberlain knelt to place the slippers on the King's feet. Bontemps drew a dressing gown about his shoulders. Monsieur de Mailly offered him holy water in a gold and porcelain cockleshell. The King signed himself, and prayed. And then getting to his feet, with pain he walked into the next room and seated himself in his chaise percée. The little throng of family and retainers followed, and the privileged gentlemen of the Entrée des Brevets were admitted, one by one. Then, the chaise percée having been removed and replaced by an armchair upholstered in red velvet, the King washed his hands, and was shaved. Slightly refreshed, he rose to have his breeches pulled up, and seated himself to have his slippers removed and his legs encased in silk stockings.

In breeches and dressing gown he replied to the inquiries of his physician. His health was not a personal matter, but an affair of state. He replied patiently, while Fagon went through his routine list of questions and set down the answers in his notebook. Fagon recorded everything which pertained to the health of the King, even to the number and description of the King's evacuations during the preceding twenty-four hours. He was a hunchback, an asthmatic, so deformed that his head seemed to protrude from the middle of his chest; when he wished to look up, he had to twist it sideways. His eyes were very dark; his glance had always, because of the position of his head, an oblique quality which made it appear very shrewd. His skin was sallow, his features irregular, his teeth very yellow and decayed. He wore his own hair, which was straight and thin and dark, and a plain snuff-colored suit. He was very intelligent and very witty—a master of the biting epigram—and his zeal for safe-guarding the King's health was beyond question very great. The King trusted him. Monsieur detested him because of his ugliness, because of the King's trust in him, and because that trust had been inspired by the recommendations of Madame de Maintenon.

The Grand Chamberlain stood holding the King's shirt wrapped in white taffeta, waiting for Fagon to be done, but Fagon, gasping for breath between each question, like a winded horse, went on and on. At last the King said, very courteously:

"I repeat, my dear Monsieur Fagon, I do not feel ill. But I am very tired."

"As I suspected, Sire," replied the hunchback. "I recommend that Your Majesty drink a bouillon before going to Council, and I further recommend that Your Majesty hold Council before going to Mass."

The King assented with a gesture. It was true, he did not feel ill, but he was depressed to the point of exhaustion. He could not rid himself of the thought of Fénelon's letter. *France is become a vast desolate almshouse.* He dreaded the moment when he would again meet the eyes of the young priest and know himself powerless to lift a finger against him, powerless through his own most conscientious self-control. The business of the *lever* went on.

The Duc du Maine and his brother the Comte de Toulouse helped the King their father to remove his dressing gown, which they then held before him as a screen between him and his audience while Monseigneur helped him off with his nightshirt. Monseigneur accepted from the Grand Chamberlain the shirt in the white taffeta, and with Bontemps and Monseigneur each holding a sleeve, the King put on his shirt. The dressing gown was let fall, revealing the King to his court as Bontemps and Monseigneur each knelt to fasten a wrist band. There was no lace on the King's shirt this day; the King was in partial mourning. He had all but forgotten the necessity for it, but Bontemps had remembered.

All this stepping forward and back, of bowing, presenting, of withdrawing, like figures in a ritualistic dance, all this fluttering about him of hands which served him, which he had no need to direct, left the King free to pursue his thoughts. And although he made an effort to assemble in his mind those matters which he intended presently to lay before the Council, he found his thoughts returning constantly to the accusations of François de Salignac de la Mothe-Fénelon. He began to look for the abbé in the crowd before him, dreading to meet his gaze, and yet, when he did not find him, feeling a dull and suffocating anger rise slowly within him. He believed himself very secure, this young abbé, to ignore the King's *lever*.

The feeling of suffocation increased. The air seemed very close. It was, in fact, both stinking and stuffy, and small wonder; when the Entrée de la Chambre and the Entrée Générale had taken place, nearly three hundred gentlemen had pushed into the room. Few of them had bathed recently, and most of them used pomander. The King had an intense dislike of perfume in any form, a dislike which was well known and universally disregarded.

The small wig of the *lever* was removed, and replaced by a large perruque, and the *lever* came to a halt. The King waited for his bouillon. The bouillon was always ready, whether the King called for it or not, and so were the vergers with white wands, and the other persons whose business it was to convey the bouillon to the King, but bodies cannot move with the speed of thought. It took a certain number of minutes for a page to run with the message to the Commons, and for the procession to make its way from the Commons, through the courtyard, up the marble stairway, through the three ante-chambers to the Grand Salon. Monsieur de Mailly, whose duty and privilege it was to present the King's nef to the King, betook himself to the Salon du Grand Couvert, and waited there with the ship in his hands for the procession from the Commons.

The King in his shirt sleeves waited, and surveyed the gentle-men of his court. His eyes, which in the shaven head, or under the white nightcap, had appeared small and beady, in the shadow of the chestnut curls of the great perruque appeared large and velvety. There was in their reserve and in their unhurried and unembarrassed scrutiny of his gentlemen something feline. No man present but wished to be noticed by the King, and no man present but felt a slight sense of discomfort as the royal gaze seemed to pause upon him. The King continued his search for the abbé Fénelon, and did not find him.

The little Duc de Bourgogne, at the elbow of Monseigneur, shifted his weight from one foot to the other, and dropped his head. His mouth was unhappy. The King remembered his fer-vent "Oh, yes, Sire," in reply to the question, "Are you content with Monsieur Fénelon?" and thought, "He steals the affection of my grandson from me."

The King's glance fell upon the figure of Monsieur de Pont-chartrain, Secretary of State, alert and elegant, who stood nearby, balancing like a bird about to quit a bough, and Pont-chartrain, catching the King's eye an instant, took advantage of the moment to begin a conversation. The pause in the *lever* had become awkward.

"I have been informed, Sire," he began, "that old Monsieur de Valavoire is dead."

The King replied, after the slightest possible hesitation, "I am sorry to hear it. He was Governor of Sisteron, was he not?"

"The same, Sire."

"It is long since we have seen him at court."

"He was eighty years old, Sire, and Sisteron is far from Versailles."

"He needs no apology. He once gave valiant service to the Crown."

"And held a brevet for it from the late Cardinal," said Pontchartrain, the problem of the King's expenditures uppermost in his mind, "for fifty thousand livres, which terminates upon his death."

"Eighty is a good age," said the King, and resumed his search for the face of his grandson's tutor. The room had become almost unbearably stuffy. Then he saw a face which brought with its appearance a sudden memory of fresh air, of space, and of well-being. He signaled with one finger for the owner of the face to approach.

"Monsieur La Violette," said the King, when the huntsman stood before him, "we have missed you."

"When Monseigneur is at Choisy, so must I be," answered La Violette.

"Even so," answered the King graciously. "But today, with your permission, I shall ask Monseigneur to lend you to me."

Monseigneur bowed his consent. La Violette bowed also, straight from the hips, and straightened himself easily. He was a good six feet tall and magnificently erect. The King continued:

"We shall hunt today."

"As you like, Sire."

"What sort of day shall we have?"

"A pleasant day, I trust. I heard the larks singing behind the mist as I came here. The mist will clear by noon. We shall have a good afternoon for the pheasants."

"At three we shall shoot." The King smiled very kindly, and La Violette, thinking himself dismissed, took a step backward in withdrawal. But the King checked him.

"Monseigneur has told me that you are recently turned eighty. It would be a great loss if all gentlemen of eighty were to remain away from my court." La Violette bowed again, but the King was not yet ready to let him go. "You carry your-self like a stripling. If you were to turn your back on me, and I did not know you, I would swear that you were no more than twenty. Tell me, what do you do to remain so young?"

"I hunt with the King," said La Violette, "or with Mon-seigneur, and I never drink water in my wine."

Someone laughed. The King did not smile.

"I am told," he said, "that you will not even drink water in your soup."

"True, Sire. Soup is mostly water. Therefore it is weakening."

"I am the victim of Monsieur Fagon, who has ordered me to drink a bowl of soup."

"Advised, Sire, not ordered," murmured Fagon with a whis-tling breath. The King disregarded the interruption.

"If you had not such a bad opinion of my soup, I should be tempted to share it with you."

The face of the old huntsman reddened beneath its tan, but he stood his ground and answered plainly, "Your Majesty may do as he likes, but as for me, who am an ordinary person, I should still find it weakening."

The King permitted him to retire then, and as he retreated the crowd parted before the white wands of the vergers, and the bouillon arrived. The King's Almoner, the King's butler, the King's taster, and a fourth gentleman, whose business it was to hold a plate beneath the chin of the King as he drank, formed a semicircle. Monsieur de Mailly had been so recently appointed to his office that his new duty had as yet lost none of its solemnity for him. He was beset by little fears. What if he should stumble? What if he should find himself about to sneeze? He made his reverence without mishap, and then, still full of anxiety, waited with the ship upon his outstretched hands for Monsieur to perform his part in the ritual.

Monsieur was abstracted. He seemed to have forgotten his duty. Then he suddenly came to himself, smiled at his brother, and saluted the ship. He shook back the lace from his wrists, and delicately removed from the ship the royal napkin. With his ruffles still clear of his wrists, like a cardplayer who demonstrates that he has nothing up his sleeves, he turned to his brother, and with another low reverence presented him the napkin.

The King shook out his napkin upon his knee. As he did so, there fell from it a small pamphlet which glided to the floor and came to rest against his shoe. Monsieur de Mailly saw it, plainly, leaning against the diamond buckle, but, encumbered by the ship, could not stir to pick it up. Monsieur was to all appearances transfixed with surprise. Pontchartrain leaped forward, but the King was quicker. He had the pamphlet in his hand; he inspected it.

Monsieur de Mailly felt an illness, a sudden pressure at the pit of the stomach. No one had ever suggested that he should inspect the napkin before presenting the nef; the ship itself was guarded day and night. He looked at Monsieur and saw in his face no hint of disaster, but only an expression of amused interest. Monsieur, however, was privileged. His composure was not, for Monsieur de Mailly, altogether reassuring. As for Monsieur, he saw in the face of the King a great serenity—too great a serenity—which gradually assumed a certain iciness. Monsieur was familiar with the expression. His faint smile deepened slightly.

The King's attention was caught by an engraving which at first glance seemed to be a representation of the statue in the Place des Victoires. But something was wrong with the representation. The statue of the King surmounted the pedestal, as it should, and the pedestal was surrounded by four figures, but the figures were not those of captives, nor were they chained. Instead, they were women, four women whom the King had loved, and they held the King enchained. In order that his meaning should be perfectly clear, the engraver had indicated their names: Madame de Montespan, La Duchesse de La Vallière, La Duchesse de Fontanges, and Madame de Maintenon. The precaution was well advised. The portraits bore no resemblance

to their subjects. A cold fury struck the King; he gave no indication of it. He opened the booklet, and met upon the title
page another and greater insult.

Scarron Apparu à Madame de Maintenon, he read, in large
type, and then, in smaller letters, *et les Reproches qu'il lui fait
sur ses amours avec Louis le Grand. A Cologne chez Jean le
Blanc. M.DC.XCIV.*

It was remarkable with what ease, with what effrontery,
they accused him, they insulted him, through these anonymous
pamphlets, these unsigned letters, men like Fénelon, like Jean
le Blanc, who had not the courage to speak these insults to
his face. John White. John Blank. John Nobody. They were
many, and they were not worth his anger. He was wounded,
nevertheless.

Presently he heard Monsieur cough judiciously and then remark in the silkiest of voices:

"The soup will be cold."

The King looked up. He observed Monsieur's faint smile,
the dismay in the face of Monsieur de Mailly. He ignored the
half gesture of Monsieur de Pontchartrain to relieve him of the
booklet. He closed the pamphlet upon his knee.

"The soup is always cold," said the King, and reached for the
bouillon. The *lever* continued.

The King put on his coat and, when he did so, slipped the
pamphlet into his coat pocket, where it fitted as if it had been
made for it. He chose a cravat, and tied it himself. He selected
a handkerchief, gloves, a hat, a cane. The blue ribbon of the
Order of the Holy Spirit was placed upon his shoulder so that
it crossed his breast diagonally. The emblem of the Order hung
from a knot beneath his left hand. His sword was thrust through
the sword pocket of his coat, so that he could rest his hand
upon its jeweled hilt. He stood at last with his left hand upon
his sword, his right upon the knob of his tall cane, and with
his eyes found and drew about him the members of his Monday
Council.

Monsieur de Mailly, relieved of the burden of the ship, and also, to a very great degree, of his distress, offered the prayer for the day, and the King led the way into his Council Chamber.

When the door closed upon his brother, Monsieur, who was not a member of the Council, put his hat back on his head and went to pay his respects to Madame, his wife, a most unusual procedure.

Chapter Four

PAUL DAMAS, the morning after Easter, woke to a time-less moment and did not know where he was. The voice which wakened him was familiar, yet he could not place it. He lay so far beneath the surface of consciousness that, although he heard the voice, he could not reply.

The voice evoked another which said, also from a great distance, "Call back the wandering soul," and this voice he recognized as that of the priest who had taught him to read, had taught him his catechism, and had taught him a smatter-ing of the ancients, an old man in a grease-spotted soutane with a face as brown as a nut, with high cheekbones red as apples. One morning in a sunny garden the priest had explained a notion held by the ancients, that one should waken gradually a sleeping body in order to give the wandering spirit time to return to its carnal habitation.

The voice continued to call. It was the voice of an old man, and it was tinged with a remembrance of kindness shown to him, and yet, he now remembered, it could not be that of the priest, for the priest had been dead a good ten years. With a great effort he opened his eyes and saw bending over him a countenance familiar, but not the face of his preceptor. It was wax-colored with fatigue, and rough with grizzled, unshaven beard. From beneath the black ringlets of a periwig a few grey locks straggled about the hollow temples, and the eyes were anguished.

"Your morning is here, my friend," said the lantern lighter. "Your morning and my night, and I need my bed."

From the vast enchantment of sleep the memory of Paul Damas was suddenly delivered into the cold dim light of day. He sat up in bed and looked at his host with concern.

"You are tired," he said. "I was comfortable, thanks to you. I slept like the dead. But you? Was it a bad night?"

"Do the dead sleep so well?" said the old man. "It was no worse a night than many. With me, it's age, not the weather. It flows through the veins and chills the flesh, little by little. When I lean over, my head whirls. Help me off with my shoes."

"You're not so very old," said Damas. "What you need is food. We will find you a breakfast."

But the lantern lighter shook his head. "For nothing in the world would I climb those stairs again today. Help me into bed. All that I need is to lie down."

Without his hat, without his wig, without his laced and padded coat, the old man appeared very small, like a plucked fowl. Damas helped him into bed, tied the cotton nightcap under the lean chin, pushed the covers down about the bony shoulders. The old man's eyes, full of misery and gratitude, looked up at him.

"I'll bring you some coffee."

"No coffee," said the old man firmly. "It's a foreign drug. The King never drinks coffee."

"Brandy?"

"Nothing at all. I shall sleep. There's nothing to equal sleep,

for nourishment. If you come back . . ." He paused, closed
his eyes, and then resumed, rather indistinctly, "If you come
back tonight, I'll be at the Place des Victoires at sundown, on
the King's business." The eyes opened briefly, flashing a quick
look up at the young man. "Come back," he said imperiously.
"You'll see. I'll be there. I'm tough. Tough as an old rat."
He closed his eyes again, and a grin made its way slowly through
the bristling growth about his lips.

"Very well," said Damas, "and meantime, many thanks for
the night's lodging."

With eyes still closed, and the least possible motion of the
lips, the lantern lighter replied, "It was nothing. A small favor
from a tough old rat." Then the eyes flashed open once more.
"Will you come back?" he demanded.

"Certainly," said Paul. It was a promise. What else could he
have said? But it was pleasant to think that the day, however
it went, would have a meeting at its end. It was also pleasant
to be sure of a night's lodging. Whether or not he would eat
that day was another question. He had forgotten, when he
suggested brandy to the old man, that he had emptied his
wallet the night before. Between them they had this morning,
he and the old man, exactly nothing in the way of cash. However, now that he was fully awake, he felt an upsurge of hope.
Somewhere in Paris there must be a job waiting for him.

He put on his shoes and buttoned up his coat, and then,
remembering the advice of the Ballad Singer—if you have a
clean shirt, put it on—he unbuttoned his coat and changed his
shirt. He combed his hair, and brushed his hat with the sleeve
of his coat, and with his thumbnail did his best to remove the
dried mud from the shoulder of his coat. He could not wash
his face or hands—there was no water in the tin ewer—but he
could wash later in the street, at some fountain or other, and
when he reached the rue St.-Jacques he would not look too
bedraggled. It was a bit of luck for him that the Beadle was
out of town, and that it was the wife of the Beadle to whom

he would make his application. She would be less likely to ask him questions which he would find it difficult to answer.

He returned to the bed before leaving the room for a last word with his host, but the old man was sound asleep. All his pride and his resistance were undone. He lay on his back. His breathing was rhythmic and deep, and each breath blew out his relaxed lips in a little puff, but there was a struggle for each breath, and Paul felt, observing this struggle, that each breath might be the last. He could do the old man no good by remaining with him, however, and he was eager to be off.

He groped his way down the stairs, past one closed doorway after another, and his uneasiness about the old man went with him. When he made the last turning and started down the last flight of steps, he saw that the door to the street was open. The damp, fresh air mounted toward him, the street was full of mist. In the doorway, filling it completely, stood a woman with a basket on her arm. Her back was toward him. She was talking to someone in the street whom he could not see. He thought that he would speak to her about the old man. If she lived in the building, she probably knew him and would be glad to look in on him in the course of the day.

Paul came down the last steps, formulating a little speech to her, but the woman, turning about, blocked his passage with her basket and herself, and forestalled him by inquiring sharply, "What are you doing here?"

Stung by her tone, he forgot his speech, and answered, "Do you take me for a thief?"

"And why not?" she answered. "You don't belong here."

"I slept here."

"I didn't open the door for you."

"The old man let me in."

"The old man?"

"Father Lanterns."

"Oh—that one. So you slept in his room. He has no right to sublet his room. What did he charge you?"

"I was his guest."

She laughed derisively. "He charged you nothing? He was a fool to charge you nothing, in view of the fact that he's not paid his rent."

"That's the story," said Paul.

"A silly story."

"May I pass?"

But she continued to block his way. He could not see her face clearly, since the strong light was behind her, but her expression was visible in her voice.

"You may pass when you pay me for the lodging. That's no more than right. I collect the rents for the buildings. It's not in the contract for the old man to sublet his room."

"I don't believe you," said Paul, and then, "Besides, I have no money."

"Ah, there," she said, "I might believe *you*. But you still owe me money, and how do I know that you aren't a thief?"

Paul did not answer. He put his hands on the edge of her basket and tried to push it aside. She turned slightly, lifting the basket above her thick waist, so that the light fell on her face and on the contents of her basket, equally; Paul saw a bunch of turnips, long, cold and dead white, slightly purple at the tops, and beside them the spotted teats of a cow's udder, the cheapest meat for sale in any market. He lifted his eyes from her basket to her face, and the face appeared as dead white as the turnips, fat, jowled, and unhealthy. Her mouth was thin, her eyes little and black as beads. She resisted his pressure, and called into the street:

"Mathilde! Run for the police."

Her voice was not alarmed, and the woman in the street did not obey her.

"A thief?"

"For sure. You heard him. He was in the lodging of Father Lanterns while the old man was out. Call the police."

She might have been jesting, but there was no mirth in her

voice. Paul could not judge the seriousness of her intentions. She held her basket solidly before her, braced her back against the wall, and stared at him truculently. He wrenched the basket sideways with both hands, exerting all the strength he could muster, and managed to slide past her. In the street he found himself face to face with another woman, who stepped back in surprise and made no motion to stop him.

The woman with the basket cursed her acquaintance for letting slip a thief. Paul, running, heard behind him the voice of Mathilde, ironic, calm.

"What could he steal from the old man? Candle ends?"

He escaped into the mist, and it was only when he had turned a corner, and felt himself safe, that he stopped and remembered that he must take note of the street and the house, in order to find it again at nightfall—to find it if, by ill chance, the old man should fail the rendezvous at the Place des Victoires.

At three that afternoon, when the King kept his appointment with La Violette, when the sun had burned away the mist and the sky was clear and tender blue above Paris as above Versailles, Paul Damas stood in the kitchen-bookshop in the rue des Lions. His luck had turned, if Larcher would take him into his employment, but he had not yet seen Larcher.

The room pleased him. It was provincial in its plainness, its quiet, and its smallness. The stone floor, the great hearth, the extreme utility of every piece of furnishing, the economy of the fire banked with wood ashes made him feel at home. He had had enough of Paris for the moment. Even the figure of the woman who was seated at the table when he entered was a part of the same picture. She was dressed like any peasant woman of moderate fortune; the only concession to the fashion of the day was the upstanding ruffle of her coif. She came to meet him, unhurried, taking time first to set her pen upright in the dish of sand, and to put a weight upon the opened page of her account book.

She wore that day a brown woolen shawl, three-cornered,

drawn smoothly over her breast, the ends tucked under the belt of her apron. The apron, dull blue, reached to the hem of her skirt. Her skin, very smooth, had the pallor of the city dweller; the pallor became her, setting off the warm grey of her eyes, the darkness of the hair which showed beneath the fluting of her cap. He thought she was about the same age as himself. He felt at ease with her; they were of the same class, artisans. Behind her he glimpsed the copper fountain, polished like an autumn oak leaf, and on the chimney shelf plates of spotted blue and brown faïence.

He asked nothing better than to work here, and for a long time. This was where he belonged. The world of Father Lanterns, the Ballad Singer, the fat woman with the basket of turnips were part of a queer dream.

He explained his errand and asked to see the master of the shop.

"He is in there," said Marianne, indicating the door to the bindery.

"Will he see me?" said Paul.

"Go in and ask him," she said with her amused, quick smile.

Still he hesitated. He wanted the job so much that he was overcareful. He remembered that there were times when to open the door to the bindery without due permission was to invite damnation. For the laying of gold leaf upon leather the air must be absolutely without motion. The least breath of air . . . It was, of course, unlikely that Larcher would be working with gold leaf without mentioning the fact to his wife. Nevertheless, Paul hesitated, his eyes on Marianne's face. He looked at her, in his curious anxiety, a moment too long. The color began to appear in her cheeks. She turned from him abruptly and pushed open the door to the bindery.

"But go in, since I tell you to." She stood aside to let him pass.

The bindery was much more light than the kitchen, a fact

which gave Paul the momentary illusion that it was larger. But it was just as small, just as crowded, longer, narrower, but with the same fine proportions of an outmoded elegance. Here, too, everything welcomed him, the sewing frames, the presses, the cutting tables, particularly the screw press with its huge oaken uprights, and the air with its familiar smell unlike any other blend of odors. He could see through the long windows into the sunlit court.

Jean and Nicolas were both at work, Jean at a sewing frame, Nicolas at a high table near the door. They both looked up as Paul entered; there was no possible doubt which was the master of the shop. Paul was surprised at Larcher's age. He had assumed that Marianne was the wife of the master; now he wondered if she could be a sister of the boy who was so obviously Larcher's son.

"Someone from Bourdon," said Marianne.

Jean left his sewing, and came in deference to the name of the Beadle of his guild to meet the visitor.

Again, Paul explained his errand. He opened his bag and got out his journeyman's credentials and his chef d'oeuvre. Jean listened without interrupting. When Paul had finished, Jean said only:

"I did not ask Bourdon for an assistant."

"I left the request," said Nicolas. "I left it this noon with Mademoiselle Bourdon."

Jean merely looked at his son.

"I have no need of an assistant," he concluded quietly.

The tone was final. Paul, without reply, gave a farewell look at all the familiar objects, the pleasant room, the mass of rich color against the grey-green wall where the dyed skins were hung, and turned to leave, his papers and his master-work still in his hands. His disappointment was beyond words. He meant to keep his dignity, however, until he was well out of range of the eyes bent upon him, particularly the grey eyes of Marianne.

But as he turned, Jean said, "What have you there?" and took from Paul, not his credentials, but the book.

It was a small volume, bound in garnet morocco, tooled in gold, both on the spine and on the covers, the top of the pages gilded also. Larcher stroked it with the flat of his hand, ran a knowing finger down the boards next to the spine, testing the fanning out of the cords, examined the headbands, let the book fall open naturally, cradled in the palm of his hand, and closed it. Paul recognized in the touch of his hands his approval; but the stubbornness remained in his face.

"The gilding is yours, also?"

"Everything."

"It is well done."

Paul drew a deep breath. Larcher would relent.

"Nevertheless," said Jean, retaining the book, "you have still something to learn concerning headbands."

"I thought it well sewn."

"Very well sewn. But look here. You have placed your cord at the very top of the spine, and sewn your band over it. So, as the book is taken from the shelf, what happens? The finger tugs at the headband, and what comes loose, eventually, but the cord, the very structure of the binding."

"It seems firm," said Paul.

Larcher shook his head. "I will show you examples. We repair books here, as often as we bind them new." He looked about the room. Nicolas, before he could be asked, found what his father wanted, and handed it to him. "You see," Jean continued to Paul, "this is what happens. In Paris we no longer place the cord at the top. In the provinces they are slow to change, even for the better. Here we lower the top cord a little; we retain the careful sewing of the headband. Then the book will last. When it comes to lasting a hundred years, two hundred years, as a book should, these little matters are important."

Paul listened attentively, with the growing sense that Larcher had retreated from his absolute refusal, and for the very good reason that he had seen and liked Paul's work. Nicolas stood listening to his father's unusual discourse with the same happy confidence. Then Jean, unsmiling, but kindly, returned Paul's book to him, and Nicolas signaled to Paul to present his other credentials once more. Jean saw the gesture. He said to both young men, without undue emphasis, but in his slow deep voice which carried finality:

"Still, I do not need an assistant."

"But you said you would consider," Nicolas exclaimed.

"Well?" said Jean. And then, "I have considered."

"No, Jean," said his wife. "Nicolas acted reasonably—you must admit. And the young man has come in good faith. We should not waste his time. Let him stay the week out, and see how things go."

The double, unexpected protest startled Paul, but very agreeably. Jean was also astonished. He stared at the faces before him, eager, hopeful, reproving, and then lifted his two hands, palms out, in a gesture of resignation, and turned his back upon his wife, his son, and Paul Damas. It was as much as to declare, "Have it your way," but there was also in the gesture, it seemed to Paul, an immense and unexplained sadness.

Jean said not another word, either then or in the course of the afternoon. He brought unfinished work and set it before Paul, and went back to his sewing. It was Nicolas who showed Paul what he needed to know about the shop, who smiled at him in a comradely way, and who exchanged a few words with him from time to time, although he never attempted to carry on a conversation. This in itself did not trouble Paul, nor did he find the quiet of the shop depressing as they worked together, the three of them. There was a certain amount of activity in the courtyard, women's voices, the sound of wheels, of horses' hooves, the jingle of harness as the horses were led into their stalls, excited quacking of ducks. The place was not a tomb. But more than once he caught Nicolas looking at his father, his father unaware that he was observed, with an expression that was a blend of anxiety and speculation, and it made him wonder how long the victory of the mother and son over the father would hold good. In the morning, or even by nightfall, Jean might reassert his authority, and Paul would find himself again one of the unemployed of Paris.

The clear light dimmed gradually. Dusk began to rise in the corners of the workshop. At seven o'clock it had become difficult to see and to work with precision. The sound of bells from churches nearby and churches far away began to float over the courtyard, and as they began Jean dismissed Paul with a sign, without a word, and his face was sad, Paul thought, far more sad than stern. The situation was puzzling. But, being dismissed, he gathered together his gear, took his hat and coat, and went into the kitchen, where Marianne nodded to him cheerfully, and wished him good evening.

Partly as a subterfuge, to delay his walking out into the street with so much unsettled, his wages, his privileges—in Auxerre he had supped with the master—he held out his soiled hands and asked if he might wash them before he left. Her response was quick. She poured water into a basin and brought him a towel which was only slightly crumpled. She said, while he soaped and rinsed his hands:

"Where is the book which so pleased my husband?" And then, in possession of the book, "It is very pretty. Since you work here, it should be on display. It might attract custom."

"Have you read it?" said Paul.

She glanced at the title. "Is it the play? There was a play by that name."

"Perhaps you saw the play."

"We don't go to the theatre."

"I admire it," said Paul. "One of my greatest desires is to see it on the stage."

She shook her head. "They don't give it any more," she said. "I never hear it spoken of."

Still Paul delayed. The bowls were set on the table; there

was a very appetizing smell of chick-peas cooked with parsley and leeks. Another moment, and she might ask him to stay to supper, but as he hovered over his book, where she had placed it before the window, Marianne said:

"It will be quite safe. We will see you at seven in the morning."

She had her reasons for wishing to get him out of the kitchen promptly. She was as uncertain as Paul that Jean would not reverse his position, given a little more time. If Nicolas was due for a reprimand, the continued presence of Paul might either postpone it or precipitate it, she had no way of knowing which. Or if complete surrender and reconciliation were possible, Nicolas and his father would be better off alone.

She saw Paul out of the doorway before she called to Jean to cut the bread.

Supper went as always, quietly. Both men were hungry. But when Nicolas had emptied his bowl, he began, "Papa."

Jean looked up without lifting his head.

"We will not talk of it," he said.

"But Papa," began the boy again. Marianne, rising, laid her hand on his shoulder, warningly. She refilled his bowl, and he ate what she served him, but in his silence, and in every motion of his hand or head, she saw the tension mounting. With the last spoonful, asking no one's leave, he got up and took his hat, and fairly bolted from the room.

Marianne looked at Jean, who returned her look as if nothing had occurred. He cut himself another piece of bread and wiped his bowl clean with a portion of it. The muscles of his jaw stood out as he chewed. He kept his eyes blindly upon the middle of the table, and his wife watched him, half in exasperation and half in pity. By and by he also stood up, and took his hat and his pipe, and walked out of the kitchen to the consolation of the Golden Harrow.

Nicolas made straight for the river. He had no plan in mind except to get away from both his parents. He could not be charitable toward his father, nor even grateful. If he had won the argument, his father's grimness took all pleasure from the occasion. If he had not won and Paul was to be sacked at the end of the week, or the next day, there was nothing to be grateful about. So long as his father refused to talk with him, he could not know what to count on. He felt nothing but indignation as he rounded the corner from the rue du Petit-Musc and started on a diagonal across the Quai.

Paul Damas was sitting on the parapet above the Port St.-Paul, watching the rivermen on the beach below. He saw the last passengers debark from the *coche d'eau* from Auxerre, climb the stone stairway, and disappear into the streets which led from the Quai or through the doorway of the Petite Bastille, a cabaret. The market women had removed their stalls and baskets sometime earlier. The sky filled with a soft golden light behind low clouds. Lights began to appear in the buildings across the river channel, and the men on the beach hung their lanterns at prow and stern of the barges and smaller boats, and built a fire on the silted gravel. The evening was balmy, the air much milder than on Easter evening. The stone beneath Paul's hand was still warm from the long afternoon of sun.

He sat there, one knee cocked before him on the broad parapet, happy enough to enjoy the scene, troubled only a little by a sense of hunger, the question of where he would pass the night, the uncertainty of his new employment. He had not eaten since the night before, but a little fasting, he reasoned, never hurt anyone. Rather, it tended to clear the brain. As for a lodging, there was still the old man of the lanterns, who must by now be at his work, unless he was in fact ill. If the old man was ill and had not left his room, Paul would have to face again the fat woman with the basket. And on this night he could offer the old man nothing in the way of food or drink. The prospect was uninviting. He remembered then how easily the wife of Master Larcher had dismissed him from her kitchen, and cursed himself lightly for not having stood his ground and asked her for a small advance on his earnings. A total lack of money was a definite inconvenience. He was thinking of Nicolas at the moment when he actually caught sight of the boy crossing the Quai, walking, not running, but as quickly as if the devil were at his heels.

Nicolas, being hailed, stopped short. He was delighted to see Damas. He tried for a moment to explain his hurry, and then, laughing, said only that he needed to stretch his muscles. He had no destination. He would go wherever Paul was bound, and they could talk as they went. The upshot of the meeting was that they spent an hour and more pacing the Mail, under the sculptured torches of the Arsenal, between the Arsenal and the river.

They talked, not of the shop, nor of the boy's desire to leave it, nor of women. They talked of books, and this led on to a discussion of the So-called Reformed Religion, the *Religion Prétendue Reformée;* and from that to the *Provincial Letters* of Pascal. Paul had read a good deal among the books which were no longer printed avec privilège du Roi, and was untroubled by what he had read, but not because he was extremely devout. Nicolas had read little and was passionate about every new idea.

He wanted to know, among other matters, why the *Letters* of Pascal should be forbidden him. What was this Jansenism which Pascal defended and which had made saints, it would seem, of the men and women of Port-Royal? Why must the Jesuits and the King seek to destroy it? Did it truly lead to the heresies of the So-called Reformed Religion? What of Molinos and those strange people called Quakers? He had read enough of Pascal to feel a tremendous admiration for his mind and spirit, although he had never owned a copy of either the *Letters* or the *Pensées.* There were phrases which had seemed to him pure flashes of spiritual lightning. Must he give up his admiration for Pascal before he could be reckoned a good Christian and a loyal subject? If so, he was not sure that he wanted to be either. He poured out all this to Paul with what seemed to Paul great indiscretion, in view of the fact that he had known Paul only a few hours. And Paul, who had made a point all his life of not enlisting his devotion completely in any cause, was flattered by the boy's confidence. Not very well informed himself, but better informed by a great deal than the boy, he tried to answer some of the questions. They were on dangerous ground; both of them knew that. It was a pleasure for them both to talk without constraint, as if they were old friends.

Between them and the main channel of the river was an island, the Ile Louviers, where green lumber was piled to weather and the firewood for the city was stacked as well. Above their heads the elm trees were just breaking into leaf. The sharp, fresh, slightly bitter scent of the leaf buds and new leaves mingled with the smell of water and of freshly cut wood.

Meanwhile, Marianne entertained a visitor.

Jacques Têtu, abbé de Belval and prieur de St.-Denis-de-la-Chartre, was a very eccentric old man. Among his many strange habits was that of going about the city on foot like any common man, instead of riding in the coaches of his friends or of hiring a sedan chair. It was known that he could not afford a coach of his own and that he gave away much money to the poor. No one presumed, however, that his charities had reduced him to the necessity of walking. He liked to walk, and he preferred to walk unattended. In that spring of 1694 he spent a great deal of time prowling about the Quartier St.-Paul by himself.

His fondness for the neighborhood was incomprehensible to his friends. It was no longer fashionable, had not been so for thirty years, and the abbé himself was that winter one of the fashions of Paris. Great ladies visited him on his "day." But the Quartier charmed him. It had once been royal. The names of the streets were reminders of the palace gardens; the name of the rue des Lions was all that was left of the menagerie of Charles the Fifth. But at the corner of the rue des Lions was a little *tourelle* which had once been part of the royal Hôtel St.-Pol, and within the memory of the abbé, a long memory, the Marquise de Sévigné, her husband, and her little daughter had lived in the rue des Lions. To walk these streets gave the abbé something of the pleasure of walking in the country or in the autumn woods, but pleased him more because, in spite of his melancholy and his desire for loneliness, he was a very social man. He liked to be in solitude among his fellow men. Moreover, the neighborhood was convenient to the cathedral and to the church of St.-Denis-de-la-Chartre.

On this evening he turned from the rue Beau-Treillis into the rue des Lions, and saw, where he had not before observed that there was a shopwindow, a flash of crimson. He had not known there was a bookstore in the neighborhood, and since he could not pass either a bookstore or a pretty woman without a second look, he paused, and was charmed by the garnet-covered volume.

Marianne, deserted by her two men, had tidied up the kitchen and washed the supper dishes. She opened the door to throw the dishwater out upon the stones of the covered passageway just as the abbé appeared. She could not check the gesture. The water fell in a wide, silver arc, breaking as it fell, just short of the abbé's feet.

Marianne had seen the abbé before; he was not a figure to be overlooked. He was the tallest and the thinnest man she had ever seen. However, she knew nothing further about him save that he must be a person of importance. She was surprised when he stopped before her, and distressed that she had almost wet him with her greasy water. She apologized; she curtsied, but the abbé brushed aside her apology with easy grace. He wished to enter the shop. Once in the shop, he went directly to the window, and, asking no permission, took up the volume which had caught his eye and began to examine it.

He fondled the book, stroking the leather, as Jean had done, and let it fall open in his long and bony hand. Then he inquired, "Have you no candle?"

This was what she had hoped for, that someone would be drawn into the shop by the display of the book. She had not counted upon the visit of anyone so extraordinary. When she had lighted the candle, the abbé appeared even more extraordinary, a sort of beneficent apparition. He was not merely thin; he was gaunt. He wore the short black soutane of the lay priest, which made his legs, in their black stockings, seem even more long and bony than they were. He wore no wig. His hair, which had once been blond, had grown rusty with the years and was mixed with grey. His eyebrows, shaggy and blond, and his eyelashes caught the candlelight, and yet the brows projecting over the deep sockets of his eyes seemed to make them deeper still. His face, his whole head, was in structure long and narrow, and his shoulders were high and uneven. One of the wits of the court had said, "He is shaped like a vial of perfume. Whenever he takes off his hat, I have the impulse to put my finger on the top of his head, to stopper him." As he stood there, with Paul's book in his hand, he was both curiously awkward and curiously at ease.

He began to read, silently. He turned page after page. Marianne waited, hopefully. Then he closed the book upon one finger and, looking at her sadly with his shining, deep-set eyes, said in a beautiful, deep voice, "It is outrageous, Mademoiselle."

"Why, what is wrong, Monsieur l'abbé?"

"It is," answered the abbé Têtu, "that so fine a binding should enclose so pernicious a text."

Marianne tried to remember what she knew about the *Phèdre* of Jean Racine besides the fact that it was no longer played at the Comédie, and, realizing that she knew nothing, held her peace.

The abbé looked about the shop, and inquired if it had been long at this location.

"Oh, yes, Monsieur l'abbé, a good many years."

"I am guilty," said the abbé with a sigh, "of not observing

adequately the world I live in. Is your husband responsible for the binding?"

"My husband's assistant."

"An excellent craftsman," said the abbé. "A pity that he had not a better text on which to exercise his skill." He looked thoughtfully at the book in his hand, and then said with decision, "I will give him a book which shall deserve his pains; and which will become a treasure in my library. You are puzzled, Mademoiselle. I will explain."

He dropped his black hat upon the table, seated himself in Jean's chair, crossed his long black legs, and said, "Listen to this." He opened the book and began to read.

His voice was low and unforced, yet it filled the room. It reminded Marianne of nothing so much as the humming of bees in a warm garden; and the contrast between his appearance, a man made of sticks to frighten crows, and the quality of his voice, cultivated to the last degree, so fascinated her that she did not altogether follow the sense of the words. He read in disapproval, yet he read so well that the long alexandrines swept by, balanced, monotonous, subtly varied, giving her great pleasure, although she did not fully understand them. Then he repeated a line.

"*C'est Vénus toute entière à sa proie attachée.*" He stopped short. "Is that a line befitting the pen of a Christian gentleman? In this whole drama, what has become of the Christian will to resist the power of the flesh? A drama of desire triumphant, with no saving grace." He laid the book on the table. "Mademoiselle," he said, lifting a bony forefinger to emphasize the statement, "the man who wrote those lines has himself repented of them. He so disapproves of them that he has renounced the drama and the theatre, and goes in daily sorrow for having once lavished all his talent on them. For we must admit that he possessed a certain talent. A limited gift. Yet there we have his most notorious play bound with such loving care that the little book appears almost a reliquary." He sighed, and looked past Marianne into the shadow of the hearth. When he resumed his voice was very low.

"A very great lady of my acquaintance, herself a poet, a beauty in her young days, a learned lady, was not duped by the talent of Monsieur Racine. She is dead; not two months dead. She was long dying. It is her poems that I will ask your husband's assistant to bind with as much care as he has lavished on this *Phèdre*. That volume will indeed be a reliquary. I am an old man. I saw her beauty unfold and fade under the blight of pain. She had a growth in her breast. She died of this growth. Rejoice in your youth, Mademoiselle, for it is like the branch in May."

"Oh, Monsieur l'abbé," said Marianne, "I have a son grown."

The abbé seemed not to hear her. "*Tant qu'on est belle . . .*" he said very softly, looking into the darkened hearth, and then, "*Mais on a peu de temps à l'être, et longtemps à ne l'être plus.*"

He looked about him vaguely, picked up his hat and stood up, unfolding himself slowly to his full height.

"I trespass on your time," he said. "I cannot sleep. Opium is of no use. I lie awake, night after night, and I am haunted by memory. Tomorrow I shall send you the poems of Madame Deshoulières. I ask to have her initials enlaced in a monogram, like those of Monsieur Racine." He put on his hat and moved slowly toward the door, accompanied by his shadow, looking himself, in his black garments, like a tall shadow. In the doorway he paused and said, "I may send also, at some future date, a little drama of my own on a Scriptural theme."

He went off, leaving Marianne with the assurance that the designs of Nicolas would not miscarry, that Jean would not dismiss a workman who had brought the shop an order from this strange but distinguished abbé. She had forgotten to inquire his name. If only he did not forget, among his memories, to send the book.

Almost as soon as he was gone his visit began to take on the quality of a dream. He had communicated his sadness to Marianne, and he had evoked a disquieting pleasure, a personal gratitude. "He thought me young," she said to herself, closing the shutters upon the still luminous twilight, "I who have borne five children and buried four; who have a grown son."

Chapter Five

*M*ONSIEUR found his wife writing letters. At her feet was a basket of honey-colored Spaniel puppies. About her shoulders, over her dressing gown, was an old fur pelerine which she had brought with her years ago, at the time of their marriage, from the Palatinate. Her hair, uncovered, had not yet been arranged for the day. She wore no paint or powder on her face—but she never did. Every freckle and pockmark and wrinkle showed as plainly as God intended it to. A short, thick-set old woman, more stocky than fat, for she exercised daily, she greeted Monsieur without comment, returning, for his elaborate reverence, a look of frank inquiry. She had not expected a visit from Monsieur, but if she had, she would not have changed her routine in any respect.

The windows were wide open, the room full of damp air. Monsieur shivered, but made no motion to close the windows. He did not intend to remain there long. Beside his wife's writing case stood a silver tray on which her breakfast had been brought her from the Commons. Monsieur looked it over and did not see what he was looking for. He observed, with skillful casualness:

"The King received a pamphlet with his broth this morning."

"Indeed?" said Madame. "Was it the same as this?"

She lifted a sheet of paper and took up a copy of *Monsieur Scarron Apparu à Madame de Maintenon.* She offered it to Monsieur in her small, firm, freckled hand, and Monsieur leaned toward it long enough to verify the title.

"If you care to read it," said his wife, "it is yours."

"Thank you," said Monsieur. "If you received one with your *petit déjeuner,* I shall probably receive one too."

"It was in my napkin," she said, "as you imagined. Do you imagine also a general prevalence of pamphlets this morning?"

Monsieur smiled. "Since you and the King have been favored, why not all the family?"

"La Reine Scarronique," said Madame, taking up her pen, "will be interested." She knew that the visit was over. She dipped her pen in the ink and considered her interrupted letter. Monsieur, withdrawing, gauged the extent of his wife's good humor by the term with which she referred to her enemy. She had a vast number of other titles in two languages, less kind and less decorous. He envied her invention and her vocabulary.

The King sat in Council that morning the usual three hours. On the stroke of twelve he entered the Salle des Glaces and proceeded through it to Mass in his chapel, followed by most of his court. After Mass he dined in the Salle du Grand Couvert, and then, since the day was Monday, he remained there for another hour to receive petitions from anyone in the land, high or low, who cared to petition him. After that he retired to his bedroom, where he changed to hunting clothes—coat, boots, hat, wig, everything. Bontemps, receiving the King's coat of that morning, removed from its pockets the King's handkerchief, a fistful of holy medals, and the libelous pamphlet. The King, seeing the pamphlet, said, "Give it to me," and thrust it into the pocket of his hunting coat, with the intention of turning it over to Monsieur de Pontchartrain. His mind was full of the business discussed at Council. The pamphlet had become a trifling irritation which he forgot for the next few hours.

La Violette had promised the King good sport, and he kept his promise. The birds rose often, the King shot and never missed. But several times he felt a dizziness which forced him to lower his gun, as he was about to take aim, and wait before he could again lift it to his shoulder. The sun was still shining, the birds still rising, when the King left the field, a little before six o'clock, and went, still in his hunting clothes, to the apartment of Madame de Maintenon. He was greatly fatigued.

He entered the apartment unannounced, earlier than was his custom, and found the mistress of it seated in her sheltered corner between the bed and the fireplace. It had not occurred to him that she would not be there and ready to receive him.

She held on her knees a portable desk, littered with papers. As the King entered, she swept all these together with a startled gesture and handed the desk to Nanon, who hovered near. Nanon the devoted, Nanon the treasure, curtsied to the King, the desk balanced upon her outstretched hands, and disappeared into the adjoining room. Madame de Maintenon advanced to meet the King. The King, embracing her, intent only upon his own malaise, did not observe any reluctance in her manner, nor that her eyelids were wet with tears. She was there when he needed her, as she always was, the smooth soft cheek, the lace, the velvet untainted by any artificial perfume, in the lace the faintest odor of incense, as if she had just come from chapel. Yet he had intruded upon the only hour of the day which she attempted to reserve for herself.

At St.-Cyr, her school for impoverished gentlewomen, although to be there was her greatest happiness, she was seldom or never alone, and never without responsibility. At Versailles there was always the long evening with the King, and when the

King had left her, visits from his courtiers, visits from his children, between whom and the King she was mediator. Tensions, jealousies, malice, she met them with charity and common sense. There were always letters to be written, books to be read. She rose at seven and was seldom permitted to retire before midnight. She was approaching sixty—she was older than the King—and although she had lived without dissipation, the strain of such long and crowded days was making itself felt. Her headaches were more frequent, her neuralgia more painful.

She had married because her spiritual adviser had convinced her that it was her duty to do so. She prayed daily that she might be for the King all that he needed, but she did not love him. Children she loved with great tenderness, even those who no longer deserved her love, and old servants, but no man had ever been able to rouse in her an equal tenderness. The King was her responsibility. She esteemed him, she was grateful to him. She was especially grateful when she remembered St.-Cyr; it was his gift to her, a gift of labor, more precious than jewels. But as a woman she received the King's attentions as a form of penance, and marveled that they continued, year after year. She could recognize the existence of sexual passion as she recognized the existence of evil. She encountered proof of its violence daily, in one person or another, and externally she knew how to deal with it, but she did not understand it. She had never experienced it.

When Nanon Balbien had brought her the writing desk that evening, the old woman had said, "There it is, that horrible libel. I would have destroyed it, but that you have told me so often, destroy nothing, conceal nothing. Ah, Madame, in the old days when I boiled your little pot there was nothing but kindness in the broth. You torment yourself needlessly, if I dare say so."

"It is no more than simple wisdom," Madame de Maintenon had replied, "to be informed of the activities of one's enemies, as well as of one's friends."

She knew herself hated. The pamphlet itself had come as no surprise. She had considered calmly, and even with a puritanical satisfaction at suffering in the performance of a duty, the cartoon of the statue and the four women who held the King enslaved. The raising of the ghost of Scarron had troubled her a little; she had never forgotten her deep gratitude to Scarron, as a girl. His offer of marriage had freed her from the necessity of entering a convent. It had been a gesture of protection offered gallantly by a man in his forties (and a cripple) to a girl of seventeen. She would have been glad to find a little of his wit and courage in the pages which followed. But there was nothing. She had not found even a touch of his genial ribaldry. Nothing but an extravagant narrative in which characters from Scarron's romances appeared and disappeared, in which the King made improper advances to his guest, the Queen of England, and in which she herself went upon some strange sort of pilgrimage. She had been ready to lay it aside when she came, midway in the text, upon a passage which struck her at the heart. She had read that at St.-Cyr she maintained and educated a group of well-bred but impoverished young women from among whom she chose, at her discretion, concubines for an aging King. She had felt the tears rush to her eyes, and had cried out to Nanon, "Why must they attack St.-Cyr?"

At that moment the King had entered, too early, as if he had some disaster to report to her. But, having embraced her, he flung himself into his armchair on the other side of the fireplace, and sat there without a word, while Nanon went lightly up the few steps at the end of the room, bearing the little desk, and returned, after a brief interval, with the distaff and spindle, and the wool with which the mistress liked to busy her hands during the King's conferences. The King then remarked that the room seemed very warm. He asked Nanon to open a window, and requested that Monsieur de Pontchartrain be sent for.

Alone with the King, Madame de Maintenon left the spindle untouched. The tears which he had not noticed dried on her eyelids. Composed and serene, she observed the King, and wondered if this was to be one of those evenings she had learned to dread, when he brought her in silence the burden of his gloom, profoundly courteous, profoundly inconsiderate. There was no escape for her from those evenings, even when she pleaded a headache or a great fatigue. The King would wait, while Nanon prepared her for bed, and when she was ensconced against the pillows, he would remain, in his chair beside the fire, preventing sleep and refusing solace. But when Monsieur de Pontchartrain arrived, the King roused himself from his brown study.

Monsieur de Pontchartrain, slender and erect, perched on the folding stool before the King, spread out his portfolio upon another stool, and the evening's work began.

The King signed letters, listened while his minister read for his approval other letters, amended, rejected, dictated replies. He rested his eyes by closing them while Monsieur de Pontchartrain read to him, and when he opened them the room swam in a dazzle of candlelight. This routine business went on for some three quarters of an hour. Then Monsieur de Pontchartrain brought up another subject.

He described a new tax; it was to be a poll tax, levied throughout the kingdom, and based upon the estimated wealth of each individual, the proceeds to go directly to the Crown.

"The Crown is in desperate need of money," said Monsieur de Pontchartrain. "The usual sources of revenue are no longer adequate. We have no other recourse than to tax the nation as a whole." His enunciation was fine, his phrasing rapid. The statement, as he pronounced it, admitted of no argument. In the mind of the King another voice spoke, just as clearly. "France," said the voice of Fénelon, the tutor of the King's grandson, "France is become a vast desolate almshouse."

"And now," said the King to himself, "I am asked to lay a further burden on my poor."

The King glanced at Madame de Maintenon, as if she must

have heard, also, the voice of the young priest. Her eyes were upon him, in an expression grave and tender and expectant. Her hands, those beautifully shaped white hands, lay quietly, palms up, upon the black velvet of her lap. The eyes of Pontchartrain were also upon the King, without insolence, but very bright in their direct gaze.

The King said, "There remains the question, however greatly we are in need of funds, as to whether the Crown has the moral right to draw upon the wealth of the entire kingdom."

"But, Sire, since the entire kingdom belongs to the Crown, the Crown does no more than take a small part of what already belongs to it in entirety."

"It is a question for the Church," said the King. "I wish to consult Monsieur the Archbishop of Paris."

Pontchartrain bowed his head. "I venture to urge you, Sire, to do so without delay." He closed his portfolio and waited to be dismissed.

The King did not move. He was wondering if his wife could have conspired with the young priest to have that letter put into his hand, and the thought brought with it such a mingling of jealousy and hurt that he felt a sweat break out upon his forehead. He dismissed the thought almost as quickly as it had sprung into being, but it made him feel very ill. It was a grief which he could not lay before her in hope of consolation. He had bound his own hands in regard to Fénelon. He was not yet ready to acknowledge the existence of the letter. Then he reached into the pocket of his coat for a handkerchief with which to wipe his forehead, and his fingers encountered the rough paper of the pamphlet.

"Before you retire," said the King to his minister, "pray send word to Monsieur de La Reynie that there is in present circulation a libel entitled *The Ghost of Monsieur Scarron*, which we require him to suppress. Make your letter very strong. You cannot make it too strong. The pamphlet is an attack upon Madame de Maintenon." He turned to his wife and saw a deep rose color mounting to her cheek, suffusing her throat, her forehead. If she blushed like this at the mere mention of Scarron, how she would blush if he accused her of complicity with the young priest! But he would never accuse her. He said in his usual, altogether courteous manner, "I am sorry to mention this matter in your presence."

Madame de Maintenon, painfully aware of her blushing—it was a weakness which she had never been able to control—nevertheless answered with no confusion, "It is not for myself that I am distressed, but the pamphlet attacks St.-Cyr."

"Ah," said the King, with a glance of great significance to Monsieur de Pontchartrain. Then, "As you leave, be so good as to send word to Bontemps that there will be no *grand coucher* tonight, and that I will retire immediately."

But when the minister had withdrawn, he still sat on, silent, while Madame de Maintenon waited, the color ebbing slowly from her face. At last he got to his feet slowly, as if with difficulty. She rose also, and moved forward a few steps to meet him. He lifted his hands, placing one on either of her shoulders, and said gravely, "You endure many things for me."

Only that, and suddenly, bowing his head upon his right hand, he leaned with all his weight upon her shoulder. The stiff curls brushed her cheek. She straightened herself to support this weight, feeling all the King's grief, all his loneliness, all his great responsibilities bearing down upon her single body.

They stood so for a long moment. Then the King turned away, and she watched him go with a great pity mixed with a great relief. The door closed behind him, and left her free to write her letters, to make her prayers, to retire alone to the curtained bed in the deep alcove behind her.

Chapter Six

THAT MONDAY NIGHT in Paris, Paul Damas and Nicolas Larcher walked for a long time on the Mail between the river and the Arsenal. The stars came out in pale clusters above the clotted new leaves of the elms; the smell of the river dominated and then obliterated the various scents and odors of the day. The coldness of the water seemed to rise and flow about their ankles. The Quai was deserted, the Port below so quiet that the young men could hear the water lapping at the sides of the boats. Nicolas decided that he must go home. He offered to accompany Paul part way to his lodgings, wherever they were, and it then came out that Paul had no lodging for the night nor any money with which to pay for one.

Paul had not forgotten the old man of the lanterns. The image of the fat woman with the basket was even more vivid in his mind. At some moment during his long conversation with Nicolas he had decided against looking to the old man for shelter again. He had formulated no other plan for himself, and his declaration to the boy that he was homeless was not consciously a cast for an offer of hospitality. It resulted, however, in a quick invitation.

"Sleep with me," said Nicolas. "We will be only a little crowded."

So it happened that Marianne, going in the dark of the morning on Tuesday, candle in hand, to waken her son, drew back the curtain of his bed and looked down upon the face of Paul Damas. Nicolas had already risen and gone down to the court.

Paul lay upon his back, his eyes wide open, one arm flung outside the covers and across his chest. His shirt was open at the throat; the candlelight, gliding over the flesh, made the short hair sparkle, and showed the iris of the eye, dazzled by its brightness, to be reddish brown, very clear, and almost the color of fox fur. Marianne dropped the curtain at once, and Paul saw the glimmer of her candle through the cloth as she moved away.

When Nicolas entered the kitchen, the window was un-shuttered, the fire burned brightly, and his mother was washing the back of her neck with a white cloth. She stood before the copper-framed mirror on the kitchen wall. The mirror was cheap. A flaw had developed in the quicksilver. The flaw hung between her reflection and her face like a blemish. The glass had a greenish cast, and, where she stood, neither sunlight nor firelight fell upon her skin to relieve the pallor. The effect was not encouraging. It made her look ill. She had been searching her reflection to learn, if she could, why the strange, tall abbé had called her young, and as she appraised her features she also wondered how her unwashed, sleepy face had appeared to Paul; she had not even combed her hair.

She had taken her features for granted for a long time now, as she had accepted her status. She was the mother of a grown son, therefore she was no longer young. As soon as Nicolas entered, she abandoned her scrutiny. She bent her head, lifting the mass of dark curls from the nape of her neck with one hand, and with the other scrubbed her neck vigorously. She rinsed the cloth in cold water, wrung it out tightly, shook it, and hung it up, all before she acknowledged the presence of the young man. Then, "You are taking in lodgers," she said crisply.

Nicolas smiled and began to cut himself a piece of bread.

"Does that annoy you?"

"Personally, no. But your father may very well feel that things are moving too rapidly. He did not engage the young man. He merely permitted him to remain. It is a bit early to be taking him into the family."

"Damas had no lodging," said Nicolas. "He has no money. He should ask Papa tonight for a day's wages."

"Don't rush your father," said Marianne. "I will pay him a day's wages. He can pay me back when your father pays him; and say nothing to your father about it."

She returned to the mirror to comb her hair and tie on her cap. It seemed to her that she risked very little. If the abbé was as good as his word and remembered to send the work, Jean would keep the new man. The more she thought of the abbé's visit, however, the less certain she became that the abbé would remember his promise. She had neglected to inquire his name. That should not be difficult to learn. If he did not send the book, she would go to him herself and remind him. So she counted out the coins for Paul, and kept her counsel regarding the tall abbé.

Extraordinarily, the abbé Têtu remembered. By midmorning a servant brought to Larcher the poems of Madame Deshoulières, with the instruction that they be bound by his assistant.

"Mademoiselle," said the servant, "understands all the particulars."

"The abbé Têtu came himself to the shop?" said Larcher, incredulous, when the servant had gone. "But the abbé Têtu is an intimate of Madame de Maintenon."

"He did not speak of that," said Marianne. "He spoke of the lady who wrote the book." But she felt strangely reticent concerning what he had said of Madame Deshoulières, or of Monsieur Racine's *Phèdre*, or of herself.

"It is a great honor for you," said Jean to Paul, and led him away to choose a piece of leather for the abbé's book. Nicolas said to his mother teasingly:

"Now you have a friend at court. You will know where to go when you wish to petition the King."

"And now," she returned, "you have what you wanted, help for your father. Can you wait a few days before you pack your portmanteau? You are very gay at the prospect of leaving us."

Paul, receiving at the end of the day the money which Marianne had counted out for him from her own market money, put two and two together in his own fashion. He gave Marianne all the credit for obtaining the abbé's commission for him, and he gave himself not a little credit for having obtained her interest in his affairs. He had seen her face bent above him, tender, unguarded, in a look not meant for him. She was prettier than he had realized in his first view of her. He was willing to assume for himself the look not meant for him, and he was also prepared to be cautious. A woman had gulled him in Auxerre. With money in his pocket, feeling quite as gay as Nicolas, he went off after work to find himself a lodging. He succeeded, by being as flattering as he knew to the bedraggled woman who showed him up five flights of crooked stairs to a room as small as that of Father Lanterns.

"It is dark," she said, "but what of that, since you will not be working here. I rented it formerly to a seamstress who never went out and did nothing but complain."

"I shall never complain," said Paul, pocketing the key.

"I believe you," she said, "nor shall I, with a pleasant young gentleman in the house."

She looked about the room, wiped the table with a wet rag, and concluded, "I supply sheets. There is a privy on the first landing. The door to the street is never locked."

The room was over a stationer's shop in the rue des Deux Boules, between the Grand Châtelet and the church of St.-Jacques de la Boucherie.

AT VERSAILLES the King slept badly. There had been no grand coucher; there was no *lever* the following morning. Fagon declared that the King suffered from a tertian fever, and treated him according to his usual methods. He gave the King quinine and purgatives, alternately, repeating the doses until the King purged blood. He buried the King under feather quilts until his nightshirt was soaked with sweat. He prescribed a clear broth and a thin old burgundy, so old that even its rich color had grown pale, and diluted it with water.

The King bore the treatment heroically, but because of his physical exhaustion his thoughts swarmed through his aching head in uncontrollable disorder. The greater part of each night he passed between waking and sleeping. In the daylight hours, since he was unable to convene his Council, he found time on his hands. He had time to remember and further examine with a perverse interest the pamphlet which he had unconsciously re-titled *The Ghost of Monsieur Scarron*. It contained all the possible elements of insult, it seemed to him. It struck at the deepest emotions of his heart, at his most generous gestures, at his most sacred responsibilities. It dredged from the past passions and griefs which he thought he had put away forever, and in his weakness he could not again dismiss them.

He lived again through the self-reproaches of his dying passion for Louise de La Vallière; he suffered again the bitter quarrels with Madame de Montespan and the bitter fear of the Great Poison Trials. He felt once more the profound revulsion of the moment when La Reynie presented him evidence that Madame de Montespan herself had been involved with La Voisin, that she had, with La Voisin, taken part in the Black Mass, and that she had most certainly with her own hand given the King as aphrodisiacs filth compounded in sacrilege. He remembered as well his brief and now incomprehensible passion for La Fontanges, which had ceased as suddenly and as incomprehensibly as it had begun, and he asked himself once more, impatiently, why he should blame himself for her death. He could not command himself to love. She had died in childbirth, fortunately without living issue, but this was not his fault. She had been neither destitute nor unattended.

A rumor that she had drunk poison in a glass of milk offered to her by Madame de Montespan had been brought to him, and he had been urged to have an autopsy performed in order that the story might be either quashed or confirmed. The possibility that the rumor might be true was more than he could face. He had required no autopsy. He wished only to forget the girl, beautiful and adoring as she had been; but the pamphlet and his illness would not permit him to forget her.

He had done all that he could. He had gone to Madame de Maintenon and asked her to reason with the girl, to explain to the silly child that the affair must end. He had been certain that Madame de Maintenon would approach the girl with kindness. He had hoped that she would be able to impart some of her own reasonableness to Fontanges.

She had but small success with Fontanges, but she had applauded his own effort to terminate the affair, and she had never once reproached him for having become involved in it, nor had she thought him heartless in the conclusion of it.

She had never reproached him. But the pamphlet reproached him, the anonymous letter reproached him. The pamphlet was without merit, literary or otherwise, but the letter, had it been couched in gentler terms, might have been of value to him. The letter and the pamphlet alike reproached him for the continuation of the war and for the poverty of his kingdom. The letter attacked his self-esteem; the pamphlet attacked St.-Cyr.

Much later in the week, when he woke finally with a clear head, although drained of bodily vigor, he had made two decisions. The abbé Fénelon must continue undisturbed in his work with the young prince and in his pleasant conferences with Madame de Maintenon and her dear friends; and all those who could be held responsible for the pamphlet—the author, the printer, the engraver, the distributors—must be punished.

Before he began his morning's work with Monsieur de Pontchartrain, he sent for the chief of the police of Paris.

Nicolas Gabriel de La Reynie came seldom to Versailles. When he appeared there toward noon on a day in midweek, it might fairly be assumed that something had disturbed the King. Monsieur, encountering the Lieutenant of the Police at the head of the marble stairway, assumed as much, and smiled, and there was a quality of complacency in his smile which the Lieutenant remarked because at the time he saw no reason for it.

Although La Reynie came seldom to Versailles and the King almost never visited Paris, the King and his Lieutenant of the Police were at all times in close touch with one another. Before the establishment of the King's Police in Paris, the city had been kept in order only by the retainers of the many great houses, a situation which tended to create disorder rather than to dispel it. La Reynie, taking control in the King's name, established order, if not absolutely, at least to an extraordinary degree. He instituted a number of reforms in the management of the city which made his name respected both in the city and at court. The illumination and the cleansing of the streets were his work. He was, for those who knew him personally, as for those who knew him only as a legend, the walking embodiment of honesty and justice.

He was also for the King both eyes and ears in that city which the King avoided. What names were entered as guests in the records of the hostelries, or as criminals in those of the prisons, what books were published, what songs were sung on street corners or in cabarets, the exact number of beggars or of homeless sick, the prices of grain, of bread, all these and an infinite number of similar details were available to the King through his chief of police. The condition of the city seemed as clear to him as the lines in the palm of his hand. Through La Reynie he could, when the occasion warranted it, bypass the Parlement, which was the court of justice of the city, and so quietly maintain his personal control of the law.

The King and La Reynie had not always seen eye to eye on all subjects. La Reynie had more than once, in the name of abstract justice, held out most stubbornly against the King's personal wishes. During the Great Poison Trials, for example, the King had wished not only to suppress but to destroy all evidence against his mistress. La Reynie had wished it presented. The King had won the major issue, but the documents had not been destroyed. They had been entrusted to La Reynie's personal keeping, and this matter of the little casket which contained them remained perpetually between La Reynie and the King as a challenge and a bond.

La Reynie was approaching seventy. He had served the King since those first years after the death of Mazarin when the King had asserted his own authority, and through the years the King's reliance upon him had deepened steadily. His own devotion to the King was as great.

When, after a brief conference with the King on matters which he had anticipated, La Reynie received from the King's hand the noxious pamphlet, he understood the true reason for the summons, and he was not pleased. He said so frankly, and the King, without comment, drew his eyebrows slightly together and waited for an explanation.

"Your Majesty knows better than anyone," La Reynie reminded him tactfully, "the present condition of Paris."

Surely the King had not forgotten the bread riots of the past few winters. One of these had resulted in a hanging, necessary, but unfortunate. In spite of the King's enormous personal generosity, the people still suffered from a lack of bread. There were more than three thousand homeless wandering the streets of Paris. The King had understandably been unable to increase the size of his police force in proportion to the growth of the city because of the inevitable expenses of his war. La Reynie's men had more work than they could handle properly; he could ill spare any of them to make an all-out search of the city for a pamphlet. He regretted the insult to Madame de Maintenon; he agreed that insult to the King was the equivalent of blasphemy, but, with due respect, he submitted the opinion that the pamphlet itself was of small importance compared to the risk of rioting in Paris.

"Nevertheless," said the King, "I wish the authors of the libel found and, once found, I wish them punished to the full extent of the law."

La Reynie bowed. "The galleys?" he inquired.

"I wish them hanged," said the King flatly.

"We will do what we can," said La Reynie, bowing once more. "But, Sire, permit me to remind you that it is extremely difficult to find a needle in a haystack."

On his way back to his carriage, which waited for him in the Court of Honor, he passed the spot where he had encountered Monsieur. Monsieur was not waiting for him, but his disembodied smile was there; and La Reynie, remembering it, felt suddenly enlightened. He did not for an instant assume that Monsieur had performed a sleight-of-hand in offering the napkin and the pamphlet to the King; he did assume that whoever had placed the pamphlet in the King's ship had done so with the knowledge and protection of someone of such high position as to be quite beyond the reach of the King's police. There would be no profit in beginning his inquiries at Versailles. Nor had the King suggested it. The source of the pamphlet, he was certain, was in Paris, and it was there that the search must begin.

Chapter Seven

THE TITLE of the pamphlet as the King had given it to
Monsieur de Pontchartrain had already been sent to the rue
St.-Jacques to be added to the list of proscribed publications
which Denis Thierry printed for the King. La Reynie, having
examined the pamphlet, sent further identifying information,
such as the name of the publisher and the date, and a description
of the format—in duodécimo, 136 pages, *y compris la gravure*—
and requested that the revised list be distributed as soon as possible. It did not occur to him to correct the title. In due time the
list reached the bindery in the rue des Lions, where Jean Larcher
called it to the attention of Paul and of Nicolas, and then forgot
it.

On Saturday evening Paul received his first week's wages, five
livres and ten sols, a good handful. It would have been six
livres except for the half day on Monday before he had begun
work. Larcher, tying the strings of his purse, called to Marianne

for glasses and for wine. She brought three glasses and a carafe of claret.

"We are four tonight," said her husband. "Bring one for yourself."

"Thank you. I am not thirsty."

"Nevertheless, bring a glass for yourself, because we drink with Damas." He shoved his purse into his pocket, and poured the wine, filling each glass to exactly the same level. "A family is a firm," he said, as they gathered about the table. "Therefore we must all drink together." They lifted their glasses in the time-honored ritual. Larcher leaned back his head and poured the wine down his throat in one swallow, but Marianne delayed, holding the glass as if to admire the color or the clearness of the wine. A regret, unanticipated and unreasonably poignant, filled her heart at this formal declaration of a decision which she already knew and had approved. Nicolas was to leave them. This strange young man whom she neither liked nor disliked, as she told herself, was to take his place. The decision did not warrant such regret. She hesitated so long that Larcher said to her:

"But drink. For the sake of the bargain."

She smiled, and emptied her glass.

Paul, as Larcher turned away, dismissing the little group, repaid to Marianne the money she had lent him. She accepted the coins with reserve, in silence; both silence and reserve were explicable because Jean was still so near them in the room, and she had enjoined a secrecy upon the loan. Nevertheless, he was struck by a certain coldness in her manner which puzzled him. Once again he was disappointed that no one asked him to remain for supper, but his disappointment did not last long.

The taste of the wine was still upon his lips when he emerged from the shadowy street upon the Quai. The evening lay before him, untouched, with infinite possibilities. The sky above the island where the cathedral stood was pale gold.

He knew what he wanted: first of all, food, and then a young companion, preferably a girl. And he knew where he could find them, at the Petite Bastille and at the Pont Neuf. The thought of Father Lanterns, recurring to him as he looked at the gold sky, he put aside with hardly a flicker of conscience. He would look up the old man on the morrow. Sunday would be a day of freedom also.

At the Petite Bastille he ate extravagantly and well of a hot beef pasty. He had another glass of wine, a heavier burgundy, and as he sat there, he thought of Marianne holding her glass before her in that long moment of hesitation. He saw no significance in her delay. He remembered the color of the wine and the look of revery in her grey eyes only because the whole picture had pleased him, and to remember them became part of his immediate contentment. "And yet," he thought, "she is not especially pretty. She could make more of herself." He had observed her during the week with a natural curiosity. She controlled his future to a large extent, he was sure of that. She seemed always very reserved, except with Nicolas. Her coldness of manner this evening, as she accepted his coins, was not very different from her usual behavior; and for that he had an explanation of a sort. She seemed contented with Larcher. "Then," he thought with a vanity encouraged by the wine, "with a little effort I could make her discontented. But it is not worth upsetting the applecart for that." He paid his bill, and set off toward the Pont Neuf, toward the sunset.

In the rue de la Mortellerie he lost sight of the river. He passed a man who was hoisting into place one of La Reynie's lanterns, and who grinned at him as he went by, and said with macabre joviality, "Up the rope she goes." He saw the river again when he crossed the Place de Grève. Beyond it the cathedral loomed broadside against a sky which had grown violet and was pin-pointed with stars. He passed the Grand Châtelet, the stronghold of La Reynie's police force, ominous under its old turrets, guarding the old approach to the Pont au Change, and went on until he again found the river.

He was then on the Quai de la Mégisserie, and he stopped to lean against the parapet and look down upon the water, and from the water to the sky, savoring the beauty of the evening and his own personal satisfaction. His goal, the Pont Neuf, was at the western end of the Quai; he could see the lights, and hear voices and an occasional burst of song. Upstream, to his left, the Pont au Change carried a double row of houses, tall and narrow, with small, pointed gables, all alike, above its series of darkened arches. The river rushed through the arches with great force and, below the arch nearest the right bank, turned a water mill, which creaked and splashed. A few barges, hooded with canvas, were moored nearer the Pont Neuf, waiting, perhaps, to be towed farther upstream in the morning. There were no boats and no landing place on the opposite shore.

The river flowed smoothly in its deep channel, its luminous surface unbroken by any eddies or ripples, but he knew how the water piled itself against the stone piers of the Pont Neuf. The Quai was deserted, the air as soft as when he had walked with Nicolas on the Mail.

The Quai was deserted because it had acquired such a reputation for robberies that La Reynie no longer permitted the setting up of any stands or booths which might serve as ambushes for the brigands. Paul in his ignorance felt no sense of danger. He was aware only that he had come upon one of those unfrequented places which were so common in Paris, near to the main centers of activity, and yet curiously sequestered and tranquil.

Water had always charmed him, its deception, its variability. He thought, leaning over the parapet, that this was the same river as the sunny tide that had brought him to Paris, the river that he had known as a country stream with grassy margins, the same and not the same. He was himself the same and not the same young man who had lived in Auxerre, preoccupied with objects and people whom he would probably never see again. He hoped tonight that he would never see them again. It seemed very long ago, that life, yet it was only a few weeks behind him. There was a stone stairway near where he stood, leading down to the beach. If he cared to, he could descend those steps and dip his hand into water which had followed him from Auxerre. And that, he told himself, was the only link remaining between his old life and his new, a link that was in itself a symbol of obliteration.

It was fortunate that something had occurred to get him out of Auxerre. He had been duped; that was unpleasant to remember. Also, he had behaved dishonorably. The realization became clear before he could again marshal excuses and disguises for his conduct. It caught him, in his contentment, with his guard down. He bowed his head on his hands, his elbows resting on the stone before him. The attitude was that of prayer, but he was not praying. He was merely waiting to be relieved of the sudden bitterness which he felt so sharply; he might have waited so for a sharp intestinal pain to resolve itself and pass. After a time he lifted his head and looked down again upon the river. The sky had grown much darker; the surface of the water was still luminous.

He was just about to turn away when he saw the milky pallor broken by a wedge of blackness drawn in mid-channel by a boat which shot from beneath the central arch of the Pont au Change. It was followed at once by another boat, somewhat larger than the first, and from the maneuvering and the speed of the rowers, Paul surmised that this was either a race or a pursuit. The drama caught his interest, and he stayed.

The first boat held only two passengers, one rowing, one steering. The other had two sets of oars and a man in the stern and another in the sharp prow, who leaned far overboard and lunged to catch at something in the water. He did not succeed. The boat passed too quickly, and when it had passed Paul saw the object bobbing in the water. It spun, catching a gleam of light upon a flat side. Then, as if caught in a hidden eddy, the object sailed directly after the smaller boat and overtook it, so that

the steersman of the small boat managed to get both arms around
it and lift it, dripping, onto his knees.

Meanwhile the rowers in the larger boat, in an effort to check
their craft, backed water furiously, fighting both the current
and their own impetus. The four blades waved in the air, dipped,
rose again wildly, making Paul think of an insect lying on its
back, helpless. The steersman also tried to do his part; he succeeded in turning the boat sideways, so that it swung across the
bow of the smaller boat, and then, like an iron rod against a
magnet, swung parallel with it. The two locked boats began to
revolve, the current moving them all the while downstream. It
was easy to foresee that if they did not disentangle themselves
promptly they would both be flung against the piers of the
bridge, and that would be the end of them.

Paul leaned forward, pressing against the stone, as if the few
inches he gained in nearness would make the struggle more
visible. He could not see exactly what was happening. He heard
some choked cries, as if the men were too busy to cry aloud.
Even so, a sense of their anger and their fear rose to him through
the semi-darkness. One boat lost an oar; he saw it float away.
The boats continued to revolve; then the smaller disengaged itself and began to pull for the beach. The other, which he now
saw had lost the oar, still spun, and with increasing speed. One of
its two oarsmen was on his back in the bottom of the boat.
The other, alone, was trying to regain mastery of the craft. It
was heavy for one man to handle, and the steersman's efforts did
not help the oarsman. Quite the contrary. With a pleasurable
horror which released him from any thoughts of himself, Paul
watched the current seize upon the boat with greater force, and
waited to see it crash and capsize. At the last possible moment,
however, the single rower managed to get it straight with the
rush of the current. It went under the main archway, centered
like an arrow, and safe. Then Paul noticed that the smaller boat,
which he had forgotten to observe, was making a landing
directly below where he stood. The drama continued.

The men climbed from the boat and, lifting the prow, dragged it a safe distance up the beach. They stood a moment, resting, and looking down-river. There was no sign of the other boat. One said, "So they made it."

"More than they deserved," said the other. "It was ours. We spotted it first."

"Who are they?"

"Never saw 'em before. If I see 'em again, I'll crack their skulls. Nearly drowned us, they did." He took off his cap and wiped his forehead. His companion merely said:

"I wonder what we've got."

He reached into the boat and lifted out the package, which was square, perhaps two feet in dimension. He hugged it to his chest as if it were fairly heavy, and walked with it a little higher up the beach, toward Paul, before he set it down. The two men knelt over it then, so that Paul could no longer see it. He heard them curse the knots, which were water-swollen; then one of them whipped out a knife. They were some time unwrapping the package. Paul felt his interest growing all the while, as if he were watching a show, or as if he had got involved in a game with these men. Then he heard one of them exclaim in infinite disgust:

"Books." The word was followed by a stream of softly spoken invocation, calling upon all filth, and especially upon the ultimate, the human.

"For this," said his companion, "I nearly bust a gut. I wish they had 'em. Let's chuck 'em back in the river."

At this Paul cried out, before he could think to check himself, "Wait," and before they could do more than rise from their crouching position about the opened package, he ran down the steps and joined them. At close range he could see little more of them than he had been able to distinguish from the Quai. The gleam of an eye, the outline of a beaky nose, the silhouette of a head wrapped with a rag, like a turban. But he was immediately aware of their suspicion and a suspended hostility.

He wished that he had counted ten before he spoke. But it was too late to retreat. He tried to tell them that books were often of great value.

"You want them? I give them to you," said the man in the turban. There was no generosity in his voice.

"No," said Paul hastily. "You salvaged them. They're yours. But it would be foolish to throw them away without finding what they are."

"For me, one's as bad as another," said the man in the turban. But the other said in a slow, nasal voice:

"It makes sense, what he says. Show the gentleman the little stinking books."

The package, Paul now saw, contained four smaller packages. One of these had been ripped open. The riverman, taking it up, extracted from it a small book, small indeed, less than half an inch thick and about five by eight inches in width and breadth, a size to fit conveniently into a pocket. Paul, taking it into his hand, thought automatically, "A duodecimo." There seemed to be a picture on the cover. He could not see it clearly. The riverman obligingly got out his tinder box and struck a flame.

For an instant Paul saw an engraving, the statue of the King in the Place des Victoires, but with certain changes. He did not have time to read the names of the women before the light flickered and went out. He could guess what he had not been able to observe.

"Well?" said the man who held the tinderbox.

"I don't know," said Paul, temporizing.

"Make it your business to know," said the same man. Paul heard the threat under the slow inflections. He explained nervously:

"It depends upon how you feel about the police."

"Can you see us? Not much to brag about, eh? And I inform you of what you cannot perhaps see: we are very hungry."

"There are people who would pay good money for the books."

"Libels?" said the riverman.

"Against the King," said Paul.

"Where does one find these people?" said the same man, and then the other said:

"Perhaps the gentleman would care to buy the books himself. We won't ask much—just what you happen to have in your purse. You needn't burden yourself with the books, either, if that troubles you."

"My purse," Paul began. "Listen, I spend my money before I earn it. But these libels——" He described the cartoon to them as rapidly and vividly as he could. He went on from that to tell them of the Ballad Singer. He promised them that the Ballad Singer would know how to market the books. He promised them a munificent profit. He spoke with an eloquence he had not suspected in himself, and all the while he felt his knees trembling. He ended, in order to convince them, by promising to approach the Ballad Singer himself, and to make his offer the more authentic, he demanded a third of the profit. Fortunately for his argument, the Ballad Singer was well known to them by sight and by reputation. They believed that Paul knew what he was talking about.

All this took quite a long time. The rivermen were not very quick in the head. They had no scruples about the police, but they were not used to dealing in this kind of commodity. They were slow to give up their original suspicion of Paul, a man who could read. They reached the point, however, of agreeing to take charge of the pamphlets while Paul approached the Ballad Singer. After that they must have a rendezvous. Paul made several suggestions of place and hour. The man with the tinderbox refused them, one after the other. At last the other man said flatly:

"A rendezvous, how do we know it won't be a trap?"

"I will tell you," said Paul. "Do the police ever give a reward?"

The question was never answered. The man who still held

the bundle of pamphlets saw the enemy first. He forced the package upon Paul with such suddenness that Paul staggered backward. Without thinking, he thrust the single pamphlet, which he still held, into his pocket, and took from the riverman the torn bundle. The eyes of the riverman were focused on something to the right and beyond Paul's shoulder. Paul doubled over and wheeled to the left, and the intruder made a rush past Paul at the riverman. The riverman, his hands free, caught the intruder coming in and curled him up with a couple of hard blows. The intruder stumbled on the package and fell forward, catching the riverman about the knees as he went down. Paul saw all this from the corner of his eye as he wheeled about.

He saw also two other figures emerging from the darkness, gaining in size as they came, like figures in a nightmare. They were the men from the other boat, who had made a landing below the Pont Neuf and returned along the shore, noiselessly. There were but three of them, the fourth having not yet recovered from his fall in the boat, and so for a moment it was three against three. But the other two of the enemy, seeing the opened package on the gravel, and not seeing, apparently, the bundle which Paul was clutching to his middle, made straight for the brawl over the package; and Paul, taking advantage of the direction in which his maneuver had brought him, headed for the steps. He reached them without interference, and went up with wings on his heels.

The fight was silent, except for the sound of blows, an irregular tattoo at which Paul winced, until, just as he reached the head of the steps, a scream cut the air, sharp, thin, agonized. Paul looked down at the tangle of struggling figures in time to see an arm rise above the tangle and fall again. The light which made the surface of the river luminous showed him the blade of a knife. Before he had gained the street, the cry was answered by a whistle, thinner and finer, but equally alarming: the police on the Pont Neuf.

Paul had begun to run toward the bridge, toward lights, toward safety. He saw, as he ran, a group of figures approaching from the bridge. He doubled back, running toward the Pont au Change, and then, realizing that this would be a second mistake, since police would be appearing from the Châtelet, he took the only way out remaining, and ducked into the street directly across from where he had been standing by the parapet.

He had no idea where he was going. A lantern above the entrance of the street cast a dim circle of light on the paving. On each side the walls rose straight and windowless. He knew that the street where he lodged was north of the river and not far from there. He judged it to be more to the east, and at the first opening in that direction, he turned right, and found himself rushing toward the main entrance of the prison of For l'Evêque.

Once more he doubled on his track. He looked toward the Quai and saw a horde of the King's police pouring down the stairway to the beach. He turned about and ran, panic urging him on and counseling him to change his course whenever an opportunity presented itself. In this way he became in a short time not only out of breath but completely confused. Beside a high blank wall he came to a halt and leaned against the wall, breathing hard and wondering where he was. When his breath began to come more evenly, he lifted his head, felt the air cool and quiet on his face, and became aware of a fragrance of plum blossoms. Reassurance flooded him, restorative. He knew where he was. He had noted the white blossoms lifting above the wall that morning when he set out through the usual thin mist of six o'clock.

Being reassured, he became aware also that he was still clutching the bundle of pamphlets. He could drop them here; no one would see him. But curiosity woke also. He had barely a glimpse of the cartoon, and the fact that he had stood, himself, in the Place des Victoires made him wish to study the cartoon. As he hesitated, a hurrying figure emerged from the street he had just quitted. In that light he knew that it was the figure of a man, nothing more definite, but his reassurance was not proof against the idea that he was pursued. He set his legs in motion, proceeding toward the street where he lodged. He hoped, at the first turning, to lose his pursuer, but the man turned also. An excitement filled him, such as had been both fearful and pleasurable when he was a child, running down darkening alleys. The thought that he might be picked up for having been part of a brawl which had ended in murder—he was sure, by then, that it was murder—made him break from a walk into a run. The man behind him began to run also.

Paul did not dare to turn his head to verify or to dispel the image of a gendarme at his back. He reached the rue des Deux Boules, still followed. He saw the door to his lodging. He made a sudden burst of speed, gained the door, pushed it open, thankful that it was never locked, and shut it firmly behind him. He ran a few steps up the pitch-black stairway. Here he stopped, the blood pounding in his ears, and listened to hear the footsteps of his pursuer going on down the street. To his horror, the steps halted, the door was shaken roughly, for in his closing of it he had wedged it temporarily. Then the door flew open, a man entered and began to climb the stair. Paul flattened himself against the wall, and held his breath.

Incredibly, his pursuer passed him, pressing against the opposite side of the wall as if groping his way. Then Paul heard the now familiar rattle of the latch to the privy on the first landing. A door opened and closed. Choking a hysterical desire to laugh, still not daring to make a sound, as if fear had already become a habit, Paul climbed the remaining flights of stairs to his own room.

When he had locked the door he groped among his belongings and found his tinderbox. He hung his bag upon a nail by the head of his bed, rubbed his shoulder reflectively, and kicked off his shoes. The fatigue of reaction began to set in. He saw the package, which he had tossed on the bed. Forgetting that he had a copy of the pamphlet in his pocket, he extracted one from the package and, wadding a pillow behind him for comfort, settled down on his bed for an evening of quiet entertainment. He had looked his fill at the cartoon of the King and his four enslaving loves, when he turned the page and saw another engraving, a picture of Madame de Maintenon and the ghost of Monsieur Scarron.

Chapter Eight

*I*T WAS ALMOST NOON of the following Monday, April
the nineteenth, before La Reynie's men brought their search
to the rue des Lions. Paul and Nicolas were alone in the bindery;
it was the first time since Paul's hiring that such a situation had
occurred. They both worked steadily, but a little while after
Jean's departure Paul, unthinking, began to whistle softly.

He was rounding the back of a book. His hammer fell with
light, even blows, accurate, identical, monotonous. Over its
unaccented, unvarying beat, the tune floated, stopped, began
again, in no relation to the tapping but blending with it happily.
The book, held upright in its vise, was smeared with glue, the
glue become firm to the point of tackiness, of the consistency to
be malleable, and through it Paul was shaping the back to the
proper even arc. If the back was well rounded, when the binding
was complete the book would open easily and lie flat. It was an
art to round a back, an art in which Paul excelled.

The gluepot stood on the floor behind him, cooling slowly.

The sun, moving toward the meridian, sent its rays steeply into the courtyard and shortened the oblongs of sunlight on the floor near the windows.

The sun had shone every day since Paul had come to Paris, an unprecedented stretch of fair weather. It had given him on Sunday a long warm afternoon, which he had spent wandering and resting in the meadows by the Bièvre, with a girl whom he might see again, or might not, as he chose. She had been pretty in a certain way, not witty, but companionable. He found her on the Pont Neuf.

He had recovered completely, after a night's sleep, from his terrors of the evening before. Even his certainty that a murder had been committed faded under the influence of the sunlight and the soft air. As for the fantasy of Monsieur Scarron, after the first ten pages he had found it dull. It had put him to sleep and, waking, he was no longer interested. As he whistled and tapped, his thought was on the girl, on the grass where they had rested, and on the willows hung with pollened catkins. He thought of the girl dispassionately, critically. He was pleased with himself because he had enjoyed the day without permitting himself to be taken.

Nicolas was preparing a pile of sections, or signatures, for the press. He built the structure of the book: upon a sheet of tin, a piece of clean paper, upon that a section, and then another piece of paper, another sheet of tin, and so on, until all the sections were assembled and the book was ready for the press. The press was old, a standing press with two great uprights, taller than a man, and a strong crossbeam, all in oak, stained and darkened and polished with the passage of time and the touch of hands. The wheel, manipulated by three knobs, rose or descended upon a central screw. It looked, in its hugeness and darkness and its latent power, like an instrument of torture. One man, with his hands on the wheel, could have exerted enough pressure to kill his victim. It stood domesticated, amid the sewing frames, the tables, the cheerful daily litter of the shop. Nicolas placed his pile of signatures in the press; Paul laid down his hammer and went to help him. While the boy steadied the pile, Paul turned the wheel. Too much pressure would force the imprint of the letters from one page to the next; too little would permit the damp sheets to pucker and warp. At the precise moment when the pile had solidified into a block, and before the pressure had become too great, Paul lifted his hands, held them poised a moment over the knobs, and smiled down at Nicolas. Then he returned to his work. They had not exchanged a word. But shortly after, as if resuming a conversation, Nicolas said earnestly:

"Naturally, I love my mother."

"Naturally?" Paul repeated in surprise. "What's so natural about loving your mother? I didn't love mine." It was not the answer that Nicolas had expected. Paul, in explanation, went on. "She didn't love me. As for my father, I never saw him. You say *naturally*. It's not natural at all. You are simply very lucky."

"Then you don't think it's strange, and unnatural, of me to want to leave home?"

"It struck me as odd," said Paul, "when you first mentioned it."

"Odd?" said Nicolas, defensive.

"Because everything you want to leave," said Paul, "is what I never had and always wanted."

"It isn't enough," said the boy, "to be fed and clothed."

"And loved?" said Paul calmly.

"I am loved too much," said the boy. "You don't understand. They don't talk about it; they don't show it. But I know. I feel smothered. I wasn't always the only child."

Paul took time to reflect upon this, and then replied with an unpleasant little laugh, "To be entirely free, a man must neither love nor be loved. I have never been loved. Today I love no one. Therefore I am free. It is not altogether an enjoyable state, although there's much to be said for it."

"And another thing," said the boy, disregarding Paul's bitter-

ness, "those books we talked about that night by the river—
I can't mention them here."

"There are many places where they can't be mentioned," said
Paul. "Most places."

"I know," said the boy. "That's part of it. Everything must be
published *avec privilége du Roi.*"

"This would be the same in Paris, or out of Paris, so long as
you remained in France."

"I know," said the boy.

"Louis the Great," said Paul, quoting from the inscription on
the base of the statue, "the Father and Leader of his Army. The
Ever Fortunate."

"But why must he forever decide what's fit to read and what's
not?"

"Without the constant authority of the King," said Paul
soberly, "the kingdom would come to ruin."

"Do you believe that?" said the boy.

"That's what we're taught," said Paul.

It was then that they heard a stir of voices and steps in the
adjoining room, and Larcher entered with the men who had
been detailed to search his shop.

Larcher was annoyed but resigned. The search was a formality, the men insisted. They knew his reputation; they expected to find nothing censorable in his shop, but an order
was an order.

"What do they want?" said Nicolas to his father as if the
officers did not exist.

"Some pamphlet about Scarron," Jean replied. "As if there
weren't a multitude. The pamphleteers outdid themselves when
he died."

"But this is new," said an officer. "Moreover, it is against the
King and Madame de Maintenon. A duodecimo," he read from
his instructions, "of one hundred and thirty-six pages, including
the engraving. Now if you will show me an inventory of the
books, leaflets, engravings, and so forth, in your holding——"

"Go on with your work," said Jean to the young men.

Nicolas lifted his eyebrows in an expression of extreme exasperation, and obeyed his father. Paul, taking up his hammer, could observe in the face of the boy nothing but his exasperation, no fear; neither was there any fear in Larcher's face or manner. As for himself, he began to feel a distinct nervousness. At the words, "a duodecimo of one hundred and thirty-six pages," he remembered not only the bundle of pamphlets in his room, but the single pamphlet which he had stuffed so hastily into his pocket during the fight on the Quai.

When the police had completed their investigation of the bindery, and had examined, in the kitchen, the account books, and had gone upstairs to examine the contents of the room where Nicolas slept, Nicolas said:

"Well, how do you like it now?"

"Like what?"

"The constant authority of the King."

"No better than you," said Paul. He resumed his tapping; he was in no mood to continue his little tune. To allay his nervousness, more than to satisfy his curiosity, he began a conversation.

"What could happen if they found what they wanted?"

Nicolas shrugged his shoulders. "That would depend. A fine. The Bastille. I don't know. The Widow Créstien—they seized her presses because of a history she published. Three years later she was still trying to get them back."

"Never the galleys?"

"Not to my knowledge," said Nicolas with a faint smile, "but look, I don't know everything."

"The profit could hardly be worth the risk."

The conversation had not diminished Paul's nervousness. Nicolas, obviously untroubled, and even complacent at the timely demonstration of his grievances, looked at Paul with a new feeling of solidarity.

"Now you see what I mean."

Paul nodded. "But you knew these men," he said. "They knew you, the son of Larcher, an honest man. What if they take it into their heads to question me?"

"My father will vouch for you," said Nicolas.

Chapter Nine

IT HAD BEEN AGREED that Nicolas would pay his own way on his adventure. Therefore, on the morning when at last the boy was to take the coach to Rouen, while he was still packing his portmanteau, it came almost as a shock to have his father place in his hand first a roll of coins sewed tightly in a bit of blue silk, and then an old money belt of chamois, stained and stretched about the buckle. He had braced himself to keep his bargain, to be entirely responsible for himself. He had braced himself also against his father's disapproval.

The hour was still before daylight, and though the wooden shutters had been thrown open above the court, Nicolas had been moving in a semi-darkness. Jean stood with his back to the windows. His face was hard to decipher, but what he offered his son was so expressive that the boy stammered as he thanked him. Jean said:

"Pull up your shirt and fasten it next to your skin. You may not need it. In that case, bring it back." And then, as Nicolas obeyed, fitting the roll, which was not large, into the belt and then fastening the clammy leather about his waist, Jean further startled the boy by adding, "In Rouen there used to live a man with whom I had some dealings. He kept a bookstore between the cathedral and St.-Ouen. He was a good man, though a Huguenot. He was not young at the time of the Revocation, and he died soon after. His widow, if she is still in business, will have been converted. You would risk nothing in looking her up."

"Behind St.-Ouen?"

"The name is Cailloué."

The boy, too surprised for comment, repeated the name. Jean added, "She would remember me."

Nicolas had not asked his parents whether they meant to accompany him to the inn from which the coaches set out for Normandy for fear of a refusal. Also, he was unwilling to show that it mattered to him one way or the other. He was prepared to say good bye at the door of the shop. He drank the hot broth which his mother had prepared for him, and received from her a package containing food for his journey, bread, cheese, and a dried onion, and then, ready to depart, saw his father take his own hat from the peg by the door, and was pleased. Jean took up the portmanteau. Nicolas protested, but his father, as if he had not heard a word, set it on his own shoulder and led the way into the tunnel of the porte-cochère.

The great door to the street was still locked, and had to be unlocked and locked again before the three of them could start off together. Jean still led the way. From the deserted rue des Lions they entered the larger thoroughfares and joined the crowd of carts and market folk traveling toward Les Halles. From time to time strangers intruded between Nicolas and his father, but he could see a little way ahead his portmanteau riding along on his father's shoulder, just as he had seen it when as a child he had followed his father across the city in the opposite direction to become apprenticed. On that day his mother had not been with them. He did not know the streets, and all his safety depended upon his keeping that portmanteau in view. He fought against the recollection consciously, reminding himself that this day was different, that he did not need his father's help, but when his mother put her hand on his arm to warn him of an approaching cart, he shook her off with a violence that startled them both.

Nevertheless, his spirits rose as they neared the rue St.-Denis and the hostelry of Le Cerf. The coolness of the morning, the long brisk walk, even the clatter of voices all around him, were very pleasant to his young strength. When the portmanteau had been strapped in place on the roof of the coach, he felt that he was off. He turned to face his parents as someone who had already left them. The farewell would be a formality; it would not touch him inwardly. Yet as he faced them standing there side by side, waiting for his embraces, he had the sensation of seeing them for the first time. It was something like the moment in the kitchen when his mother had spoken to him of her girlhood and her marriage, but what he felt here in the innyard was different. The surprise of his father's generosity was still with him; he had not yet become accustomed to the idea of his father's speaking well of a Huguenot. He did not know either of these people, whose external appearance was so familiar, as familiar as the comfort of an old shoe.

He had thought of them as looking alike, in some vague fashion, as if his mother's shawl had been a triangle of the stuff of which his father's coat was made, as if her features had taken on some conformity with those of Jean, by long association. He knew, of course, that they were different, but they had never before appeared to differ so much as at this moment. His mother stood with her chin lifted, her back very straight. Her eyes were bright, and she glanced from his face to the activity beyond his shoulder with an excitement kindred to his own. His father's face was clouded. And there was nothing to say, nothing that had not already been spoken of in private, at home. There was no reason to prolong the moment; and the coach was beginning to fill. If he wanted a seat, he must climb into it promptly.

He bent his head and kissed his parents on both cheeks, and as he did so, emotion had him suddenly by the throat. He turned away brusquely, and when he had found a place in the coach and looked for them through the dusty, greenish glass, they had disappeared. Either they had left the innyard immediately or the crowd had pushed between them and the coach. He was alone and on his journey even before the first crack of the whip.

Marianne had not hoped that Jean would put his arm about her to console her and direct her progress as they left the innyard, but she had hoped to put her hand in the crook of his arm and walk beside him. He moved too quickly for that. As she followed him he seemed to her a lonely figure. His shoulders were as solid as ever, but his motion was despondent. "In the shop," she thought, "it will doubtless be the same—not an unnecessary word spoken until Nicolas returns." After a while she said, "There will be Paul, of course, but he is more clearly of the generation of Nicolas than of mine. He is none of my affair, but he will at least be someone about the shop. So few people visit the shop since the war. It used to be different, in that respect. Who comes now? The bailiff. Police agents. An old abbé." Remembering the old abbé, she could not escape remembering his words, "Rejoice in your youth, for it is like the bough in May."

Thanks to his bulk and his singleness of purpose, Jean moved forward rapidly. Hurrying to keep pace with him, she exclaimed within herself with bitterness, "My youth! It's on its way to Rouen with Nicolas." Then a surge of traffic separated her from him. She thought, "He will wait for me." But when she could move again, although she could see him in the distance, she could not catch up with him, and he did not stop.

"He should wait," she thought with hurt and indignation. The effort to keep up with Jean had set her blood in motion.

With defiance she demanded of Jean's steadily retreating head and shoulders, "Is it a tragedy that a boy grows up? What would become of the race?"

Thereafter she proceeded as she wished, more slowly, taking time to look about her. She did the first marketing for the day at the Port St.-Paul, bargaining, visiting a little, and returned to the rue des Lions not long after six o'clock. Jean was already at work. Paul, who was not required to come before seven, had not yet appeared.

She left her purchases in the kitchen and went to the rooms over the shop, and stripped the sheets from the bed where Nicolas had slept. She knotted them in a ball and flung them into a basket where six weeks of soiled linens had accumulated, and then hung the other coverings from the *barre d'appui* of the windows over the court. She made the bed in the front room, opened the shutters upon the street, and the window also, since the day was so fair. She had returned to the inner room and was engaged in a thorough cleaning of the cupboard shelves when she heard a slow footstep upon the stairway. Jean pushed open the door.

He came forward into the room, surveyed the dismantled bed, and then the piles of books and paper by which his wife had surrounded herself as she worked.

"That was in order," he said with grave disapproval.

"I will put it back exactly as I found it," she answered, "less the dust."

"Throw nothing away."

She made no reply to the unnecessary instruction. She did not assume that he had come to express regret for having outdistanced her on the way home from The Stag. She continued her work and waited for him to perform whatever errand he had in mind. But he remained where he was, watching her for a time before he made his announcement.

"So long as Nicolas is gone," he said, "I shall offer Damas room and board, to be taken from his wages. A profit for him."

"You mean to lodge him here, in this room?" said Marianne sharply.

"Yes," said Larcher, the single word heavy with irony, as if to say, "Where else?"

"But we cannot have him here. We will be walking through this room at all hours. And we need the space for storage, and for other things. Where will I hang the washing?"

"The bed is curtained, is it not? What we store here will not disturb him."

"You would put a stranger in your son's bed? No, Jean, I protest."

"I don't intend," Larcher said calmly, "to pay rent for an empty room." He glanced again at the unmade bed. "Count on it."

A ferment of emotion filled her after he had gone back to the shop. She was at a loss to explain even to herself the deep repugnance which she felt at the thought of Paul Damas asleep at her door, asleep in her son's bed. She was neither a prude nor a spinster. There had been nothing revolting in the appearance of the young man upon whose face she had thrown the light of her candle when she had gone to wake Nicolas, nothing insolent, only a surprised stare in eyes widened and blinded by the sudden light. As for herself, she had been decent; she had thrown a shawl over her nightgown. The incident was nothing. To have Paul in the room would be the most trivial of inconveniences; and the arrangement would save them all a good bit of money, and yet—she resented the proposition. She added the resentment to the exasperation she had felt at being deserted on the way home from Le Cerf, and went on with her cleaning in a very bad state of mind.

She did not hear Paul's arrival, but when she went downstairs to prepare the noonday meal, she caught a glimpse of him working beside Jean, absorbed.

Toward noon Jean left the shop, his hat set firm on his head, a bundle in his hand. He did not say where he was going. A little later Paul came into the shop and went on into the court. When he returned, he halted short of the door to the bindery. Marianne was near the table, her lap full of some white stuff which she was mending. Paul had hardly spoken two words with her since the day he had begun to work for Larcher. He was uncertain whether she liked him or disliked him. He felt that he owed it to himself and to his job to form some sort of understanding with her. He saw on the table three bowls, three spoons, as he had seen them on every day. Today one cover was for him. He came back a few steps, so that he stood before her. She drew her thread through the cloth to its full length before she looked up, her expression neither cold nor kind, simply inquiring.

"I wanted to thank you," said Paul, "for offering me room and board. It was a handsome offer."

Marianne dropped her eyes to her mending; he saw her shoulders lifted in the slightest of shrugs.

"Indeed, it was very kind of you," he said, and waited.

She looked up, accepting his appreciation with a deprecating half-smile. "It was Jean's offer."

"I told the master that I have a room, not as pleasant as this, but where I'm paid up in advance. It would be awkward to change. As for meals, I can shift for myself mornings and evenings, but I will be very happy to take the noon meal with you." He smiled engagingly. "It would have been a great inconvenience for you, Mademoiselle, and much added work, to have a lodger."

"If you have a room entirely to yourself," said Marianne, "of course you wish to keep it. For the rest, it would have been no great trouble to me."

Her expression was clearly that of relief, and in spite of Paul's protestation, it piqued him to learn that she did not care to have him at all hours as one of the family. Jean had been frankly annoyed at his partial refusal. The moment had come for him to return to his work, and he had made no progress. He searched his mind for a means of prolonging the conversation. He spoke of Nicolas and his journey and saw her face close. Then he remembered the pamphlet which he had perversely carried in his pocket since the day of the search. Out of curiosity to see how she would respond, he pulled it out and laid it on her knees.

She thrust her needle firmly in the cloth and took up the pamphlet about the apparition of Scarron without undue excitement or interest.

Paul watched her as Monsieur had watched the King, but whereas the face of the King had remained impassive, Paul saw the beginning of a smile tug at the corner of Marianne's mouth. She studied the cartoon, then ruffled the pages, as the King had done, and then, controlling the smile, glanced up at Paul.

"Why do you show me this?"

"To amuse you. My faith, I know better than to show it to the master."

"Where did you get it?"

"I found it," Paul replied soberly, "in the gutter on the Quai this side the Pont Neuf."

"It is clean to have been in the gutter."

He made no reply to that. He knew that she did not believe him, but the truth was too elaborate and would do him no more good than the statement he had given. He could tell her one more thing.

"It was in my pocket the day they searched the shop. I was in a cold sweat when I remembered it."

"I believe you," she said.

"But it is amusing."

Again she considered the picture of the King enchained, and thought that it was chiefly amusing because it was forbidden. She wondered if Jean, if he saw it, would consider it his duty to report it to the police, and, knowing his extreme loyalty to the King and to La Reynie, especially to La Reynie, she decided that he would. She held the pamphlet out to Paul. He shook his head, refusing it.

"Destroy it for me."

"I should," she said, smiling at last, freely and completely, "show it to my husband."

Paul said nothing. He returned her smile, pleased at his small triumph, and enjoying also the warmth and color which came into her face as she smiled. He knew that she would not betray him. He went back to his work, and she heard him presently whistling to himself as he had often whistled when Nicolas and he were alone in the shop. It was an air she knew; she could not remember the words.

She was aware that Paul had put himself into her danger, to use the old and courtly phrase. She was also aware, as Paul was not, that his security, which she had all but promised him in the long smiling look which they had just exchanged, sprang from defiance, and the defiance, in turn, sprang from her double resentment against Jean that morning. It was a private revenge which could do Jean no harm. It was a taking of sides with Paul against Jean, and the sharing of a secret.

So it began. Paul fell in easily with the ways of the Larchers. By nature tactful and patient, finding it simpler to evade what displeased him than to grapple with it, he bore Jean's taciturnity with no indication that he was aware of it. Larcher's gloom was more noticeable at the table at noon than during the working hours. For Marianne her husband's silence was nothing new, and a gloomy silence not very different from a merely preoccupied silence. The presence of Paul made her the more conscious of it; she watched him covertly that first day to see how he met it.

He made no attempt to begin a conversation with Jean or with herself. After a few days Jean himself began to talk a little with his assistant. At first the talk was of matters pertaining to the shop, immediate matters, but it became gradually more general and embraced the news of the day. It rarely approached such controversial subjects as Paul and Nicolas had discussed under the elm trees of the Mail, and when it did, Paul bent with the prevailing wind, a pliant spear of grass. He agreed with Jean less than he agreed with Nicolas, but he was under no compulsion to champion the ideas of either man. He kept his own counsel.

Neither Jean nor Paul addressed himself to Marianne, and she found little of interest in their conversation. But Paul, having made his first successful approach to her, continued to entertain himself by a leisurely campaign for her favor.

He complimented her upon her cooking. The food remained as simple and economical as ever, but she began to take more pains in the preparation of it. There were small garnishings; mushrooms and cress were in season; and since Paul did not dine with the Larchers on Sundays, the best meal of the week was shifted without apology to Saturday. He complimented her also, but not too frequently, upon a cap or a kerchief, and when the effect of his compliment became apparent, some days later, by a prettier cap or a knot of colored ribbon at her throat, he felt an enjoyable sense of power.

He had no intention of abusing his power. He had told himself, in a confident mood, that he could make her discontented with her husband. He became subsequently less confident, but even when his confidence returned, he had no thought of disturbing the situation. He appreciated her good will, and he enjoyed seeing her blossom. The lace above her forehead, the crimson satin at her bosom enhanced his day. Her earrings were of copper, plain loops, and rather small, but when the light was right they cast small circular shadows on her throat or her cheek, depending on the tilt of her head, and this he found delightful. He woke one day to the realization that the pale smooth skin with its undertone of warmth, the heavy-lidded grey eyes, the round throat and chin had become for him immensely seductive. He spent the following Sunday with the girl from the Pont Neuf, a corrective measure, but on Monday he found his master's wife more attractive; more to his taste.

As for Marianne, when she fastened the first knot of ribbon at her throat, she told herself that she did so in response to the advice of the abbé Jacques Têtu.

She had learned more concerning the abbé after a few visits to the fountain in the rue St.-Antoine. The servants from the Hôtel Carnavalet filled their pitchers there. He was indeed a friend of Madame de Maintenon, and of many other ladies of high title and irreproachable reputation. She learned of his fondness for the company of women, his weakness for a pretty face or figure, but she also learned of his great piety. He was a man of the Church; she could trust his advice to be good.

The sunny days went on, stunting the young wheat on the plains of Beauce, warming the beggars of Paris. The women of Paris carried their soiled linens to the river to be washed. Marianne and the girl who lived in the mansard apartment above the rooms of the Larchers went together to the Ile Louviers. Paul carried their wooden tubs, following the two basket-laden women across the footbridge leading from the corner of the Quai des Célestins to the Ile Louviers.

On the Mail, now high above his head, the elm trees were in full leaf. The beach was secluded. They were in the country, the three of them, and not more than a good stone's throw from the Port St.-Paul. The girl Simone promptly removed her shoes and tucked up her skirts, and, taking her tub from Paul, waded into the river to fill it. From the water she called to Marianne sitting beside her basket, "How slow you are! Lazy woman!" Marianne, clasping her arms about her knees, feigned fatigue and waited for Paul to go. But Paul loitered, lifting his nose, like a fox, to sniff the sweet air.

The day before, since Jean kept no apprentice, Marianne, performing the duties of an apprentice, was folding sections. There was no one in the bindery save Paul and herself, and the room was so quiet that every stroke of the blunt-edged ivory folder was audible as a sigh. Paul was working at the other end of the room and had not spoken in half an hour; there was no reason to suppose that he was even thinking of her. She had not consciously been thinking of Paul, yet she had suddenly felt herself desired. The emotion, half alarm, half pleasure, had swept through her so strongly that it left her trembling. She had not dared look toward Paul for several minutes. When she did lift her eyes, she saw him, exactly as she had seen him earlier, bent above his work, oblivious, to all appearances, of everything else in the world. At noon, and at evening, when he had paused as usual, leaving the shop, to wish her good night, there had been nothing in his voice or manner to suggest that he had any thought of her except in an easy friendship. She had berated herself. Her loneliness had played a trick upon her. She did not deny her loneliness, even as she lay beside Jean that night, but she did deny the validity of her instinctive apprehension.

Now, while Simone called to her from the river, she felt the same irrational sense of extreme modesty that had troubled her when she had seen Paul in her son's bed and when Jean had proposed that Paul become their lodger. It was a feeling that she could neither explain nor indulge. Under Paul's gaze, she slowly removed her own shoes and stockings and trussed up her skirts. There was nothing to be ashamed of. She had, on the contrary, reason to feel a little vanity. Her feet were clean, small, and well shaped, with strong, high arches. She picked up her tub and walked across the sandy gravel to the water's edge, feeling the breeze about her ankles, and disregarding Paul. Simone called to Paul:

"How I pity you! Having to work indoors today!"

When she brought her tub dripping to the beach, Paul had regained the bridge.

At noon the women stopped to rest. Marianne stretched herself beneath the willows, and Simone came to sit with her, her arms upon her knees, her head on her arms. She was very young, not more than a year older than Nicolas. She had been married a year and was five months pregnant. Her husband was a riverman, almost as young as herself; they had no relatives in the city, and her friendship with Marianne had begun on a day during her first months of nausea when Marianne had found her on the stairs, clinging to the railing, dizzy and fearful. For another month Simone could not pass a fish peddler without vomiting. Then her natural good health and cheerfulness reestablished themselves; she gave Marianne credit for the change, and consulted her endlessly upon the ways in which pregnancies may develop, children may be delivered.

With her head on her arms, she watched the flicker of shadows as the breeze, moving the willow branches, shredded and filtered the sunlight. Her face was full of contentment, a round, rosy face, not too pretty, but very likable. Her hair was bound up in a blue cloth which left her ears uncovered. She smiled vaguely, like a child half awake, half asleep, a child without a thought. Out of this revery of the flesh she presently remarked, without preamble:

"The little Damas is in love with you."

Marianne opened her eyes wide. "Nonsense," she said.

"Oh, but he is," said the girl peaceably.

"He could be my son," said Marianne.

"I could be your daughter," Simone corrected her, "but Damas is much older than I. He must be thirty years old. Besides, what has that to do with it?"

"Everything," said Marianne.

The girl laughed, her childlike face became knowledgeable and mischievous.

"At your age, my little Simone, what makes you so wise?"

"I saw him look at you," said the girl.

Marianne held up a hand as a screen from a ray of leaping sunlight. It was extraordinary how well she felt, stretched there on the dry ground, how light her body was, how remote from such miseries as Simone had lately known, and others that she had still to know before her child would be born.

Simone did not pursue the subject of Paul. She wanted to talk about herself. Marianne replied to her questions, was sympathetic to her speculations, and repeated for her the often-given advice, all the while thinking, "I was as young as that once, as heavy with child. Is it possible that I have seen four children die, and wept over them, and that I now lie here, unsorrowing? I do not even feel the lack of Nicolas."

"And so do you promise to be with me at the time?" said Simone.

"I am not a registered midwife."

"But I would feel more safe with you than with a stranger," said Simone.

"I promise," said Marianne.

She could feel no concern for Simone. The girl was well built for childbearing, and as healthy as a little animal. There would be no difficulty for either the midwife or the patient in her delivery. Her concern was now for herself, a new self, yet not a stranger. In the enlightenment which followed on Simone's corroboration of what she had fearfully denied, she understood that her fear had not been that Paul had desired her but that she had invented his desire. She understood also her dismay at the thought of Paul asleep in her son's bed. It had nothing to do with Nicolas, but with the fact that she herself slept just beyond the closed door. She felt this great immodesty because she slept there not alone but with her husband. All this should have alarmed her. It paved the way for trouble. Instead, she felt a gaiety such as she had not known in years, such as, perhaps, she had never known.

Sitting up, she observed that the bindweed in the grass had opened all its blossoms, small trumpets spread wide to catch the sunlight. The water flowing about her ankles, the light on the broken ripples as she dipped and rinsed her linens delighted her. With Simone's help she wrung her sheets and spread them on the grass to bleach. The afternoon went by, and gradually the reality of the situation redefined itself. A sense of worry worked through her new happiness like an old water stain upon a plastered wall, making itself known through a fresh coat of plaster. By the time Paul came to help them carry home their gear, the worry had made itself distinct.

Over the bridge they went, and past the evening hubbub on the Quai St.-Paul. At the rue des Lions they left their tubs in the courtyard, and Paul carried the basket of damp linens for Marianne to the room above the bindery. She had strung clotheslines diagonally across the room. She turned her back on Paul and put her hand upon a cord, testing it for security, when she felt Paul come close behind her. She froze, holding her breath, and then she felt a kiss, not on her throat, which the loosened kerchief left bare, but upon her shoulder, on the kerchief itself. The kiss was light. She barely felt the touch. It was such a kiss as might rank as stolen, unobserved; or, if she chose, she might acknowledge it. She chose to ignore it, and Paul withdrew a step. He said:

"May I help you more?"

Without turning her head she thanked him and declined his offer. "You have done enough for today," she said, her voice steady and light, without, she flattered herself, any undertone of feeling which might be misconstrued.

He said good night then and left the room. She heard him, as he descended the stairs, begin to whistle his little tune, always the same tune. She lifted a sheet, unfolded it, and spread it over the line. The linen was almost dry; it smelled of the river, of the sun, of the willow trees, it seemed. Paul's whistle dwindled; she began to hum the air herself. Then all at once she knew the words again, and she began to sing them under her breath. It was a song from Brie. Her mother's sister had been fond of it.

> *La rose de ton blanc rosier*
> *Est une rose blanche.*

*J'ai pas demandé un baiser
En découpant la branche.*

Indeed he had not asked a kiss. He had merely stolen one. She would never speak of it, and neither would he.

"No," she said to herself, "he will never make me any trouble."

Chapter Ten

ON THE DAY that Nicolas left for Rouen, Monsieur Rob-
bert, Procureur du Roi au Châtelet, paid his usual Monday visit
to Monsieur de La Reynie. He passed La Reynie's barber in the
antechamber and found La Reynie himself freshly shaven but
still in his dressing gown, writing a letter.

"To Monsieur le Commissaire de La Marre," the letter began,
"the 26th of April, 1694.

"Send me today, early, a note upon what you have found concerning the last booklet, and what proof we may hope to obtain
against those who printed it; because the King desires this offense
to be punished at all costs. This is only the beginning of the requests made by the King concerning which I write you. Let
me know if any peddler has been arrested, or any declaration
taken from among the peddlers, which gives any information
regarding the printer, or even if this piece was printed in Paris."

He interrupted himself long enough to greet his visitor and

pray him to be seated. Then he concluded his letter, and sealed it, and gave it to the hand of a servant to be delivered.

Robert was an old friend, the Monday visit a long-established custom, since the courts of the Châtelet held their first sessions of the week on Tuesday. The son of Robert, a rising young lawyer, also served the King as *conseiller du Roi au Châtelet*. It was of him that the two older men exchanged their first remarks. After this they proceeded to the problems of bread for the city.

It struck Robert, as La Reynie outlined his plans, that his friend had aged greatly within the last months. The room was full of morning sunlight. Perhaps it was because of the brightness which illuminated every line in the face of his friend, or because he himself had been questioned recently concerning the number of his years, which closely paralleled those of La Reynie, that he made a conscious observation of the familiar face, and inescapably noted there the marks of advancing age. There was a deep vertical line between the heavy eyebrows. The eyes were sad, and about the full, equable lips were other lines which indicated a long-continued strain.

Monsieur Robert had made a resolution to quit the service whenever La Reynie should tender his resignation to the King. The day might be soon; he would be glad of it, although he did not feel it suitable for him to urge the resignation.

La Reynie spoke without emotion, summing up the problem, and discussing the practical means taken to cope with it. The conference drew to its end, and Monsieur Robert bent to take up his hat, which he had placed on the floor beside his chair.

"One thing more," said La Reynie. "You have certain prisoners at the Châtelet who were arrested during the bread riots. Your son understands my reluctance to have them punished severely."

"I will remind him," said Monsieur. Robert. "I agree with you. It's not the time to make an example of them before the people. Another matter, which I almost forgot. A week ago

Saturday last, our men broke up a fight among some water rats. One of them was taken, being hurt, and unable to run away. I don't wish to trouble you with trifles. The brawl was like any other brawl along the quais, except for one thing. They were fighting for the possession of a bundle of pamphlets. Something about the ghost of Scarron appearing to Madame de Maintenon."

"Ah," said La Reynie.

"When I learned this," continued Monsieur Robert, "I advised my son to have the men questioned more thoroughly. It was an extremely insolent libel."

"We have been conducting a search for it," said La Reynie dryly.

"My son had not been informed of your search."

"The King makes an issue of this libel," said La Reynie. "What did you learn?"

"Only that the pamphlets were thrown into the Seine between the Pont au Change and the Pont Notre Dame from the Cité, and nearer to the Pont au Change. One lot of men saw the package fall and retrieved it. The others tried to rob them. It may have been thrown from a window, or from the Passage des Oeufs, which is the only direct approach to the river at that point. The man admitted that he knew of the subject of the pamphlet, but he did not know how to read."

"In that case," said La Reynie, "one of his friends must have been able to read. Have him questioned again."

"Impossible," said Monsieur Robert. "He had an eye gouged out in the fight. A fever set in, following an infection of the eye."

"Have him cared for by a competent physician."

"Too late. He died yesterday."

La Reynie remained silent for so long that Robert said, "The city is full of such libels. Songs, pamphlets, snuffboxes even. Can we suppress them all?"

"If the people had bread there would be no bitterness in

their songs—nor sedition in their snuffboxes. We would do well at this time to ignore the ghost of Monsieur Scarron. But, here is the situation. The King desires this offense to be punished at all costs. At all costs. You understand?"

Monsieur Robert understood very well. He made his farewells and departed, leaving La Reynie to ponder the extreme unwisdom of the King's desire.

One did not argue with the King; but the King was usually observant of advice. The King was usually reasonable; and although the remarks about Madame de Maintenon in the little pamphlet were unusually insulting, particularly those which made her out to be a procuress for the King and St.-Cyr a seraglio in which she educated young women for the King's pleasure, still, the King's insistence upon an intensified search, and his demand of the ultimate penalty for the culprits, when found, all seemed to La Reynie most unreasonable, considering the circumstances.

"Considering the circumstances," he repeated to himself. And the circumstances were that the people of the city—not the rich, but the people—had lived during the last few years on the edge of famine. Tempers were short. It would take very little to set off a revolt; and what happened in Paris affected the whole of France. A hanging as punishment for a jest, although an ugly jest, might be the very thing to set it off. The King knew the circumstances as well as did La Reynie.

Well, he had promised to do what he could, and, being an honest man, he meant to keep his promise. In the meantime, he had other things to worry about, and one of them was the case of the grain merchant, Roger.

It was the opinion of La Reynie that a great part of the scarcity of grain was due to hoarding on the part of the farmers and of the grain merchants. Actually, it was due to several things, the diminished value of the metal currency, unseasonable droughts, destructive rain and hail, the stoppage of river traffic by flood and by freezing, and, probably most important of all, the cutting off of import by the war.

In August of the previous year, when grain was selling at the unheard-of price of thirty-five livres the *sétier*, La Reynie wrote to Monsieur de Harlay, First President of the Courts of the city, "Roger has a boat at l'Ecole. He asks forty-two livres the sétier." The incident was fixed in his mind by a report made to him that very same day; it concerned the body of a dead child found in a well. The parents had drowned it because they could not feed it. He had concluded his note to Harlay with, "This man seems not to have a French heart." In March of 1694 Roger was back at the Port de l'Ecole, again with grain for sale, and Monsieur de Harlay had devised a plan for dealing with him.

Roger had been formerly an acknowledged Huguenot. With the revocation of the Edict of Nantes, which laid severe economic penalties on members of the Reformed Religion—or the So-called Reformed Religion, depending upon the point of view—he had permitted himself to be converted to Catholicism. The First President proposed to accuse him of being *mal converti* and arrest him on that charge without a trial, since he had been unable to arrest him merely for asking a high price for his wheat. Roger would lose the privileges of a first-class citizen, his accounts could be investigated, his warehouses searched, with no need of a warrant from the King.

Far more than the First President, more than the King, La Reynie wanted to make Roger disgorge his hidden wheat. It was at the door of La Reynie in the rue du Boulloy, the previous autumn, that the mob of women had gathered. He had himself gone out to speak to them. He had heard the uproar; he had seen their faces, and he had written to Harlay, "These women who had seen their children die were little concerned for their own lives." He could not forget those outcries nor those faces. Nevertheless, he replied to Harlay:

"In regard to your proposal touching Roger, the wheat merchant, and the idea of using the pretext that he is ill converted in order to arrest him because of his bad conduct in regard to the wheat—I can't imagine what the source might be of such a proposition; but I find no difficulty in replying very clearly (since you command me to explain myself on this subject) that I should never agree, and that such a proposition would appear to me incomparably more odious than the evil which one might think to remedy by such a process."

That terminated, for the time being, the affair of Roger, for though Harlay, as first jurist of the city, officially outranked La Reynie, La Reynie spoke for the King and was answerable to no one save the King.

The problem of feeding the city remained. The dole had been tried, a dole from the King's purse; and ovens had been set up in the court of the Louvre. There had been a distribution of bread, parish by parish. In March of 1694 they had attempted to fix the price of grain, with the result that almost no grain had been brought to market. The ban on price-raising had been removed, and there was bread, but at a sum that many could not pay.

La Reynie pinned his hope on the coming harvest, but as the unclouded days grew into weeks, he began to lose hope of that, and his correspondence more and more often bore witness to a new preoccupation. "If God does not send aid, I do not know what will become of us."

The people also thought that the time had come to ask help of God. This was the city of Sainte Geneviève. She had interceded for her city in times past. In the most desperate hours, when her shrine had been carried in solemn procession from her church on the hill down to the cathedral on the island, she had worked miracles. It had been a long time since they had disturbed her. Surely the time had come to beseech her to intercede for the most humble of favors, rain for the new harvest.

The request for the ceremony came from the people and was eventually returned to them in the form of a proclamation.

But matters of great formality and ritual proceed slowly.

Through April and the first weeks of May throughout the country the earth continued to harden, the young wheat drooped. It was not until the twenty-first of May that the proclamation was made public, stating that "His Majesty, full of kindness for his people, and having a singular affection for the inhabitants of the city of Paris, desires that the solemn procession of the shrine of Sainte Geneviève be made, in order that everyone should unite in prayer, asking of God through the intercession of the saint, a fortunate harvest, and all the graces of which the Kingdom has need." By that time all was so well arranged that the date of the ceremony could also be made public, along with the orders of the Church for the great procession, complete in every detail, down to the last prayer and genuflection. The procession of the shrine was to take place on Thursday, the twenty-seventh of May, three days before Pentecost, and from Monday through Wednesday the city would prepare itself spiritually.

Announcement of the proclamation and of the instructions was made by cry and trumpet in every market place in the city, before the churches, on the Pont Neuf, and beneath the statue of the King in the Place des Victoires. This was on Friday. On Saturday the proclamation and the orders of the Church appeared on printed sheets, posted throughout the city, and on sale at the bookstores. On Sunday they were read and explained from every pulpit. There was no possibility of anyone's not knowing what was to take place.

On Monday the pilgrimages began from every church—conventual, abbatial, parochial—first to the Cathedral of Notre Dame, and then up the steady incline to the church of Sainte Geneviève on the Mont, then back to their own altars. The clergy were followed by their people. They went with crozier and incense, singing penitential hymns, and bearing with them whatever their church possessed of holy relics. On every hour and half-hour they set out, two churches, each from a different quarter of the city, and since the way was often long and the procession slow, those congregations returning from the Mont often encountered those just setting out, and all day long each day from dawn on Monday until twilight on Wednesday, the sound of chanting was continuous. It mingled with the noises of the street, the sound of hammer and chisel, the cries of vendors, of animals, and the creaking of ungreased axles.

Before the cathedral and before the church of the saint the chanting never ceased. The bells of the churches rang incessantly. Each pilgrimage began with the singing of the *Exsurge Domine*. At the cathedral, Our Lady was implored, and then the other patrons of Paris, Saint Denis and Saint Marcel. At the Montagne Sainte Geneviève the people intoned: *"Parce Domine, parce populo tuo; ut dignis flagellationibus castigatus, in tua miseratione respiret, per Christum."* Where they knelt they could look up at the shrine, still veiled, upon its exceedingly high pedestal. They observed the pillars of jasper, the carven cherubim, and tried to imagine the casket itself as they had once seen it long ago, or as they had heard it spoken of, a small box, hardly a yard long, with a pointed roof, like a little church, made of silver washed with gold and studded with jewels, a casket of fabulous value. In it were the ashes of the good and simple saint, the shepherdess who in her mortal life had never worn a jewel.

Forty days' indulgence was granted by the Church to each individual taking part in these pilgrimages, and lest any man or woman of whatever degree be deprived of this benefit, the Procureur Général was charged with the responsibility of leading in pilgrimage the poor of the city, those who received alms either from the Church or from the King, who were lodged in the Hôpital des Petites Maisons at the expense of the city. To make all certain, the Commissaires de Police in charge of each parish informed their people that they must be present on Tuesday, with their chaplets in their hands, ready to make the pilgrimage, on penalty of forfeiting for a month whatever charity they received.

At four o'clock, led by the verger bearing the cross, shepherded by the commissaires, and marching four abreast, all the men together, followed by all the women, and then by the few clergy of the almshouse, the procession of the poor set out. Their route was prescribed, and the procession timed to arrive before the cathedral at seven. They bore each one a mark on the left forearm as proof of their participation in the pilgrimage. They marched in the given order of their parishes, and the procession was long. They were the living testimony to Sainte Geneviève of the great need of her city; yet they marched without precious relics and without incense, and the few clergy from the almshouse made so small a showing at the end of the cortege that it seemed a procession only of the poor and the police.

Wednesday was declared a day of fast; and on Wednesday evening the pilgrimages came to an end. The sun, hot and red, hung above the horizon in an enormous ball, pouring a fiery light upon the waters of the Seine.

In the rue du Boulloy, Monsieur de La Reynie retired early. He had a part to play in the ceremonies of the morrow which would tax his strength. He was glad of the occasion, not only because an appeal was being made to heaven, but because he might contribute his personal effort.

"But all this," he reminded himself as he laid aside his wig and his coat, "does not mean for a certainty that we shall have rain or that the harvest will be saved. I have no lack of faith in the good saint, but God will grant or will deny this mercy in accordance with His own obscure plans. Should the procession bring no rain, I must feel no bitterness in my heart either toward Him or toward His saint. Nevertheless . . ."

Chapter Eleven

*J*EAN LARCHER and his wife made their pilgrimage on
Tuesday morning with the parish of St.-Paul. They marched
under a cloudless sky, leaving the rue St.-Paul at eleven and returning to the rue des Lions late in the afternoon, exhausted.
Paul Damas accompanied Jean, considering himself more a
parishioner of the quarter where he worked than of that where
he lodged. He had not been to confession at any church since he
had come to Paris.

On Wednesday, long after sundown, Marianne lay awake.
The heat was not excessive; it was not that which kept her from
sleeping. Jean slept, snoring a little and sometimes making short,
strangled sounds in his throat, so that she prodded him until he
turned on his side and slept quietly. But the day-long radiant
sky had left the air very warm, and the three days of prayer
and chanting and the constant sound of bells had left the city
drenched in emotion. In Marianne the pilgrimage of Tuesday,
her own effort of prayer below the veiled shrine had intensified

a longing which reached back into her girlhood, as well as into the dim, monotonous future.

She lay beside Jean, straight and unmoving, and remembered her first imaginings of love, centered on no one, mere stirrings of the awakening blood. She had married, and love had become something no longer mysterious nor overpowering; a burden, a weight on the breast, and also a shoulder against which to shelter on a cold night. The children had occupied her hands and absorbed her affections. She had worked very hard. The shop, the kitchen, the market, the children again, sickness and death, the midwifery she had practiced, without making a profession of it, had filled her hours. She had not had time to mourn her children properly; she had had no time in which to speculate on the nature of love. She had never asked herself if she was in love with her husband. She had assumed that she was. He had been a good husband; according to the measure of her world, a very good husband. Secure in this belief, and in the consciousness that she had been a good wife, she had seen no reason why she should not take pleasure in Paul's unspoken devotion. This was a face of love which she had never seen before. The sweetness which it afforded her was extraordinary.

She was not so naïve as to assume that the situation could continue indefinitely as it was. Her own position was fixed; it did not even occur to her that it could change. But Paul would change, she knew, and since he could not advance, he must retreat. He had already, in the few days since he had touched his lips to her shoulder, begun his retreat. She had observed the little indications and had felt a sadness.

Kneeling below the shrine in the church of the saint, she had tried to pray fo the good of France, for a safe return of Nicolas, but it had been difficult to concentrate upon her prayer. Her thoughts had shifted continually to her husband's young assistant, kneeling beside her husband, some distance from her. And moved by the devotion of all those other men and women who were bowed in prayer with her, as much as by her own religious feeling, she felt rising and mingling with her devotion a fierce desire which she had long ago dismissed as part of the pain of being young.

Since she could not sleep, she sat up in bed, her hands about her knees. Jean did not stir. She left the bed and crossed to the window, which she opened. An arch of starlit sky overhung the neighboring roofs. The whole city seemed deserted. Everything was tranquil. Everything waited for the morrow, and the miracle.

She leaned out, her hand upon the scaling paint of the window frame wet with a heavy dew, and, breathing the soft air, noticed a scent, unfamiliar to her, but very sweet, of some night-blooming shrub in one of the walled gardens nearby. In the country, on a night as warm and still as this, a nightingale should be singing. Her longing seemed intolerable. She undid the ties of her bonnet de nuit, removed it, and shook out her hair. She loosened the neck of her gown also, for the refreshment of the air upon her moist skin. She might just as well have removed her gown entirely and let her whole body breathe. The street, with every shutter closed in every house, was as private as an empty room. But even in such solitude, nakedness would have seemed libertine. She remembered what she had heard of the country girls of Brie, how they "welcomed March" by coming at dawn of the first day of the month to the doors of their houses and throwing their skirts up over their faces. The young men doubtless rose at dawn also and watched through the closed shutters. A good, frank custom, she thought, with a certain envy.

Across the river, on the hill which the Parisians called the Mountain of Sainte Geneviève, in the abbey church of the saint, the priests of the order kept their vigil.

Midnight passed. After Nones the abbé in pontifical robes approached the high altar, and after the liturgy and the Confiteor, he gave absolution to his priests as if it had been Ash Wednesday. The benediction over, two priests in alb and stole withdrew the veil which had covered the shrine. At that moment, all the bells of the abbey began to ring, the kneeling choir chanted *Beata Virgo Genova*, and the joyous pealing and chanting continued while the shrine was lowered by ropes to the shoulders of the four oldest priests of the order, who, with prayer and fasting, had prepared themselves for the great honor.

This was between three and four of the morning. The sound of the bells rang out over the city, and a slight wind lifted and carried their jubilance over the countryside. Marianne did not hear it, being then sound asleep, but in chapels in every part of the city the religious, keeping vigil, knew what was being accomplished on the Mont.

At dawn the carriage of Monsieur de La Reynie stopped before the churches of Sainte Geneviève and of Saint Etienne-du-Mont, and Monsieur de La Reynie, descending, dismissed his coachman with the instruction to meet him at six that evening at the Palace of the Archbishop. It was to be a long day.

In his red robe, hatless, bewigged, he crossed the space before the two churches. The birds were singing in the abbey garden, a mixed choir, warblers, thrushes, and chaffinches. The sun was not yet above the horizon, but the great luminosity in the sky announced another clear day. The pavement shone with moisture. The façades of the churches rose up shadowless before him, shoulder to shoulder, a unit, but as different from each other as they could very well be. The façade of Ste.-Geneviève was old and plain, severe in its simplicity; that of St.-Etienne elaborate with every richness of the renaissance.

A group of gentlemen in red robes like his own waited for him in the portal of the church of Sainte Geneviève, officials from the Châtelet, among them his friend Robert, and also Monsieur Lamoignon the younger, who would this day stand as hostage from the Châtelet for the shrine during its absence from the church. A canon from the cathedral of Notre Dame, a counselor from the Parlement de Paris, and a master from the

Court of Accounts would remain with him, hostages also. La Reynie lifted his gaze, as he approached, from the figures in red to the stone figure of the saint in the space above the central door, a figure upright and narrow as a column, a young woman holding before her a book and a lighted candle, while over her shoulders leaned a demon who attempted to extinguish the flame of the candle, and an angel who protected it. The saint stood smiling, untroubled by the celestial struggle about her sloping shoulders. La Reynie saluted her inwardly before he greeted his friends. The last time he had come to take charge of her shrine he had been many years younger and much more solid in health. The saint was as young as ever.

He presented himself with his group to the abbé, who in turn led them to the shrine, where they made their devotions. He then received from the abbé, with verbal and written promises, according to precedent, custodianship of the shrine from that hour until the hour when it should be returned to its high pedestal. He swore, and his companions swore also, not to let the holy relic out of their sight, but to remain at all moments near it. Monsieur de Lamoignon assumed his role as hostage. The documents which had just been signed were placed in safe-keeping, and the gentlemen of the Châtelet were led to their seats, near the shrine.

At seven arrived the members of the Court of Parlement, all in red robes, who made their devotions, presented their hostage, and were seated near the police. At nine came the clergy from the cathedral, bringing the relics which were the treasures of Notre Dame, to remain in the abbey church until the return of the shrine. Last of all came the shrine of Saint Marcel, carried by representatives of the Corporation of Goldsmiths, and received at the portal of the church with due honor, so that there might be no departure from the old saying that Sainte Geneviève goes not forth unless Saint Marcel comes first to find her. At ten the procession was ready to start out. It was to be a procession of the clergy, the Court of Parlement, the chief magistrates of the city, and the beadles of the corporations. On this day the people would be audience.

They set out at last. The abbé of the church of Sainte Geneviève, in white, and barefoot, went with his priests, a figure full of the grace of humility, extending his hand in blessing as he went. The Archbishop of Paris, an old man, and infirm, was carried in a chair tapestried in purple velvet and embroidered with golden fleurs-de-lis. His head was bowed under the weight of his white and gold mitre. A servant walking behind him held a parasol over his head. The chair swayed as it was carried forward; the Archbishop swayed also, turning from side to side to bestow his blessings. And behind him came the shrines of the two saints, with their guard of honor, a double guard of clergy and of police.

The crowd was silent as the procession advanced. La Reynie could hear, above the sound of chanting from the clergy which preceded him, the clicking of rosaries, the murmur of prayers, and then, as the people caught sight of the shrine with its crown and its cross dazzling in the sunlight, he heard the cries of ecstasy, like a prolonged sigh which moved forward beside him as the crush of foam moves forward beneath the prow of a ship. All the way down the rue St.-Jacques he heard this hushed, ecstatic sigh, broken occasionally by a sharp outcry of adoration or of supplication.

The procession moved slowly. The way seemed more long than it had seemed on that other occasion so many years ago. On that other occasion there had not been this continued weight of sunlight; the appeal had been for fair weather, that time. It was a relief to find himself at last moving across the comparatively small parvis before Notre-Dame, and to know that soon he would enter that great cool Gothic cave and be able to rest for a while.

Jean Larcher and Marianne were among the massed crowd which knelt within view of the cathedral for the passage of the saint. They had taken their positions early; the wait had been long. Jean had told his beads many times. They had never hoped to be able to enter the cathedral, huge as it was. They waited outside while the service was conducted within, and then rose rather stiffly from their knees and made their way back to the rue des Lions.

Marianne had not seen Paul since the evening before. The day was a holiday for everyone. There was no reason why he should have appeared at the shop that morning, but she had hoped, since he had made his pilgrimage with them, that he would come with them for the procession. She had dressed with special care, as was befitting the occasion. She had been satisfied with what she could see of herself in the mirror in the kitchen, and she was disappointed that Paul did not arrive before it was time for them to leave home.

She kept a lookout for him in the crowd, but neither on their way to the cathedral nor in the crowd which surged about the parvis did she see any sign of him. When Jean and Marianne turned back to their own quarter, Marianne caught a glimpse of Simone and her husband Jules at a distance. She waved, and urged Jean to try to join them, but Jean was bent on getting home as quickly as possible, and the crowd was thick. She lost them before they had left the Ile de la Cité.

However, Marianne and Jean had been at home only a little time before the voice of Simone was heard calling at their door. She came in without waiting for Marianne to open the door, pulling Jules by the hand. They were bravely dressed, both full of wonder and excitement. They had seen the shrine; they had been very close to it as it passed. Simone had been blessed. She was sure she had been especially blessed by the Archbishop himself; she had been almost under his hand. Jules had bought her sweetcakes and an orange. Jules was going to take her on the river. Jules was so good to her; he would surely make a good father, would he not? Through all this chatter Jules stood calmly, full of pride. If hard work and generosity would make him a good father, he could take care of that. He said to Jean, one man to another, when Simone stopped for breath:

"I saw your friend Monsieur Bourdon walking in the procession."

Larcher nodded.

"He looked very hot," said Jules.

He waited, and the women waited for Jean to contribute something to the conversation. Jean let his eyes rest kindly on Simone's flushed face. He said:

"I saw Monsieur de La Reynie. A great man."

The soberness of the statement stopped the conversation. Jules could think of no suitable comment. Jean turned away, and Simone remembered that Jules and she were going on the river and into the country. They had left the kitchen, when she opened the door again and, looking around the edge of it, called to Marianne:

"I told him that when my time comes you will take care of me. He was very pleased."

She disappeared, the round blue eyes, the rosy face, the young smile, and Marianne set about preparing dinner. An hour or more later, when the meal had been eaten and all traces of it removed and the kitchen swept, Jean, coming from the workshop, found Marianne still in her festive clothing.

"Are you going to another procession?"

"Someone might come."

Jean looked skeptical, but made no further comment.

She was loath to take off her finery, and thereby to end the holiday. The great ceremony was over, for her. The days of anticipation and prayer had reached their climax when she saw the shrine floating above the kneeling crowd, and as yet there had been no miracle. Nothing was resolved within herself.

There would be festive dinners in the great hôtels when the ceremonies were completed. The inns would be crowded with family parties, and there would be more than one picnic in the fields. What had Paul done with his holiday? She knew the answer. The water meadows of the Bièvre, the lanes between the hedgerows were full of couples on a warm afternoon.

Even the building where she lived was more than half abandoned. She went slowly through the court and up the stairs. Slowly she undid her ribbons, her hooks, and removed her lace-edged cap and her taffeta dress. The dress was the same that she had worn when she was married. It had not been new then. It was a crisp stuff of woven stripes, a fine red stripe, as bright as blood, between two small stripes of apple green, and then a broader stripe of black. The fabric had begun to crack; there were little slits along the edges of folds. She must wear it soon, if she was to get the good of it. She wished that Paul had seen her in it. And then she wished that she need not think of Paul so much. In blue and brown denim and plain linen she went back to her kitchen.

For an hour she fought with her restlessness. Then, with no clear intention, but in response to her great need of action of some sort, she walked out of the shop and into the street. The street was empty, save for an old woman and a very young child some thirty feet away. Marianne passed them, exchanging a look of understanding with the old woman; it was no one she knew, a straggler from the crowds which had come to the ceremonies. And there was still no miracle. The air was dead and hot.

She thought, "Perhaps we have not prayed enough. Perhaps we have not prayed purely. I myself, I hardly kept my mind on my prayers half the time. I must not think so much about Paul. I am sure that he does not think about me all the time, and the day will come—the sooner the better—when he will not think of me at all."

It seemed to her then that it would be a very good thing to return to the church on the Mont and to pray again, and this time to pray to be delivered of her vanity.

She crossed the Pont Marie, and then the footbridge to the Cité. She felt happier already. The air seemed fresher. The crowd which had surrounded the parvis of the cathedral had dispersed. The area that had been closed to traffic was now traversed by a few carriages. About the doors of the cathedral and about the booths set up at the edge of the parvis, a few people stirred, gathered in groups of two or three, like bees which remain hovering about a branch after a swarm has taken flight. A few white clouds drifted above the towers. A breeze had sprung up.

Marianne saw beneath her feet, as she began to cross the parvis, a ribbon, some withered flowers—cornflowers—and a spiral of orange peel. A child darted before her and snatched almost from under her feet the bit of peel. At a safe distance he stopped, and turned and smiled at her in triumph, and then ran on, biting his prize. She had once seen a rat gnaw on such a bit of peeling.

The wind quickened to gustiness as she climbed the rue St.-Jacques, and shook the tapestries which still hung from the windows. But the sun still shone; the heat was oppressive.

The steadily rising slope fatigued her. She passed beneath familiar signs, before shops which she knew well, but everything looked strange and unfamiliar. The tapestries, the garlands, the very lack of traffic, made it another world. She almost forgot why she was climbing the long street, alone and hot and tired, and when she at last reached the Mont and entered the darkness of the church, she needed to make an effort to collect her thoughts and to resume her intention.

She was not alone. Others were kneeling in the darkness. Toward the end of the narrow nave candles glimmered before the altar. The shrine had been returned to its high platform, the hostages released, but the shrine was not yet veiled. She began her prayers with the Pater Noster, as she had begun them with Jean, two days ago. She could not resist turning her head to look at the spot where Jean and Paul had knelt together. Then she devoted herself to the supplication which she had planned: rain for the fields, victory for the King's armies, a safe return for Nicolas, and for herself, a pure heart, a quiet heart, a heart without vanity and without the pain of desire. She prayed well. She felt immensely solaced, and when she had kissed her chaplet for the last time, she rose and made her way cautiously among the kneeling forms to the door of the church, and then stepped into the open air and the sunlight.

A strong gust of wind struck her immediately and veered from the face of the church in an eddy. She made a few steps forward, then turned, and, looking back, saw the façades of the two churches white against a mass of black clouds, those clouds which had floated like snow above the towers of Notre-Dame. Above the central door of her church, in a blaze of western sunlight, the statue of Sainte Geneviève still held her book and taper and smiled mysteriously. While Marianne stared, the black cloud was split by a tremendous flash of lightning. A few drops of rain struck the pavement, and then the thunder rolled above and below the clouds, carried overhead by the rising wind, echoing from the stones beneath her feet.

It was already raining in the country and in the suburbs. In almost no time at all, it seemed, the curtain of rain reached the Mont. The spires disappeared. The clouds moved directly overhead; the western sunlight was eclipsed. Marianne found herself standing in the sudden night in the pouring rain.

It never entered her head to take shelter in the church. Startled, almost frightened, and then exhilarated by this overwhelming miracle, she picked up her skirts and began to run downhill, toward home. The lightning continued, the thunder continued, full-throated. The mercy of God resembled his wrath.

The coolness, the relief of tension in the sultry air revived her. She felt the rain joyfully on her face, on her bare arms, penetrating her clothing. She ran. The wind snatched at her cap. In the first doorway which offered a little shelter she removed the cap and, looking back, saw the street running with water, a shallow brook with a pattern of ripples braiding into the central gutter. The rain struck with such force that every drop bounced upward to a height of three or four inches, and it fell so thickly that there appeared to be a layer of raindrops spread continuously three inches above the shallow cascade, the crests of innumerable small fountains.

She shivered, being wet. There was plainly no chance that the storm would slacken for some hours. She picked up her skirts and ran on. Before she reached the river, at the Place Maubert, she took shelter again in a doorway to catch her breath. She was enjoying her encounter with the weather. She had not felt so light of heart since the pilgrimages had begun, and she was already so wet that it made no difference if she became wetter. She was glad that she had changed her clothes. As she stood there, breathing quickly and pushing back the drowned hair from her face, the door of an inn across the street flew open, and a young man dashed precipitously over the roadway. It was Paul. He pressed himself against the door beside her.

"What a fine miracle!" he shouted above the sound of falling rain.

She made no answer except to smile at him, too surprised to conceal her delight. He had never seen her look like this, her flesh so bright, her look so unconstrained. He laid a hand lightly upon her wet shoulder and, leaning forward, kissed her upon the mouth with passion. It was a long kiss. It seemed to taste of honey. He felt her lips grow warm under his. Then he released her and drew back in order to look at her again. She was not angry—he had not expected her to be angry; she had returned the kiss too well. But he wanted to look at her eyes. The pupils were dilated, the grey iris almost disappeared. Then the full white lids closed over them slowly. Her face grew white, and for a very brief moment he thought that she was about to faint. She swayed a little, her lips remained parted. He took her hands, which were cold and wet, like her face. He did not know what to do next.

She opened her eyes and, snatching her hands from his, gave him a look which he did not understand. Then she brushed past him, jumped from the high doorsill to the street, and ran on down toward the river, through the rain and the darkness.

Chapter Twelve

*T*HE RAIN CONTINUED all that night, and all the next day, and all the day after that. The city was purified as it had not been in months. Pentecost dawned fair on a refreshed world, and on Pentecost it was announced in the churches that on the very day and hour of the descent of the shrine to the cathedral a great victory had been awarded the King's army in Catalonia.

In profound gratitude to God, the King requested the Archbishop of Paris to have a *Te Deum* sung on June the ninth in the cathedral. On that day the King would present to the cathedral the sixteen Spanish banners which were being sent to him from Catalonia by the Duc de Noailles. On the evening of that day there would be *feux de joie* throughout the city and dancing in the streets.

By the afternoon of the ninth Paul was nearly desperate in his need to speak to Marianne alone. What had begun for him as a game, a test of skill and ingenuity, had become with that kiss in the rain a passion from which he suffered. He found no consolation in the company of the girl from the Pont Neuf. What he felt for Marianne eclipsed the memory of what he had felt for his master's wife in Auxerre, and yet, as Marianne avoided him, and invoked, at such times as it was necessary for them to be alone together, the full authority of her position as mistress of the shop, he was reminded of the woman at Auxerre, and the bitterness of that rejection was added to his new bitterness.

Because Marianne had responded to his kiss he made her responsible for his suffering. He felt that he deserved an accounting, but he could not get her to himself long enough to place his accusation. She took shelter from him in the presence of her husband. She had run from him, that evening in the rain; she had run from knowledge of herself. But she was no green girl. He had given her time to regain her courage. She should now let him approach her. She should admit her passion honestly; and if she felt herself too good to accept his love, she should at least stand still and hear his reproaches.

For several days he devised speeches by which he might bring her to terms. Then he decided to give her what she was giving him, silence and the back of her hand. He could renounce her. She was not the most attractive woman he had ever seen. He had intended, and he still intended, to keep out of trouble. She had asked for that kiss, standing there with her hair uncovered, her bodice wet through and clinging to her breasts, smiling like a wild girl. But the betrayal at Auxerre worked in him like a poison, until he began to feel unsure of the thing he was most sure of. He must touch her once more to reassure himself, and then he could turn his back on her. He was never once concerned that she might speak to Jean against him.

On Wednesday evening, while Jean was still in the bindery, Paul made a pretext to enter the kitchen, and, approaching Marianne before she could escape, said quickly:

"You know where I live?"

"I know the name of the street."

He made an impatient gesture with his hand, as if to say that was not enough.

"I will wait for you tonight in the Place de Grève. I will wait all evening."

It had been a day like Pentecost, the air light and pure, the sunlight brilliant. White clouds had sailed across the city, and at sunset grey ones floated, edged with gold in a pale gold sky. The air was soft. Heat exhaled from the stones of the city as from a healthy animal body. Paul patrolled the Place de Grève, from one end to the other. He did not know by what street she would arrive, if she came. He made allowance for the time it would take her to give Jean his supper, and then made a further allowance for her hesitation, for accident, for her meeting a neighbor on the way. He had no appetite for supper himself. He marched from one extremity of the Hôtel de Ville to the other, looked toward the river and beyond the mass of the cathedral looming broadside above the pointed roofs of the Cité, looked at the Great Cross which stood where the scaffolds were erected for executions, and turned and walked back to the point from which he had started.

When he remembered her avoidance of him during the past week, he thought she would not come. When he remembered the pressure of her lips against his, he was certain that she would. He did not know how he could endure to enter the shop on the morrow if she did not come. He decided that he would not be able to remain with Larcher. Then he understood that the pain of his uncertainty would continue whether he worked for Larcher or elsewhere, if she did not come.

Wood had been stacked for the fires of celebration. The crowd was late in gathering. A man with a musette sat on the steps of the Great Cross and tried out a few tunes. At the corner of the rue de la Mortellerie some papers affixed to a post fluttered in the draft of air from the river. They were well weathered; they had been posted the day of the procession. Idly, Paul stopped to read them.

He realized almost at once that he had heard the contents cried with trumpet that day, and more than once, first in one part of the city and then another, as he had wandered about by himself. It was the most recent effort of La Reynie to empty the city of the homeless. It declared that all vagrants who were healthy enough for employment and who were still not employed, and who had their origin elsewhere than in the city, should leave the city within the next three days and return to their former habitations. Those not complying with the decree, should they be found in the city after three days, for the first offense should be detained for a week at the Hôpital Général, that is to say, at the almshouse, where they would be employed by the city in return for their nourishment. For the second offense, should they be again taken in the city, they should be condemned to the galleys for three years. This was for the men; as for the women, for the first offense they should be treated the same as the men; for the second, they should be shaved, whipped, and stood in the pillory for two hours.

The decree did not apply to him, thank God. He wondered how many beggars were still able to evade the almshouse and the galleys, and was about to turn away when he felt a touch on his shoulder. He spun about, expecting to greet Marianne, and found himself confronted by a tall and gaunt young man with a gaunt and honest face. He had seen that face before, but he could not think where—the bony forehead, the deep-set eyes, and, shading them, the dusty, broad-brimmed beaver hat.

"You don't remember me?" said the young man, smiling, the smile incising two curved lines at each side of his mouth. "The printer from Lyon, in the shop of the Widow Charmot, rue de la Vieille Bouclerie? Rambault. Pierre Rambault." He brought out the items of identification hopefully one after the other as Paul stared at him, dazed by his disappointment. "You are the little bookbinder from Auxerre. You came looking for a job. I can see that you found one. You are brushed, well fed. I am glad for you. Upon my soul, I was sorry for you that day."

Paul could not but remember him then, the only person, before he had encountered Father Lanterns, who had found a kind word for him. His first acquaintance. He protested that he had not forgotten. He had been startled only. He crowded back his disappointment and tried to be cordial.

"I'm on the way to a friend," said the gaunt young man. "Come along and have a drink with us. He's a printer too, also from Lyon. I knew his brother there."

"I'm waiting for a friend myself," said Paul.

"Bring him along. Chavance won't mind."

"It's a woman."

"Bring her, then. She'll be an addition."

"She's not that sort."

"So . . ." said the printer from Lyon. "I'll wait with you until she turns up. Tell me about your job."

"You'll embarrass her," said Paul. "Be a good fellow, go along and find your friend."

"No need for her to be embarrassed. What do you take me for? A boor? Chavance, also, is a good sort. He has connections —the best. He even lodges with the monks."

"Some other time," said Paul, pleading.

"A man you should know, yourself."

"Some other time. I'll look you up, and then I can meet your friend."

"Chavance is the name."

"From Lyon," said Paul. "Now goodbye. I see my friend."

He did not see Marianne, nor any woman resembling her, but the pretense let him escape from under the shoulder of the printer. Halfway across the Place he looked back. The gaunt young man from the shop of the Widow Charmot had disappeared.

In the rue des Lions, Marianne said to Jean:

"They'll be lighting the bonfires presently. Shall we go to see them?"

"I prefer the Harrow," said Jean, "to any more standing on my feet. I've seen bonfires in my life."

"I'll walk to the Harrow with you," said Marianne. "There will be a tremendous fire in the rue St.-Antoine. We can see it from the door of the Harrow."

"As you like," he said, and took his twist of blond tobacco, his pipe, and a few spills from the mantel.

She followed him down the street, saying to herself, "If he asks me to go into the Harrow, I will stay with him all evening." But at the door of the inn he cast a brief look toward St.-Antoine and remarked that the fires had not yet been lighted.

"You will have something of a wait," he said, and left her in the street.

Oddly, she felt a disappointment. She bit her lip and looked after him. If he had invited her to stay she would have felt a different disappointment, and probably rebellion, along with the bitter satisfaction of doing what she knew she should do. There was still nothing to prevent her from following him into the Harrow, nothing except a sense of being slighted, which, however, was strong. She lifted her chin and turned to the rue St.-Antoine.

The bonfires had not yet been lighted, that was true, but the crowd was in readiness. There was music, sackbutts and fiddles, and a smell of wine, as if someone had broken a bottle. She told herself that she had asked Jean to come with her, and she had given him a fair chance to ask her to remain with him, and he had refused her, twice. She could not have stayed quietly at home on an evening like this, nor could she have been content for two hours in a smoky room at the Harrow. The restlessness which stirred her, and which was so like the restlessness of that hot afternoon before the storm, was not caused by the sound of fiddles merely. It had sprung into existence with Paul's hurried words, and lived in her with a terrible force. She knew quite well what would happen if she went to meet him, and she knew also, beneath her delays, her hesitations and her subterfuges, that she would go.

She had brushed her hair after supper and had bathed her face. She had taken a red satin ribbon in her fingers and was about to knot it at her throat when she remembered Jean's observation.

"Are you going to another procession?" he had asked.

She drew the ribbon regretfully through her fingers, then folded it smoothly and tucked it in the pocket of her skirt. It was the first deception. When she had gone as far on St.-Antoine as the fountain before the church of the Jesuits, she took the ribbon from her pocket and tied it about her throat. Then she went on toward the Place de Grève.

"There is no point in waiting here to see the fires," she said in the surface of her mind. "There will be a better celebration before the Hôtel de Ville, naturally." If she were challenged for leaving her own quarter, this would be her answer. Naturally. But no one challenged her, no one paid any attention to her at all, as she went on past the familiar landmarks, drawn by a force which was wholly unfamiliar and not to be denied; and in the Place de Grève she found Paul waiting for her.

At the Place de Grève there were three huge bonfires and a crowd to match. The lone musician had been joined by some fiddlers; the orange seller, the man with the flask of eau-de-vie and the little cups hung from a belt over his shoulder, the seller of sweetcakes were all there, and doing business. The cakes, very thin, were sprinkled with sugar while still hot and rolled up into horns. They were called *oublies* by some, but more popularly *plaisirs*. Marianne and Paul, attempting to leave the Place, found their way blocked by the seller of sweetcakes, who thrust his tray at them and roared his usual song.

Voici le plaisir, Madame, voici le plaisir.
N'en mangez pas, Madame. Ça fait mourir.

The cakes were fragrant, like the scent of locust blossoms on a warm night. The sweetcakes man was sure of his sale. But Paul took Marianne by the hand and led her imperiously past. The sweetcakes man bellowed with laughter.

"She's afraid to die!" he shouted after them. He had other customers at once.

In the closed stairway there was a smell of stale urine at the first landing; at the second a smell of rancid cabbage. Marianne went first, Paul following close behind her, saying, "A little bit more and we shall be there," and then, "It is here."

She stepped into a room which had not been opened all day, which was still warm with the personal odor of its one occupant, holding the odor as a coat or a shirt might hold it. This was a sensual pleasure for Marianne. The room embraced her before Paul did.

He paused to lock the door. The sense of security reached her. She turned to meet his hands, and to feel, as she had expected, his lips upon hers. What she had not expected was the great release from the restlessness which had driven her during the last hours, and from the doubt and almost physical pain which had plagued her for the last week. Desire remained, but it remained like a warm tide of life and of delight. She moved into Paul's arms without the least sense that she was committing a mortal sin.

She had disrobed herself for Jean, laying aside her clothes in an orderly way. She let Paul remove her fichu and drop it on the floor, undo her bodice. The room was dim. His hands told him all that he had longed to know, and guided her toward the bed which she had not seen.

After the last shuddering breath, the stifled cry of astonishment, she lay at peace. Paul rolled away, keeping one hand upon her shoulder, as if to assure himself of her reality, and presently slept. *Voici le plaisir, Madame. Ça fait mourir.* This, she told herself, was what it meant to die. This was what it meant to love. She had thought of her husband at this first contact with a different man, but she had thought of him with such a sense of the impersonal, at such a distance, that she had felt no intrusion of one experience upon the other. The experiences had so little resemblance to each other that she had all at once forgotten Jean completely, as she had forgotten herself, the hour, the day, the year. What remained in her moment of great contentment was the astonishment. All her life she had ignored this extraordinary extent of passion. Yet she had once thought herself happily married, or happily enough.

She seemed to have come alive in a new existence, yet she remembered the details of her old existence; it had been no dream. Its reality was still with her.

Paul stirred. He was awake, she felt, although he had said nothing. The rhythm of his breathing had changed. The sky had darkened, and through the dusty window which looked upon the steep roof of the next building came only the dimmest of light. Time had passed. She did not know how much time.

"I must go."

"Why?" Paul's voice, very softly.

"What time is it, do you think?"

"Time does not exist. We have slain it."

"I must be home before Jean leaves the Harrow. Had you forgotten Jean?"

"No. I have sometimes wished that he were dead. Or, more simply, that he did not exist."

"He's a good man."

"Yes."

"We do him no harm." She was certain of that.

Paul's hand moved from her shoulder across her breasts. He said, "I take nothing from him that belongs to him. Is that not so?"

She answered that it was so, and lifted his hand to her lips, and laying it gently aside, sat up in bed. She looked about her. The floor seemed piled with dust, furnished with shadows.

"Where are my clothes? I must go."

"You are so sensible," he answered with a sigh. Then he added disarmingly, "And that is a very good thing."

He got up from the bed, which was very low, and searched for his tinderbox. But, fumbling between the copper ewer and the basin, finding the iron candlestick, he made himself a promise that he would one day overpower her to such a point that she would no longer remember to be sensible; and then he would remind her to go home.

Chapter Thirteen

IN THE WEEKS that followed, Marianne learned many deceptions. Most of them were simple. She learned to look at Paul in Jean's presence so that her feeling was not visible in her face. She learned to accept with pride, knowing the reason, Paul's disregard of her when they were not alone together; and she learned to multiply occasions when they might be alone.

Life was no longer monotonous. Any moment might yield an encounter which would make her tingle with pleasure to her heels. And since any moment might betray her through some chance gesture or sudden change of color, she needed to be constantly alert, aware of herself as of the others. She had begun weeks before to take pains with the food she served, the way she dressed. Now she wanted to sing as she scrubbed or swept. She contented herself with silence and with a freer and happier way of moving, so that even Jean looked at her with pleasure as she came and went. It seemed all a part, for him, of the well-being of his shop since the advent of his young assistant, the well-being of the city since the miracle of the saint. He could see that others besides the tall abbé Têtu appreciated the work which issued from the shop. His business improved, in spite of the bad times. He enjoyed, also, when his depression over the absence of his son grew less extreme, having Paul to converse with, in his laconic way.

As for Paul, he was happy. He was almost satisfied. Deception was nothing new to him; he sensed its novelty for Marianne and took a certain malicious pleasure in observing the ease with which she became adept. He noted also that the fear of being surprised heightened her pleasure in a kiss. The knowledge that he had persuaded an honest woman into his bed increased his triumph. The first time, after her visit to his room, that he embraced her as he found her standing midway between the table where she served their meals and the hearth where she prepared them, she was shocked.

"Not here, in my own kitchen," she protested, with all the years of her unquestioned fidelity surrounding her.

"Why not?" said Paul. "Is it less a sin to kiss on the street or in a stairway?"

"Here I am Larcher's wife," she would have answered if in her confusion she could have found the words, but no words came, and Paul went on:

"In my room you were not embarrassed, and my room is an unworthy place for you. A rat hole, filled with the stench of poverty, for you, who sleep in a great bed with red curtains, with clean white sheets that smell of the sun and air, who sleep in that great bed with your husband." He was amused and brutal, and yet careful not to go too far. "But how beautiful you were in my room," he said, turning quickly from the accusation of adultery which he had almost made. He kissed her under her chin, so that she smiled, and said, "You are a good wife, Mademoiselle. It pleases me that you put lavender between your sheets. I like to see you scour the copper. If I must envy Jean, I will envy him for everything."

In theory it was an excellent situation, beneficial to all three of them. The theory was Paul's, which he expounded to Marianne. He relieved Jean of the responsibility of keeping his wife content, and at the same time provided him, in his bed and in his kitchen, with a woman who was even more attentive to his welfare than she had been before the ninth of June. He himself worked better than he had ever worked before. He exerted himself to be considerate of Jean.

With all this assurance that she was not greatly wronging her husband, Marianne found it a little matter to excuse herself to Jean for not going to early Mass with him. She left the shop later, alone, and went not to Mass but to Paul's stuffy little room, from which she returned with clear eyes and a deepened color. It seemed as if things might remain in this fine balance indefinitely. It was Marianne who in her new assurance became a little careless.

One day in midsummer, Paul and Marianne being alone in the bindery, Paul remarked that he had lost a button from his shirt, and Marianne offered to sew it on for him.

It seemed an innocent activity, especially in view of their relationship. She performed the task deftly and quickly, then looked about for her scissors to snip the thread. Not finding them, "Lend me your knife," she said to Paul. "No, never mind," and, bending toward him, she bit the thread. The action brought her head against his breast. Perhaps she held it there the fraction of a moment longer than was necessary. It seemed to Paul that she delayed the moment, for, looking over her head, he met the surprised gaze of his master. Jean had returned, with no undue quietness of step, with no intention of taking anyone unawares, but absorbed in themselves, neither Paul nor Marianne had heard the opening of the door or the advancing step. A rigidity in Paul warned Marianne of something amiss. She lifted her head, looking first at Paul, then followed his glance toward her husband.

Midday, midsummer, the air was warm and moist after a

morning shower. Marianne had discarded her cap and her fichu. Her arms were bare almost to the shoulder, as she had pushed back her sleeves. The air, the informality of the moment, the two figures standing like one in a rectangle of sunlight, all combined to give Jean an impression of what was in fact the truth. But the moment itself was innocent.

A sense of revelation rushed upon him, bringing to mind a hundred hitherto unquestioned gestures, poses, inflections. They were lovers, these two. He had taken his wife in adultery. The knowledge hit him with the force of a heavy blow on the forehead. He stopped dead where he stood. Then the moment resolved itself naturally, without drama. Marianne came toward him, holding on the middle finger of the hand poised before her, her silver thimble, and between the thumb and first finger, a needle threaded with white.

"I mislaid my scissors," she said. "I had to use my teeth."

Jean stared at her, not comprehending the connection of her words with what he had just witnessed, still shocked by a knowledge which had presented itself as a certainty. She explained.

"He lost a button from his shirt. Something had to be done, for the sake of appearances."

In fact, Paul was then reaching to button his shirt just where her head had seemed to rest. His grin was embarrassed.

"I don't have another clean shirt," he said. "I didn't think it would be so noticeable."

Larcher still blocked the door to the kitchen, and Marianne, wishing to pass him, put out her hand to push him aside. The gesture, again, was natural. She passed him, brushing him with her body as she did so, as she had done unnumbered times before, as she had every right to do, being his wife; and to the stunned look in his eyes she said:

"I couldn't ask him to take off his shirt, as I do you, when I wish to sew on a button."

Jean's fear and knowledge turned about him and then leveled into an illusion. Nothing was wrong. The people whom he had trusted were still worthy of his trust. Relief and then repentance took possession of him. He said nothing at all, but removed his coat, put on his apron, and resumed his work.

But that evening at the Harrow, stuffing the tobacco into his pipe and tamping it down with his little finger, he tried to evaluate his appalling suspicion. It was as unbased, it now seemed to him, as it had been sudden, and, he added for his own peace of mind, evanescent. But like the flash of lightning which it resembled, in the ensuing darkness it left the image of what it had starkly illuminated. He summoned up for scrutiny the gestures, the laughter beyond the door, all the little indications which had seemed to him in that instant warnings which he had ignored. Reconsidered, they seemed as innocent as he had thought them at that time. He had noticed them, that was all. He had noticed them doubtless because he was jealous. The reason for his jealousy was baseless. The fact that Marianne was more than ever thoughtful of his needs did not occur to him as a reason for suspecting that she might be enjoying the love of another man. Since there was no reason for his jealousy, there was no reason for giving importance to all those trivial incidents which it had pointed out. Before he had finished lighting his pipe his thoughts had come full circle.

Outwardly he appeared as calm as ever. Looking up, he asked for his usual thimbleful of brandy, and then relaxed behind a cloud of smoke. He had come full circle, and what remained in his mind was the sense of having wronged his wife. This was much more pleasant than the suspicion that she might have wronged him. He built up a solid wall of resolution against the very fear of such a catastrophe. He smoked his pipe and drank his brandy, paid for his drink and left the Harrow, much earlier than was his habit.

More than once on a warm clear evening such as this, Paul and Marianne, relying on the extraordinary regularity of Larcher's routine, had met, sometimes no farther from home than the Mail beneath the Arsenal. Sometimes they went to the Ile

Louviers. Those who frequented the Ile at dusk paid little attention to other couples. From across the river floated the sounds of
cattle and horses being led down to drink on the far shore, and
sometimes there were shouts and laughter from people bathing.
Frogs sang in the dampness of the moat. On this night, however,
Paul had asked for no rendezvous.

The shop was silent and shuttered. The windows of the bindery were also dark. Jean saw a light in the upper room. On the
half-enclosed landing he paused, hearing beyond the door Marianne's voice. One last pang of doubt constricted his heart before he heard the answering voice. Reassured, he opened the door
upon Simone and Marianne.

"I'm lending her a garment big enough to cover her and the
little one under her ribs," said Marianne. "That skirt covered
Nicolas once upon a time. Under a clean apron it should look as
good as new."

He went on into the front room, removing his clothing, and.
stretched himself in bed, leaving the bed curtains open. He
pulled a sheet halfway up his body, and lay looking up into the
dark corners of the canopy. He listened to the interchange of
voices in the next room, unable to distinguish what they were
saying, and then, after the voices fell silent, he listened to the
opening and shutting of cupboard doors. Simone must have gone
to her own rooms. Marianne was busy with her own affairs,
not his; they detained her a long time.

The skirt which had covered Nicolas—he did not remember it
well. Some blue stuff, much faded. He would not have recognized it on Simone. Women kept track of such things. He made
an effort, however, to remember the days when Marianne had
first worn such a skirt, lifting at the hem in front, her apron tied
high, close under her breasts. Her bosom had grown rounder. It
was not so very long ago. Eighteen, or less. than eighteen years,
a small part of a lifetime. She had changed very little. There had
been some bad years when she seemed to age, but lately, being

less burdened with hard work, she had grown younger in appearance.

He had not done badly by his family, after all. He was proud to have been able to care so well for his parents-in-law in their old age; it was a satisfaction to him that he had seen them decently buried. As for Nicolas, he was proud that he could offer his son a share in an honest business, well established. The sense of injury which accompanied his thought of Nicolas lessened the satisfaction which he had begun to feel in the achievement of his life. He tried to hold to the satisfaction. Marianne understood what he had accomplished against odds, and one day his son might realize it too. He called to her:

"Come to bed, Marianne."

"In a moment."

He waited. She was very quiet. Two people passed below in the street, talking. Overhead someone moved a chair or some other piece of furniture. By and by Marianne came and sat on the edge of his bed, toward the foot. She folded her hands on her knee and looked down at him.

"Close the shutters and come to bed."

"It's too hot," she answered without moving.

Through the twilight they could see each other clearly. She looked down at him patiently, attentively, like a child or a servant whom he had summoned and who had come obediently. She saw that he had not put on a nightshirt, that his broad chest was exposed in the shadow of the bed. The cord of his scapular and the scapular itself lay upon the matted dark hair. It was the scapular of the Carmelites, dedicated to the Holy Virgin, a fold of brown cloth sewn carefully together and containing she knew not what images or prayers, square in shape, darkened with sweat and shiny at the corners. He had worn it ever since she had known him. He would doubtless be buried in it. He appeared very large lying among the pillows, his throat and chest exposed like this, larger than when he was clothed and on his feet. She looked at him, feeling neither repugnance nor desire, and waited for him to speak.

"The English have bombarded Dieppe," he said, "and set fire to the town. The whole town is destroyed. It is frightful to think of the homeless of an entire town turned loose upon the country-side."

She made no comment; there seemed none to make. The frightfulness was remote. It did not touch her inner com-placency, nor did it have much to do, that she could see, with Jean's early and unaccustomed return. She knew quite well how she must have looked as he opened the door upon them, Paul and herself, that morning, nor was the significance of Paul's casual good night, spoken in Jean's hearing, lost upon her. She was not yet alarmed, but she knew that she had a problem. She waited for an accusation, her answer prepared, and then, since none came, she tried a diversion.

"Are you ill?" she asked.

"I am worried about Nicolas."

"Rouen is unharmed," she said.

"We do not know that he is still in Rouen."

"But would he have gone to Dieppe?"

"If he did not find work in Rouen," Jean said, "he might have gone anywhere."

"If he can't find work and he runs out of money, he can always come home."

"The war has an attraction for a boy of his age."

His voice was sombre. "To hear him," Marianne thought, "the boy is already dead." She could not feel alarmed for Nicolas, she did not know why. He was young and capable. She did not think that he would enlist, but if he did, he would be able to take care of himself. Her detachment, she felt, was natural, and at the same time she wondered at it. It was all of a piece with what she had felt lying under the willows with Simone, a sur-prise that his absence should trouble her so little. Yet she loved her son. She was sorry for Jean, also.

She had waited for an accusation. Now that the conversation had turned away from herself, she made an effort to fall in with his mood.

"Those people at Rouen, perhaps they could tell you something. Why don't you write to them?"

"The Cailloué? I have avoided correspondence with them since the Revocation."

"You wouldn't have sent Nicolas to them if you thought there was danger."

"If they are still in business, they are converted," said Jean. "I don't even know if they're still in business."

"It would do no harm to write."

"The old man died in his bed, unmolested—that I know," Jean said slowly; he had said as much to Nicolas in April. "You are right. I will send off a letter to them in the morning." He removed his hands from behind his head, stretched out one hand upon the sheet, palm up, toward his wife. "Come to bed, Marianne," he said, his voice tender.

In the morning he did dispatch his letter and felt some relief for having done so. But the weight of an accusation which he had not made still oppressed him and demanded atonement. At noon, eating the good food which Marianne had prepared, he looked from one to the other of his table companions as he had looked formerly at Nicolas and Marianne, troubled and paternal. He addressed himself to Marianne.

"You spoke of a trip to Pincourt today."

"Beyond Pincourt. For some honey. My mother's uncle—he is very old—keeps a few hives. He sent me word that he would open them today, and that if I cared for honey he would let me have some. Of course it is not a gift, exactly, but I would pay him less than they ask elsewhere."

"I ordered leather at Pincourt. It would save me a trip if you could bring it when you go for your honey. It's not much out of your way."

She demurred. "Of course, Jean, but . . ."

He turned to Paul. "She is right. It would be too much for her to carry. You will go with her. And I ask you to look over the skins before they are wrapped to make sure they give us no faulty ones."

Paul was immediately acquiescent. Marianne said:

"But it will be late. He never opens the hives until sundown, when all the bees are home."

"That will make no difference to me, Mademoiselle. I am free in the evening."

"But we must stop at Pincourt before sundown."

"That can be arranged," said Jean. "Go a little early. Have a visit with your uncle—your great-uncle." He included them both like his children in a benevolent glance, and closed the subject.

They spent a long time in the shop of the leather merchant, examining the skins, checking one shade of red or green against another, closing the deal. Paul shouldered the bundle and they went on, still in the sunlight, into the narrower lanes of the faubourgs between Ménilmontant and the river.

They found themselves shortly before sundown in an enclosed garden, very long, narrow as an alley, where there were straw-covered beehives on a long bench facing the east, and fruit trees espaliered against a high stone wall. The place smelled of ripe and rotting fruit and of gillyflowers.

They sat down on a bench at a distance from the hives, and the uncle picked up a fallen peach, shook the bees from it, and offered it to Marianne.

"They steal as much from me as they can," he remarked, stooping to find another for Paul.

It was a white-fleshed peach, an early variety; the juice ran down her wrist as she bit into it, and she leaned away from the bench to avoid dropping juice on her skirt.

"As soon as the shadow hits them, they will abandon all this," said the uncle. "They will all be in their houses presently, and then I'll give them something to put them to sleep."

"Do they never sting you?" Paul asked.

"Never. I understand them, and moreover, I'm old. The skin is dry. It rouses nothing in them. If you were to go among them," he said to Marianne, "they would doubtless sting you. Your skin is young and moist." He smiled, showing the stumps of a few yellow teeth. His eyes, a grey-green, were shadowed by a wide straw hat. He had trimmed his grey beard with scissors as close to his chin as he could cut. Marianne, smiling back at him, took her handkerchief from the pocket in her skirt and wiped her forehead and cheeks.

"It is sweating weather," she said, "especially on the road." Then to Paul, "He is really remarkable. I have seen him with his bare hands reach into a swarm of bees, and rummage there, and bring out the queen."

"It is a good trade, that of bee-keeper, but one must be educated, and also constitutionally suited for it."

He left them in order to prepare his gear for robbing the hives.

Since the moment when they had left the rue des Lions they had behaved with as much decorum as if they had been continually in the presence of Jean. Now that they were alone and in privacy as complete as they could have desired, the decorum continued.

Marianne balanced the pit of the peach in her hand, and remarked that if one had a little piece of land one could plant it and in time have a tree with fruit; and Paul smiled at her with happiness, and made no offer to touch her. She thought of the many times when she had suggested to Jean that he should invest his hoarded money in a property, suggestions which he always refused, but she did not speak of it. She laid the pit between them on the bench and again wiped her face and her throat with her handkerchief. Putting the kerchief back in her pocket, she felt the beads of her chaplet huddled there, and remembered the day of the great procession, the storm, and her meeting with Paul, and turned her face toward him in pleasure, living, in this relaxed and quiet half hour, in two worlds, the world of herself and Paul, and of herself and her husband. There seemed no great conflict between them.

The sun moved slowly up the wall and, as the old man had predicted, the bees left the earth and the rotting fruit which had been damaged while still on the tree and had dropped before the careful hands could rescue it. The sky began to change color slowly, the light softened. Paul removed his hat and laid it on the bundle of leather.

"When the moon rises there will be nightingales," he said.

By that time they would be again in the city in their separate lodgings. The old man returned in his costume for robbing the hives. He carried a contraption of copper with a long spout and a kind of small bellows. It contained live coals, and over the coals he had stuffed scraps of old cloth, damp straw and leaves. He still wore his hat. His hands were bare, but he had tied the sleeves of his smock at the wrist, had tucked the loose ends into his belt, and had twisted a large red kerchief about his neck, all this so that the bees would not crawl under his clothing. His breeches were tight at the knee. His cloth stockings were thick.

Only a few bees were visible through the dusk, hovering at the doors of the hives. He approached the long bench quietly and, using the bellows of his smoke pot, puffed a little smoke into each hive, moving down the line, stooping, an enchanter employing a practical magic. He laid the smoker aside, went into the house again, and returned with wide dishes of copper and of faïence which he set near the hives; then he approached the hives again, tapping them, shaking them a little, and listening. When he heard or thought he heard a stirring beneath the straw, he gave them a little more smoke and waited for it to take effect.

Marianne and Paul watched from a safe distance. In due time the old man lifted the straw cover of a hive, removed the honey to the waiting dishes, breaking the full comb from the supporting withes, discarding old and dirty masses of comb; then he replaced the supports and the conical straw cap.

Remembering his guests, he broke some smaller pieces from

the comb and came to offer them, a piece in each hand. A bee crawled over the hand from which Marianne received her piece. There were others on his sleeve and on his shoulder. They did not try to fly, but clung, dazed and confused, nor did the old man try to brush them away. The smell of smoke approached with him; he carried it away with him when he went back to the hives, but the honeycomb tasted of smoke, still. The wax was soft from the heat of the sun, the honey sharply sweet and fragrant with some quality besides the scent of flowers.

On the way home, walking almost in darkness, Marianne, carrying her pot of honey, Paul shouldering the roll of leather, they came to the Porte St.-Antoine and lingered, crossing the bridge above the moat. The scent of water plants, of ooze, rose from the marshy bottom. It was the odor they had often breathed, resting in each other's arms in the shadows of the Ile Louviers. They saw the mass of the Bastille from the other side now, a huge black shadow with a level, crenellated top. Beyond it lay the quarter where Marianne lived, where Paul worked. They had not kissed, they had not touched hands once all afternoon. They had behaved like good children, and they had been curiously happy.

"He has given us a fine outing," said Paul.

"He has been worried over Nicolas and the war," said Marianne, as if in answer to a question.

"It was not for that he sent us out together," said Paul.

"Greatly worried," she persisted. "He has written to Rouen for news of him."

"He knows about us," said Paul quietly. "He knows and he refuses to know."

Chapter Fourteen

IN MID-AUGUST came a letter from Rouen, signed by Mademoiselle Marianne Cailloué.

"Since my mother is very infirm because of her advancing age, in order to spare her fatigue, I permit myself the honor of answering your inquiry regarding your son. Unfortunately we were unable to give him employment since our business is small and Monsieur Jean Dumesnil, who is my mother's partner, is able to handle most of our work alone. He has also the assistance of his brother Jacques. We were happy to receive your son. He passed several evenings in conversation with Monsieur Jean Dumesnil before he left Rouen. Although I did not make one of their company, I can assure you that Monsieur Dumesnil was favorably impressed with this handsome young man whose prolonged silence must quite naturally distress you. I regret with all my heart that I can give you no further news of him nor of his intended destination upon leaving Rouen."

"He never wrote a letter in his life," said Marianne. "And by now, even if it occurred to him to write, he would say it wasn't worth the trouble, since he'll be home again soon."

"How soon?"

"By autumn. That was what he said. Summer is almost over."

Jean folded the letter and placed it in the pocket of his vest. His eyes were unhappy, and he did not look at the letter as he folded it, nor at his wife.

The abbé Têtu established himself in the rue Neuve St.-Paul that summer. This was the street, as one came from the river, which lay next after the rue des Lions. Like the rue des Lions, it had once been a part of the King's gardens. The grave hôtels where the aristocracy had once lived were now inhabited largely by lawyers and rich bourgeois. The Marquise de Brinvilliers had lived there, and not so very long ago. Her poisons, her adulteries, and her murders were still fresh in the minds of the abbé's acquaintances. To the common people, after her execution, she became a saint because of her touching repentance. When her body had been burned, they scrambled for a handful of her ashes, to be hoarded like holy relics. The Marquise de Sévigné had remarked, when the flames had died and nothing remained of La Brinvilliers except her ashes and a little smoke, "She is in the air now. We breathe her."

Madame de Sévigné left Paris for Provence before the miracle of Sainte Geneviève, declaring herself happy to quit the scene of so much misery. But even in Paradise—"this life is too sweet; the days fly by too quickly, and we do no penance—" Madame de Sévigné longed for news of her friends in Paris, and her ,cousin, Monsieur de Coulanges, supplied her in detail. He wrote of his wife's illness, of the Italian doctor who undertook to cure her, and of the abbé Têtu's remove.

"Monsieur l'abbé Têtu is, as ever, most extraordinary; he has rented a house in the rue Neuve-Saint-Paul . . . Madame de Coulanges had a very bad night, but the remedies she is taking cannot cure her on the dot. We need a little patience. But the person who is most likely to die of all this is the abbé Têtu, who cannot endure either the presence or the conversation of Carette, and to such a point that he has deserted the house of Coulanges, because Carette comes there every day, and passes an infinity of time with her. Madame de Coulanges is of the same opinion as the abbé, but when life itself is at stake . . . The abbé continues to admire Madame de Coulanges, and fumes inwardly because she does not get rid of Carette . . . The abbé also disapproves that she has placed an orange tree loaded with blossoms in her gallery; in a word, he is very extraordinary, and I fear lest his next remove be to the Incurables—to soften the name of the retreat where he will actually wind up."

The disapproval of Coulanges did not disturb the abbé. He liked his house, the rent was suitable to his purse; but his self-imposed exile from the salon of Madame de Coulanges troubled him sorely, and he lacked the company of Madame de Sévigné. His insomnia increased. The laudanum which he took to induce sleep left him, in his waking hours, deeply melancholy. At the worst of his melancholy he left Paris for the Abbaye de la Trappe, and spent some expiatory hours with Monsieur de Rancé.

Te Deum succeeded *Te Deum* that spring and summer as the King's armies advanced from one victory to another. The announcements of new taxes followed with equal frequency. After the decree of late May which had required all homeless and unemployed persons to quit the city, it became necessary to post guards at the city gates to prevent reflux of the tide of unfortunates. On Corpus Christi day the beggars so crowded Versailles in hope of alms and scraps from the tables of the court that they created a sanitary problem. There was illness in Paris. Fagon feared an epidemic under the King's windows. At his instigation, the day after the fête, the streets and courtyards were washed down in a great cleansing operation. The King watched the procession of Corpus Christi from a window and performed his devotions for the day in his private chapel.

Meanwhile the harvest advanced. In late June, to prevent

speculation, the King issued an order forbidding the sale of standing grain; but as the heads of wheat began to ripen, the outcasts of Paris, and starving country folk as well, made havoc in the fields, snatching the grain to eat from their hands, as the followers of Jesus of Nazareth once ate upon a Sabbath.

Roger, the grain merchant, continued his operations at the Port de l'Ecole, an irritation both to Monsieur de La Reynie and to Monsieur de Harlay. Harlay, ineffective in matters of decision, goaded by the constant admonitions of Monsieur de Pontchartrain, writing in the name of the King, to do something, decided in July to do something about Roger. Since he could do nothing in this case through La Reynie, he went over the head of La Reynie directly to the King. He made a request and received from Pontchartrain an answer:

"Here is the order which you asked of me for the arrest of Roger. Be assured that everything you need for this service shall be sent you promptly. But permit me, as an old friend, to repeat to you ever the more strongly the same things, and let me tell you that the King is chagrined and impatient that nothing is done. In the name of God, act! Make use of whom you will. Feel your superiority. All the officers are under you, and in this case you are given an increase of authority. Everything depends upon you. Upon you alone will fall all the credit or all the blame."

So Roger was arrested. La Reynie could do no more than comply. He wrote to Harlay:

"The King's order was carried out this morning and Roger has been conducted to the Châtelet. His books have been seized —accounts, journals, bills of lading, and other documents, so that his dealings in grain may be investigated thoroughly. It is through examination of his papers that we hope for some light on the subject; however, the detention of his person may perhaps serve as an example."

This was on the sixth of July.

Monsieur de Pontchartrain was aware of a certain coldness,

subsequently, between La Reynie and Harlay. The arrest of
Roger did not change the larger picture. The King continued to
be chagrined and impatient, and on Saturday Monsieur de Harlay received two more notes from Monsieur de Pontchartrain.
The first said:

"Make use of Monsieur de La Reynie. Observe that though
I say to you make use of Monsieur de La Reynie, I do not say
that once you have done that, that all is done." The second
said:

"The King commands me to tell you that you should be
tomorrow at Trianon at half past two o'clock precisely. This is
in order to discuss with you the ineffective control in Paris over
bread, over grain, over public speech, with all of which you will
find him strongly displeased. He commands me also to summon
Monsieur de La Reynie and Monsieur le Prévost des Marchands;
but he will talk with you in private before seeing them."

Thus it happened that on that Sunday afternoon La Reynie
and the Prévost des Marchands de Paris paced together up and
down the marble peristyle, waiting for the King to end his
private talk with the Premier Président. Beyond the rose-red
pillars to the east the long approach of forest and lawn dreamed
in the sun. La Reynie had been much disturbed over the arrest
of Roger. He contained his impatience, hoping to make a protest
to the King.

The conference with the King began upon the dot of three.
La Reynie derived much satisfaction from it. It did not disturb
him to hear the First President reminded that everything was in
his hands. The plans presented by the King were those of La
Reynie; Harlay and the Provost of the Merchants were enjoined
to see them carried out.

The King detained La Reynie when the others had been dismissed.

"I understand that you made an arrest against your better
judgment."

"I dislike, Sire, to arrest any man for false or devious reasons."

The King smiled. "The end does not justify the means?"

"Exactly, Sire."

"I agree in principle. But we needed to encourage Harlay. And now what can you tell me of *The Ghost of Monsieur Scarron?*"

Chapter Fifteen

THE CALM PLEASURE which he had experienced in the walled garden with the beehives deceived Paul. Tasting the sweetness of the honey, looking at Marianne, he had felt in control of himself and of his passion. He had substituted one sensuous delight for another, and he had flattered his self-love by behaving for an afternoon like a man of honor. It seemed to him that he could lay by this love or take it up as he pleased, and although on the morrow he felt the return of his desire, refreshed, and sharper than ever, he believed in his continued freedom.

The hour in the garden had its effect upon him in another way. It filled him with a longing to be with Marianne in the open air, the sunlight, the clean meadows. He conceived a notion that it would be delightful to be with her in the company of other people, no longer furtive but triumphant. He wanted to parade his conquest. The small room, hot and musty, even the trampled grass of the Ile Louviers, seemed to him to the highest degree unsatisfactory. He began to entreat her for a rendezvous in the country. He spoke so well and so often of his new desire that he succeeded in filling Marianne with his own disgust of the small room and the stinking stairway in the rue des Deux Boules. Her first reply to his suggestion was that it was impractical. She could find no excuse for being away from home so long. Jean would question her absence, especially on a Sunday. But after a while Paul's urging woke in her, who was city-bred and had seldom ventured beyond the city, a desire for the unexplored lanes beyond Pincourt, and she remembered that she must return to her uncle the jar in which she had brought home the honey. It occurred to her also that country eggs are sweeter and less dear than city eggs; she had Jean's permission to go in search of fresh eggs. She set out alone on a Sunday in late August, the Sunday before St. Bartholomew's Day. Alone, she knocked at the door of her mother's uncle and returned the crock. At the first crossroad beyond, she met Paul.

Jubilant with having got his wish, inwardly triumphant and filled with a sense of power, Paul was outwardly deferential, with every trick of flattery known to man. Marianne had never seen him look so happy, his eyes so bright. His sack, slung on his shoulder as usual, contained bread, cheese, and a bottle of good wine. They would feast in a field, perhaps by the river. He lifted his chin in the gesture that had become familiar to her, of a fox sniffing the air. She had seen a fox once, when she was a little girl, and had gone with her mother and father to the woods of Meudon. The color, the gesture were all that remained of the memory. She had been too young to be frightened.

"They are cutting wheat," he said. "The earth smells good, like bread itself. I shall take off your cap by and by, and spread out your hair in the sun, and on the earth. Tonight, when you lie in your bed, your hair will smell of the earth. That will be a pleasure for Jean," he added, suddenly *méchant*.

She put a hand on his arm in protest.

"I am good to you," she said gently. "You don't need to plague me."

She dropped her hand and moved closer to him as they walked, so that from time to time her arm brushed his coat sleeve, or his hand swung against hers. To be so close enveloped her in an emotion equal to that of an embrace. Paul was aware of this emotion; he could waken it or quell it, as he pleased.

They went much farther from the city than Marianne had ever been before. In perfect security that her face would not be known, she asked at a house for eggs. She found also in the shadow of a wall a handful of field mushrooms, some with the white membrane between cap and stem barely broken, the gills pink, and yet as large as an egg. She thought that Jean should be pleased with the mushrooms, since she had paid nothing for them. The day remained fair until late afternoon, when as they turned back toward the city a summer shower overtook them, blowing in from the plains to the south. They ran, laughing, to the nearest shelter, which was the open doorway of an inn.

They found places at an empty table, the wall at their backs, so that they could sit together and face the room. They watched the entry of a christening party which had been feasting in the garden and had been driven indoors by the rain—parents, grandparents, cousins, uncles, and aunts, to say nothing of the nurse with the infant in her arms, all talking at once. The innwife scurried about, trying to make room for them, reseating her guests, pushing small tables together into a long one. A very tall young man with a companion not so tall, who were dispossessed by the hostess, came to sit with Paul and Marianne.

The tall young man pushed back his hat, a black beaver with a wide brim, and stretched his long legs beneath the table. Paul recognized the gaunt face, the big kindly mouth of Rambault, the printer from Lyon, who as quickly recognized Paul.

"The bookbinder from Auxerre! I haven't seen him since the eve of Fête-Dieu. This is wonderful. Isn't it wonderful, Chavance?"

"*Mirabile visu*," said his friend. "Likewise *mirabile dictu*. Altogether extraordinary."

"I told you he lodged with the monks. It's beginning to rub off on him. This is the man I wanted you to meet. This is my friend Chavance, most brilliant fellow I know. Say something, Chavance."

"*Laus propria sordet*," said Chavance with tolerance. "Self-praise is base."

"Let me buy you a drink, you and your pretty friend." Rambault signaled to the hostess before Paul could stop him, and, turning to Marianne, said earnestly: "The first time I saw this little Damas he was a sad object. It would have drawn your pity. Hungry, homeless, without a job, a stranger in Paris—not to mention another trouble which plagued him sorely. What touched me, Mademoiselle, was that I once felt exactly as he looked. Now his fortunes have changed. He has all the luck in the world, that's evident." The lines like parenthesis marks on each side of his wide mouth deepened as he smiled, lips closed. He turned to Chavance. "He works for Larcher, rue des Lions, a man I don't know, but who has a prodigious reputation for honesty and for being very close with his money. A King's man. Undoubtedly a good man to work for. Isn't that so, Damas?"

Paul admitted the general truth of the description. To change the subject he said to Chavance: "What's the news of the day?"

Chavance elevated his eyebrows and answered in the manner of the *nouvelliste* of the Tuileries gardens.

"Monseigneur hunts the wolf in the forest of Sénart. The King has gone to St.-Cyr to commune with his aged paramour in her seraglio."

Rambault interrupted:

"Paul's master would never approve of your attitude, my friend."

Chavance shrugged, and began a more factual account of the news. In other circumstances Paul would have enjoyed listening to him. He had been sitting with his arm about Marianne's shoulders when the two men had approached. He had withdrawn his arm, and Marianne now sat with her hands folded before her in a pose of complete reserve. Nothing could disguise the glow which surrounded her, however, the air of sensuous well-being of a woman who is happy in love. He knew what Rambault had concluded; he could hardly blame him. He put in a bad quarter of an hour.

Marianne watched the doorway. She saw the end of the rain and the first gleam of returning sunlight. She stood up and took her basket on her arm.

"We must go now," she said.

Paul had not finished his glass of wine. Rambault protested. But she was firm.

"We are already late."

She moved away from them while Rambault detained Paul forcibly. She heard them promising to meet again. Rambault was saying to Paul, "I will hunt you out in your rue des Lions." She heard Paul protesting that Larcher was inhospitable to visitors, and then she moved where she could no longer distinguish their words. She stood by the doorway, waiting. The country road lay with a few puddles reflecting the blue of the sky. Birds began to sing as if it were early morning. She was greatly disturbed by the encounter with Paul's friends, almost as much as if they had appeared at the shop. She had thought herself far from Paris. The inn was a trap. She wanted to be on the road again. Then she heard a voice say loudly and clearly:

"Good day, Mademoiselle Marianne."

She turned to confront a woman who sat at a table near the door. Marianne knew her well, a tall, rawboned creature, flat-chested, narrow in the hips, with a long face and a heavy jaw. Her mouth was long and narrow, cruel in repose. Her hair was sandy; there was a heavy growth of reddish hair on her upper lip. She bared her square, strong teeth in a smile.

"You walk abroad a great deal of late," she said, and her voice had the ring of sociability.

Marianne looked at her with mistrust.

"'I find better eggs in the country," she replied.

"Certainly. So do I. And in the rue des Deux Boules, what do you find?"

Marianne felt the chill of panic, but she replied evenly:

"Can it be that you don't know the stationer's shop in the rue des Deux Boules? I recommend it. La Règle d'Or."

The woman smiled and broke a piece of bread. Her hands were strong. They clutched and tore the bread like the talons of a hawk. Still smiling above those rapacious hands, she said:

"There are rooms to let above the Règle d'Or, are there not?"

The implication was obvious. Marianne made no reply, but stepped into the road and waited there until Paul joined her. Some distance from the inn Paul said:

"Who was that woman?"

"The housekeeper for Monsieur Pinon."

"Is she of the Quartier St.-Paul?"

"The rue des Lions," Marianne answered. "She has a great opinion of herself, since she serves a man who is a President of the Grand Conseil in the Parlement. And she talks—at the fountain, at the market, at the Harrow. I do not call her my friend."

"Well, what can she say?" returned Paul. "That she saw you in the country one day, in the rue des Deux Boules on another."

"She saw me with you. She can imply things."

"Who would believe her?"

"Ah, that would surprise you."

"She won't approach Jean."

"Are you so sure?"

"Knowing your husband, I can't imagine that even a house-keeper for a President of the Council would approach him if she could do nothing more than imply something unsavory about his wife. No, she won't speak to Jean."

"She will speak to every other woman in the quarter," said Marianne, "and I shall have to face them at every street corner."

"You have friends."

"While I'm respected, I have friends. You have friends also, it appears. What will you do, how will you feel when your friend the printer turns up at the shop?"

"Oh," said Paul, "he thinks no harm."

"He thinks," said Marianne, "that I'm your whore." She hesitated at the word, a man's word, and then brought it out roundly and bitterly. Paul smiled; she saw the smile.

"So you are," he said, "not a *putain*, but an adulteress. Is that so dreadful? Madame de Maintenon is an adulteress, judging from what they say."

"It's a jest for you," she said furiously. "No one will think the less of you, if it all comes out. It will be a very funny story to tell your friends. No one will mind at all, except, perhaps, Jean."

He sobered at that.

"But Jean knows," he declared. "I told you that. He knows and he doesn't care."

"He was suspicious," she corrected him, "and then he decided to trust us."

"He needs me in the shop," said Paul. "He doesn't love you. He's old."

The statement was an insult. She wanted to protest that her husband loved her still, but the realization of her queer position, as lover or mistress to two men, stopped the words on her tongue. She read in Paul's face nothing but a desire to hurt her.

"If he does learn——" she began.

"It won't be any neighborhood gossip who tells him," said Paul coldly.

"You mean that I——" she said, but could not go on.

They faced each other in something close to hatred. Then they turned away from each other and walked on side by side, without a word, until they reached the approach to the Porte St.-Antoine.

Gradually, during that return, the violence of Marianne's emotion faded and left only a cold fear. All that Simone's affectionate teasing or that Jean's suspicion and forgiveness had failed to do, the sharp tongue of the housekeeper of Monsieur Pinon had done effectively. Paul himself, for the sake of this expedition to the country, had roused in her a distaste for all the subterfuges of their dishonesty. Now the fear of discovery overrode all desire. Paul's cruelty threw her back upon herself. She knew that she must take steps to save herself. It was useless to look to him for help. Plans crowded through her mind, possibilities and improbabilities, and were discarded, one after the other, as she walked on, her head drooping, her basket heavy on her arm. Paul walked beside her, a stranger, a hostile presence. She was aware of every motion that he made; at the same time she felt that all communication between them was destroyed. She would never be more unhappy if she lived to be a hundred.

By the time they reached the faubourg St.-Antoine she had made her decision. On the bridge before the city gate she stopped in the semicircular embrasure where they had stopped before, returning from her uncle's house. She set her basket on the parapet. Paul, beside her, turned his back on the Porte. A cart creaked slowly past, the hooves of oxen falling in a measured beat upon the stones. Paul waited for her to speak. She said, folding her hands upon her basket and not looking at him:

"It is time to end it."

"What do you mean?"

"I shan't see you again, except as I must."

"You dismiss me?"

"From the shop? No. But Jean would dismiss you if he knew."

"Do you mean," he said, incredulous, "that I shall continue to work in the same rooms where you are, and that there will be between us nothing, no more——" He hesitated. She finished it for him:

"No love. It will be just as it was before the storm. It couldn't have lasted, in any case. Now it's over."

"Are you out of your mind?"

She shook her head. "It's ended, anyway."

"It's not ended," he said hotly.

"You ended it yourself, not an hour ago." He made an exclamation of denial, but she went on, "I shall manage to do my work where it must be done without concerning myself over you. If you can't work there also, you have my leave to look elsewhere."

He had been so sure of her, he had felt his power absolute; it had been the main source of his delight. Now she could stand before him and say calmly that she could do without him. He did not believe it; no, he would not accept it. Staring hard at her, he caught the least flicker of unsteadiness in her eyes. Then the lids descended, shutting him briefly from her sight, in a little death. When they lifted again, he saw that her eyes were full of tears. His own eyes narrowed.

"Very well," he said, as calmly as herself, "if that's the way you want it, that's the way it shall be." He turned on his heel and walked off.

She watched him through the gate until he was lost to sight.

"There is no other way," she thought, taking up her basket. "If I do not end it, the knowledge will reach Jean by one road or another. Then Jean will dismiss him, and that will be the least he will do." She felt, watching Paul go, as if she had destroyed him, as if she would never see him again.

Chapter Sixteen

ON MONDAY MORNING, however, Paul showed up for work at his usual hour. He appeared a little grey and tired, as if he had not slept well the night before. At noon, when he sat down to eat with Marianne and Jean, he was as courteous as ever to his master's wife, and more than ever interested in what his master had to say. There were no stolen glances for Marianne, no smiles, and she felt, as she had felt on the road to the Porte St.-Antoine, that a void existed between them across which no sound could travel.

She remembered the strange excitement she had once known whenever Paul entered a room where she was, whether he looked in her direction or not. It was as if some emanation reached her, a tangible shared delight independent of words or gestures. Now there was nothing. She had ceased to exist for him.

On the next day, and the next, he had recovered his good color, he appeared rested and almost debonair. It was what she had asked for. It seemed to agree with him. She had wasted her pity that Sunday evening. Indeed, he worked so well, with industry and exactness, that Jean praised him to his face, and again, in private, to Marianne.

"He has eyes in the tips of his fingers. I doubt if there's a man to equal him in the city."

"You would be sorry to lose him," said Marianne.

"I don't intend to lose him," said Jean. "When Nicolas returns, we'll talk of a partnership."

She had all but forgotten the return of Nicolas, yet she had never envisaged a future without him, nor a future without Jean, nor one in which she could not hold up her head before the housekeeper of Monsieur Pinon or any other neighbor.

She had time in the following week to visit more with Simone. Her round blue eyes, affectionate and confiding, were a comfort to Marianne. At the fountain before the church of the Jesuits she met, inevitably, the rawboned housekeeper. She had come to realize, as Paul had said, that the woman could no nothing more than imply. There was no substance to her accusation. Secure in her own consciousness that the illicit relationship was ended, and the more secure since she herself had taken the step to end it, she met her enemy with assurance.

In anticipation of the return of Nicolas she gave his room a thorough cleaning. She went through all the cupboards, as she had done upon his departure, ranging things in order, and she made for Jean a new inventory of his supplies. Still it seemed to her that she had time on her hands. She even went to the church around the corner in the rue St.-Paul with the thought of confessing. She had not confessed nor taken communion since Pentecost.

She knelt for a long time in the semi-darkness, trying to prepare herself for the ordeal. She thought of herself in the abbey church of Sainte Geneviève. She had prayed for a quiet heart, and had felt her prayer accepted. Then she remembered the first kiss that Paul had ever given her, in the rain. Her determination to renounce him remained firm, but with that memory came a defiance. She could not repent of having kissed him, of having slept in his arms. She regretted only her loss, now that the affair was ended, and her sense of loss was as great as Paul could have wished. She left the church with the sense of sinning by being unwilling to repent, rather than with any actual sense of having sinned by loving.

She worked hard in order to fatigue herself, and she slept badly, waking in the morning with her teeth clenched tight and her jaws aching. By the end of the week the aching had concentrated in a molar which had previously given her trouble from time to time. Sunday night she hardly slept at all for the pain, and woke Monday with her jaw visibly swollen.

"Have it out," said Jean, as she sat up in bed, cradling her chin in her hands.

"It will cure itself," she said. "It has always cured itself before."

"You have my advice," said Jean.

"I don't want to lose the tooth."

"If you're too much a coward to suffer briefly, then you may have to suffer long," said Jean.

She made a compress of salt and oil of cloves and set it inside her cheek against the swollen gum and told herself that the pain had begun to lessen and would soon go away. She had brought it on herself by clenching her teeth. She would sleep with a knotted handkerchief between her jaws for a while. She had a quite reasonable horror of dentists, and to lose a tooth, and for the first time, was a symbol of disintegration. It was the beginning of old age. She overlooked the fact that most women of her own age had already lost several teeth, and that even Simone's young smile showed a gap at one side. She looked at herself at the mirror in the kitchen and decided that the swelling did not show in any just proportion to the pain. This reassured her vanity so that she was willing to sit at the table with Paul and Jean, although she turned her head so that Paul could not see the swollen cheek.

The day was warm and cloudy. Jean, having eaten, leaned back in his chair, his chin on his chest, disinclined to move, and Paul, who had eaten his soup and the crust of his bread, continued his remarks to Jean. He was speaking of nothing important, as far as Marianne could understand. It was something about a Spanish heresy and the love of God. Then Paul said:

"I tried to explain this to a girl yesterday. She had her own version of the idea."

He held up the morsel of bread for his own observation, turning it right and left, and then dropped it to the table, where he continued to play with it, without intention of achieving any particular form.

His thoughts reverted to the girl. He was lying in the grass with his head in her lap. She had been stroking the hair away from his forehead, and their talk had got around, God only knew how, to the subject of sin and confession.

"What do I tell the priest?" she had said in answer to his question. "That I have sinned in the flesh and am sorry. Which is true. Then he gives me absolution. Without that, how could I go to Mass and take communion?"

"But you don't change your way of life," he had pointed out.

"How can I? Would you want me to steal? A girl must live. What I do harms no one. Of course it offends God, and for that I am sorry. For that I am heartily sorry—I always mean it when I say it in confession. But it would offend Him even more if I were to throw myself in the Seine."

Paul addressed himself to Jean.

"She said that she loved God, and that was the main thing, wasn't it? I couldn't get any farther with the idea."

"The heresy of Molinos," said Jean, "could not be more simply stated. What have you there in the bread? A portrait of her?"

"An unintentional portrait. It doesn't do her justice." He held up the bread for Jean's inspection.

"Pretty enough," said Jean.

Paul considered his modeling.

"In a way," he said judiciously, "it does her more than justice. Her skin is very badly marked from the smallpox. The scars have spoiled the shape of the features. Her eyes are pretty, a cornflower blue, but her chief beauty is her smile, which I cannot model. Her teeth are like those of a little girl, small, white, even, not one missing. Otherwise . . ." He closed his hand upon the bit of bread, squashing it out of any resemblance to a head.

"That reminds me," said Jean. "My wife has a toothache." To Marianne he said, "Have you decided to follow my advice?"

"Of course," she answered with a bitterness that made him stare. "Your advice is always good."

She left the table, hesitated just a moment, as if she had something else to say, and then left the room swiftly.

When she had changed from her felt slippers to her leather shoes and had assured herself that she had money in her pocket to pay the dentist, she set off for the Pont Neuf. She was angry with both men, and on the verge of tears, as well. She was jealous. She had never known true jealousy before; it was far more painful than the toothache. She was certain that Jean had told Paul earlier that she had a toothache and that Paul had directed his remarks toward her to mock her, to tell her, in short, that she was old and that the world contained young women with perfect teeth.

She walked quickly, preoccupied with her grief. She kept seeing Paul's hand, the clever hand that had, as Jean said, eyes in the tips of the fingers, playing with the bread. She knew on her throat, on her breast, the touch of those fingers that saw while they caressed. How could he be so cruel, she asked herself, as to plague her with this tale of another woman when he must know how she suffered? Had he made it all up, this story of a girl? No, surely not. For what else would he do on a Sunday afternoon, if she were not with him herself, but take another woman into the country? His hands were always restless. He did not smoke. He had no pipe or tobacco to occupy them. She re-

membered the hands of Nicolas playing with the knife his
father had given him, and the hands of the printer, Paul's
friend, at the inn, twirling his glass of wine as he talked. They
were the hands of a printer unmistakably, large hands with long
fingers and big knuckles, with every line and roughness of the
skin engrained with ink. No matter how often he washed them,
they would still be stained.

Her rapid pace stirred up the blood which beat against the
nerve of the tooth. The tooth throbbed, increasingly painful, and
her head ached also. She could not think coherently. She could
only feel. But what was that idea of sin, of confession, of loving
God, that Paul had been discussing with another woman, a girl?

There was a dentist on the Quai de la Misère near the Pont
Neuf, a Monsieur Carmelline. His sign hung from a window in
an upper room, where he was visited by persons of quality.
There was also in the Place Dauphine at the tip of the Cité
another Monsieur Carmelline, his uncle, who was patronized by
the nobility. Between these two famous practitioners, one at
either end of the longer stretch of the Pont Neuf, there were the
wandering drawers of teeth, who traveled not only from town
to town but from country to country. They were strangely
dressed. They surrounded themselves with mysteries. Marianne
had always regarded them with fear and suspicion quite apart
from the fear of physical anguish which they could inflict. It
did not occur to her to call on either Carmelline; their fees would
be prohibitive. She must make her choice of what chance offered
her on the bridge.

The first drawer of teeth whom she saw, she passed by, for
one reason, because he was at leisure—a bad recommendation.
His costume was extraordinary; something in green velvet with
loops of gold braid on the shoulders, and a long fringed scarf of
scarlet and gold, and on his head a turban of scarlet and gold,
as if he were a Turk or some other kind of infidel. He had for a
servant a young Moorish boy, slight and girlish, who leaned
against his master, who, in turn, leaned against the parapet,

scanning with his black eyes the passing crowd as if he might suddenly take it into his head to swoop upon a victim. Marianne liked nothing about him, neither the extravagance of his costume nor his vulturine glance, nor the servile, enchanted posture of the young Moor.

Neither did she greatly like the next dentist whom she saw, but before his booth there was a little boy and an old woman. The boy's face was tear-stained. The old woman crouched, in a great billowing of rusty skirts, wiping the boy's face and admonishing him to be a man. Behind his table the dentist washed his hands proudly and tossed the suds from the basin on the pavement. He took something small from the table and held it out between his large thumb and forefinger.

"That's right, be brave, *mon petit bonhomme*," he said. "Since it is over, and there's nothing more to fear, this is the moment to be brave. And behold, you can show this to your friends, all bloody as it is. You don't have many friends, I wager, with as bloody a tooth as this."

His eyes were small, set deep between heavy brows and heavily fleshed cheeks, and they were bright with amusement. A short, thick mustache, grizzled and bristling, left his lips clear. His teeth were square and short and widely spaced, the teeth of a peasant who had never known a toothache. His costume was far less extravagant than that of his competitor, a dark coat with a red fringed sash about his middle, a furred cap with a green velvet crown, clothes odd enough to advertise his calling, but not completely outlandish. His accent was pure Burgundian.

The child gulped, and accepted the tooth. The dentist turned his small bright eyes upon Marianne and noted the swollen cheek.

"Come," he said. "You'll not be less brave than a child."

She let him open her mouth and explore the painful tooth with a huge finger.

The afternoon traffic on the bridge was heavy. It moved in a channel between two raised sidewalks, the only sidewalks for pedestrians in all the city. To Marianne, her head tipped back and held by the hands of the dentist's assistant as in a vise, the sound of the traffic became a steady dissonance pierced now and again by the sharp cries of hawkers. The dentist pried and poked with something sharp and fine. Then he exchanged his tool for something heavier; she could not see what it was. A ballad singer approaching on the sidewalk began a madrigal in a great rolling bass that soared above the traffic, making the traffic an accompaniment.

> *"Sous Fouquet, qu'on regrette encore,*
> *On jouissait du siècle d' or.*
>
> *"Le siècle d' argent vient ensuite——"*

Marianne, in order to avoid thinking of what was happening in her mouth, tried to concentrate upon the words of the ballad singer. He came so near that as he passed she was able to catch a glimpse of him from under her lashes. The ballad singer, in curiosity, without pausing in his song, turned to look at the dentist's victim, and Marianne saw a face, dark, heavily lined, which would have been handsome in an heroic way if it had not been for the cancerous condition of one eye which had spread into the cheek in a red and running sore. The sight was so horrible that she forgot the pain which was being inflicted upon her.

She closed her own eyes in a sensation of faintness. The grinding of cartwheels, iron upon stone, seemed to enter her head and merged with a grinding of forceps upon her tooth. She felt as if her jaw were being wrenched apart. The grip of the assistant tightened upon her head, the hands spreading over her ears and round the back of her neck. Even with her ears covered she could still hear the voice of the ballad singer, clear, rich, and flexible. It was fantastic that any man with such a horrible face should have such a beautiful voice.

An increase of violence on the part of the dentist obliterated the phrases of the singer. Marianne choked, cried, "Ah!" The enormous hands and the enormous instrument were suddenly withdrawn from her mouth. The hands gripping her head and ears also dropped away. She stood dizzily alone, and heard from a great distance the ballad singer enunciate with perfect clearness:

> *"Et La France aujourd'hui sans argent et sans grain,*
> *Au siècle de fer est réduite*
> *Par le turbulent Pontchartrain."*

"There, Mademoiselle," said the voice with the Burgundian accent, "you are in luck and I am too. You made me sweat. The tooth is broken, but not the root." Then, as if it were no concern of hers or of his either, but in cheerful comment, "That singer will get himself into trouble one of these days." He wiped his forehead with the towel and prepared to wash his hands.

Marianne's dizziness increased. She leaned with both hands on the table, dropping her head forward.

"His eye," she said thickly, finding it difficult to move her tongue, "his eye made me sick."

"You are kind to blame it on his eye and not on me," said the dentist. "That will be only one livre, Mademoiselle, since you were an excellent patient. If all women had such straight roots to their teeth, a dentist would need only half his art. But you had an infection, Mademoiselle, of the first order. You came to me just in time."

The assistant put a glass of water in her hand.

"Spit on the pavement," he said.

The cloud of blackness dispersed from before her eyes. She looked up and saw the dentist smiling at her as if he had never tried to strangle her.

"I advise," he said, "a thimbleful of brandy before you go very far. Wash the mouth with warm water and salt. Do not eat much for a day or two."

A little crowd had gathered to watch the operation. "On the Pont Neuf," she thought, "nothing happens without a crowd." She pushed by her audience and encountered immediately a vendor of brandy who knew his business. He had been waiting for her. His flagon was already poised above the tiny pewter mug.

She got as far as the Samaritaine before she collapsed. She found a place on the dusty pavement against the parapet near the fountain and sat there, her knees huddled under her chin, her head bowed, her face hidden, but not for shame. She was incapable of caring whether she was observed or not. Footsteps passed her, a garment occasionally brushed her, but no one disturbed her. Another sick woman, another drunk, another beggar fainting with hunger, it was all one to the crowd. She heard below her the cries of boatmen echoing between the water and the vault of the bridge. Above her the wheels of the various dials of the Samaritaine revolved. At three the hour was struck. The machinery which drew the water from the Seine ground and creaked without ceasing. She lifted her head only to spit out the blood which gathered in her mouth. Her jaw ached horribly. The reassurance of the dentist did not reach her. She felt mutilated, rejected, and derided. She felt old.

Chapter Seventeen

"SO YOU HAD IT OUT," said Jean when she returned home. "It was time. Your eyes look like two holes burnt in a blanket."

By the next morning she was recovered physically. The swelling was imperceptible. The hole in her jaw no longer bled. No one would have suspected, to look at her, the ordeal of the day before. The sense of desolation remained, however. She was as firm as ever in her resolution to have nothing more to do with Paul, but the thought that he had so quickly replaced her was a torment.

She went to market early, as usual. Being short of money, because of the livre spent on the Pont Neuf, and unwilling to ask Jean for more that morning, she could buy little in the way of meat but a dozen chicken legs. She spent a long time preparing them for the soup kettle; it was a task which she disliked. If the legs were dipped into boiling water for a minute and then cooled, the horny covering, thin and semi-transparent if the hen had been young, or scaly and yellow if the hen had been old, could be removed like a glove without tearing the flesh. The legs then boiled slowly with herbs and salt gave a rich gelatinous broth, very nourishing, and there was often a little good meat which could be gnawed from the bone. Once cooked, it was good fare; Jean liked it.

This morning the claws, as she took them up one by one to be peeled, sometimes encrusted with dirt which could not be scalded away, curved viciously, lengthened by much scratching in hard earth. They seemed to her cruel and brutal, and the gesture she made, in order to rip the outer nail from the claw and clear the scaly case from the clean meat, seemed to her brutal also. Cleared of its befouled and calloused sheathing, the claw appeared clean and intact, unchanged in outline, bearing still a nail on every crooked finger, still with its heavy padded palm, a hand bestial in shape yet purified. It was a fantastic thing, innocent in its new purity and helplessness, cruel in its old unrelinquished predatory pose. Marianne, ripping the old covering from the flesh again and again, put into the motion a part of her own distress, opposing the cruel gesture to the cruel fact. She permitted herself no pity for the dead birds, nor for her jealous heart.

While she worked, Jean came into the kitchen and drew himself a drink of water from the copper fountain. After that he rapped on the fountain with his knuckles and, having determined that it was almost empty, took up the buckets and went off, presumably to refill it. It was a task which had formerly belonged to Nicolas. Marianne occasionally carried water for it, but in the main, Jean had made himself responsible for keeping it filled. The fountain held eight bucketfuls, and refilling it meant four trips to the rue St.-Antoine. A month ago—ten days ago—Jean's departure with the buckets would have been the signal for Paul to leave his work, to put his arms about Marianne. On this morning she braced herself against the knowledge that Paul would not appear.

Yet the door to the workroom opened. Marianne without lifting her head knew that Paul had crossed the room and stood before her. She would not look up; he did not go away. He said in a low voice:

"I suffer."

She had heard him say the same words once before, she could not remember when. She believed him. She looked up and saw his face full of pleading, and her resolve melted, evaporated, became as if it had never existed.

When Jean returned with his two buckets of water, setting them down in the porte-cochère while he opened the door to the kitchen, Marianne was still peeling chicken legs, and Paul was back in the shop. But Marianne kept on her lips the pressure of Paul's long kiss. She could still feel in the embrace of his slight, agile body the violence of his passion and of his triumph. Nothing else mattered. Nothing else had reality.

Jean poured the water into the copper tank, took the two empty buckets in one hand, and prepared to leave again.

"Still at it," he said to Marianne, looking at the dish heaped with chicken legs and the bowl half filled with unskinned claws which she held on her knees.

"It's tedious work," she said.

He nodded and went off again, and on his exit Paul appeared from the bindery, and Marianne laid aside her work. So, like a comedy, it continued, while Jean patiently made three more trips to the fountain before the church of the Jesuits. While he was away, Paul held Marianne in his arms and whispered fiercely what they must do, or he paced up and down the kitchen, returning to take her hands in his and press them against his heart or against his lips. All the while he argued and protested; and when they heard the footsteps outside the door and the sound of buckets being set down heavily, Paul disappeared like a puppet in a clock, only to reappear the moment that Jean was gone.

He declared that the situation was impossible, that Marianne had been right to say that it must be brought to an end, but that to end it like this, within sight of each other and ignoring each other, was also impossible. It was killing him with slow torture. He could not bear it. Marianne protested that she had been mistaken, that everything could go on as it had, that her fear had been groundless, that Jean suspected nothing, and that there was no reason why, treated with caution and consideration, Jean should not continue as blind and contented as he was. To this Paul retorted:

"Jean may be blind, but what of Nicolas? Will he be blind too? Think of yourself observed by the eyes of your son. Think of it, I say. Could you bear that?"

At this Marianne had covered her face with her hands, and Paul, pulling them from before her eyes, holding them tightly in his own hands, had continued:

"There is only one way out. I shall leave."

"No," said Marianne. "No."

"Why not? It's the honorable thing to do."

"I couldn't live without you."

"Ah," said Paul, taking a deep breath, his grip on her hands growing tighter, "then you must come with me."

"How can I?" she answered.

In the end he convinced her that flight together was the only possible course of action, and furthermore, since flight, in times like the present, was impossible without money, he persuaded her that it would be no crime to take from Jean's hoard a sum equivalent to the dowry she had brought him. It was more than he had ever hoped to accomplish. It was more, in fact, than he had dreamed of attempting. The sense of his power to make her suffer, to make her smile, to make her do as he wished, had gone to his head. When Jean had made his last trip, poured the last bucketful into the copper fountain, and so cut short grotesquely their conversation, Paul found himself again before his sewing frame, amazed at what he had demanded and received, and somewhat at a loss to know what his next step would be.

Jean worked beside him while he tried to map a plan of action. He felt no conscious hatred of Jean. He was trying to form a plan for his own survival. The ten days during which he had been a discarded lover had in truth made him suffer. And he had suffered not only Marianne's naïve defection but also the betrayal of Auxerre. He had feared, from moment to moment, that the story would repeat itself and that Marianne would betray him to Jean. Then he had argued himself out of that fear, saying that if Marianne betrayed her lover she would also have to betray herself, and of that he did not believe her capable. The woman in Auxerre had been capable of it, however. She had rearranged the facts, he did not know exactly how, and she had come off with her own position stronger than ever. He dared not let himself regret the train of incidents and unconsidered impulses which had brought him to this moment. The compulsion to possess Marianne, and to possess her as sole and undisputed master, left him, it seemed, without a choice.

There were two problems. They could not leave together, nor could Marianne simply remove the money from the chest at some time when she held the key, as she had suggested. No, he would have to leave the city first on some valid excuse. He could return, unknown, and take the money. But he would have to break the lock to remove suspicion from Marianne; and Marianne must be with Jean at the time of the theft, to prove her innocence. After that she could join him someplace outside the city after a safe interval. The money would be gone, and Jean would know that Marianne could not have taken it. He would inform the police. The police would accomplish nothing in the way of a search; Paul himself would be out of the city by then, and Jean would testify that he had left Paris well before the theft. If Marianne should disappear then, some weeks later, there would be no way to associate her disappearance with the theft. She must disappear, taking nothing with her, not so much as a ribbon, nothing but her empty market basket, so that her disappearance would indicate only that she must have met with an accident, one of the many accidents of the city. Her body would not be found. Jean would believe himself a widower. He would perhaps hire a housekeeper. He would go on working. He would smoke his pipe at the Harrow as he did now, every night. Nicolas would return and work with his father. As for Marianne and himself, they would establish themselves with new names in a new life in some provincial city, far from Paris, where he would buy his master's papers with Marianne's dowry, just as Jean had done. He would be a master binder at last.

He worked it all out in the hours remaining to that day, which was the last of August. Jean had spoken lately of the return of Nicolas as if it were imminent; he would return in September, Jean had said. For this reason, and because he did not dare let Marianne have time in which to change her mind, he decided that he must put his plan into action at once, as quickly as possible, that very weekend. He was not a master criminal. Certain details troubled him. He did not know how to go about breaking a lock. He realized that he was counting heavily on Marianne's assistance, that he was asking her to play a part of skillful deception, and he also realized that if she should weaken in her intention after the plan had been carried beyond a certain point, she could send him to the gallows.

It was a big risk for a big reward. If he did not take the risk because he did not trust his dominance over Marianne, he would never be able to bear the inner humiliation. If he won, he would have everything he needed, love, money, and a pride in his own powers.

He continued to mull over the details, checking the logic of the plan for security, that night and the next day. He needed, the next day, to confer with Marianne. He could not call the plan complete until he had her agreement. But on that day Jean was incredibly sociable. "What has got into him?" Paul thought. "He is at my elbow every minute." Yet there was no indication in Jean's constant presence of a budding suspicion. It was simply that on that particular day the work in which he was engaged seemed to dovetail with the work which he had laid out for Paul.

There was no moment when Paul could speak to Marianne alone in the shop. Just once, toward the end of the afternoon, there was an interval when he could name to her an hour and a place when they might meet. She waited for him, after Jean had gone to the Harrow, inside the portal of St.-Paul, nervous lest some neighbor enter, and nervous also since the hour for locking the church for the night approached.

Paul did not keep her waiting long. He saw her enter from his lurking place across the street in the Passage de Charlemagne. He made sure that no one whom he could recognize saw him enter the church. He was already observing the precautions which he would have to practice when he returned alone to make the theft.

She saw him before he found her, her eyes having become accustomed to the gloom, and she put out her hand to touch his elbow as he was about to pass her by. Fearful of other eyes unobserved in the darkness which might be observing them, they stood modestly a little distance apart, as if they were on the street. Paul gave her his plan rapidly. There were no alternatives involved; everything was quite clear and already decided. She had only to assume her part in it. He wished that he could see her face. He had to take it for granted that she had not changed her mind, that she was accepting what he told her without question.

"So you see," he concluded, "it is logical. It will work. But you must describe for me the chest, where I shall find it, and how Jean keeps his money."

"It troubles me," she answered softly, "that we must take his money. It means so much to him."

"You think first of Jean," he said, his voice very low, still discreet, but charged with a bitterness engendered by his fear. "Think what it means to me, to us. But no, you can't forget Jean. You were right. It's all impossible. I was a fool to suppose you were capable of passion. Let's end it now. I'll leave Paris, and whether I live or die, that will be no concern of yours."

"Paul," she entreated in a hushed voice, "don't desert me. I'll do whatever you say."

"Forgive me," he said, and there was no play-acting in his words. "You could betray me, Marianne, don't you see? You could destroy me with two words. I love you so much that it makes no difference to me whether you drive me from you now or whether you have me hanged. I've been all these months only the assistant in the shop. You always thought first of the master. It's difficult for me to believe that you have the same passion for me that I have for you. Jean is the master. Jean sleeps with you in the great bed with the red curtains. Oh, I have seen it through the open doorway. I've never stepped inside the room. I would give ten years of my life if I could enjoy you in that bed."

"Be careful," she said, "be careful. We could be overheard." She moved against him, wishing to console him, but he stepped backward, maintaining the discreet distance. "What shall I do? I'll do whatever you wish."

A tall, skirted shape passed them silently. Marianne caught a breath of unwashed flesh and woolen, beeswax and incense; a priest.

"Did he overhear us?"

"He doesn't know what we're talking about."

"The money, as much as my dowry, will be in two rolls in the center of the chest under a fine linen shirt."

From the doorway the voice of the priest, low-pitched but aimed at the farthest recesses, intoned:

"We close."

Other shapes emerged from chapels, from behind the thick

pillars. A bent figure eclipsed momentarily the lights of the sanctuary. They moved toward the door. The outer twilight illuminated them one by one as they went out.

"You go first," said Paul.

Chapter Eighteen

*P*AUL *MADE HIS PREPARATIONS.* They were simple.
He bought a chisel on Wednesday on his way home from
work. On Thursday evening he sauntered toward Les Halles,
and outside the charnelhouses of the Innocents he found what he
wanted, a scribe, to whom he dictated a letter. He mailed the
letter that evening, and went to bed feeling confident that all
was in order.

He avoided Marianne during those two days with greater
caution than ever. On Friday morning he began, at his own
request, a project which would occupy him uniquely for nearly
a week to come. It was a privileged task, involving the designing
and gilding of a new volume. He worked, surrounded by the
smell of the gluepot, the smell of leather, with the window open
upon the courtyard, hearing the quacking of the ducks about
their wooden tub, the footsteps of household servants coming
and going, the occasional nicker of a horse from the stables. It
was a morning of solid peace, and altogether commonplace. He

began to whistle, "The rose of your white rose-tree," but after a few measures the tune faltered and fell into silence. The sense of advancing into danger moment by moment, without moving from the spot where he stood, dominated the whole morning. A little before noon the letter arrived.

Marianne brought it into the bindery and handed it to Larcher.

"This is for Paul," he said, and handed it on. Paul looked at it curiously, with apparent surprise.

"I recognize the hand," he said. "At least it is very like that of the curé in Auxerre who taught me my Latin. I wonder what he would have to write me about."

"Why not open it?" said Jean.

Paul broke the seal—there was no envelope—and read the letter through. Then, without comment, he handed it to his master.

"My dear child, I take advantage of this opportunity to send you a few words. A man who leaves Auxerre tomorrow for Paris will take this with him, and, if he cannot deliver it to your hand, will post it upon his arrival, which will still save some time. My news is unhappy, but cannot take you by surprise. Your father is dying of that old injury which you know of, and which has made life painful for him through these last years. I cannot urge you too strongly to return as quickly as possible, so that you may speak with him once more. He asks for you continually. I cannot doubt but that you are well off in Paris. All that you have written to your mother concerning your master is good. However, for her sake, after your father is gone, we must make plans to keep you near Auxerre. She will not have the strength to follow you so far from home. Of making many books there is no end, as the Preacher saith; I doubt not but that we shall find you books to bind. And much study is a weariness of the flesh, I could add, but that is for myself, not for you. I urge you, return without delay. You have my constant blessing. Hébert. At Auxerre, end of August."

"Well," said Jean, "that's a pity."

"It distresses me in more ways than one," said Paul. He passed a hand over his eyes as if the gesture would help him collect his wits.

"What's the trouble?" said Marianne anxiously. Paul's distress seemed genuine. Jean said to Paul, "With your permission," and handed her the letter. The writing was elegant and clear, and a little shaky, as if the hand that held the pen were old, and, as she read it, her first thought was, "How strange that this letter should come just when Paul really plans to leave." Halfway through, a remembrance came to her of Nicolas remarking that Paul had no father living, or that Paul had no knowledge of his father—which was it?

"But I thought your father——" she began.

Paul dropped his hand from his eyes and looked at her, a brief look, cold and menacing. She stopped short.

"Thought what?" said Jean, who had not seen Paul's face.

"Nothing. I was confused. Something I heard—but now I remember, it was the father of Simone." She continued her reading of the letter, hearing Jean say:

"It's a pity, but you have no choice."

"Yes, yes, I must go," said Paul. "But I was never so content as I've been here."

"It will leave me short-handed," said Jean.

"I know," said Paul. ●

"But you have no choice."

"No," said Paul. He accepted from Marianne the letter, without looking at her, and stood irresolute. "I can finish this day's work," he said. "I can't leave town before tomorrow in any case."

Jean had repeated himself in conversation, a thing which Paul had never known him to do. At noon, when they were all seated at table, he again betrayed the extent of his concern by saying for the third time, unhappily, that Paul had no choice in the matter. "The coche d'eau leaves for Auxerre on Saturday," he said.

"I know," said Paul.

"Buy your place this afternoon, or you'll have to sit below deck."

Paul nodded. Tickets were on sale in the rue St.-Paul at the Ville de Joigny. But he had no money. He had spent the last of his cash on his preparations. He mentioned the subject of money to Jean, who consulted his wife. Paul should be paid this evening; the week lacked only one day. She explained that there was not sufficient money in the cupboard in the kitchen where they kept the small cash. Jean handed her a key across the table.

"Take what you'll need for market, also," he said.

"The bailiff will be here any day now for the quarter's rent," she reminded him.

"When he comes, we'll find him his money."

She returned after an interval during which Paul and Jean waited in silence. She handed the key back to her husband, together with the coins. He counted out a pile for his assistant, another for his wife. Then he put one livre back in his pocket. Marianne had brought a full week's salary for Paul. He rose from his armchair and went back to his work. Paul understood from his nod, before he entered the bindery, that Larcher's assistant was free to make his visit now to the Ville de Joigny.

The day came to an end with nothing unforeseen to spoil his plan. He took his sack from the peg where it had hung every workday for the last four months and longer, and slid the strap over his shoulder. He shook hands with Jean, bowed to Marianne. He looked about the kitchen, a farewell glance, and noticed his chef d'oeuvre, the garnet *Phèdre*, still on display. For the fraction of a second he thought to claim it. Then he made a silent farewell to it, leaving it as a token of his good intentions, a sacrifice to his passion and his plan.

"I'll come back as soon as possible," he said to Jean.

"But your mother?"

"Wouldn't it be better to have a working son at a distance than a son at home who earns nothing? Hébert, my old friend, is over-optimistic about the book trade in Auxerre. I'll come back ——" He hesitated, as if he had not the heart to say, "when my father's dead." He finished, "when I can," without rhetoric, but with a good effect.

When he had gone, Jean said:

"I wonder how long this business will keep him. I may have to finish that volume myself." His expression was bleak.

Paul woke often that night, fearful of being late to the coche. When four o'clock rang from St.-Jean de la Bouchérie he left his bed. He had little to pack; his possessions were still few. He had bought only a new pair of shoes and a new shirt in the course of the summer. He put on his new shoes and packed his old ones. Emptying the cupboard, he came upon the package of pamphlets which he had hidden there the April before and had almost completely forgotten. He could not leave them there. The room would be searched as a matter of routine when Jean reported the theft. If he had remembered them sooner, he could have thrown them into the river at the spot where he had seen them retrieved. He did not want to take them with him, but he could think of nothing better to do. He removed his old shoes from the satchel, and tossed them into a corner for the police to find, and replaced them by the pamphlets.

He saw the stars above the mist when he stepped out into the rue des Deux Boules. By the time he reached the Port St.-Paul the sky was growing light and the mist was beginning to thin. In the middle of the Place de Grève he realized an oversight in his plan. Unless Jean saw him actually on board the coche d'eau, Jean could not testify to his departure. Jean might believe that he had left the city, but his story to the police would be weak, very weak. Why had he not thought of this before? He must devise some way to get Jean to the Port St.-Paul before five o'clock.

The coach was loading when he reached the Quai. He turned into the rue St.-Paul, as if he were still going to work. He would have to get Jean out of bed, perhaps. He would have to invent some plausible excuse to entice him to the Port. He had as yet been able to think of nothing reasonable, nothing that would not seem calculated to make Jean suspicious of his whole story. He went on, nervously inventing and rejecting excuses, down the familiar street. At the corner of the rue des Lions, under the small tourelle, he met Jean Larcher himself, who put a hand on his shoulder and turned him about. The hand rested there paternally.

"You're going the wrong way," said Larcher. "The river is there. Did you forget your chef d'oeuvre? I brought it."

Paul had indeed forgotten it, the perfect excuse; but he did not want to take it with him now. There was no room in his sack.

"I meant to leave it," he said. "You'll take better care of it than I would. No, I was coming to say goodbye again, on the chance that you'd be up."

"I brought also a bite of lunch for the journey." He put the package in Paul's hand. Paul thanked him awkwardly. What had happened? Had he become Nicolas for the day? He did not understand this man who, the evening before, had silently declined to pay him wages for a day he had not worked, and who now brought him this paternal gift. He tried to study Jean's face as they walked together to the Port. He could see only a cheek rough with stubble more white than grey, sprinkled with droplets from the mist, and the shoulder of a coat likewise bedewed.

They crossed the Quai where the Saturday market had already begun, and descended the broad flight of steps together. At the edge of the crowd which pressed about the gangplank of the coche d'eau, Larcher gave his hand to his assistant in a firm, slow grip.

"We'll make it worth your while to return," he said.

Paul watched him mount the steps alone, his back broad and solid, his step assured. "That's the last I'll see of him," thought Paul. On the deck of the coche he wormed his way through the crowd to a spot from which he could look back at the Port and the Quai. From the level of the water the Quai itself was largely invisible. Larcher should have by then crossed the Quai and disappeared into the rue du Petit-Musc, but there he stood near the head of the stairway, watching patiently. Paul lifted his hand in a signal, and Jean replied with a similar gesture. Then Larcher turned away and was immediately lost to sight.

He had seen Paul on board; it had happened exactly as Paul had wished. He should have felt satisfied and reassured that all was going well for him. He felt instead a resentment heightened by the pressure of Jean's hand lingering on his palm. The resentment was familiar. He had felt it at intervals throughout the summer, blending with his increasing jealousy. He liked the man. He did not hate him; he merely wished to be what Jean was, master of his own shop, husband of Marianne. He was a better craftsman than his master, a better lover, also. Even Larcher's forbearance, which had permitted the progress of Paul's affair with his wife, had become a reason for resentment. Jean was responsible for the present state of affairs as much as either of the lovers.

Paul found a place on a bench and waited for the barge to be pushed out from the shore. The vision of the stocky figure at the head of the stairs confronted him still. The cloth stockings, the fustian coat, the plain felt hat, and the kindly regard under the shadow of the hatbrim remained clear in his mind because he knew them, more clear than they had actually appeared through the intervening fog.

He could not forgive the kindliness.

The barge began to move upstream against the heavy current. At the Pont de Bercy the towlines were carried across the river to the left bank. The Ile de la Cité with its mass of buildings surrounding the cathedral, Ile Notre Dame with its fine hôtels, Ile Louviers with its trees, all drew slowly away from the travelers on the water coach. The mist cleared. They passed the Ile de Bercy and were soon between the fields. The man next to Paul took his breakfast from a basket between his feet and began to eat. Paul also yielded to hunger, put aside his scruples and his resentment for the time being, and unwrapped the bread which Larcher had handed him.

At Choisy-le-Roi, where the coach stopped while the oxen were changed, Paul left the barge, and when it swung out from shore again, he remained seated in a waterside cabaret. He had taken a ticket to Auxerre, but there was no reason why anyone on board should notice his absence. He was within a few hours' walking distance of Paris. At this point in his adventure, when the sense of release was strong, before he left the cabaret, he asked himself why he should go on with the affair. He was not yet too involved. He had committed no wrong. He could walk out upon the road and turn toward Orléans or any other city save Auxerre, and find for himself a new life. He could walk out from the bondage of his passion and of his ambition, a free man. While he twirled the stem of his glass and considered the last red drops of wine, this seemed a most attractive possibility. Then he paid his score, slid the strap of his satchel over his shoulder, and set out upon the road to Paris.

He journeyed at an easy pace. At Ivry he crossed the river. His intention was to avoid entering the city through the rue St.-Jacques, where he might be recognized. He made a long detour and at dusk entered the city from the north through the Porte St.-Martin.

He had reasoned that a crowd would be the best place in which to hide, and that Paris would be safer for him than a village. For the same reason he had instructed Marianne to meet him at Fontainebleau three weeks from that Saturday. At that time the court would have moved to Fontainebleau. Great numbers of people would be going there from Paris, and the coche d'eau would leave Paris every day in the week for Fontainebleau to accommodate them. No one would take note of Marianne at the Port St.-Paul on such a day, nor think anything of her taking passage on the coche d'eau. At Fontainebleau, where they would both be lost in the crowds, he would find her.

He made straight for the Place des Victoires. He had decided that there would be no safer place in Paris for him to spend the night than the bed of the old man of the lanterns. The time had come to keep his promise to the old man. He had always meant to return; he had just postponed doing so from week to week. But now he would buy the old man a truly royal dinner. It would help to pass the evening.

He entered the Place from the north this time. The King and the Victory stood with their backs to him. The four lanterns were lighted and beneath them the usual swarms of beggars, peddlers, and lackeys had begun to gather. At the far side of the Place a sedan chair was being carried across the circle, a linkboy running beside it. The torch glowed yellow and smoky. To Paul's left, above the line of roofs and chimneys, the moon began to rise, almost at the full, enormous and yellow in the autumnal air. Everything was the same as when he had first seen it, everything except the season and himself.

He began to walk around the Place, looking for the old man. He circled the Place entirely without catching a glimpse of the lean figure in the ancient coat and wig. He felt disappointed, and then worried. All the emotions of the day—his jealousy, his resentment, even his respect for Jean, which he found hard to bear—merged and transformed themselves without his realization into his desire to find the old man and treat him handsomely. After a second fruitless turn around the Place, he quitted it in search of the inn where he had supped with Father Lanterns, or, failing that, the door to the old man's lodging.

The moon rose steadily, becoming paler and brighter and less huge as it cleared the roof tops. Paul came upon the door of the old man, or one resembling it, before he found the inn. He remembered a peaked gable reinforced by a half-moon of wood. He stepped into the shadow of the projecting upper stories and laid his hand on the latch. It did not give. He rattled it, then pounded on the door with his fist. After a delay of several minutes, during which he continued to pound and to rattle the latch, alternately, the door was opened and a short thick figure confronted him, the figure of a woman. It might have been the woman who had blocked his passage on that April morning. He could not see her plainly enough to be certain.

"The old man they call Father Lanterns," he began.

"Is up there. He's been sick for the last three days." He remembered the beady black eyes, the turnips, and the spotted cow's udders, and became cautious.

"But the lanterns were lighted. Who lighted the King's lanterns?"

"Should I know? Perhaps La Reynie's men. Is the old man the only soul who can strike a light? So you don't believe me. Go on up. He's there. He's ill."

"What sort of illness?" said Paul, thinking of exhaustion or semi-starvation.

"A fever. How should I know what sort? But I inform you for your own good, if you're susceptible to fevers. Go up, if you like."

His indecision was easy to read. "This is no time to be ill," he thought, and before he could speak she went on:

"I go up there from time to time, but I've had all the illnesses. I take him a bowl of soup, a bit of bread, what I can spare. I'm not rich. It would be inhuman to let him die without any attention."

He believed her partly.

"He's as sick as all that?"

"He's very sick, most certainly. He might recover. These stringy old men are hard to kill. He might recover if he had proper nourishment. I can't spare him all that he ought to have. But you, if you're his friend, you could give me a little money, and I would prepare him some proper nourishment."

At this he ceased to believe her even partly. He turned away, and she shouted after him:

"Go up! See for yourself, and leave a few deniers in his old hand."

He did not answer. As before, his whole desire was to escape from her. He walked rapidly toward the Place. His generous impulse, balked, turned in upon itself; suspicion and distrust of his suspicion fought in his mind. One more hurried search through the Place told him nothing. He was sure she was lying, and again he could not be sure that the old man was not sick. Money put into her hand would never reach the old man in any shape or form. He had not the courage to approach the old man himself.

"I cannot risk coming down with a fever now, no matter who is sick, or who dies," he told himself, but the decision gave him no peace of mind. He had built up a fine picture of the evening, of companionship which would lighten the hours of waiting, and of a safe place to sleep and hide until it was time to proceed with his plan. He could not bear to face the evening alone.

He remembered the girl from the Pont Neuf with the pock-marked skin and the pretty teeth. She was called Louise Pijart, and he found her, most improbably, after he had crossed both arms of the bridge and was descending to the Quai de Conti. They dined together in a place extravagantly beyond his means, and returned afterward to the Pont Neuf to watch the mountebanks. After that she took him to her room and he made love to her with a passion which astonished her.

They slept late. Louise, waking before Paul, pushed back the curtains of the bed, opened the window upon a rainy morning. It was a warm, slow rain. It freshened the room without chilling it. She returned to the bed, barefoot, quietly, and looked down at Paul, the closed eyes, the tossed hair, a bare shoulder, an arm lifted and flung back on the pillow, the hair in the armpit showing darker, more russet, than the hair on the forehead. The mouth was closed, the expression relaxed but controlled, and from the controlled mouth she knew that he was feigning sleep.

She put one hand on his breast and leaned toward him, waiting for his lids to fly open, and when they did so, she leaned closer still, so that what he saw first on that Sunday morning was the blue of her eyes. She did not kiss him. She slipped off her peignoir, standing naked as she draped it across the foot of the bed. Then she lifted the covers and slipped in beside him.

He watched her with interest but without passion. He observed again the round, white body which the smallpox had not marred, as it had marred the face. He did not compare her with Marianne. He put all memory of Marianne sternly to one side. It was a form of purity and of devotion. He did not wish to confuse her with these casual adventures, yet he had wakened with a complete sense of her, a complete realization that this was the day when he would take the money. He was rested. His head was clear. He had waked at the first sound of the iron curtain rings sliding upon the bar above his head.

Louise put her head upon his shoulder, her hand under his chin; he dropped his arm about her mechanically. He stroked the smooth skin and stared into the canopy.

"Last night," said Louise, "you made love as if you really loved me."

"Perhaps I do," he answered.

"It never happened before like that. Why must you go away now?"

"I told you. I must live where I work."

"Is there no more work in Paris?"

"Not for me."

She sighed. "What shall we do today?" she asked. "If it weren't raining we could go to the country, to that place where you took me the last time. If it doesn't stop raining we'll have to stay indoors."

"It would be agreeable to me to stay here all the rest of the day."

"You are nice," she said, and Paul, remembering his role, lifted her wrist with his free hand and methodically kissed her fingers, one at a time.

An hour later she stretched herself, lifted her head, and then slowly disengaged herself from Paul's absent-minded embrace. She put on some petticoats and the peignoir over the petticoats, and left the room. In her absence Paul rose and dressed. The rain fell quietly beyond the open window. Bells rang the hour of noon from far away and from nearby, as they had rung over and over through the Sunday morning. He took note of them because they informed him that he had still a long afternoon to pass somehow.

She had sent out for food, a roast chicken and a bottle of wine. Paul in his shirt sleeves, his coat, vest, and satchel hung upon her prie-dieu—she had a prie-dieu like a great lady, this girl—and Louise still in her peignoir, they picnicked.

The boring afternoon went by. "Shall we play cards? Shall I show you my clothes? I'll put on my new dress for you."

Paul watched her busy herself with cream, with powder, with the rouge pot. She arranged her curls on the top of her head with bits of lace and ribbons, all held in place with wires. She put on the new dress, paraded like a peahen, and took it off. He watched all this with no other feeling than a mounting impatience with the slowness of time. She closed the window when a breeze began to blow the rain into the room. The air became sticky. The rain beat on the window, and Paul stretched himself in the only armchair, folded his hands behind his head, and stared at the ceiling.

Louise stopped before him, half in and half out of the dress which she was putting on.

"Paul, what is the matter with you? You're so different."

"I'm worried," he said.

"About what?"

"About money. Because I haven't any."

"But you said you'll meet this man who owes you money. And after that you'll have the new job."

"Suppose I don't meet him," said Paul. "What then? How will I get to my new job?"

"Do you want me to give you money?" She struggled to finish putting on the dress. Paul stood up unwillingly and helped her, pulling a little here and there. His hands did not linger on her shoulders.

"Would you really give me money?"

"I'm a fool," she answered. "Yes, I would."

"I can walk," he said. "I can walk as far as Amiens and beg my bread as I go."

He put on his coat, slung his bag over his shoulder, and looked about for his hat. She handed it to him. He accepted it without a word. He had had enough of this room.

"Will you come back tonight?"

"If I get the money I'll come back."

"You and your money. Don't you think of anything else?" She called after him, her voice sharp, "Come back if you like, but don't be surprised if I have other company."

Chapter Nineteen

THE WIND which had driven the rain ended by clearing the sky. The gutters ran with water for a while, and water dripped from the eaves. At dusk the streets filled with the usual evening mist. After supper in the rue des Lions, Marianne said to Jean:

"What are you looking for?"

"My pipe and my tobacco."

He ran his hand along the mantel as if he might find by touch what he failed to see. The tinderbox, the iron candlesticks, the copper tube for blowing the coals to life were all there. The pipe and tobacco should have been there too.

"They're upstairs."

"I thought I brought them down," he said.

"I'm sure I saw them in the bedroom."

"That's strange," he said.

"What's strange about it? You put them there every night of your life when you take off your coat."

She sat near the window, sewing a button on a shirt. Jean,

turning from his search of the mantelpiece, saw her plunge her needle downward, pull the thread through the stuff, take several small quick stitches, and bend her head to bite the thread. A memory solicited his consciousness and was refused.

"It's strange that I forget what I do," he answered slowly. "It must be the years."

"You did not forget anything. You thought you had done today something that you did yesterday, and the day before that." She did not offer to fetch his pipe and tobacco for him. She folded the shirt and said:

"You'll never wear this again. You're too broad in the shoulders. It's fine linen. We could sell it."

"Save it for Nicolas," he said.

He left the kitchen and she delayed until she knew he would be at the top of the stairs. Then she ran after him, overtaking him in the bedroom.

"Give me the key to the chest so that I can put this away."

The key turned smoothly in the lock. She pushed the tapestry aside and put up the lid. Before her lay the striped taffeta skirt. She laid the shirt on top of it, and then plunged one hand down into the corner.

But Jean was not staying to observe what she did. He had possessed himself of his twist of tobacco and his clay pipe and was already in the next room, doubtless on his way to the Harrow. He must stay in order to witness that his money was all there, safe, when she closed the chest.

"Jean," she called in panic.

He was at the door in an instant.

"What is it?"

"Where's the green rouleau—the long one?"

"But where I left it, with the others," he replied, coming behind her.

She made a great scramble in the chest, thrusting the green roll out of sight, bringing up the others, one by one, and placing them on the white shirt.

"The blue; the other blue; the short one with the pistoles—it's heavy; the white canvas. But the green one, I don't find it. Did you put it someplace else?"

"Where else would I put it?" said Jean reasonably. "It must be in there. What's come over you?"

"I thought I'd put it on top, where you could lay your hand on it easily tomorrow. You'll want it tomorrow, had you forgotten? The bailiff comes tomorrow. Now I can't find it. But you must be right. It must be here."

"Look again," said Jean.

She had his entire attention now. She slid her hand along the bottom of the chest and came up with the green rouleau. "Now how could it have gotten there?" she asked with a nervous laugh. "Could I have put it there myself? It's like your tobacco."

He watched her while she put them away again, the harvest of his life, his hard grain in small sacks, well hidden in the center of the chest; all save one, the green rouleau, which remained near the top, under the shirt.

"Now we both know where they are," she said, and handed him back the key. She faced him, smiling and apologetic. "It gave me a scare. I'll come with you to the Harrow. I'd like a brandy."

On the landing outside the storeroom she made a pretense of locking the door while Jean went slowly down the steps.

"The wet weather makes it stick," she said, rejoining him. They fastened the shutters in the kitchen and locked the door; lock after lock, they left everything secure, except the door on the landing.

"Mademoiselle Marianne," the hostess of the Harrow greeted them, "we see you little enough. Is this an anniversary? What news of your son?"

"It's the King's birthday," said Jean, ignoring the inquiry about Nicolas.

"So it is," said the hostess. "Well, since he pays so little attention to it nowadays we may be excused for forgetting it. It used to be different."

"Very different," said Jean. He had his own reason for remembering the King's birthday. He and the King were the same age. They advanced into old age together, the King, because of his gout, in his little three-wheeled chariot, Larcher, he thanked God, on his own two feet.

Paul, meanwhile, came to the rue des Lions and, seeing no light either upstairs or down, assumed that Marianne had made things ready for him. The door on the landing opened at a touch. He went through the room where he had slept with Nicolas, and on into the dark bedroom which he had never before entered. Rather than strike a light, he opened the shutter a crack. The forcing of the lock of the chest did not go as easily as he had expected. He had to gash the wood before he could insert the chisel far enough to get any leverage on it, and while he struggled he was aware through the slit in the shutter that the moon was rising. He had forgotten about the moon. It would flood the court with light, especially the side toward the bindery. He got the chest open finally. He laid his hand on the smooth linen of the shirt and felt beneath it the shape of the roll of coins, as Marianne had promised him. But he was curious. He must lift the other garments, coats, kerchiefs, under petticoats, all the wardrobe of Jean and Marianne. The violation of their privacy gave him pleasure. He plunged his hands into the corners of the chest, disarranged things deliberately, and, in doing so, came upon a nest of other rouleaux. There was more money than he could have suspected. She had said merely that a sum of money equal to her dowry would be under the shirt. He knew that she did not expect him to take any other money. But what kind of thief would he seem to be who considerately took only one rouleau? It would betray their plot, if he took only the equivalent of her dowry. He felt a sudden gluttony for all those coins, so carefully swathed. There was no telling what they were, louis d'or or simple livres. He opened his satchel to put them in it.

From that moment his line of action was determined. Since he had not discarded the pamphlets earlier, he must leave them here. There was not enough room in his bag for both the pamphlets and the money. He could not carry such heavy rouleaux in his pockets.

He dropped the lid of the chest. He replaced the tapestry. He closed the shutter firmly upon the street filling with moonlight, and groped his way into the next room.

The money, smaller in size than the bundle of pamphlets, but heavier, made the strap of his satchel dig into his shoulder. He held the pamphlets in the crook of his arm. Standing between the door and the bed, he remembered a row of cupboards to his left where Jean kept supplies for the shop. He opened one and, reaching as high as he could, thrust the pamphlets into a corner behind a stack of folded paper, so that they would seem hidden.

He knew then what he could do to cover his retreat. A letter to the police, arriving at the same time or a little before Jean's report of the theft, would bring a search of the shop, and when the pamphlets were found, Jean's appeal would be lost sight of.

A month or so in prison, a temporary closing of the shop, a small fine, these would protect Paul and would do small harm to Larcher. Marianne, in the event of Jean's arrest, could leave Paris unremarked. He wondered that he had not thought of it before. It was like something that he had planned unwittingly. He could not have shared the idea with Marianne. He thought that he had intended all along to drop the pamphlets in the river. Fortunately a suitable opportunity had never seemed to arrive.

Larcher's good reputation would doubtless work to his advantage and his punishment would be light. But even Larcher's reputation would not prevent the rising of a thick cloud of dust, and by the time it had settled both Paul and Marianne would be safe. He ran his thumb under the strap of his satchel, smiling, and stepped out confidently into the moonlight.

AT THE HARROW Marianne sipped her brandy, and, beside her, Jean read his *Mercure*. From time to time he laid down the gazette to attend to his pipe. Once he inquired if she would have another brandy. He did not comment to her on what he read. The presentation to the King of the Dictionary, the arguments in the continued battle between the Ancients and the Moderns did not interest him greatly and probably would not interest her at all.

She listened to the voices around her without trying to make sense of the broken snatches of conversation. One thing concerned her only. Had Paul returned to the rue des Lions, was he now in the bedroom, had he managed to open the chest? Or had something prevented him from carrying out his plan? It seemed a very long time since she had seen him, two nights, two days. She had missed him.

She handed Jean a light, she accepted his offer of a second drink, and she thought how strange it was that she should be sitting with him serenely while he was being robbed. She could feel nothing where he was concerned, neither guilt nor affection. He had become of no importance to her, and although she wondered at it, she could do nothing to alter her detachment.

She had spent the day in doing things to please him. She had sewn a button on a shirt which Nicolas would wear, when he returned, which she would never see him wear. The thought would have broken her heart at one time. Now she considered it without emotion. She had ceased to exist as Jean's wife, as the mother of Nicolas, but with every beat of her heart she felt for the safety of Paul. She wished she were with him. The need of him had become a sort of madness. From the strength of her desire she made an involuntary gesture, a mere stretching out of the arm, accompanied by a sigh, and Larcher lifted his head to look at her curiously.

"Are you tired? Shall we go?"

"Tired? No. Why should I be tired?"

"It's late," said Jean, and a short time after he closed his gazette, knocked out his pipe.

"Don't go on my account," she said. But he stood up and, without answering, made his departure. She followed. It was not yet curfew. She was afraid that Paul might not have made his escape. She lagged behind Jean, but her lagging did not slow his progress. When they reached the building in the rue des Lions the porter was just coming to lock the outer doors. The moon had cleared the roof tops. The courtyard was as light as day. Marianne went first up the stairway in order to pretend to unlock a door which had not been locked.

The rooms were empty; she was sure of it the moment she stepped inside. She could feel no trace at all of Paul's presence, and, as she waited for Jean to open a shutter—why should he light a candle when there was all that moonlight out of doors?— a thought came to her which was desolating. Paul had given up the plan. He had abandoned her. He had not come.

Jean pushed open the shutter. In the bedroom everything appeared exactly as they had left it, the chest covered with the tapestry, the porcelain shell and rosary on the wall above it, the chair standing at exactly the same angle, all wan and yet distinct in the pale light.

With Jean, she began to disrobe. She had only removed her bodice and skirt, her coif and fichu by the time he had stretched himself in bed. She hung them over the back of the chair, lingering, fatigued. The thought that Paul might have abandoned her seemed to drain her energy. In her underbodice and petticoats she seated herself on the chest to remove her shoes and stockings.

She did not really believe yet that Paul had deserted her, but the idea was plausible. It would be better for Paul. It would save them all a great deal of trouble. Jean would find his money in the morning when he opened the chest. Perhaps Paul would return in six weeks or so, and she would see him briefly before he went to find work elsewhere. Leaning forward to remove a shoe, she slipped her hand under her knees, under the edge of the tapestry, and groped for the lock of the chest. Her forehead rested against her knee. Her fingers touched a bit of splintered wood. It was as if she had touched Paul's hand. A wave of inexpressible delight swept through her and left her trembling. She was glad that her face was hidden. She pressed her head against her knee and thought that if anyone had tried to describe to her, six months earlier, such an experience she would have been unable either to imagine or believe it.

"Close the shutter," said Jean, "and come to bed."

She slept lightly, woke earlier than Jean, and could not lie still. The day began. She went to early market, as usual. She gossiped a little with Simone in the court when she carried down the slops. She dreaded the moment of Jean's discomfiture; it would be the worst part of the whole undertaking, for her, although the loss of one rouleau out of five should not be more than a man could bear. She wished for it to be over. By midmorning she saw the punctual bailiff pass through the courtyard to the apartment in the rear. She reported to Jean.

"He'll be here next."

Jean nodded, left his work, and stopped to wash his hands.

"He comes at an inconvenient moment," she said nervously. Again, Jean nodded.

"Put the lid on the gluepot," he said, and went upstairs.

She did as he asked, and before she left the workroom looked about to see if anything else needed attention. Everything was in order. A pile of loose sheets lay upon a table by her hand. She lifted a paperweight and set it firmly on them as if she expected a great wind to sweep the shop presently.

She went back into the kitchen and began to pace up and down in the restricted space, pressing the palms of her hands together.

"I must do something," she said. "I must work. What was I about to do when I saw him come into the court?"

She saw her market basket on the table, still unemptied. She took the copper tube from the mantel and knelt before the hearth to revive the fire. She had been on the point of preparing her vegetables for the kettle. She put her lips to the tube and blew. Then she heard Jean's cry at the door.

"I've been robbed," he said, entering the kitchen. His voice was hoarse. Behind him Simone followed. She had seen his face as he rushed from the foot of the stairs to the shop, and had run after him, her net bag swinging wildly from her arm.

"We're ruined," said Jean. "Ruined."

Marianne put out her hands to him in protest and sympathy. "No, no," she said.

"Every last denier is gone."

"No," she said. "Something must be left."

He shook his head. "Nothing," he said. "See for yourself." He put Simone aside gently, and led the way back to the upper rooms. Marianne, at the foot of the stairway, said to Simone, "Wait here," and went on after her husband.

Her dismay when she verified his statement was almost as great as his. She had planned to make a convincing show of surprise and distress, but she had no need to pretend.

"I cannot believe it," she said at last, sitting back on her heels after she had shaken every garment. "How will we eat? How will we pay the rent?"

"We must go down to the shop," said Jean presently, beginning to collect his wits. "There is no one caring for the shop. Lock the door, Marianne."

At the foot of the stairs a little group waited for them; Simone, the stableboy, the cook who had come out with a panful of apple peelings for her ducks, and a man in a bottle-green coat, the bailiff.

"Bad news travels fast," said the bailiff. "They tell me you can't pay your rent."

Jean refused to discuss it until they were once more in the kitchen, the bailiff, Marianne, and himself, and the door shut firmly on the gossips. Jean turned to the bailiff with a look of despair.

"We cannot pay the rent today. But you must understand. We've never been late in a payment. But we've been robbed. What have we in the little cupboard, Marianne?"

"The market money. Not much."

"You see, Monsieur l'Agent? Who could have foreseen this?"

"It was a considerable sum?" inquired the bailiff. "Well, then, you must notify the police. Perhaps they can recover it for you. Or a part of it. If it was a considerable sum, it's worth going to the police. Monsieur le Commissaire de La Marre is an energetic man. You may mention my name."

"Do you think so?" said Jean.

"That they can recover it? Monsieur le Commissaire is one of La Reynie's most valued men. I would put great hope in him."

Jean took his hat from the peg by the door and set out for the Châtelet without another word. Before he reached the Place de Grève he said to himself, "It's not a question of a small theft. It's a question of my life's savings. Why should I go to the Commissaire de La Marre when I can go to Monsieur de La Reynie himself?"

He felt better after that. Except for the King, there was no man in France who seemed to him more powerful.

In the rue du Boulloy he waited. Monsieur de La Reynie was in conference. Jean was alone in the antechamber. He took off his hat and mopped his forehead with his handkerchief. Then he began to put his ideas in order for the interview.

He was convinced that the theft was the work of professional lock-pickers. The door on the stairway had been opened without damage to the lock. The lock of the chest, older, and perhaps unusual because of its age, had given them trouble. They had come from outside the building and had needed to make their escape before curfew, and had therefore been pressed for time. For this reason they had broken the lock of the chest instead of working on it. They had not been prepared for the chest, therefore they had not known of his money; they must have been astonished by what they found. If they tried to spend it, their sudden affluence would give them away. The members of the Guild of Lock-makers were all sworn men, but perhaps there were defective members, men who had been expelled from the guild, or men who betrayed the secrets of the guild. Monsieur de La Reynie would know how to find such men.

The door to the inner chamber opened and a man entered the room where Larcher sat. He was of about the same age as La Reynie, and the same height. Larcher rose to his feet and brought upon himself a very observant glance, the glance of a man who has made a life-long habit of seizing upon the essential detail. Larcher had seen La Reynie in person, but always in ceremonial garb. He knew very well the features of La Reynie in the engraving made by Nanteuil from the portrait by Mignard. Everyone knew that engraving. It was on sale in all the book-stores, along with the portraits of the King. It portrayed a man at the height of his career, in his full strength and maturity. The man before him was not the Lieutenant-Général. Disappointment clouded his honest face. A voice said behind him:

"Your carriage is ready, Monsieur Robert." The gentleman let his glance pass rapidly from the figure of the artisan. He left the room, and the servant said to Jean, "Monsieur de La Reynie will see you now." The conference of Monday morning was over.

The man who waited for Larcher was wigless. The wig lay upon the table before him, among scattered papers and an ink-stand. His skull was well formed and covered with short grey hair; his face was deeply lined. It was not exactly the face in the engraving by Nanteuil, but it was undoubtedly that of Nicolas Gabriel de La Reynie. La Reynie and his most devoted admirer faced each other across the inlaid Boule table. Then

Larcher took heart and told his story. La Reynie listened without interruption.

"So you think I can restore your money to you," he said when Jean had finished.

"If you cannot, who can?"

"The theft was brutal."

"Monseigneur, it was an insult to the police."

La Reynie took up a pen and fingered it, frowning slightly. He said, "Your name is, for some reason, familiar to me."

"I have done work for Monsieur Bultault, who is, in a manner of speaking, your neighbor. I have repaired books for him."

"So you are a bookbinder," said La Reynie thoughtfully. "Do you ever publish books?"

"One craft thoroughly mastered is enough for a man," said Jean.

"The sum you mention is very large."

"Monseigneur, I have told you no more than the truth."

La Reynie laid down the pen and signaled to an attendant.

"That letter which Monsieur Robert brought me this morning, where is it?"

"But on your desk, Monsieur."

La Reynie shifted the papers, lifted his wig, found what he was looking for, and read it through carefully. Then he drew another sheet of paper toward him, dipped his pen in the ink, and wrote three words. While he waited for the ink to dry, he spoke to the attendant. The man bent his head, and La Reynie spoke into his ear, so that Larcher did not hear a word. The man bowed and left the room. La Reynie again read the letter before him, scrutinized the sheet on which he had just written, and regretfully, it seemed to Larcher, folded them together and laid them to one side. Larcher thought himself forgotten. But then La Reynie looked up at him.

"We shall do for you all that justice can do," he said gravely. "I have sent for officers from the Châtelet. They will escort you to your home. When you are there, tell them what you have just told me. We will hope for the best."

In the rue des Lions, Marianne sliced her cabbage, scraped her carrots, put the kettle on the fire. Simone stayed at her elbow, chattering. She did not send the girl away. Distraction was welcome. Fits of shivering came over her, dissipated and returned. The best way to keep her hands from trembling was to use them. There was no danger for her. She was sorry for Jean.

"I can't think how anyone could get in the room," said Simone. "Perhaps someone came in early yesterday and hid under the bed, or in the fireplace. But then how would he escape? Was the window open?"

"The window was closed," said Marianne.

"It couldn't have been anyone from the building. They're all honest folk."

"And how do you know that?" said Marianne.

"Nothing has ever been missing before."

"There's always a first time."

"Well, then, what do you think? What does Paul think? Where *is* Paul?"

"On his way to Auxerre. He left here Friday."

"Everything happens at once," said Simone.

Jean arrived with the two officers. He brought them into the shop and asked his wife to pour them each a glass of wine.

"One for me, too," he said. The dazed look had gone from his eyes. He was far from gay, but he seemed to have pulled himself together.

The first officer hesitated, accepting his glass.

"It is irregular," he said.

"You have had a long, hot walk," said Jean, "and I have had a shock. Drink." To Marianne he could not resist saying, as he set down his empty glass, "Monsieur de La Reynie himself assured me that everything possible will be done to help us."

"The scene of the trouble is above, as I understand," said the officer. "Shall we go up?"

"First, I will describe the situation," said Jean.

His account was brief and to the point. The police seemed satisfied with it. They passed through the crowd which had collected promptly in the courtyard and which trailed them up the stairway. Marianne unlocked the door. The two Larchers, the two officers entered. The police closed the door upon the curious.

"Now," said Jean, "I will show you exactly how the money was disposed."

But the officer had unfolded the papers which La Reynie had entrusted to him. He conferred with his companion, who then, instead of following Jean into the front bedroom, seized a stool and, placing it before the cupboard across from Nicolas' bed, climbed up on it and began to search the higher shelves. In a moment or two he handed down a package. The officer who held the papers folded them carelessly and stuffed them in his pocket. He accepted the package, which was already torn, and, widening the tear, pulled out a pamphlet in duodecimo, unbound. Larcher watched first with annoyance, then with apprehension. When the officer handed him the pamphlet, and when he could read the title, he turned white. Guilt itself could not have looked more betrayed. And yet he managed to say:

"This has nothing to do with my complaint. I have been robbed."

"You know this pamphlet?"

"I've heard of it."

"You admit it's in your possession?"

"I admit nothing of the sort."

"Then what's it doing in your cupboard?"

"I don't know."

"Who sleeps in this room?"

"My son."

"And where's your son?"

"I don't know. He's traveling."

"Is it possible that your son could have left these pamphlets in your cupboard?"

"No," said Larcher.

"No possibility at all?" said the officer with a slight smile.

"This is a waste of time," said the younger officer. "We don't need to try the case. We only need to bring him in if the pamphlets are found, and we have the pamphlets."

"But my money——" said Jean.

"Is out of the picture for the present. My friend, you are under arrest."

"But that's impossible," said Jean.

For answer, the officer drew the papers from his pocket, unfolded them, and selected one, which he held out for Jean's inspection, the sheet on which La Reynie had written three words. In his mind's eye Larcher saw again the lift of the pen after each word. *Jean François Larcher.* His name. That was all. The warrant had been made out in advance and signed for the King by his minister.

"Marianne!" he cried.

But Marianne had covered her face with her hands and would not look at him. She knew, as clearly as if she had seen the act, who had placed the pamphlets on the shelf, and it seemed to her that her knowledge could be as plainly seen in her face.

Jean drew a deep breath, realized that he was still holding the pamphlet.

"*The Ghost of Monsieur Scarron*," he said quietly. "An evil apparition." He gave the pamphlet back to the officer. "It is a mistake," he said with dignity. "It will be cleared up at the Châtelet. Very well. Why do we wait? Marianne, mind the shop till I come back."

The younger officer then said, with no intention of a threat, but out of simple kindness:

"If you care for her, give her a proper goodbye. You may be gone longer than you think."

But Larcher shook his head.

"Monsieur de La Reynie promised me justice, and I have confidence in him."

Nevertheless, when Marianne presented her cheek to his lips, he kissed her.

Chapter Twenty

*T*HE BOOK TRADE of Lyon and that of Rouen were perpetually under suspicion. Both cities had chalked up against them, since the beginning of the reign, a long list of offenses. Lyon in especial, being so near the frontier, and Rouen, a harbor city and once the home of many Huguenots, were also suspect at all times on general principles. In August, following the arrest in Rouen of a small bookseller by the name of Lebrun, Monsieur de Pontchartrain ordered sent to Rouen an investigator from the Paris police, who was to report to the Président de la Berchère, the King's prison at Rouen, and point out to him the booksellers of that city whose activities were dubious.

Pontchartrain had occasion a little earlier to write to the King's representative at Lyon a letter containing a long paragraph of reprimand in the name of the King for the laxity of the police of Lyon in regard to the publishing trade. The occasion was the seizure and suppression of a book, the book was *Les Intrigues Galantes de la Cour de France.* It had been printed secretly in

Paris, the title page naming as publisher the mythical P. Marteau of Cologne. It had been printed publicly in Lyon without the privilege or permission of the King. The letter was calculated to set off a search of all doubtful shops and a check of those artisans of the book trade who had lately removed to Paris.

The search of Jean Larcher's account books, seized after his arrest, yielded nothing of interest, but a letter found in the pocket of the coat he was wearing was sent to Leclerc, the investigator at Rouen. By the eleventh of September the Commissaire de La Marre had advised La Reynie of a number of suspects, in Paris and in the other two cities, and was ready to proceed with their arrest if he should be supplied with the order.

La Reynie read his report carefully, and then replied, in substance, that what the Commissaire had written him was considerable, but that he had neglected to state precisely what sort of proof he had, written or otherwise, "against the accomplices of the provinces as well as of Paris." If he considered that the proof was certain, or might become so upon further examination, the King would doubtless agree to have the accomplices arrested where they were and brought to Paris for trial. It seemed to La Reynie that the evidence of the Commissaire de La Marre was regrettably vague. However, he could not afford to refuse to co-operate with the officer. Something might come of even such vague suspicions, and the pressure from the King by way of Pontchartrain continued as strong as ever, straight down through Monsieur de La Reynie, through Monsieur Robert of the Châtelet to the Commissaire de La Marre. The King had his finger on them all. De La Marre made his arrests.

On the twenty-third of September the King from Fontainebleau dispatched to Paris a document which listed the names of the suspects and which placed the entire jurisdiction of their trial in the hands of Monsieur de La Reynie, forbidding jurisdiction to other courts or judges, and "this notwithstanding all oppositions or appeals, made individually or otherwise, to the contrary."

"Having been informed," went the order, "that the following named persons, François Larcher, compagnon bookbinder, Pierre Rambault, compagnon printer, Jean Chavance, apprentice bookseller, Simon Vers, compagnon printer, and Charles Charon, peddler, carried on a commerce of all sorts of libels and forbidden books, having printed some such in our good city of Paris, had others printed at Lyon, and that they sold and distributed them in the said city of Paris, as well as in the provinces and even outside the kingdom, we have arrested them and hold them prisoners, in our castle of Vincennes, and in the prisons of the Great and the Little Châtelet, and of For l'Evêque."

Monsieur Robert, commanded by the same order to assist Monsieur de La Reynie in every possible way in his conduct of the trials, on that same September twenty-third wrote a letter to Monsieur le Commissaire de La Marre.

"Monsieur de La Reynie does me the honor to emphasize that we must hasten the examination of the evidence in the trial of Chavance, and in order to complete it, we must interrogate the wife of Larcher, and if she makes any accusation, confront her; for that I have need of a writ, which the clerk of the court cannot deliver to me until the transcription of the procès-verbal on which he is at work be completed. I beg you therefore, if it hasn't yet been done, to have a copy written out fair, so that I may have the order to send out tomorrow morning.

"I enclose a long letter by Chavance which contains important evidence. You may see the Widow Roblinel, and ask her, on behalf of Chavance, for his coat, his linen, a louis d'or, and the other things which he requests. You may show her the letter, but don't on any account give it to her."

After this he set to work on the selection of the seven judges who were to hear the trials, subject to the approval of La Reynie.

Prisoners were lodged at the King's expense, and in accordance with their social station. Usually the lodging for an artisan was fifteen sols a day or, in some cases, ten. Luxuries such as a fire, or better food than that provided by the prison authorities, could be bought by the prisoner if he had a little money. Whether or not he was kept incommunicado depended upon the nature of his offense, the evidence against him, or the King's wish. In general, prisoners were not treated inhumanely. The King's prisoners were better off than most.

The method of procedure when a trial was involved—and a trial was not always considered necessary—was to begin with the drawing up of the procès-verbal, the statement of facts against the prisoner. When the evidence seemed incomplete, or the prisoner unwilling to contribute information, the *question* was employed. The leg of the prisoner was encased in heavy planks, the planks were bound together with chains, and when all was bound as tightly as possible, wedges were inserted beneath the chains which tightened them still further. There were eight wedges, no more, and very often not more than two or three were required to persuade the prisoner that it would be wiser to contribute information than to withhold it.

The question was of two kinds, that which preceded the sentence, and that which followed it, the theory being that a man under sentence, no longer hoping to escape punishment through silence, yet desiring to escape present and immediate pain, might be willing to give information which could lead to the conviction of others.

The insertion of the first four wedges was called the question ordinaire, and that of the last four the question extraordinaire. The whole procedure, in comparison with the torture commonly in use a half century earlier, was mild. It was considered routine, and, although La Reynie had more than once pointed out to the King that information obtained after the fifth wedge was not to be relied upon, the brodequin, or boot, as it was called, continued in daily use.

Marianne did not know to which prison her husband had been taken. She knew that he left in a coach; she saw it from the window. That meant that he went as the King's prisoner. No prisoner entered the Bastille on foot, she knew that, and she was free to assume that he had been taken to the Bastille, but the Bastille was not the only possibility.

Simone and Jules were waiting for her in the courtyard when she came down. Simone would not believe in Jean's guilt.

"Not Jean," she said, shaking her head loyally. "Jean would never touch such a libel. Someone else must have put them there."

"I cleaned that cupboard after Nicolas left," said Marianne, "and I cleaned it again Saturday. There were no pamphlets. I know."

"I don't suspect Nicolas," said Simone quickly. "If he were only here now, to help you!"

"If he were here," said Jules, "then he would be arrested too."

"Do you think so?" said Simone. "Then it's lucky for Paul that he's gone too."

"Paul may be arrested, wherever he is," said Jules. "When they begin to arrest people, they don't know when to stop."

"But Paul left the shop on Friday. He left for Auxerre on Saturday, early. Jean saw him off. I cleaned that cupboard on Saturday afternoon."

"I don't accuse him," said Jules, "but in his place, I'd be worried."

"You should warn him," said Simone.

"How can I?"

"Much better," said Jules, "that he should know nothing at all about what's happened here, if they decide to arrest him."

"They won't be able to find him," said Marianne unguardedly.

"Oh, if they decide to arrest him, they can pick him off the coche d'eau anywhere along the way."

"But will they know——"

"Jean will tell them. Don't suppose that they won't inquire about him."

"But I can clear him."

"If they accept your testimony. You could clear your husband, too."

"Oh yes," said Simone. "That's right. Jules, you think so clearly."

"But it would be better if someone had been with you when you cleaned the cupboard."

"How could I have known?"

"I was with you, wasn't I?" said Simone. "Didn't I come in while you were working? Or was that the day before? No, I came in, I'm sure."

"Don't be too sure, little rattle-brain," said Jules with a smile. "The police aren't fools."

"Then they'll believe Marianne," said the girl. "They'll certainly believe Jean."

"Jean believes," said Marianne slowly, "that he'll be given justice."

"Then we shouldn't worry so about him," said Simone. "Nor about Paul."

"I wouldn't worry about Paul in the least," said Jules with a curious look at Marianne, "unless they decide to hold Jean."

The police returned that afternoon and, having seized the account books, closed and sealed the door of the bindery. No business of any sort was to be conducted in Jean's name so long as he was a prisoner of the King. They informed Marianne further that she would be questioned in due time, and that she should hold herself available for their questioning, and that she was on no account to quit the city.

All this did not look as if Jean were to be released very soon. On the following day the bailiff, calling again, explained to her that the collecting of rent was in abeyance, pending Jean's trial. The contract for the apartments was in Jean's name. Neither Jean nor his wife could be evicted so long as Jean's case remained undecided.

"If he is released," said the bailiff, tapping on the lid of his snuffbox, "we'll have a little talk about extending the time of payment. If he's convicted, we'll have to settle the account from his estate." Marianne looked blank, and he elaborated. "From the sale of equipment, furniture, personal articles."

"But he's innocent," said Marianne. "They must release him. What is this talk of conviction?"

"All beyond my knowledge," said the agent with a wave of the hand. "I only say that for the immediate present you need not worry about the rent."

For a week she expected every day either to be sent for or to see Jean return. At the end of the week there was nothing to eat in the cupboard, and no money; no money at all. With the permission of the police she went to the Bureau des Recommanderesses in the rue de la Vannerie and asked for work.

She was angry with Paul, and for two reasons. The first was that he had taken more money from Jean than the sum agreed upon. She had not made him promise not to touch the other money, but he knew that she felt entitled to no more than her dowry. She felt betrayed. The second was that he had unloosed the activities of the police against them instead of for them, as had been planned.

Why had he done this? He must realize that he had put himself under suspicion, along with Jean. The only explanation for both the planting of the pamphlets and the total theft which made sense to her came to her very early in the week, and she wished that she had not thought of it. If Paul meant never to return, not even to their rendezvous at Fontainebleau, the greater the confusion in the rue des Lions, the better his chances for leaving the kingdom safely. She knew then that she had never trusted him. She had loved him, not for his virtues, but because she could not help it. Strangest thing of all, she loved him still. She weighed quite coldly the chances of his deserting her, now that he had the money, against what she remembered of the despair and passion in his voice when he had thought of losing her, and she believed that he would be at Fontainebleau on the twenty-fifth. She would reproach him, she would demand explanations, and then she would forget everything in his embrace.

She asked for work as assistant to a registered midwife or, failing that, as a housekeeper, but she could not wait for a good situation to be offered. She had to take what was immediately available. She accepted without murmuring a place as kitchen maid in a house on the Ile Notre Dame. It was near the shop, which was a convenience, and she did not expect to work there long.

On the tenth of September, Monsieur Fieubet, who owned the great hôtel at the corner of the Quai des Célestins and the rue du Petit-Musc, died at his place in the country. The entrance to the hôtel, on the Quai, was draped in black, and Marianne, returning from work and seeing the funeral hatchments, although she had never laid eyes on the man for whom they were raised, felt them an ill omen. She crossed herself, and in the act remembered that it had been a long time since she had been to confession. She wondered if it was true that the soul withered, deprived of the holy wafer. It might be true. She felt herself changed. The sin of her passion for Paul Damas had less reality to her now than when she had first gone to his room. The great reality was her need of seeing him again.

The second week went by, and most of the third week. In two days she would meet him at Fontainebleau.

Simone, whom she had seen infrequently since she had been working out, stopped her in the courtyard and asked for news.

"No news," said Marianne.

"Jules says——" the girl began; then stopped.

"And what does he say?"

"He says it's very queer that the police do not get around to questioning you."

"I think it queer myself."

"He thinks they may have taken Paul. And he thinks—— I can't tell you all that he said, but I'm sure he's wrong, very wrong."

She could not be persuaded to say more, but she flung her arms around Marianne's neck and kissed her on the cheek.

That night, alone in the big bed, Marianne wondered less about what Jules might have said than that Paul might have been arrested. If he were put to the question he would not be able to bear it; he would tell everything, and they would hang him for theft. She had been forbidden to leave the city, but the police seemed to have forgotten her. She must be at the rendezvous whether she heard from the police or not. How else could she know what had happened to Paul?

On the twenty-fourth of September the copyist of the Châtelet provided Monsieur Robert with the writ which he had requested, and by nightfall Marianne was informed that she must be at the Châtelet early on the morrow.

She obeyed the summons. The habit of compliance, the fear of authority were strong; but while she sat in the antechamber, waiting to be called, she counted on her fingers the hours until her rendezvous, and she thought that if the police did not detain her too long she could still be there, and on time.

Hours later she was led into a rectangular room somewhere in the heart of the Grand Châtelet, remote from the round towers of the donjons and lighted inadequately by one high window. Candles had been furnished for the clerk and for the examiner. There was a fireplace in which no flame was burning, a door opposite that by which she had entered, and in one corner a pile of lumber—planks, chains, and two wooden buckets turned upside down. If she could have looked more carefully, she would have seen also a pile of wedges and a wooden mallet.

"This is not a trial," her examiner said, "nor am I a judge. You may speak freely to me. I make inquiries for the sake of the defendant as well as for the King. You understand that it's to the advantage of the defendant, if he's innocent, to have the whole truth known."

His tone was kind, but the room frightened her. She wondered where Jean was and if she would see him. She began to answer questions such as she had expected to be asked. She explained how she had cleaned the cupboard twice since the departure of her son and had seen no copies of the pamphlet on the shelf.

The examiner nodded. Then he asked, "Have you ever seen a copy of this pamphlet?"

"*The Ghost of Monsieur Scarron?* Yes," she said, without thinking.

"And where did you see it?"

"It was but one copy, Monsieur. I found it."

"Where?"

"In the gutter on the Quai de la Mégisserie."

"And what did you do with it?"

"I burned it."

"Did you show it to anyone—did you show it to your husband before you burned it?"

"No, Monsieur."

"And why did you burn it, instead of reporting it to us?"

"I was afraid, Monsieur."

"Your husband says that he has never seen a copy, and yet he recognized it promptly."

"But Monsieur, we were warned against it."

"Warned?"

"It was on the list."

"Of course, of course," said her examiner. He consulted the papers before him, while she twisted her hands beneath her apron. Then, "I shall ask you to try to identify four men," he said. "If you have ever seen them, no matter how briefly, whether you know them or not, you must say so."

There was a pause, during which she tried to keep her eyes from the pile of lumber in the corner. If they had taken Paul, they would need to ask her to identify him. Then the first man was brought in. To her relief, it was a man whom she had never seen before. Nor had she ever seen, to her knowledge, the next two. The third man was seized with a severe fit of coughing as he stood before her, which bent him double. One thing the three men had in common; they all limped.

The examiner had left his place behind the table and had moved to where he could observe both the face of Marianne and the face of the man who confronted her. He did not question her during these confrontations. He merely took note of her answer and signaled to the jailer to bring in the next man.

The fourth man to enter was tall; like the others, he limped. He was hatless; his clothing was wrinkled, and he had a week's growth of beard. Nevertheless there was no mistaking the long, gaunt features, the eyes deep-set under the bony forehead, the wide mouth encircled by the deep curved lines, of the printer from Lyon, Paul's friend. She had seen him last across a table in a country inn, with Paul beside her and the summer rain pouring down outside the door. He recognized her too, but gave no sign of greeting. He simply stared at her with his surprised and honest eyes. He was led away, limping, before the examiner asked his first question.

She could not deny that she had seen him before, but she did not know his name. She knew nothing about him. She thought he was a printer, "because of his hands." He was only a man who had sat across the table from her in an inn one day last August. She could name the day; she had forgotten the name of the inn. She was asked only one more question.

"Was your husband with you that day?"

No, she was alone.

Her examiner, leaning his elbow on the table, rested his head on his hand in such a way that his fingers covered his mouth. He looked down at his papers, and Marianne could not tell what he was thinking.

Presently, he dropped his hand from his mouth and said, as if he were conversing with her, not examining her:

"Do you suppose that the man whom you have just seen could at any time have entered your husband's shop, and placed the pamphlets where we know they were found?"

"It would have been difficult."

"But not impossible?"

"I suppose, not impossible," she said unwillingly, "but——"

"But?" he prompted her, still with his easy, almost kindly manner.

"I don't think he did."

"Why not?"

"Because he seems an honest kind of man."

"But honest men sometimes assume for themselves privileges beyond permission, such as the printing and distributing of books insulting to the King. They forget that the King is the anointed of God."

"My husband never forgot that," said Marianne quickly.

"You are loyal to your husband, Mademoiselle. Now try to remember. You said there were no pamphlets in the cupboard on that Saturday afternoon. But couldn't you have been mistaken? You didn't see the pamphlets. Granted. They were well wrapped. And the package resembled any other package, of books, of paper, of what you will. You would not have remarked this package. It could have been placed there days earlier, could it not? Weeks or months earlier? It looked as if it belonged there."

He was plausible, he was kindly; she did not wish to offend him. She assented. She saw too late where her assent was leading her.

"Your son Nicolas was a young man of independent ideas, was he not? He had friends who may have amused themselves at the King's expense."

"But Nicolas——" she began. He went on smoothly:

"There was also your husband's assistant, who had frequent access to the upper rooms."

She froze at that, and the examiner, more interested in trying to establish confidence between them than in chivvying her for information which he already had, abandoned that line of speculation.

"Let us talk of your son. I understand that you expect his return very soon. We have reason to believe that he is no longer in France. We believe that he is in England. You are surprised. In Rouen he fell in with company which influenced him strongly, it would seem. Isn't it possible that in Paris, also, he had companions whom you didn't know? Or did you know his friends?"

She looked at him in increasing bewilderment. He leaned forward, crossing his arms before him on the table, and said:

"What you must understand is this. Your husband has been put to the question, ordinary and extraordinary. He will tell us nothing. He insists upon claiming absolute responsibility for everything in his shop. Unless he will give us the name of a person who might have left the pamphlets, or unless you will help us by telling what you know, we have no choice but to assume your husband to be guilty. And in that case, I must warn you, it will go hard with him."

"You would imprison him?" she said with terror. "You would confiscate the shop?"

"It would be much worse than that."

"But he's an honest man, Monsieur. He doesn't deserve such punishment."

But Monsieur Robert the younger had finished with her. He did not reply. He indicated that she might go.

Chapter Twenty-one

MARIANNE STOOD outside the doors of the Grand Châtelet, dazed, and tried to think which way to turn to regain the Place de Grève. It was broad daylight. She judged the hour to be sometime after noon, but the long wait, the penumbra of the candlelighted room, the twisting passages through which she had been led back to the daylight and the open air left her without a proper sense of time or of direction. She followed the first people who passed her, and presently found herself approaching the Great Slaughterhouse. She turned about, passed once more under the archway of the Châtelet, and crossed the Place de Grève.

From the terror inspired by Monsieur Robert's last admonition, and the horror at the thought that Jean had been tortured, another idea emerged, as she found herself able to move freely. Paul had not been arrested. Neither Nicolas nor Paul was imprisoned. The hope that Paul would be waiting for her this day at Fontainebleau became a certainty. She began to run in order not to miss the next coche d'eau, not to be more late than she already knew she was.

She could not run all the way to the Port St.-Paul. She walked, until she caught her breath again, then ran a little way, then walked. She paid no attention to the people whom she met or passed. She came from the rue de la Mortellerie, as Paul had done, to the Quai above the Port, and saw in a glance that a coche was still there, and taking on passengers. She still did not know the hour exactly; she did not dare waste any time by returning to the rue des Lions. She boarded the coche exactly as Paul had told her to, in her humblest clothes, without any treasure of any sort; in her pocket was the little money she had saved from her daily wages. She could pay her fare. From habit she thought of the kitchen in the rue des Lions and in what condition she had left it. She had not had time this morning to kindle the fire. The coals were banked with ashes; they might last through the evening. She did not think that they would still be live by morning. She had left a cupful of soup in the kettle. It would sour by the next day. She had not made the bed, nor emptied the slop jar in the bedroom; and none of this mattered. She would never again see the rooms in the rue des Lions.

It was midafternoon when she approached the gates of the château. She was surrounded by a crowd intent on merrymaking. There were also the beggars who had followed the court from Versailles, as they would follow wherever the King went, to enjoy the scraps from his kitchens. And there were the mountebanks, the peddlers, the ballad singers, all the concours of the Pont Neuf. She was surrounded by a gabble of voices. Suddenly, very near, she heard a seller of sweetcakes.

"*Voici le plaisir, Madame, voici le plaisir.*"

The voice was as raucous as when she had heard that same cry with Paul in the Place de Grève, although it might not have been the same man. They were all hoarse as rooks, the sweetcake men.

"*N'en mangez pas, Madame. Ça fait mourir.*"

She turned her back on him. The death of which he sang so

harshly was not the death which threatened Paul if she should obey the admonition of the examiner of the Châtelet, not the death which had raised the funeral hatchments on the Quai des Célestins, but the mention of it was an ill omen, like the black draperies. Or perhaps it was the same. Love, death, love which is mortal sin, the death of the soul, how could she tell them apart? She must find Paul. Then she would feel alive again, and be able to think more clearly.

He was not at the gates. This did not surprise her. She herself had not been punctual, although through no fault of her own. He might have left the spot briefly for any of several reasons. But he would return. She was prepared to wait for him.

Beyond the gates the gardeners were raking the gravel. People like herself, ordinary people, walked through the gates and across the gravel toward the château, and entered. Carriages passed her, and coaches, and men on horseback. The crowd thinned and clotted, moving past her, pausing before her, but never noticing her. She could have been invisible.

She was glad of this respite. She had longed so for Paul that she dreaded the emotion she would feel when he should actually appear. Once when she thought she saw him through the crowd, his arm and shoulder and a part of his face only, her heart had stopped, and then pounded so that it hurt. The afternoon passed, slowly. She became very tired. She had eaten nothing that day and had been on her feet for a long time, but she did not dare leave her post near the gates for fear of missing him.

She heard the hours chime from the chapel of the château. She began to think that he would not come or that he had perhaps come at noon, and then gone away for good. She tried to remember the exact words of her examiner. What, exactly, had he said that had made her so confident that Paul had not been arrested? And as she thought of this, all that had been said concerning Jean's possible fate returned to her the more strongly. Jean had been tortured, and was threatened with something more severe than imprisonment or the loss of the shop. What was that? The galleys? It seemed impossible that for so small an offense he should be sent to the galleys. He was a strong man, but he was not young; five years at the galleys was enough to kill a strong man. It would mean his death. Paul, whatever he had intended when he left the pamphlets, had surely never intended that.

She knew quite well what she ought to do. The man at the Châtelet had made that quite clear. But she could not betray Paul. She had not understood what they were doing to Jean; but now she knew, and if he died in the galleys, his suffering and his death would be upon her soul all the days of her life, and after; whereas Paul, who could not have known what had happened, who could not have foreseen such disaster, could not be held one half as responsible.

Her first anger against Paul revived, and her first suspicion. Paul had brought this upon her. He had meant never to return. Yet even in her anger she knew that if he came to her now through the crowd, she would forget everything. She would go away with him, and forget Jean's danger. She waited, hoping that he would appear, until it was time to take the last coche back to Paris. Then, because she knew that she would have to be at work again in the morning on the Ile Notre Dame, she joined the sight-seers who straggled toward the river.

The coche was very crowded. She sat on the deck, huddled within herself, between a very tired priest, who promptly went sound asleep, sitting up, and a family of petit bourgeois, more prosperous than she, but more or less her own class. They had reserved their afternoon lunch or supper to be eaten on the trip home. They opened their covered hampers and picnicked on the deck. If Marianne had shown herself at all friendly they would have offered her food, no doubt. They were very talk-ative among themselves. They would have welcomed another voice. But she felt herself estranged from all humanity at that hour, deserted by Paul, and in her turn abandoning Jean. Bread would have stuck in her throat. She could not help overhearing their chatter. From it she formed a picture of their afternoon.

They had been at the château early in the day. They had seen not only the King but the young Princes returning from hunting. The King had been at the hunt in a carriage with the Princesses. They had seen, which was most remarkable, the mysterious Madame de Maintenon arrive in a closed carriage with only one attendant, and had marveled at the number of shawls and hoods that swathed her on this warm day. Marianne, who had been at Fontainebleau as well as they, had seen nothing but a crowd which she might have seen on the Pont Neuf. There had been only one image in her mind, that of a slight young man in a brown coat with a russet vest, with a worn satchel hung from his shoulder. If she had seen him, she would no longer have a decision to make. Whether for right or wrong, she would have made her choice, and she would no longer have been alone. Now she had all the problem to turn over in her mind again. She could not forget it.

The most simple way out of her torment was to go to the man at the Châtelet and tell him all that she knew of Paul; their plan; her relations with him. This would free her husband. If Paul had deserted her, he should be out of the country by now, well out of reach of the police. He had three weeks' head start of them. To confess, if that were the case, would do him small harm. As for herself, they might choose to hang her for her share in the plan. At that moment this did not seem to her greatly to be dreaded. She could never again live with Jean. She would never again be able to look him in the eyes. And if Paul had deserted her, after leading her to this state in which she damned her soul forever for his love, she did not want to live. If she were hanged she would at least die confessed. But she could not stop here in her reasoning.

She was increasingly in doubt about whether Paul had been arrested. Jules was right. The police were not fools, although their acts were unpredictable. Her examiner had mentioned Paul, and then had veered away from the subject, as if he knew

far more about Paul than she could tell him. But the police did
not as yet suspect her, or they would not have permitted her to
walk out freely from the Châtelet. This meant, in her reasoning,
that neither Jean nor Paul had spoken against her. If Paul were
in prison, then she could not accuse him of deserting her, and
if she confessed, she would be giving him over to the hangman.
So long as she had expected him to meet her, there had been no
question in her mind of betraying him, no matter who suffered,
or how greatly. She could feel free to expose him only if she
knew he was safe. And how was she to know that? Would he
someday send her a message from Holland, or from Spain?

Paul had said that Jean "knew" about them. "He knows, and
he refuses to know." In all her misery her complacency was
gone. She wondered how she had ever dared believe that Jean
did not know he was cuckolded. She had been blind, not Jean.
Jean could put two and two together. "Let Jean accuse us.
Let Jean accuse Paul; it is Jean's responsibility, not mine," she
thought, and bowed her head on her knees, hiding her face.

At her elbow the man of the family made a ribald remark
about Madame de Maintenon which brought a cackle of laughter
from his mother-in-law and a protest from his wife.

"Not that word," she said. "You mustn't call her by that word.
She's a good woman, all the world knows, and very charitable."

The husband laughed, and sang a scrap of a ballad.

> *"The Maintenon, tra la tra la,*
> *Still sends our Louis out to war.*

"You've spoiled my rhyme," he interjected.

> *"She regulates His Majesty,*
> *And keeps us all in poverty."*

"That's very unjust of you," said the wife, "when you've had
such a good bottle of wine, and as tender a capon as could be
served the King, and altogether a very pleasant day."

The jesting went on, without Marianne's attention. She had other things to remember. On a certain day Paul had said to her, "You are a putain, are you not?" That Paul! If she could but learn to hate him.

She remembered also that the abbé Têtu was a friend of Madame de Maintenon, and the remembrance offered an avenue of escape to her tormented mind. All the trouble over the pamphlets went back to Madame de Maintenon. She climbed the stairs at the Port St.-Paul in an immense fatigue, but with a new resolution. Before thinking any more about her problem she would visit the abbé.

She unlocked the door of the cold kitchen, saying to herself, "Tomorrow I'll talk to the abbé." But after she had drunk a cup of water and bathed her face, she was too troubled to sleep. She removed her cap, and combed her hair before the copper-framed mirror, seeing within the frame a dim face, the face of a stranger. She made herself as neat as she could. She rubbed her cheeks, trying to bring back a little color to the skin, and then she went around the corner to the rue Neuve St.-Paul.

Chapter Twenty-two

*J*ACQUES TETU suffered a severe migraine on the afternoon of September twenty-fifth. He had wished to attend
complines at the cathedral; instead he attended vespers at St.-
Paul, which was so near his dwelling. Returning from the
service, he declined the supper which his housekeeper had
prepared for him; he took a dose of laudanum and seated himself
before his fire to wait for the effect of the drops. When the wife
of the bookbinder in the rue des Lions was announced he could
not immediately remember her, as much because of the pain as
because of the opium. He had never revisited the shop, and the
memory of his evening there had resolved itself more or less
into a recollection of reading, or reciting the verses of Madame
Deshoulières. He had been pleased with the book they made for
him; he remembered the name of Larcher, and since his housekeeper stated that the woman seemed in great distress, he said
that he would receive her.

As Marianne entered, he drew his long legs beneath him, and

rose with unusual courtesy to greet her. He had been sitting without candles. The evening light, shining through small panes of tinted glass, pale green and amethyst, illuminated the apartment dimly. Têtu, looking at Marianne with care, recognized the features of a small woman who had sometimes smiled and curtsied to him in the street, and from this salutation he had derived pleasure without quite knowing who she was. She had seemed young and happy, and he had enjoyed her happiness like a passing fragrance. She was changed; greatly changed.

"How can I aid you, Mademoiselle?" he asked. The voice was as she remembered, musical and deep. His courtesy touched her. She could not think how to begin, and while she groped for words he went on, "Do I owe you money? I have become more forgetful than ever, I regret to say. If I owe you money, that's a problem easily taken care of." He divined that it was not money, but he continued to talk, giving her time in which to compose herself. "It's my old trouble, Mademoiselle. I do not sleep. Lack of sleep affects the mentality in the long run. I neglect many things. You must pardon me if I have neglected my affairs in regard to your husband or your shop."

"The shop is closed, Monsieur l'abbé."

"I am sorry to hear it. Through the general illness?"

"Through the police."

The abbé drew his sandy brows together and bent his head in surprise and incredulity. He clasped his hands behind his back and, in so doing, thrust his shoulders higher, so that he appeared even more tall and narrow than he was in fact.

"This is strange news," he said, and waited for her explanation. He had heard nothing of Jean's arrest. It was necessary to tell him the whole story from the beginning, and when that was done, it was necessary to describe the pamphlet. Her account of the pamphlet seemed to affect him as strongly as her statement that Jean Larcher was a prisoner of the King and in danger of the galleys. He turned from her, and with his hands behind his back, his head lowered, he paced up and down the room, shaking his head from time to time, and muttering expressions of distress beneath his breath.

"Infamous," she heard him say as he approached her, only to turn away; and again, "Infamous."

Finally he stopped before her and, shaking his head very sternly and sadly, said:

"I am indeed sorry that your husband is involved in this affair. If he is guilty, he deserves the galleys."

"You know his reputation, Monsieur l'abbé. You know it's not in his character to slander the King."

"A man's character is judged by his deeds, not the other way round. One must have knowledge of a man's deeds before one can be assured of his character."

"All his life——" she began, and then, lifting her clasped hands beneath her chin, said, "I implore you to believe that Jean had nothing to do with the wicked pamphlet."

The abbé suffered from a tic which in moments of great emotion or of great fatigue drew the corner of his mouth toward his ear so violently that his whole face seemed to go to pieces. His friends were well acquainted with this infirmity. It struck him now, and Marianne, unprepared, was terrified. He saw in her terror, as she lifted her clasped hands to her mouth, a reflection of his grimace. He extended his hands helplessly. Then he turned his back on her abruptly. He went to the window, and stood looking down through the tinted panes upon the garden. He could not master the tic. After a time, still with his back to her, he said:

"Let us assume, Mademoiselle, that I agree with you; that your husband is innocent. What can I do to help you? Nothing. You do not fully recognize the iniquity of this pamphlet. It is not only blasphemous. It touches the King in his best and deepest affection. It assails a lady who has committed no offense, a great and good woman who deserves no slander. It is understandable that the police must exert themselves to punish such a slander."

"Ah, Monsieur l'abbé," said Marianne, "if only you could make an appeal for Jean to someone higher than the police."

The abbé turned about and, shielding his cheek with his hand, stared at her with surprise.

"My dear child, I have no influence with the King." His voice became bitter. "I am not a Père Lachaise. The King has not esteemed me sufficiently to make me a bishop. I cannot presume to offer him spiritual advice."

"If you would appeal to Madame de Maintenon, she could approach the King. It's true, isn't it, you are one of her friends?"

"It is true," said the abbé gently.

He seated himself where he had been resting when she entered. He had been very tired then, and in great pain as well. Now the pain had grown less sharp, but the fatigue had increased, a part of the gradual relaxation caused by the drug. He was confused. The bitterness of his old aspiration for a bishopric began to take possession of his mind, pushing aside a better sentiment, his pity for this artisan's wife, and even eclipsing his indignation over the insult to Madame de Maintenon. He struggled against it. The tic continued to torment him. He held his hand against his face and tried to concentrate upon the thought of Madame de Maintenon.

"I have known Françoise d'Aubigné," he said in a remote and fading voice, "since she was a very young woman, in fortune and in position far below the place she holds today. I have seen her in a society which was a test of any woman's virtue, and I have known her to behave not only with virtue but discretion. I have had some measure of proof that her esteem for me continues, although, when we meet, which has not been often of late, we fall into an old habit of badinage, and nothing is said of doctrine, or of policy, or of other serious matters. But of these matters we do correspond. No, I can see no harm in appealing to her for the sake of your husband. If he is innocent, if the police cannot find out the truth, then we must fall back on simple kindness."

He spoke so quietly that Marianne could hardly hear him.

"I will write to her," he concluded in a stronger voice. "I will write to her at once."

Marianne fell on her knees beside his chair and, lifting the long and bony hand which lay upon the arm of the chair, kissed it in gratitude. The skin was delicate and smooth, the skin of an old man. He withdrew the hand without embarrassment.

"As you go out, my child," he said, "have the kindness to request my housekeeper to bring in the candles. And one thing more." He rummaged with a long finger in the pocket of his soutane and brought out a gold coin. "Take this."

"I didn't ask for charity, Monsieur l'abbé."

"No matter. Take it. Consider it a loan. It will please me."

He dropped the protecting hand from his face and was able to smile at her with an expression of singular sweetness.

For a long time after she had left him he sat and watched the fire. The windows darkened. The candle flames made mirrors of the glass. In the fire small flames climbed like vines through the twigs of a fresh faggot. He watched the flames, which were hypnotic, like the drug he had taken, and felt himself sinking into a warm inertia. He was fully awake, but the pain was gone from behind his eyes. Perhaps he was able to move, but movement would have demanded a great effort. It was a pleasure to feel that he was unable to stir, as if he were dissociated from his body, his mind free, his body resting. The dose had been tripled this last winter from that with which he had begun, and still it did not make him sleep. But this state of being was better than sleeping. He could think; above all, he could remember, and in his memory the images were wonderfully distinct.

He would begin his letter to Madame de Maintenon with a protestation against the scurrilous pamphlet, and then he would praise her kindness. The kindness was real. He could remember an infinite number of examples. He admired most of all in her the tender heart. It would not be a difficult letter to compose, but he could not write it tonight, because of the circumstances. He would write it in the morning, when his head was clear.

In the meantime he sat with his long legs stretched toward the fire, his hands relaxed on the arms of the chair, his head drooping. He could not remember when he first met Françoise d'Aubigné. His first clear recollection of her was certainly after her marriage to Scarron, and early in that marriage, for he remembered her in a gown of yellow taffeta, a color which set off her dark hair and eyes to perfection. She had a warm soft skin, very white, which was unusual in a woman with such dark hair and eyes, and glowing with youth. She blushed easily; it had been a wonderful thing to see the rich color sweep up from her white bosom to her face. It was the only way in which she had ever betrayed her embarrassment at the conversation or the manners of her husband's friends.

He knew her better in the days when they had both frequented the Hôtel d'Albret, where the conversation had been scarcely less libertine than at the house of Scarron. She never wore colors after the death of her husband, but her wit had remained bright and her composure incomparable; yet she was only a girl. He knew her best in the company of Madame de Sévigné and of Madame de Coulanges. At dinner at the house of Madame de Coulanges—Monsieur de Coulanges, incorrigible gadabout, was often absent—with the blond Marquise on one hand and the dark-eyed Madame Scarron on the other, the abbé had been in the company he most enjoyed. She was still Madame Scarron at that time, although she had already become governess to the King's bastard children, for he remembered well one evening when he had dined with the three ladies and later driven with them to that house on the road to Vaugirard where Madame Scarron lived with her royal nurslings. They had left Madame Scarron there, and returned to the rue des Tournelles, where the Coulanges had then lived, and all the way there had been a flow of wit and compliment, easy exchange of sentiment and idea, and applause for his own erudition, an erudition often wasted on less cultivated companions. An evening to remember, indeed. And all the way home Madame de Sévigné had praised her friend and rejoiced in her good fortune. The carriage had been that of Madame de Sévigné, but presently Madame Scarron had her own coach. Then she was hailed as Madame de Maintenon; now she was the King's wife .The abbé Têtu was as sure of that as if he had seen the wedding contract. In all this good fortune she had remained loyal to her old friends. Her friends remained devoted to her, as well, although now they seldom met. "How should they meet?" he thought. "She never leaves the King, and the King dislikes me."

He had not so far forgotten the wife of the bookbinder but that the remembrance of the King's dislike warned him that he should revise the letter which he planned. For the sake of Larcher, it would be wise if Madame de Maintenon, in making her request, omitted the name of Jacques Têtu. He pondered for a while on how he might phrase this warning to the lady without implying a criticism of the King, or seeming to cherish unduly his own disappointment. His state of mind, which did not permit him to sleep, did not permit, either, continued coherence of thought.

His attention slid from the letter to his old grievance. Whether the King had let himself be affected by gossip, at the time of that unpleasant affair with the Duc de Richelieu, or whether the King was simply unable to appreciate the virtues of a learned literary style, the abbé could not know. He had been expelled from the Hôtel d'Albret by Richelieu, a man of fantastic jealousy, and he had been censured by the King. The King, a man whose gallant-ries had been both excessive and factual, condemned a man who had practiced merely the manners of gallantry, and upon rare occasions. The King's taste in letters was deplorable. He cher-ished Racine. So, for that matter, did Madame de Maintenon. The abbé had his friends, and he had known his triumphs. Member of the Académie, Fauteuil numéro 27, since 1665, he had enjoyed an established reputation long before the admission of Boileau-Despréaux or of La Fontaine. Let them remember that.

He had seen La Fontaine lately, in the street. The mark of illness and of age had been upon him. He had turned uncommonly devout, so they said. It was said also that Despréaux was now so deaf that he never appeared at court.

The abbé shifted a little on his lean haunches. His lips moved, but no words came from them. He thought of Madame de Coulanges suffering from her continual colic, abusing herself with the remedies of an Italian quack, and of Madame de Sévigné and her rheumatism. He thought of Françoise d'Aubigné's neuralgic shoulder and of her headaches, similar, though not equal, to his own. The mark of age was on them all, on his old friends, on himself. How had it happened? He had busied himself with his writing, his devotions, his friendships, and suddenly he found himself aged, and all his generation with him. It was like a trick of magic performed while his back was turned for an instant. Madame Deshoulières and Madame de Lafayette had already vanished. He would be fortunate to follow them before his mind dissolved, as it seemed to be dissolving now, in this waking sleep in which it was so difficult to distinguish between the past and the present. He must pull himself together. In the morning he must write to Madame de Maintenon.

In the morning, which was Sunday, the abbé remembered his resolution, but was delayed in the execution of it. Between the hour for early Mass and for dinner he had another visitor, the lawyer Antoine Bruneau. This was a man who, but two years earlier, had been no more than a *huissier* at the Grand Châtelet. Now he had his connections with the Parlement de Paris. Since he had attained the privilege of wearing the red robe and discarding the black, he aspired further. He had never been one to neglect the formalities and courtesies by which a man could acquaint his superiors with the knowledge of his existence, as well as of his most obedient desire to be of service. Eventually he became *avocat au Parlement*. Now he took good care to visit those persons who could help him further.

On the twenty-sixth of September he paid his compliments to Monsieur Pinon in the rue des Lions. Then he called upon the Président du Grand Conseil, Monsieur Feydeau de Brou, in the rue Neuve St.-Paul, and then, since he was practically at the abbé's doorstep, he decided that a compliment to Jacques Têtu would not be amiss. In spite of his reputation for eccentricity, the abbé was welcomed in houses where Antoine Bruneau would have given his eyeteeth to be admitted.

The abbé received him with absent-minded courtesy. He was in the state of depression which invariably followed upon his taking the drug. In such moments he thought the comfort of the drops hardly worth the aftermath of gloom. He knew, at the same time, that when the migraine returned, or the long insomnia held him in its grip, he would again have recourse to the little vial, and the knowledge did not increase his esteem of himself. He had found it more difficult by daylight, also, to believe that the letter which he intended to write would greatly aid the case of the bookbinder.

This doubt was no help to him as he began to formulate the sentences by which he might introduce the subject. He laid aside his pen, still dry of tip, and seated himself near the window where he could look down into the enclosed garden while his visitor talked.

Antoine Bruneau spoke of one thing and another in a flat voice. He was well informed, this humorless, obliging, servile man. He intruded his presence upon groups at the Palais de Justice where he had no business. His method was to give news in exchange for news. Sometimes he learned more than he told. This, he felt, was profit.

The abbé listened to him first with inattention, then with active boredom, and then realized, all at once, that the man was connected with the courts of justice, and asked him a tentative question on the subject uppermost in his mind. The lawyer planted his hands on his knees and replied with assurance that he had heard all there was to hear about the *libelle sanglant* against the King and Madame de Maintenon, and the trials connected with it.

"Can you tell me," said the abbé with a reserve the opposite of Bruneau's assurance, "how the case is likely to go for the persons accused?"

"I can tell you first that the Parlement is to have nothing more to do with the case. Within the week an order was received at the Châtelet which places the whole affair in the hands of Monsieur de La Reynie, removing it thus from any possible clemency of the Parlement."

"This is unusual, is it not?"

Bruneau lifted a deprecating hand.

"Monsieur de La Reynie has always acted for the King in matters of libel."

"You spoke of a possible clemency from the Parlement."

Again the deprecating hand and a shrug of the shoulders from Bruneau.

"The Parlement acts for the city of Paris. It assures justice for its citizens. Representatives of the guilds, for example, can make their voices heard. Whereas La Reynie is the puppet of the King, and there will be through him exactly as much clemency as the King desires."

The abbé nodded thoughtfully. Bruneau continued:

"You understand that though I call him a puppet I have the greatest respect for La Reynie. There is a certain jealous element in the Parlement, however, which resents the removal of its power."

"The matter of clemency," the abbé suggested.

"The case deserves no clemency. It would have been adequately judged by the Parlement. We are not insensitive to blasphemy."

"But in the event that one or even several of the accused should be innocent," the abbé interposed gently.

"They would receive justice. You have a particular interest in the case, Monsieur l'abbé?"

The abbé admitted that he had, that he was concerned for a man of the neighborhood, a man with a good reputation.

"You think him innocent?"

"Frankly, I do."

"Then, Monsieur l'abbé, if I were you, I would cease to worry about him. For, whatever else may be said regarding Monsieur de La Reynie, it has never been said that he was either incompetent or impetuous. He is the soul of justice. If your man is innocent, believe me, he won't suffer."

"Things are said, then, regarding Monsieur de La Reynie?"

"Only that his power undermines the power of Parlement. As you well know, between the King and certain powerful elements in Paris, there have been, shall we say, certain differences? Do not misunderstand me, I beg of you. I am completely devoted to the King. As completely as yourself. As the great Bossuet has said, '*O rois, vous portez sur vos fronts un caractère divin.*'"

The abbé inclined his head in agreement, and the lawyer, feeling that he had made a good impression with his quotation, and wishing to do even better, said:

"The most effective way to aid your man, if you are deeply concerned for him, is to entreat the King directly."

"Your suggestion is interesting but impractical," said the abbé very coldly.

Bruneau knew when he was dismissed; he had been dismissed too many times in his importunate career not to recognize the tone. He rose and went through the motions and speeches of his ceremonious leave-taking. He had blundered, and just when he had thought he was doing so well. He could not understand his blunder.

He left the abbé in a mood of deep bitterness. "I am a priest. Why should I meddle with the affairs of La Reynie?" But the cause of his bitterness was deeper than that. He could not bear to be reminded, even by a fool who did not know what he was saying, that the King had no use for him. It roused the old struggle between his vanity and the humility he owed his God, and, in his depressed condition, the struggle went badly for his humility.

Chapter Twenty-three

*A*T THE END OF A WEEK the abbé had not yet written his letter. Neither had he abandoned altogether the thought
of writing it. He had given a promise, and although for sufficient
reasons he could have absolved himself of the promise, the
reasons he mustered were not, to his scrupulous mind, sufficient.

October had come with weather that was golden and serene,
the air sweetened by showers which passed and left the yellow
leaves upon the ground to dry in the sunlight. Madame de
Maintenon had requested of Racine a canticle for her girls at
St.-Cyr. On Friday evening, which was the first of October,
Racine read aloud to the King and to Madame de Maintenon the
paraphrases from Saint Paul which he had made for her that
day.

> *Mon Dieu, quelle guerre cruelle!*
> *Je trouve deux hommes en moi.*
> *L'un veut que plein d'amour pour Toi*

Je Te sois sans cesse fidèle;
L'autre à Tes volontés rebelle,
Me soulève contre Ta loi.

My God, what cruel war!
I find two men in me.
One begs me to adore
Thee with fidelity;
The other drives me still
Rebellious to Thy will.

Madame de Maintenon, her hands resting quietly in her lap, her
head, swathed in black lawn, leaning against the red damask of
her chair, listened attentively, and approved of the verses. The
King did more. He passed his hand across his eyes as if to clear
them of a drop of moisture, and said, deeply moved:
"Ah, those two men. I know them well."
Racine could not have been more greatly rewarded. Madame
de Maintenon begged him to give the verses to the composer
that very night so that Monsieur Moreau could begin work on
the music at once. Moreau had applied himself to the task; on
Saturday afternoon the music was ready. Madame de Maintenon's wing chair was again carried from her apartments to the
King's room and placed near the head of his bed. The harpsichord was brought in by six lackeys. The musicians assembled,
two violinists, two flutists, a cellist and four singers from the
Opéra at Paris. Jean Baptiste Moreau presented himself, music
in hand.
The King that morning had found his gouty foot too swollen
to stand upon. He kept to his bed. The King and the court were
in mourning, first for the infant daughter of the Duc du Maine,
who had died at the age of two weeks, and then for the brother
of the Queen of England. The King of England had withdrawn
to the monastery of La Trappe, and the Queen to the convent

at Chaillot. Festivities at Fontainebleau were canceled, but a concert spirituel was still in order. Three o'clock struck.

"Where is Racine?" said the King.

No one could tell him. Moreau made his little speech about the imperfections of his work, the speed with which it had been composed, and the hope that the King and the lady would help him to improve it by their criticism. The musicians ranged themselves about the harpsichord. Bontemps closed the door to the antechamber.

"But where is Racine?" said the King again. "What do you think of this, Madame? Racine makes us wait. This will be an item for his history."

Racine was in the park. Beguiled, after a modest dinner, by the tempered sunlight, he had paced on and on, between the plane trees and the quiet water of the canal.

The King's Historiographer, Madame de Maintenon's poet, wished that he were at home with his wife and children, or at Auteuil with his friend Boileau. On such a day as this the garden at Auteuil would be perfection. He would write to Boileau on the morrow, and send him a copy of his paraphrases. He would invite the criticism of his friend, not because he mistrusted his own judgment, nor because Despréaux, stone deaf, had still the finest ear in France for the subtleties of the language, but in order to continue a conversation over the days and distances which separated them.

The King had arranged everything very kindly some seven years ago. They were both to continue as historiographers of his reign, but Boileau, because of his infirmities, was excused from following the King from place to place. Racine was to accompany the King wherever he went, and take notes. The notes were to be sent to Boileau, who would rewrite them for the history. Doubtless Boileau was happier in his cottage at Auteuil than was Racine as courtier and campaigner. Nevertheless, the fact remained, and troubled the conscience of Racine, that Racine received four thousand livres a year and Boileau received but two thousand. Racine was a gentleman of the King's bedchamber, and Boileau was a deaf old man in a small village.

As for campaigning with the King, it had not been a pleasure for Racine. The sight of many men in mortal danger was stirring, no doubt, but it was not a pleasure. He was thankful that this year the King did not campaign in person. He regretted, of course, the infirmities which kept the King at home, but the King's Historiographer was but one year younger than the King.

He turned about, still in good time for the concert, he thought, and retraced his steps to the château. As he entered, he heard the clock strike three. Either the enchantment of the afternoon had confused him or it took him much longer to walk the length of the canal than it had done last autumn. That recurrent pain in his side about the region of the liver made it difficult for him to hurry. Still, hearing the chime, he hurried. He arrived breathless before the door of the antechamber, and heard no music. He hurried through the antechamber; the Swiss stood aside. Bontemps opened the door for him, and the King said:

"Here is our poet, now."

Racine made his apologies, but, bowing, he put a hand to his side, where the pain caught suddenly, and the unconscious gesture made a better apology to Madame de Maintenon than his words.

The music began, clear, elegant, suitable for young ladies. Racine listened anxiously to hear his own words given back to him, and to appraise them, hoping that the music of Monsieur Moreau would not destroy his own music, but reinforce it. The King, also, behind the Bourbon mask, composed himself to listen.

He too had noticed the hand which Racine had carried to his side. Racine pleaded his age and his pain. Madame de Maintenon pleaded her aching shoulder and excused herself from taking the air with him in his calèche. They suffered, but did he not suffer too? He kept his pain to himself.

Pontchartrain that morning had brought him a message from

La Reynie. He had empowered La Reynie well over a week ago to deal with the libellistes of *The Ghost of Monsieur Scarron;* he had assumed that their affair was taken care of. Now, having made his examinations and determined the guilt of his suspects, La Reynie suggested that the case be considered closed and the prisoners dismissed with a light punishment. If the suggestion had been made by La Reynie personally in private audience with him, the King might have taken it under advisement, although unwillingly, but made by Pontchartrain in the presence of Madame de Maintenon, the King could not accept it. He knew this to be a weakness. His first wrath against the pamphlet had diminished, but he had made an issue of the case with Madame de Maintenon and with La Reynie. He did not see how he could retreat from his position.

The two men of the paraphrase exhorted him to look within himself. A high, young voice, rising like a bird above the slow notes of the violins, the flicker of the harpsichord, softened his mood. He began to feel that it might not be too late to come to some agreement with La Reynie over the fate of the libellistes. A ruler showed himself wise in his ability to use advice.

Only in his later years had he come to realize the true virtue of Christian humility, and to desire to practice it. He no longer emblazoned his coat with diamonds, but it was unthinkable that he should abandon his emblem of the sun. His revery, proceeding by association rather than by logic, brought him round to the statue in the Place des Victoires. It had pleased him once, but for years now it had been a subject for self-reproach and for grief. His dislike for the statue had become so great that it included even the donor himself, La Feuillade, who was dead now, and who had died aware of the King's coldness, a very disappointed man. La Feuillade, the King argued, had gone too far. The burning of incense, the inscription on the base of the statue, *Viro Immortali*, to the Immortal Man, this was too much. This could only be an offense to God. No man should be worshiped. No man is immortal. But the inscription was still there, blazoned in gold; the King lacked the courage to renounce the flattery publicly. The lanterns still burned; he had heard a rhyme in mockery of the lanterns.

> *La Feuillade, faudis, je crois que tu me bernes,*
> *De placer le soleil entre quatre lanternes.*

"*Tu me bernes, en effet, La Feuillade,*" thought the King. "You make a fool of me before God, and a sinner as well." Then he remembered the travesty of the statue on the cover of the pamphlet, and there seemed no reason to him why he should consider clemency for those who were responsible for it.

Madame de Maintenon also thought of those two men and fell into a revery under the spell of the innocent music. She had been full of sorrow over the death of the little Mademoiselle du Maine; she grieved for the young father, whom she loved. She needed no softening of her heart by the music. She grieved for the King also. The mourning which he had commanded had been unprecedented for a child so young, a child who had barely existed. It had brought criticism and protest which had reached her ears, but not the ears of the King. So long as she had known the King he had been a tender father. She found herself thinking of those early days, of Madame de Montespan, her friend, who had done her the great kindness to recommend her to the King; of the storms in which that friendship had broken up; of her own efforts to save it. Her thought went lightly on from one remembered moment to another, until she found herself thinking of Marie Angélique de Scorailles, who had been for a little while Duchesse de Fontanges. She remembered the day that the King in desperation had come to her and begged her to reason with Fontanges. For two hours, on a spring afternoon, she had tried to persuade the girl to be calm, to accept as final the King's dismissal of her, and to put off her unhappy passion for the King. She did not remember what arguments she had used; she had been filled with pity, and she had been very patient. The girl had been incapable of reason—simple, sincere, gentle, all that, but silly as a basket. At the end of her most reasonable pleading the girl had turned upon her with a sudden vivacity very unlike her usual manner, and had cried: "But Madame, you speak of putting off a passion as if it were a shirt!"

She saw very clearly the tumbled red-gold curls, and the blue eyes dark with emotion, the white skin, whiter than milk, and with surprise she said to herself, "How did I come to be thinking of this, on this afternoon?" Was it, she wondered, as the music came to a close, having lost track of the light progressions of her memory, because of the mention that morning of the scurrilous pamphlet? The cover had linked her with the King's former loves, with La Vallière, Montespan, Fontanges.

Chapter Twenty-four

THE MILD OCTOBER WEATHER which piled the sunny
leaves in the forest of Fontainebleau, did not prevent an increase
of illness in the city. Even before the first of October the fear of
contagion had become so great that certain ladies requested to
be excused from attending Mass in the churches. The Archbishop granted them permission to be served in their private
chapels. The harvest had been good, but the price of bread had
gone up. As in the spring, the streets were full of beggars, but
these were not country people come to the city, but city people
who could not find work. Shortly after her visit to the abbé
Têtu, Marianne was dismissed from her job on the Ile Notre
Dame. No explanation was offered. This would not have mattered if she could have found other work without delay, but
when she was questioned by a prospective employer at the
Bureau des Recommanderesses, the questioning seldom went beyond the inquiry concerning her husband's trade and his whereabouts.

She found work finally in a house where half the family was sick of the fever, work that no one else had been willing to take, that of cleansing the sickroom and caring for the sick. Strangely, she found some comfort in the work. She had returned to her old labors, and in so doing found something of her old self, the woman she had been before Paul came to the rue des Lions. Also, she performed a penance.

During the days when she was unemployed, rather than break the abbé's gold piece, she sold a few of her belongings. She sold first her holiday clothing, then her silver thimble. There was a daily distribution of soup to the needy by the Fathers of the Célestins, but pride, which kept her from asking help of Bourdon, kept her from joining the lines of beggars; nor did she return to the abbé. She had asked one great favor of him; that was enough. She was confident that he had written his letter, for he had said he would. There was nothing she could do now but wait.

She had boarded the water coach for Fontainebleau without a thought of Simone, whom she had promised to be with when she was brought to bed, but in her loneliness she remembered the girl, and managed to exchange a few words with her almost every day, usually in the evening. By the end of September she began to worry. Either the girl had made a miscalculation or the child was late. It was after she had again found employment, and had been working in that house for several days, that upon her return to the rue des Lions she saw a light in the window above her own rooms. Without pausing at her own door she continued up the stairs to the apartment under the mansards. Jules opened the door. She made her inquiry and waited to be asked inside.

"I've taken her into the country," he said.

"She was past her time," said Marianne. "I've been worried."

"I understand," said Jules. "But the air in the country is more pure. She'll be well attended." He stepped out upon the narrow landing, drawing the door shut behind him. Marianne could not see the expression of his face. She wondered why he did not wish her to see into the room. Was he lying?

"But *I* was to attend her," she said.

"I know where you've been working," he answered. "Yes, I know a little of your life, through Simone." He spoke slowly and with a slight formality. Marianne was aware that he was avoiding the ruder turns of speech common along the water-front. He spoke simply and with a gravity at variance with his youthfulness. "I'm not a rich man," he said, "but I could remove my wife from the city for her lying in. That much I could do. You will understand, Mademoiselle Marianne, I love my wife. I wish to shield her from contagion in every form."

Chapter Twenty-five

O_N *THE EIGHTEENTH OF OCTOBER,* late in the afternoon, a carriage from Rouen drove east upon the rue St.-Antoine and stopped at the narrow entry to the Bastille. The driver showed his papers, the gate was opened for him and his vehicle, and closed behind them. At the end of the passage he made a sharp turn to the left, crossed the first drawbridge and the Governor's courtyard. The second drawbridge, at right angles to the first, led directly between the two great round towers of the southern aspect of the fortress. The hooves of the horses, the iron rims of the carriage wheels resounded hollowly upon the planks of the bridge, and harshly on the stones of the tunneled passage. The driver pulled on the reins and called to his horses. He threw the reins to a servant and climbed down from the box. His first act, upon setting his foot on the pavement, was to blow his nose with his fingers. The horses threw back their heads and shook their bits, and then hung their heads, lifting and putting down their feet uneasily. The driver was stiff with fatigue. He wiped his fingers on his handkerchief, stuffed the handkerchief into his coat pocket, and opened the carriage door.

The first person to descend was the King's officer, Girard Letellier, who reached a hand to a young woman and helped her to the ground. He then extended his hand to a much older woman, who disregarded it. Clutching the carriage door with a white hand veined with blue, but firm in its grasp, and with the other lifting her dark and heavy skirts, she set her foot upon the carriage step, and so lowered herself with dignity and independence to the pavement. She was a small woman, slender and erect. The last person to quit the carriage was a man in his early thirties, dressed simply, even shabbily, in dark colors, and wearing his own hair.

The driver slammed the door of the carriage and climbed back on his seat. The horses threw their weight against the traces and dragged the carriage into the huge courtyard of the prison. Girard Letellier ushered his three prisoners into the office of the Governor of the Bastille.

Baismaux was seated in an armchair near a cheerful fire. There were lighted candles on a table at his elbow. At another and larger table an officer was seated who rose as the prisoners entered, and carried some papers to Baismaux, who did not rise.

The mother, who had refused the hand of the coachman, had accepted the offer of her daughter's arm. They stood close together, nearly the same height; the daughter was slightly the taller of the two. Cloaked and hooded, their figures were similar. Their faces were also similar, in that one prophesied what the other might become. Their traveling companion, the young man, stood behind them, a little to one side, and watched them as if he feared for them rather than for himself.

Baismaux considered the women. The younger was certainly no more than thirty, and possibly not that, but mature in her composure. Her eyes were steady, her color clear, her skin fresh and firm. The hood, pushed back from her forehead, showed smooth hair, glossy and dark, brushed without coquetry beneath a plain linen coif. It was a face full of energy and intelligence, the features compact, well formed, the mouth not pinched but very firm. The mother's face was like it save that the skin was pale, and yellowed faintly like old silk, and stretched tight over the cheekbones. The line of the jaw was delicate and strong. The eyes were as dark as those of her daughter, deeply set and calm with an intensity of calmness that made the eyes of the Governor stop upon them for a long moment. He consulted the paper in his hand, a perfunctory consultation, and then addressed himself to the younger of the two women.

"You are Mademoiselle Marianne Cailloué of Rouen?"

She bent her head in reply.

"And this is your mother, whom you accompany of your own free will?"

Again the inclination of the head.

"Your mother is a widow, and owns a bookshop in that town, in partnership with a certain Jean Dumesnil."

"I am Jean Dumesnil," said the young man.

"We will come to you in a moment," said Baismaux. "Mademoiselle, you understand that you are not under arrest. Only your mother and Dumesnil are under arrest. I have no order to receive you here."

"I was received in La Berchère, at Rouen," said Marianne Cailloué in a low clear voice with a slight Norman accent. "I was permitted to be with my mother from the first moment of her imprisonment. As you can see, Monsieur le Gouverneur, she is no longer young. She has been very ill. She needs me to care for her."

"It is irregular," said Baismaux.

"Monsieur le Gouverneur," said the Widow Cailloué, speaking for the first time, "if you will permit me the charity of my daughter's presence, it need not be an expense to the King. I am able and willing to pay for her lodging here."

The Governor hesitated very briefly.

"That will not be necessary," he said, "unless the King declines in so many words to be responsible for her board. The point is that at this moment she is free to leave us." Marianne Cailloué made no reply to this, and the Governor turned to Letellier. "Monsieur d'Ormesson sent no packets with the prisoners?"

"No, Your Excellency."

"Very well. You may go now."

"If Your Excellency will be so good as to sign a receipt for my prisoners."

The officer who had brought Baismaux the papers brought him also pen and ink. He signed the documents which Letellier presented, and then said to the prisoners, "I commend you now to Monsieur du Junca," and, having said so, seemed to be no longer concerned with them. He produced a small book from his pocket and, turning comfortably toward the fire, opened the book on his knee and began to read.

As Letellier left, two guards of the fortress entered and took their places, one on either side of the door. They had no more than taken their places when they removed their hats and held them before their faces. Marianne Cailloué observed them with astonishment.

Du Junca opened a book on the long table.

"You are invited to register," he said.

When they had written their names, Marianne Cailloué said, indicating the guards:

"Why do they cover their faces? Are we shameful to look upon?"

"You are guests of the King," said Monsieur du Junca. "When you leave us, you will leave as you are entering, unobserved. There will be no shadow on your name. Your sojourn here will be known only to a trustworthy few. Now, I must ask you to leave with me any articles of value which you carry. When you leave, you may claim these articles again. I shall make an inventory, which you will sign. However, if you desire to have certain money spent for your comfort, or for the comfort of your mother, beyond what the King has assigned for your lodging, the sum will be subtracted from the money you leave with me. I can inform you that the King assigns, as a matter of course, the sum of thirteen sols a day for your mother."

He emptied the bag which she had brought with her from Rouen, spreading out the contents on the table with a practiced hand. There were a few garments, a small bag of coins, a few books. He took the books up one by one and looked at them narrowly.

"You are of the So-called Reformed Religion," he said. "I will inquire about these, and if they are permitted, I will return them to you. I will have you visited also by our confessor."

The coins were counted, the sum noted, the garments swept up and thrust into the bag. The possessions of Jean Dumesnil were then inspected in like manner. He seemed little interested in the process. He kept his eyes fixed on Marianne Cailloué, and once he succeeded in catching her eye. A look of great reassurance passed between them quickly.

While du Junca was making his inspection, two more men came into the room and waited unobtrusively. When the business was completed, the inventories signed, du Junca beckoned to them.

"Saint-Roman," said du Junca, "you will lodge these women on the first floor of the Tour de la Chapelle and take entire charge of them. Bequet, the man on the first floor of the Tour du Coin; in your care."

The turnkey approached. Marianne Cailloué did not stir.

"We still do not know what charge has been brought against us," she said.

"Nor do I," said du Junca.

"This is harsh treatment for a woman of my mother's age."

"I do not contradict you," said du Junca.

"When may we look for an explanation of all this?"

"Later," said Monsieur du Junca.

There was nothing to do but follow the turnkey. Dumesnil

and Bequet had preceded them. They passed through the tunnel into an enormous enclosure, one unbroken space surrounded by the eight round towers and the walls which connected them. The walls were straight, the line of their summit perfectly level except for the pattern of the crenelations. It had been daylight when their carriage reached Paris; during the interview with Baismaux and his officers the sun had set. An afterglow tinted the drifting clouds. Against the cloud-filled sky, behind the crenelated parapet, the figure of a man on guard was very small.

Dumesnil and his jailer proceeded to the farthest corner of the enclosure, to the right, walking briskly. They disappeared from view before Saint-Roman and his charges, walking more slowly because of the Widow Cailloué, reached the door to the Tour de la Chapelle. It was next to the Tour du Coin, and in the eastern wall of the fortress.

Saint-Roman had made no effort to hurry them. When they halted before the open door, he waited with patience. The stairway was steep, and the women, particularly the elder, must be tired. "But," he said to himself, "they all do this, no matter what age they are." They lifted their faces to the sky. Then they entered and he locked the door behind them.

At the first floor he unlocked a door to a circular chamber.

"As you see," he said, "there are the necessities of life. For a small sum you may also have a fire. By arrangement, of the same sort, you could also prepare your own food."

The two women stood in the center of the room. It was not large, and it was very dim. Marianne could distinguish the shape of the fireplace, and a low bed, a table, a chair and a stool, by the shaft of twilight falling through the long window. The window, unglazed and unshuttered, was barred lengthwise and sunk deep in the wall, through the entire thickness of the stone.

"There is no one else in the room?" she asked.

"A mouse or two perhaps. Will you have a fire?"

"If you will be so good."

From the stairway Saint-Roman took a last look at his prisoners through the grated window in the door. They had not moved from the center of the room. They stood clinging to each other as if they were one person, and said nothing. As he went down the stairs he heard no voices, only the sound of his own steps.

When the sound of footsteps died away Marianne Cailloué said to her mother. "You must lie down," and when the older woman lay stretched on the straw mattress the daughter covered her with both their traveling capes and, sitting down beside her, pressed the thick wool tenderly about her mother's shoulders.

"We shall have a fire presently," she said. "Even a small fire will warm the room greatly."

Her mother's eyelids flickered open.

"I cannot imagine a fire," said the older woman, "that would warm these walls."

They waited in silence. Marianne Cailloué thought that her mother had fallen asleep, when she spoke, without opening her eyes.

"It's damp. It smells of marshland. Are we near a marsh?" The daughter could not answer. In a little while the mother spoke again. "You wrote for me to the father of the boy, but your father is dead now eight years, God give him rest. Moreover, to my knowledge, the boy's father was never one of us. It's a late day to make inquiries in the name of the Revocation. But I cannot think why else they would trouble us." She paused. It tired her to speak, but after a while she mustered her strength to go on. "Was there something perhaps in your letter, some phrase that might have been misunderstood?"

The younger woman considered.

"I phrased it very carefully," she said at last. "I think there was nothing in it to cause us trouble."

Again the silence fell between them. The walls seemed to have shut out every noise. The daughter could hear her mother breathing. Then the mother stirred and opened her dark eyes again, very dark in the white face framed by the white hair.

"I wish that we could have conferred a little with Jean. Your father trusted him. I trust him too. Jean Dumesnil is a sincere man. But he is also intransigent. I sometimes think it would have been best for him to go to England with others of the faith. But he had his ideas. He said he was needed in France."

Marianne Cailloué smiled a little. She agreed that Dumesnil was stubborn. He had insisted that he was needed not only in France, but in Rouen. He had wished to marry her, and he had not yet given up the idea. He had remained in order to help her care for her mother. Nor had he abandoned the Huguenots, either. Although he never spoke of it, she knew quite well what commerce he had with certain fishermen who brought their catch to Rouen and returned with other cargo to Le Havre, and who were not unfriendly to the Reformed Religion. She had observed how quick a friendship sprang up between him and the young man from Paris. They had spent a number of evenings strolling along the waterfront and conversing, those April evenings when the dusk delayed and the wind down the river was laden with the scent of new leaves and new grass. When she had inquired, after the rather abrupt departure of the boy, whether he had gone to Cambrai, as he had once spoken of doing, Jean had smiled at her with a peculiar satisfaction and had replied merely, "No, not to Cambrai, I believe."

She had been too discreet to question him further. To her mother she answered thoughtfully:

"Nicolas Larcher was not one of us."

"But he would not have wished to harm us," said her mother.

"How could he have harmed us? No, it's his father who seems to be in trouble. Although why his trouble should involve us is more than I can understand."

"I cannot understand it either," said her mother with a long sigh. "We've been very careful. We've done nothing wrong. If every decision had been left to Jean Dumesnil, it might have been a different story. More than once, my dear, I've had to remind him that it is not for us to publish certain books, no matter how excellent, nor how badly needed by the Religion. That is a work for those who have left the country. I have asked only to live quietly, in my own faith, and die quietly, in my own bed, like your father."

A question formed itself in the mind of Marianne Cailloué which she forbore to speak. The same thought seemed to have visited her mother, for she said with a faint smile:

"Jean Dumesnil would not have published such a book unknown to me. He is stubborn, but he is honorable. He gave me his word. And so, I still cannot understand why we are here."

Chapter Twenty-six

ALLHALLOWS CAME AND WENT. The churches
were hung with black, the candles burned for the dead, and
in the white frost of early morning the footsteps of those who
approached the churches were printed in black, at first singly,
then overlapping each other repeatedly until all individual prints
were merged.

Marianne Larcher lighted her candles in the old church of
Saint Paul, as she had lighted them year after year, for her
parents, for her dead children, and tried to pray. She prayed
for the dead in the words which she had been taught. When she
tried to pray for the living she found herself in an argument
with herself, always the same argument. She rose from her knees
and left the church, turning her back upon the confessional,
drawing her shawl about her head, not knowing and not caring
whether her neighbors had seen her. Since her conversation with
Jules she had come to think of them all as leagued against her
with the housekeeper of Monsieur Pinon. She saw no reason to

believe that the woman had kept her malice to herself; and when even Simone's friendly gossip had betrayed her to Jules, she could guess what stories were circulating against her.

At Versailles the King touched the sick, and the King's physicians recorded a great number of cures. In Paris the price of bread was still high. There was a rumor that the wheat had been reserved for the King's armies. In spite of all the edicts, the number of penniless within the city increased daily. They swarmed the streets, drawing together into little bands in which there was no warmth of common sympathy, but merely an agglutination of their misery. Marianne, returning home after nightfall, encountered them more than once, gathered about the doorways of the rich, as they had gathered the winter before. The poor, wrapped in anonymous rags, in old coats and torn mantles, their feet and ankles bound with strips of cloth which served as footwear, stood and cried aloud that they were famished. They attempted no violence. They merely stood and filled the darkness with their lamentations. Marianne had to pass through these crowds to continue on her way. They made no difficulty for her. When a gleam of light fell upon their faces, she saw no hostility in their eyes, and no curiosity. She might have been one of them.

One rainy night she encountered such a crowd midway in her own street, before the Hôtel d'Aubricourt, just at the moment when the police descended upon it with torches and sticks. That night she locked the door of the kitchen from within, and kindled a small blaze on the hearth, and sat close to it, drying her wet feet and rubbing them with her hands.

Her leather shoes had gone to pieces. She had no money to have them mended, and the wooden shoes, which she now wore everywhere, were cold. The margin between her condition and that of the homeless poor had grown more narrow with every passing day. She looked about the room for something more that she might sell; there was not much left. She thought of how that room had formerly been filled with the warmth and goodness of life, and a sense of despair came over her. She could not wait much longer for Jean to be released, for Nicolas to return, to have word from Paul, for something to happen to change the situation in which she was trapped. It had been a long time since the abbé Têtu had written his letter. Madame de Maintenon must have a hard heart, or else she had less power over the King than all the songs and libels led one to believe.

She hoped constantly for Jean's release, but she could not imagine, try as she would, how life would go on for them after that. She tried to think of Jean and Nicolas together, rebuilding their fortune, but she could not fit herself into the picture. As for Paul, his physical presence being removed from her life, and the memory of it constantly receding in time, there were days when she felt as if she had wakened from a trance, or from some kind of spell which had destroyed her ability to think and feel normally. Yet she sometimes dreamed of Paul and, waking, had to instruct herself again with the fact of his desertion. One thing remained impossible for her, and that was to inform upon him, even to save Jean from the galleys. She still took shelter behind the abbé's letter from the need of decision.

In spite of all this, she thought less and less often of Paul, and more and more frequently of Jean and of Nicolas, not as they would be when they returned, but as they had been. She took refuge in remembering how she had combed and trimmed her son's hair, how she had lengthened the sleeves of his shirts as he grew. She remembered the sleeves of Jean's fustian coat, how the stuff had remained creased after he had removed it, still holding the character of the man who wore it. She remembered Nicolas and the other children playing on the floor of the shop, beneath Jean's feet, who had stepped above them carefully as a horse moves its feet about familiar cats who haunt the stable. Until this last spring she had never made a move of any sort in these rooms which had not been related in one way or another to Nicolas or to Jean. Her habits kept her company in the empty rooms.

Chafing her feet before the penurious fire, she marveled that she continued to make so great an effort to live, that she had not succumbed to the infections of the rooms where she worked. She had never taken an illness from the children she had nursed. She had never had time to be sick. When the questions which she asked herself daily were answered, then she could find time to be ill, to be taken to St.-Lazare, and to die. In the meantime she squeezed the water from her woolen stockings and spread them near the fire to dry, and went barefooted through the court and up the cold stairs to her bed. In the dark morning as she set out for work she felt the mud of the gutter, stiffened by the hard frost, give underfoot like breaking wax.

Soon after Allhallows she was sent from the place where she worked to fetch water, with two wooden buckets and a wooden yoke for her shoulders. She filled them at the fountain in the rue St.-Antoine in front of the sombre magnificence of the church of the Jesuits. The water was cold. The filled buckets seemed more than naturally heavy, as if the very coldness of the water had a weight of its own. She fastened them to the yoke, and stooped to take the yoke upon her shoulders, and as she straightened under the load and turned to leave the fountain, she saw the woman she most dreaded, the housekeeper of the counselor, Monsieur Pinon. They had of late ignored each other when they met, but on this day the housekeeper approached Marianne.

"Have you had news of your husband?" she said, without other greeting.

Marianne looked up into the little greenish eyes, cold and bright, and at the heavy jaw, and at the mouth that had always seemed cruel. The mouth smiled, as if with intended kindness. The smile was filled with complacence.

"Then this may interest you," said the housekeeper in reply to Marianne's negative gesture of the head. "There is a rumor that a chain of convicts will leave tomorrow for the galleys, for Toulon. They leave early, to avoid notice. If you present yourself at La Tournelle early enough, you may have a chance to speak to your husband."

"But he hasn't been convicted," said Marianne.

"He hasn't been released," said the housekeeper smugly. "A chain leaves. If he's with them, he's been convicted. This you can learn for yourself."

"Is it certain?"

"It's a rumor, as I said. No one informs me, but since I listen, in a house such as that of Monsieur Pinon I hear interesting things. Naturally the police are close-mouthed about the departure of a chain. Too much interest, too great a crowd, in times like these——" She shrugged her shoulders, angular and large beneath her thick shawl. "It takes nothing to start a riot. I tell you this in kindness. I presume you still have some affection for your husband."

She moved away, and it was not her fault that another woman, pushing to reach the fountain, struck the edge of one of Marianne's buckets, sending a wave of icy water over her ankle and instep.

La Tournelle was not a prison in the absolute sense of the word. It was a prison in that men were confined there after sentence, and left it only to work out their sentence in penal servitude. It remained under the surveillance of the police, but the priests of St.-Nicolas-du-Chardonnet were in authority there, not the police. Over a generation ago Vincent de Paul had asked permission to use the old fortifications of the city at the Porte St.-Bernard. He brought there the men who had been condemned to the galleys and been lodged in the wet dungeons of the Conciergerie until a large enough number should have been condemned to make up a chain. In the days of the Conciergerie the chains left Paris for Marseilles on the average of twice a year, and after the ordeal of their imprisonment many of the men died on the road, some died in prison, and few lived to serve in the galleys. At La Tournelle the good Monsieur Vincent gave them spiritual consolation, as well as better physical care than they had known before, to strengthen their bodies for the long journey south, as well as to strengthen their souls. His work had been respected, and when the old Porte St.-Bernard had been pulled down to make way for a new gate in honor of the young King, the old tower had been left. The priests of St.-Nicolas carried on his work, and Mass was said there on Sundays and on holy days, as in all consecrated chapels.

Marianne came there before daylight, mistrusting the advice of the housekeeper of Monsieur Pinon, yet not daring to disregard it. She thought the woman capable of making the suggestion as a bitter jest, to send her through the dark streets fearfully and for nothing. She could not forget, however, that in the house of the counselor the woman might have picked up a word of truth. She brought with her the abbé's gold piece. There had been no time that evening to sell anything more from the kitchen, and she did not dare bring anything but money. She did not think he would be permitted to receive other gifts. His pipe, his tobacco remained where he had left them, above the fireplace.

She found at the door of La Tournelle one old woman, huddled against the wall, who looked at her curiously, and then offered the information:

"They don't open yet."

Marianne wondered why she had come so early. Did she know the habits of the prison? She replied:

"I have my place. I'm first."

Her teeth were gone, save for a few snags in the lower jaw, so that her speech was lisping and indistinct. Marianne muffled her hands tighter in her shawl, and leaned against the door by the old woman. The river mist was very thick and cold. It filled the street before the old tower, it crept beneath her shawl. She heard it dripping from the archway overhead. La Tournelle itself seemed deserted, dark within and without, but a continuous thin line of traffic entered the city through the Porte St.-Bernard. The carters' lanterns were blurred. People on foot, or with bundles mysteriously wrapped, came in darkness, trusting to the growing pallor of the sky high overhead.

Marianne began to shiver. While she walked she had managed to keep warm; standing still, she found the cold too great. She took a few steps to restore the circulation of her blood, and passed through the gate. Over her head in a bas-relief the King was seated like a Greek deity at the helm of a small vessel, while sea nymphs rose from the waves to greet him and the powers of the air hailed him joyously from the clouds. Marianne found herself on the beach where the men bathed in the hot days of summer, while fine ladies stopped their coaches on the road above to watch.

Across the river lay the Ile Louviers, invisible through the fog. She stood there, trying to think what she could say to Jean if she saw him. She did not know whether she wished more to see him and be delivered from her long uncertainty, or dreaded to see him and become certain of all the suffering she had caused him. Would the sight of him give her courage to confess? What good would her confession do him now? Would it not be better merely to lay her head upon his shoulder and give him the abbé's coin? It was possible that he still trusted her. Seeing her there, he could at least know that she had not run away, although she deserved no credit for that. Would it not be kinder, if he could trust her still, to let him go his way deceived? One question never presented itself to her, however, and that was, would it not be better to leave before the doors were opened? She walked beside the water for a good half hour, and then she returned to La Tournelle and waited.

A little group of women had gathered while she was walking beyond the gate, and the group increased until there were nearly a dozen. There must be a reason for their coming, she thought. They waited patiently, without conversing, stirring only to keep the blood moving, to stamp their feet.

At seven o'clock a priest from St.-Nicolas appeared, hurrying down the rue de la Tournelle, and the group drew to one side to let him pass, all save the old woman who had been there first. She caught at his sleeve as he was about to enter, and Marianne, on the edge of the group, heard him say:

"Not today. No. How can I tell you beforehand when I'm not told myself? Not today, not tomorrow. If you wish to trust me, I'll give him your package."

At his first words the women began to drift away from the portal. Marianne pushed between them, and as the priest put up his hand to detach that of the old woman from his arm, she cried:

"Father, is my husband among your prisoners?"

"What name?" said the priest.

"Larcher."

The priest shook his head.

"Jean François Larcher."

"No Larcher at all," he said, and, having succeeded in freeing himself from the old woman, he entered and closed the door.

Marianne was left alone with the old woman, who sucked her lips in over her almost toothless gums in a smile of unpleasant comprehension. Now that it was daylight Marianne could see how filthy she was. The skin beneath her eyes was discolored, a greenish yellow, as if from a bruise. The skin about her mouth was stained with brown. The tight unpleasant smile split in the middle and then the old woman said:

"Maybe he's changed his name, your husband. If he ever comes here, they'll keep an eye on 'im for you. You won't have to wonder where he is, night or day. They'll see to it he says his prayers, too."

"Is your husband in there?" said Marianne, revolted, but touched with pity. A hoarse cackle shook the stained lips.

"My husband? At my age? My son. And do you know what he's in for? He stole. Not something to eat. Not something to wear. Not even something you could sell without getting into more trouble. A silver snuffbox. With initials engraved on it. Such dirty stupidity. And do you think I came to see him once more, to embrace him? Do you think I brought him some bread and cheese for the journey? I'm not such a fool. You heard the Father. He eats well. He eats better than I do. He leaves me to shift for myself, at my age. No, I came to spit upon him. D'you hear me? To spit upon him."

The days of uncertainty continued. The city advanced deeper into November, the days growing shorter, the nights colder. At the end of the second week in November, Marianne was dismissed from the place where she then worked. She began to haunt the rue de la Vannerie and the Bureau des Recommand-eresses. She sold the last of the dishes of speckled glaze to buy faggots.

The seal had never been removed from the door to the bindery, nor had the account books and other business records been returned to her. Money was owed to Jean on which she could collect nothing. On the other hand, she was lodged rent-free, but it worried her to think of the workroom becoming damp, of mildew and rust forming among the tools, the sewing frames, the presses, everything which had been well tended for so many years. Since the day she had been questioned the police had ignored her as if she had ceased to exist.

On the nineteenth of November, passing through the rue St.-Paul, she saw a group of men standing before the church, reading a notice posted on the door. The apothecary from the shop directly across from the church was one of them. He was leaving the group as she approached, and was about to cross the street when his eye fell on her, and he stopped.

"This concerns you," he said, gesturing with his head toward the notice.

She was startled by his gravity. Without replying to his greeting, she walked quickly toward the church door. The men stood aside for her without a word. They had all recognized her. The notice, nailed top and bottom, fluttered in the wind. She had to put her hands on the edges to hold it still while she read.

Couched in formal language, but plain to understand, it announced that on Friday, the nineteenth of November, at six o'clock in the evening, in the Place de Grève, would be hanged for the King's justice a bookbinder by the name of Larcher, and a printer by the name of Rambault. She did not read as far as the name of Rambault, nor the names of those who authorized the statement. She turned and ran, stumbling a little, into the rue Neuve St.-Paul to the hôtel where the abbé Têtu had his lodging. It was then past three o'clock.

"Monsieur l'abbé has gone into the country for a little trip," said the housekeeper. "He left no word as to when he would return."

She looked at Marianne with curiosity, as well she might, for this woman who inquired for the abbé was pale, and extravagantly urgent. When she heard that the abbé was not to be found, a dazed look came into her eyes, and she went away without explaining her errand or leaving any message.

"Yet I spoke to her very civilly," said the housekeeper later in the afternoon to the apothecary. "Of course I didn't know at the time what was the matter."

Marianne returned to the rue des Lions and in broad daylight closed the shutters. In the darkness of the kitchen she walked up and down, beating her hands together, unable to be still, and unable to bear the knowledge which was the end of all her questions.

Chapter Twenty-seven

AT SIX O'CLOCK the wind descended upon the Place de Grève in gusts that shook the torches at the foot of the gibbet. The mass of the cathedral, seen broadside from the Place, rising above the crowded roofs on the Ile de la Cité, cut a straight dark line against the sky beneath the darkness of the clouds. A crowd had gathered about the gibbet. The archers of the guard cleared a way through it for the hangman's cart. A few drops of rain hissed in the torches, but the storm was not yet ready to break. When the cart reached the gibbet, the erratic wind ceased entirely. The crowd, which had been restless, fell silent also. The shock of the tailgate, when it was lowered, could be heard plainly, and then, less clearly, came the voice of the priest.

There were four men in the cart, the executioner, the priest, the two prisoners.

Paul Damas was in the crowd. After the failure of the rendezvous at Fontainebleau he had stayed out of Paris. He had kept the rendezvous at the hour agreed on, and in the crowd before the château he had met the one-eyed Ballad Singer. The Ballad Singer had in fact recognized Paul from his back, had tapped him on the shoulder, and so forced him to turn to meet the heroic face with the cancerous eye. From him Paul had learned with what intensity, since the arrest of Larcher, the police of Paris were searching for the distributors of the pamphlet.

"You were employed by Larcher," said the Ballad Singer with a wink of his good eye. "A word to the wise."

The extent to which the Ballad Singer was informed about him, and the ease with which the Ballad Singer had recognized him, alarmed Paul. He had met the Ballad Singer once or twice since the evening with Father Lanterns, and each time the Ballad Singer had evinced a lordly friendliness which annoyed him. At Fontainebleau he thanked his lucky stars for the Ballad Singer's good will, and made haste to leave him as quickly as he could. But after the weeks of wandering to Orléans and then to Blois and back again, when he returned to Paris, desperate for news, it was the Ballad Singer he searched for and found caroling on the Pont Neuf, as always, his songs for all factions and all degrees.

Paul had bought himself a change of clothing, a coat and vest of a very dark green, a grey beaver hat, and had thrown away the satchel in which he had carried his tools and his personal belongings. He wore a money belt.

He had seen for himself that day the notices of the execution, fluttering in the wind from church doors, at street corners, at the approaches to the bridges. He had been unable to believe that such a sentence had been passed for so small a crime, unable to believe that the sentence would actually be carried out. He had come to the Place de Grève in a state of horror, to verify for himself the meaning of the printed words.

The crowd pushed toward the hangman's cart, carrying Paul with it in spite of himself. He made an effort to get free, with no success. He pulled his hat down on his forehead and bent his

head, finding himself forced almost to the wheel of the cart.
The archers of the guard stopped the crowd, and Paul could see,
less than six feet from him the heavy shoulders, the grey head
of his master. Larcher's back was turned to him. His head was
cropped; he wore no coat, only a white shirt in that biting wind.
The executioner stood beside him; facing him stood the priest,
in black, and Rambault. His hair was cropped also. It made
the face more gaunt than ever. The smile was gone from the
wide, honest mouth. He stared straight at Paul, but gave no
sign of recognition. Paul realized with relief that the glare of
the torches built up a smoky wall between the prisoners in the
cart and the crowd which surrounded it.

So, it was true. Larcher was to die. It was preposterous, but
it was true. Paul felt a great sickness, and a great hatred for
everyone in the Place, for those in authority and for those who
had come to enjoy these deaths. The arms of the gibbet loomed
above the torches, lighted by them. The priest was speaking,
but his words were muttered and, even in the silence of the
pressing crowd, unintelligible. Paul made a violent movement
of his elbow and shoulder, thrusting back between the bodies
which held him imprisoned. They moved slightly apart, and
he managed to slip between them, moving one rank away from
the cart. And little by little, with continued, thrusting jabs,
given strength by his excessive horror, he made his way to the
edge of the crowd, where he could no longer see anything
but the arms of the gibbet high in the torchlight, and where he
was free to turn and to walk away.

At the entrance to the rue de la Mortellerie the door of a
cabaret stood wide open. In the doorway stood the host, secure
in his knowledge that emotion makes men thirsty, and waited
for the hanging to be over.

Paul plunged into the darkness of the street. Halfway down
it, he remembered another evening. It was here that he had
watched one of La Reynie's men pull on a rope which hoisted a
street light into place. "Up the rope she goes," said the man,

and grinned. Paul had grinned in return. The lantern was there overhead. It was out. The glass was broken. Paul stopped, turned to the wall, and vomited. While he was wiping his mouth he heard the voices lifted in the Place de Grève in the *Salve Regina*, which meant but one thing, that the execution was completed. If he turned, if he retreated only as far as the beginning of the street, he would see the bodies of Pierre Rambault and of Jean Larcher swinging from the gibbet in the torchlight. He proceeded unsteadily toward the Port St.-Paul. Behind him the wind shut down upon the voices for a moment, muting them, then lifted; the voices lifted with it, roughened, and filled with sorrow, but in the sudden upsurge of sound incongruously triumphant.

Paul tried the door of the shop in the rue des Lions. It was not locked. He pushed it open and saw in a darkened room a woman sitting beside a dying fire. She sat with her knees apart, her feet planted flatly on the stone floor, her forearms on her knees, and her head bent forward so that her face was hidden, an attitude of complete exhaustion, without grace, such as a peasant might assume, or a woman of the roads. He looked about the room quickly. It was changed, despoiled. The floor was tracked with mud. The copper fountain, dull with tarnish, gave back no light to the fire. The wind blasted the shutters. Marianne looked up, and saw Paul standing by the door, and stared at him blankly. He bolted the door and approached her, hesitant, questioning, unsure of his reception, after having hurried to find her, almost uncertain as to whether this woman was the one he sought. But she stood up, swaying slightly, and then moved to meet him, her hands outstretched.

Smudges of darkness lay beneath her eyes. The white coif, the white fichu which he remembered were gone. She was wrapped in dark shawls. She might have appeared at any street corner, emerging from the shadow to ask alms; but she was smiling, and before he could look at her well, before he could say a word, she was in his arms. He bent his cheek to her head and

held her close, while all the doubt, fear, and guilt which had
possessed them both for so many months found expression only
in desire which held them, clinging to each other in the middle
of the darkened room. After a while there were questions,
admissions, murmured by lips pressed against the side of a cheek,
indistinct, half understood. An awareness of their situation
returned inevitably. Marianne said:

"Do you know what they did?"

"I saw him in the cart."

She recoiled, but did not take her hands from his.

"You didn't see him hanged!"

"No. But it's finished. I heard the *Salve Regina*. Didn't you
hear the *Salve?*"

She shook her head. "I heard the bells at six," she said, withdrawing her hands.

"How was I to know they'd hang him?" said Paul. "He said
himself there was no great danger in the pamphlets. You remember, he said that? Nicolas—Nicolas said it too."

"Why did you do it, Paul? Why?"

"I don't know. It was a mistake. Yes, I do know. I wanted him
out of the place. He was always here. He never left us alone.
It was a mistake, but I couldn't foresee—— How could I have
known that they would make such a great crime from a silly
libel?"

He defended himself from the reproach in her eyes. He could
not talk it down, and it was the harder to bear in that she faced
him unresisting. He had known his own bad hours during the last
months. It was because of them that he was not by now safe over
the border into Switzerland, but this moment was the worst he
had known. He had dreamed of being alone with her in these
rooms. Now they were quite alone. Nothing kept them from
the bed in the upper chamber, and the thought of it had become a horror. He said, to break the spell:

"We can't stay here. They'll be after me. They've been looking for me ever since the beginning."

"He never accused us," she said, unmoving. "He protected us."

Since she said "us" he felt a return to his authority.

"We must go," he repeated. "Have you no fear for me?"

He had to put his hand on her shoulder and shake her before he could rouse her. He found her cloak, and put it about her shoulders, and led her to the door. Then:

"Where are we going?" she asked wildly.

"I have a lodging. Come."

Chapter Twenty-eight

THE TOUR DE LA CHAPELLE received the morning sunlight, whenever the day began with sunlight. It stood above the city fosse and the garden of Monsieur de Baismaux on the apron of the fortifications. The roofs and spires of the faubourg St.-Antoine would have been visible for those within the tower if the windows of the apartments, one room on each floor of the tower, had not been so high and narrow. The Widow Cailloué and her daughter could see only a sliver of the eastern sky.

On the Friday when Jean Larcher and Pierre Rambault met their death there was no early sunlight. The day continued dark and cold, and the wind, drawn down the great flues of the chimney in the Tour de la Chapelle, whistled and moaned, or without warning blew the ashes from the hearth into the room. At midnight the rain quieted the wind and filled the room with an increase of dampness. Saturday was another dark, cold day, and Sunday, if the sun shone elsewhere, the inhabitants of the

Tour de la Chapelle had no way of knowing it. On Sunday, in the early afternoon, Marianne Cailloué sat beside the bed where her mother lay. She held her mother's hand, stroking it, and warming it with her own hands, and sometimes with her lips. She had spent almost every hour of the last two days in the same spot.

In the early morning of each day her mother's hand was cold, and the slight form beneath the covers shook with repeated chills, although her daughter squandered on the fire all the wood that Saint-Roman had brought them. In the afternoon her mother's hand grew hot and dry, and she pushed the covers from her breast, only to have her daughter replace them, gently and firmly, each time.

"It's the fever. You'll take more cold if you expose yourself."

When Saint-Roman rapped on the grille, bringing their food, she left her mother long enough to accept what he had brought, and to reply to his inquiry:

"She's quite well, but she's tired, and bed is the only place in which she can keep warm."

On Friday night she had said this, and again on Saturday, declining his offer to fetch a doctor, and asking only for more wood. On Sunday noon she had repeated:

"She is not sick; she is resting."

The turnkey did not argue the matter, and in her heart she thanked him for it. He had been much kinder all that month than she had dared to hope. He had repeatedly let her descend on fair days to the great court, and had let her walk about quite freely, save that he never let her meet, or even see, another prisoner. These periods under the sky, in the freely moving and sometimes sunny air, had kept up her courage and strength. As he had pointed out, she was only a prisoner by her own request. Monsieur du Junca had agreed that she should enjoy a privilege granted to some who were actually prisoners, the basis for the granting of such a privilege being the judgment of Monsieur du Junca. Her mother, on the other hand, was not to be accorded this privilege. The old woman smiled when she heard this, and commented that she would not have availed herself of it had it been granted, and for many reasons, the steps to the courtyard being first among them. The smile was without bitterness, but held a faint irony and a great deal of pride. La Veuve Cailloué, her daughter understood quite well, cared to accept no favors from her enemies. She did not care to put herself on view, even in that grim enclosure. She accepted her imprisonment like a religious retreat.

It was possible that the kindness of Saint-Roman resulted from no more than the existence of a sum of money in the keeping of Monsieur du Junca, from which he received his share. If his prisoners had been difficult or brutal he would no doubt have met them with brutality of his own. But for two women who were quiet, educated, and decent, although not ladies, he had a natural consideration. He was not educated himself. He knew his work. He was a servant in a strange sort of inn, a diligent and matter-of-fact servant. The prison which held so much terror and mystery for those who saw it from without was to him banal in the extreme. He interested himself in those who were in his charge, and it seemed to Marianne Cailloué, on that Sunday, that he showed a surprising sense of delicacy in that he forbore to press his question.

Her mother was very ill indeed. There was no pretense between the two women on that subject. On Friday evening, while the wind performed so strangely in the chimney, mouthing and whistling, now like an animal, now like a mad person, her mother had said:

"I can bear much. I can bear all that is necessary, but I cannot bear the thought of arguing with a priest. If they suspect that I am dying, they will send a Jesuit."

"I'll let them suspect nothing," said her daughter, stroking the frail hand.

On Sunday, shortly after noon, the body beneath the blankets and the dark woolen capes was relaxed. The morning chills had ceased. The afternoon fever had not yet gathered force. Her mother seemed to be sleeping, and Marianne Cailloué, without withdrawing her hands, ceased in their stroking, and rested too. She sat with hunched shoulders, leaning toward the bed, her eyes on the hand within her own, noting the transparency of the skin drawn tight above the enlarged knuckles, the boniness of fingers that had formerly been as round and slender as her own, and she thought that what had come to pass for her mother and herself had been a foregone conclusion from the moment of their quitting La Berchère for Paris. The hand in hers showed lines of strength for all its frailness, but it was not the kind of strength which could hold out against the long journey, the sunless days of confinement, or the physical strain of long-continued fear. It was impossible to live behind this mass of stone without experiencing some measure of fear, no matter how serene the conscience, how deep the trust in God.

Her mother had been failing before the initial detainment at Rouen. Marianne Cailloué tried to believe that, even without the fatigue and the shock of the arrest, this hour, which was the hour of her mother's death, would have come almost as soon. Without this belief, her bitterness would have become a poison and a disintegration of the spirit.

No one had yet informed them what the charge had been against her mother. They had been visited once by Monsieur du Junca and an officer from the Châtelet of Paris, who had questioned the widow about her business, her relations with Jean Dumesnil, and had presented for her verification an inventory of every book and pamphlet found in her shop or in her personal library. The Widow Cailloué inspected the list with care. It was extraordinary at her age how good her eyesight was. She required no glasses. She went down the list, item by item, and when she reached the end, she lifted those dark, bright eyes to those of the officer and declared that the record was correct in every particular.

"However," she concluded, "you must understand, Monsieur,

that the books listed on this last sheet were never offered for sale in the shop, nor ever displayed. These books belonged to my husband. I kept them for his sake, and for my own use, only."

"You may make a note to that effect," said the officer, "and then I must ask you to sign the statement."

When she had signed and the officers had departed, taking with them their papers and also their pen and ink, she said:

"So—they found your father's books. We're back in the year of the Revocation."

Later that evening, out of a prolonged silence, she spoke again:

"Blessed are ye when men shall hate you, and when they shall separate you from their company, and shall reproach you, and cast out your name as evil, for the Son of Man's sake."

She did not again express any bewilderment at their arrest, nor any theories regarding the cause. The daughter had her own theory as to the cause of their trouble, which she did not express to her mother. The finding of her father's books could be sufficient reason for her mother's being held, as now, in the King's custody. But through all the years since her father's death no one had bothered to investigate his library. The activities of Jean Dumesnil with the Huguenot émigrés, that was another matter; they had long been a cause of anxiety with her. The mention of the name of Nicolas Larcher had confirmed her in her suspicion. That the police inquiry had been made for the father rather than for the young man himself did not lessen her suspicion.

The bitterness against which she fought, seated beside her dying mother, was not directed against Jean Dumesnil. Her sympathy was for those of the Religion who wished to escape from the kingdom, and her admiration for Jean, who ran much risk in helping them, was great. She had made a point of not knowing exactly what he did. If his "commerce" brought them all three to the Bastille, it was a curious accident of fate. She would not blame him. She had hoped, each time she descended to the court, for a glimpse of him, and each time that she had failed to see him, her disappointment had become more keen. She began to realize that, although she had refused his offer of marriage five times, if fate should permit him to make a sixth offer, she would be more than happy to accept him.

After the visit of Monsieur du Junca and the officer, her mother withdrew more and more frequently into long reveries, during which her face assumed such an expression of exaltation and serenity that the daughter forbore to interrupt them. But much as she respected these silences, and deeply as she was grateful for them, since she knew her mother comforted and sustained in them by all the passion of her faith, they left the daughter alone, and in an existence so limited that she could hardly bear her solitude.

There was little to do, once she had performed the small rites of her housekeeping. She had no pen or paper, no books, no vision of the outside world. She could not sit unmoving, as her mother did, hour after hour, her hands folded in her lap, her bright exalted gaze fixed upon the shadows beyond the hearth. She would have consented to almost anything, she told herself, in order to escape from that room, anything except to desert her mother. She was the prisoner of her mother's suffering.

Now the hour had come when the mother prepared to leave the daughter. Her eyes remained closed. A little color began to creep into her cheeks; her body, no longer shaken by chills, lay quietly relaxed in the warmth of the returning fever. It was an illusion of recovery.

The daughter thought how little she knew of this woman whom she watched. The face, which resembled her own, was the face of a stranger; it was unlike her own in its economy of substance and in its serenity. The body she knew well, from tending it in illness. The mind she knew in the strength of its belief, and in certain preferences and dislikes, many of them trivial; but of her mother's youth, or even the days of her own childhood beside her mother's skirts, she knew very little.

Her mother was acutely sensitive to odors. She liked the smell of medicinal and cleansing herbs, rue and juniper and rosemary. She disliked crowds and spent much time alone on the high cliffs above the river in spring, or in the windy days of autumn, from which sorties she returned with a basket filled with cuttings from wild plants, leaves and roots, or in the fall with red haws from the wild rosebushes.

She kept a small herb and salad garden of her own, but it was not nearly large enough to shelter all the plants she needed for her remedies, or so she said. Her daughter suspected that the lonely walks meant more to her intense spirit in the way of healing than all the simples which she found.

She remembered her mother's return from those walks, her cloak damp with mist and smelling of pungent leaves, her eyes luminous and deep, her face relaxed, the hem of her skirt muddied and sometimes frayed, and when her husband had protested that she endangered her health by walking in the damp and cold, she had only smiled.

Such roaming had been abandoned after her husband's death. Age laid a hand upon her visibly; the herbs in the small garden had not been adequate to hold it off.

The name of the Norman village where her mother had been born, her mother's maiden name, her grandfather's occupation, the daughter knew. Her mother had spoken seldom of her childhood, and never of the days of her courtship. Marianne Cailloué did not know whether her mother's passion for the Reformation had influenced her father, or if it was his influence which had drawn her mother. One thing was certain; their married love and their religion had been deeply interfused.

She remembered clearly a family council in '85, soon after the publishing of the Revocation, at which Jean Dumesnil and his brother Jacques had been present. In the small room behind the shop, crowded with tall cupboards of heavily carved and darkened nutwood, they had sat about the round table, all their hands upon it in a kind of star, and had discussed for the first and last time whether they should sell the business and leave

France. Jacques Dumesnil had urged them strongly to go to England. Her mother had not spoken. After much discussion her father had said:

"My religion means much to me; my country also. I have no desire to leave France. I am unwilling to believe that Frenchmen will not permit me to live and die quietly in my own faith if I make no effort to proselytize. We are not an intolerant nation. The King, when he was young, made certain pronouncements in the vein of his grandfather. He seems now to have abandoned them. But I trust he'll come to it again, to such a tolerance. It would be greatly to his advantage. It would spare him a war with England. What do you think?" he ended, turning toward her mother, and her mother had answered:

"I think as you do."

That had been an end of it. The Dumesnil brothers had accepted her father's decision, and because of that decision her mother, herself, and Jean were in the King's prison.

"I think as you do."

Her mother had never after referred to that decision, but she could not have forgotten it, and, her daughter was certain, she could never have repented of it.

The sound of bells floating through the narrow window told her it was one o'clock. Some half hour later her mother stirred, sighed, and opened her eyes. She said in a faint voice:

"Read to me."

"You forget, Maman. They kept our books."

An arrogant brightness shone in the dark eyes.

"We do not need a book. Read me the Psalms of David." She paused for breath, and then began firmly, although in a very low voice: "The Everlasting is my shepherd. I shall not want." But she could not continue. She lay with her eyes fixed on her daughter's face, and her lips moved soundlessly as her daughter continued. The words of great comfort fell between them softly: the valley of the shadow, the rod and the staff. "Thou preparest a table before me in the sight of those who persecute

me," said Marianne Cailloué. Before she could continue her
mother interrupted her, rising a little on her pillows, her voice
strong and perfectly clear:

"Judge me, O Lord, for I have walked in mine integrity . . .
I have not sat with vain persons . . . Neither will I go in with
dissemblers. *Fais-moi justice, O Eternel, fais-moi justice.*"

She broke off, and fell back upon the pillows, exhausted, eyes
closed. She struggled for breath, and after a time she opened
her eyes again, those dark eyes so extraordinary in her wan face,
and smiled. It was a smile of triumph more than of tenderness,
but it conveyed affection also and a great secret understanding.
After that she fell asleep, and it was not until almost two o'clock
that Marianne Cailloué observed that, the head being turned to
one side, her mother's mouth sagged in the same direction
slightly. At the same time the daughter realized that the hand
which lay in her own had relaxed even beyond the relaxation of
sleep. She lifted the hand and laid it on her mother's breast, and
crossed the other hand above it.

When Saint-Roman, climbing on his evening rounds to the
chambers on the floors above, passed her grille, she spoke to
him, and a little later he returned with Monsieur du Junca.

"It happened about two o'clock," said the young woman.

"You should have notified me earlier," said the major-domo.
"Had I known your mother was ill, I would have brought a confessor."

"It was very sudden at the end," said Marianne Cailloué.

"A pity that she died unshriven," said Monsieur du Junca.
"We have a rule not to be set aside: we cannot bury in holy
ground those who died unconfessed. Saint-Roman, you understand this. Did you notice nothing?"

"Mademoiselle always said that her mother was resting,"
replied the turnkey.

"Usually," said the major-domo pedantically, "those who die
in this bastille are interred in the cemetery of St.-Paul's, which
was formerly the King's own parish church. The interment is

made in the evening. The register is inscribed with an assumed name, to cause no embarrassment to living relatives of the deceased. The true name is entered in my register. It is all very regular. Unfortunately for your mother, since she died without receiving the sacrament, there remains only burial in the casemates of the château. You undertand? In the foundations of the prison. She cannot quit the prison."

"She wished to die in her religion," said Marianne Cailloué.

Monsieur du Junca removed his hat and rubbed the back of his neck thoughtfully. He regarded the woman before him with helpless incomprehension.

"If you think it is no pity yourself, Mademoiselle," he said, replacing his hat, "who am I to protest? We will inter the deceased tomorrow night at eight in the casemates of the bastion. I think there's nothing more to be discussed."

"My departure," said Marianne Cailloué. "I shall leave for Rouen as soon as possible after my mother's burial. I shall travel at my own expense."

"As for that," said Monsieur du Junca, "it remains to be seen. It is not so simple."

"I am not a prisoner. I was never under arrest."

"True enough," said Monsieur du Junca, "nevertheless, you must understand, you were admitted by *lettre de cachet*. Monsieur de Baismaux cannot release you without an order from the King. This matter of your mother's death, outside of the Church, may cause some hesitation on the part of the King. He may feel that you are in need of religious instruction. In his place, I should think so."

Chapter Twenty-nine

O_N *THE TWENTIETH OF DECEMBER* there was to be another hanging. A little before six a crowd gathered before the Grand Châtelet. The gallows was set up in the Place de Grève. It was assumed that two men were to die, and both for having been involved in the publication and distribution of libels. No one in the crowd knew much about the nature of the libels. Snow was falling through the early darkness. It clung to the rough edges of the stone, to the shoulders of men and women, and in the corners of the street where no one trod it accumulated in a thin white mask.

The hangman's cart appeared. As on other occasions, the patient horses dragged it to the door of the prison. The archers of the guard surrounded it with a wall of torches. The door opened, and those who stood near could see in the vaulted corridor a poor devil in a white shirt limping forward between a black-robed priest and an officer. Then a mounted messenger, arriving with a great clatter of hooves, scattered the crowd, sprang from the back of his horse, and met the priest, the prisoner, and the officer on the very threshold of the prison.

There was a conference, a showing of papers, and the door of the Châtelet was closed. A murmur ran from those nearest the door to those on the edge of the crowd: reprieve. The King's reprieve. The cart was led away. The crowd dispersed. The archers of the guard carried their torches elsewhere. Jean Chavance was not to die that night. What had happened was this.

After the hanging of Larcher and Rambault the police had devoted their energies to the investigation of Chavance, the friend of Rambault. They had learned nothing from Larcher, not even during the question after sentence. They had thought him an old man. His resistance was that of a rock. Charon the peddler was condemned at the same time as Larcher, but to the galleys, not to the gibbet. He was sent to La Tournelle, where he fell ill. On the ninth of December the King, through Pontchartrain, indicated that the peddler, since he was ill, should not be sent out with the chain which was then being made ready to leave, but should be sent to another prison. Chavance also had refused to talk, and, lacking his confession, the police had arrested his brother at Lyon and two of his friends, by name Capol and Binet. The search for the pamphlet against Madame de Maintenon and the King had become an extended inquiry into all the possible sources of offense. A peddler by the name of Friquet, either from Arras or from Amiens, the police never made certain, was also picked up, and the son of a Protestant minister in Rouen by the name of La Roque was arrested and sentenced at the same time as Chavance.

Meanwhile, on the day following the execution of Larcher, Monsieur de La Reynie received from Pontchartrain the following instruction:

"*Le Roi m'ordonne de vous écrire qu'encas que Chavance, libraire de Lyon, soit condamné à la mort, Sa Majesté désire que vous fassiez surseoir l'exécution du jugement jusqu' à nouvel ordre.*"

The examination of Chavance continued through November, and on into the third week of December. Then, in reply to a puzzled inquiry, Monsieur Robert received a letter from Versailles. Pontchartrain wrote on behalf of the King:

"The King does not intend to excuse Chavance from the pain of torture in the event that he shall be condemned; but His Majesty wishes simply to change the pain of death to that of the galleys in the event that he be condemned to death and to the question before death. Nothing should prevent you from applying the question, or from carrying out the sentence until the very moment when he shall be led to his punishment, at which time Monsieur de La Reynie will make use of the order which I am sending him to reprieve the execution of the death sentence."

The resolution of Chavance cracked under the final torture, and he talked. He had distributed copies of the libel against Madame de Maintenon. The remaining copies were hidden in a room in the convent of the Cordeliers, where one of the good Fathers had sometimes let him stay. Père Lefief was the man.

La Reynie received an order from the King addressed to the Father Superior of the convent requesting permission for the police to enter and seize the books. The books were found exactly where Chavance had said they would be. They were delivered to the police and destroyed.

The lawyer Antoine Bruneau entered the circumstances of the reprieve in his private journal:

"*Chavance eût la question et jasa, accusant les moines. La potence fût plantée à la Grève, et la charrette menée au Châtelet. Survint un ordre de surseoir l'exécution, et au jugement de La Roque, fils d'un ministre de Vitré et de Rouen, qui a fait la préface de ces livres impudents. On dit que Chavance est parent ou allié du Père Lachaise, confesseur du Roi, qui a obtenu la surséance.*"

His source was hearsay; he had no way of proving that Père Lachaise had interceded for Chavance, and the impudent books for which La Roque was held responsible were not the same as the infamous libel against the King, for which Rambault and Larcher suffered.

If Chavance in his confession at any time mentioned the name of Monsieur the King's brother, the fact remained the secret of La Reynie. However, when La Reynie again saw Monsieur Robert, he remarked:

"Let us assume that we have at last exorcised the ghost of Monsieur Scarron. We need speak of him no more."

Chapter Thirty

THE JANUARY DAY had been dark and overcast. At noon a few flakes of snow had straggled downward from the heavy clouds and been trodden into the muddy slush which filled the streets of London. On the day of Queen Mary's funeral other such desultory and random flakes had fallen upon the gold and purple of her bier, as it made its journey to Westminster, and her people had stood with their feet in the freezing slush to watch it pass. Nicolas Larcher had stood with them. He had observed that many of them wept, and since it had not seemed to him the habit of the English to display emotion openly, he was the more impressed by these unforced and unconcealed tears. He had not wept, but he had felt the weight of public grief. She had died during Christmas week, and the festivities of the season had been extinguished, not by royal decree, but by a spontaneous and universal sorrow. William, they said, had been dealt a blow by her loss from which he would never recover. He was still in retirement. Business went on in the Houses

of Parliament and in the City, but the sense of gloom still overhung all activities, and weather continued clouded. It was the
year 1695.

This day called for candles at high noon in the shop where
Nicolas was employed. It was a fairly large establishment. There
were, besides himself, two other journeymen, and half a dozen
apprentices of varying ages, and the master, an Englishman,
who had received the young Frenchman on the word of a friend.
Since he had left Rouen, he had progressed along a well-
established way, maintained by members of the Reformed Religion, accepted as if he had been one of them, all because of
that first introduction at Rouen. There were no other Frenchmen in the shop, although there were in the city of London,
by common estimate, some sixty thousand refugees from France.
He had not lacked acquaintances among his compatriots. He
had found lodging with an old émigré from Nantes, a Monsieur
Bouquet, who gave him lessons in the English language and advised him on English ways. Monsieur Bouquet was a clockmaker employed in Charing Cross Road, and when his day's
work was over, before returning home, he sometimes met Nicolas at a coffeehouse near St. Paul's. Nicolas had arranged to meet
him that evening.

He had not learned much that was new to him about his
craft since coming to London. On the contrary, he had found
himself more skilled than most of his English companions. His
English master had been glad to have him, recognizing promptly
the well-trained artisan. Most of the repair work on old volumes
was given to the young Frenchman, and while the apprentices
briskly folded sheets of new publications, Nicolas in his corner
dismembered and rebuilt old books such as his father had repaired. As far as the craft was concerned, he sometimes thought,
he might as well have been at home, but there was a difference
elsewhere. He had been handed that afternoon quite casually a
book to be rebound, and before he left for his rendezvous with

Monsieur Bouquet he opened the book and read once more the title page. It was for him an experience to be savored.

"The History of the Sabbath, by Pet. Heylan, London, Printed by Henry Seile, and are to bee solde at the Sign of the Tyger's-Head in Saint-Paul's churchyard, 1636."

Nicolas smiled, and the smile was not for the fact that the Tyger's-Head still flourished, after nearly sixty years, and that he would pass the sign that evening on his way to meet his friend. It was because this *History of the Sabbath* expounded the altogether heretical idea of a small religious group which rejected the first day of the week as a day of Christian worship, and returned to the Judaic custom and the command of Moses, in remembering the seventh day to keep it holy. He had leafed through the book and found the arguments reasonable except that they ignored the instructions of Saint Paul. But the mere fact that he held such a book in his hand without fear, that its presence in the shop caused no alarm, that its existence indicated the existence of a sect which—although it was probably not large, nor widely approved of—was not persecuted, all this struck him as amazing. It represented the whole reason for his coming to England and for his remaining there.

He was not always happy. He did not like the food or the climate, and he was often lonely. He earned no more than he could have earned in France, and was sometimes paid in clipped coins, although that was not the fault of his master, but of the abused currency. Nevertheless, he had found the freedom he had longed for, and for that, he told himself, he could put up for a few more months with the puddings and the wet.

His friend Bouquet had told him that a kind of censorship of the press did exist in England. It went by the name of the Licensing Law, and concerned itself chiefly with methods of doing business. It was considered an irritation rather than a menace. It meant, among other things, that the Port of London continued to be the only port of entry for books printed abroad, that it was a penal offense on the part of a customs officer to open a box of books for inspection without the presence of one of the censors of the press. "And how," inquired Monsieur Bouquet, "can the poor fellows know in advance what the box will contain, since a description of the contents is never marked on the box!" The censors, moreover, were dilatory in the performance of their duties. Valuable shipments of books remained in the sheds until the pages mildewed.

His friend the clockmaker had further enlightened him. The Licensing Act permitted the search of private premises under a general warrant, and this practice the old refugee considered far more serious than the mere loss of merchandise through mildewing.

"Your father's shop was searched, was it not?"

Nicolas assented.

"And without warrant, I imagine."

Nicolas laughed. "Surely no one would ask the police to show a warrant."

"Exactly," said the old refugee. "The police have the right of search. Or they have an order from the King. There is no individual security or privacy. Here in England the Licensing Act could become almost as vicious. Fortunately, under William no Englishman has thought to use it viciously. Now I will tell you something. In the Commons there are enough men of good sense to have voted this Licensing Act into oblivion at the last session. It's a pity they don't foresee what it might lead to. At the moment, it's no menace. It would be well to kill it while it sleeps."

Another day he remarked over the table in the coffeehouse:

"The House of Lords, it seems, wishes to revive the horrible Licensing Act over the mandate of the Commons. There will be a quarrel, mark my words. You and I," he said genially, including the young man in his own wisdom, "know what it means to live where free thought is throttled in the cradle."

"It's true, I felt smothered," said Nicolas diffidently.

"Exactly. It's not necessary to be Huguenot to have experienced this sensation of being smothered. I have a scientific curiosity about this world, and my curiosity was being, as you say, smothered in France. France, *mère des arts*—ah, yes. But it's in England now, in Holland, in Switzerland, that the light of science burns the clearest." He sighed. "I love my country. I would rejoice to see it again. But I could not live there without dying."

He was a small man, very lean and dark, with a pointed nose, and an undershot jaw which made his lower lip project a little. His left eye, in which he held the jeweler's glass, was by nature myopic, and he had a way of half closing it, of screwing up the muscles about it as if to hold the glass, even when he was not at work. This trick of half closing the eye, and the slight projection of the lower lip as he smiled, never showing his teeth, which were greatly decayed, gave his face an expression of complacent malice. But he was not malicious, merely shrewd. He smiled at Nicolas. His eye, his right eye, was sad.

His nostalgia touched a similar nostalgia in the young man, of which he was in fact never quite free.

When Nicolas thought of France it was almost always first with a remembrance of Rouen, of his arrival there by coach in the falling dusk, and of the gorse glowing and golden in all the uncultivated stretches of the dark land. Then came a remembrance of his last sight of France, a starlit departure before dawn, a sunrise on the open sea, the coast of France a mere greenish, greyish line on the edge of a heaving horizon. The passage had been choppy, and he had been sick. He had made in Rouen his first great friendship, but he had had no news of Jean Dumesnil since he had left Rouen, nor any news of Paris save what he found in the journals from Holland.

He seized with avidity, when he first came to London, upon a publication edited by a Huguenot gentleman with, presumably, "all the refinements of the continent," but he was sadly disappointed, for it expired in November that same year. For news he learned to wait for the packet from Holland, which brought monthly to London *Le Mercure Historique et Politique*. From this small journal, smaller than the palm of his hand, he learned a number of things which justified his suspicion that in France an honest man could know little of the actual state of France or of the progress of the war, unless, of course, he was willing or fortunate enough to read the forbidden foreign publications.

These publications were for rent for a small sum at the coffeehouse where he met Monsieur Bouquet, and once he had discovered the existence of the *Mercure de Hollande*, he called for back numbers and spent much time going over the events of the past year in a new perspective.

He read of the famine in France, so much more widespread than he had realized; of riots in Toulouse and in Brittany. He read with astonishment that the King had not campaigned that spring because it was feared that an attempt might be made on his life if he were to leave the safety of the court. He read the news from Rome and from Italy, the news from Turkey and Germany, the news from Poland and the North, the news from Spain, the news from France, the news from Cologne, from Liége, from the Low Countries, and from Holland; and he read the comments and reflections of the editors upon the news from each of these areas. He tried to take these reflections with a little salt, but on the whole they seemed so reasonable, and the writers so well informed, that he placed greater and greater confidence in them. He learned, in short, many things perfectly well known to Monsieur de La Reynie, to the King, and to the Ballad Singer of the Pont Neuf. He began to feel himself an educated man at last.

When the wind was from the west and the packet from Holland was delayed, he felt deprived, and his sense of anticipation mounted day by day. The packet had been delayed this month. He hoped that he would find that evening not only his friend the clockmaker, but the *Mercure* from the Hague.

He put aside the *History of the Sabbath* to be taken care of in the morning. He shrugged his shoulders into his warm coat, bought from a seller of used garments in Cheapside, said good

night to the boys who were sweeping the shop, and stepped out-
doors into the London slush. The falling snow had given way
to a black thick fog. He made his way toward Ludgate without
star or compass.

The old man from Nantes was watching for him as he entered
the coffeehouse, a young man with a face glowing from the
damp winter air, well built, well clothed, and with a carriage of
the head that was all confidence and health.

The old Frenchman had reserved a place beside him for his
compatriot. As the young man threaded his way between the
tables, the old man felt a pardonable national pride.

The air was full of smoke from the long pipes, and smelled of
damp English woolens, and of coffee. Nicolas had learned to
like coffee. The clockmaker handed him a brochure two and a
half inches by six inches which managed to contain the whole
of Europe and news from the West Indies into the bargain.

"I've read it," said Monsieur Bouquet. "You may have it to
yourself with a clear conscience."

He smiled benignly upon the young man's pleasure. Then he
made a motion as if to withdraw the gazette, or to delay the
reading of it. But Nicolas had placed it flat on the table before
him and framed it with his hands. He read beneath the title the
promise:

"*Contenant l'Etat présent de l'europe, ce qui se passe dans
toutes les cours, l'intérêt des princes, leurs brigues, et générale-
ment tout ce qu'il y a de curieux pour le Mois de Décembre
1694.*" Below the enlaced monogram: "*A La Haye.*" And below
that, in modest type, "*Chez Henri Van Bulderen, Marchand
Libraire, dans le Pooten, á l'Enseigne de Mézeray. M DC XCIV.
Avec privilège des Etats de Holl. et Westf.*"

"This excellent Henri Van Bulderen," said Nicolas, "I owe
him much. It would be a pleasure to work for him."

"That raises a question," said Monsieur Bouquet. "I've sometimes wondered why you chose England for your exile rather
than Holland."

"Am I in exile?" said Nicolas, and then answered his own question. "I suppose I am, for the time being. It was pure chance. I had meant to go to Holland. My father sent me to a correspondent of his in Rouen." He remembered caution, but seeing about him only familiar friendly faces, went on to tell of his adventure and, in the telling of it, felt himself once more in the bistro on the waterfront.

He heard the voice of Jean Dumesnil saying, "This man has a wife who has a way of cooking sole such as you never tasted," and the fisherman at his elbow took the cue, inquiring cordially, "You like sole cooked with little clams, with mushrooms and white wine, a little thyme, a little parsley? Come to my house for supper. Until you've tasted my wife's sole normande, you have not lived." The owner of the bistro, refilling Dumesnil's glass of apple brandy, had smiled and said nothing. So it had all been arranged by Dumesnil, the finances, the introductions, the assurances. The fisherman had not only a wife who was a marvel in the kitchen; he had also a sturdy ketch which made the channel crossing in safety if not in perfect comfort.

Nicolas suspected that Mademoiselle Cailloué knew of Dumesnil's activities. She gave him a curious smile in parting. He was sure that her mother did not know of them. He thought of all three of them tonight with profound gratitude. They had lodged him in a room overlooking a small enclosed garden. They had treated him like a son. The old woman had given him claret to drink in which red rose petals had been steeped. She had said, smiling, that it was for his health, but it had seemed a gesture of Roman hospitality. He had thought her strangely beautiful with her emaciated old face and her dark eyes. The daughter was beautiful also; Dumesnil was in love with her.

"I don't know why they were so kind to me," he concluded. "They had never met my father."

"So your father sent you to them," said Monsieur Bouquet.

"And upon an impulse, having talked with Dumesnil, you came to England."

"Upon an impulse," Nicolas agreed.

"Your father, knowing you, doubtless foresaw the impulse."

"That I would come to England?"

The clockmaker nodded.

"Never in the world," said Nicolas. "He didn't wish me to leave Paris."

"If I had a son," said the old man, "as, alas, I have not, I should have sent him to England, if by chance I couldn't have gone with him."

"Ah, but you're different. You're of the Religion and you think of the King as an enemy."

"And your father? Is he perfectly satisfied with the King and all his works?"

"Catholic to the core, and the King's man through and through," said Nicolas with conviction; and then: "He doesn't understand me at all. He merely loves me."

Monsieur Bouquet permitted himself a smile of mingled amusement and relief.

"Well, that's always something, after all," he remarked. "I'm glad to know your father is content with Louis the Great. There's some news in the *Mercure* which will interest you particularly, news of your fellow artisans in Paris."

He took the *Mercure* from Nicolas and turned the pages past the news of half the world to the news of France, and gave it back, opened, to the young man.

"There," he said, "read it without alarm, and be thankful you're in London."

"It was about three months ago," the article began, "that the authorities in Paris arrested five artisans, printers, book sellers, bookbinders, because of certain libels which they had either distributed or caused to be distributed. On the eighteenth of the past month two of these were condemned to the galleys and two condemned to be hanged. The last two, having been subjected to torture, accused several others who were promptly arrested; these and the others were convicted of having printed or distributed seditious and scandalous satires against the government and even against the King's own person. Monsieur de Reynie, Lieutenant de Police, was commissioned by a decree of Conseil d'Etat to be judge of last resort in this case with several councilors from the Châtelet; so that the Court of Paris was excluded from any knowledge of the case through appeal, according to the usual course of jurisdiction. Someone is arrested every day in Paris. The twenty-fifth of this same month they arrested Monsieur Larroque, son of Larroque who was a minister in Rouen, and who is so well known for his writings."

Nicolas read it through, once in great haste, and then again very slowly, and then said gravely:

"You were afraid that my father might be one of these men."

Monsieur Bouquet assented silently.

"I assure you, there's no man in Paris less likely to be involved in such business."

"I felicitate you. That is to say, I felicitate you on that point."

"I understand," said Nicolas. "But in spite of the fact that my father and I don't agree on all subjects, I look forward to going home. He expected me home at least three months ago. But I've delayed. I like being here."

"And your mother, is she alive?"

"Very much," said the boy with a smile.

"Tell me about her."

"She's like most mothers, I suppose."

"Stood with you against your father in any argument," said the old clockmaker, "and then privately scolded you for getting into the argument."

"How did you know?" said Nicolas. Then, embarrassed but determined to be honest with himself, he said, "I miss her. I miss them both. As I didn't expect to."

The old man surveyed him shrewdly.

"You are still young, perhaps, to found a family in these hard times, too young; although, missing your family, that's what you should do. Found a family. We must find some feminine companionship for you of the right age."

Nicolas blushed under his scrutiny. He said doggedly:

"I should go home. I know it."

"That's easier said than done."

"And why?"

"Because, though you found many who were willing to help you come here, you will have difficulty in finding anyone who will help you return to France. While the war lasts, you are better off where you are, and your friends know it."

"I have money," said Nicolas.

"It needs more than money. When Louis and William can come to an agreement, you can go home."

Chapter Thirty-one

IT WAS TWO LONG YEARS, almost three years, before Louis and William reached an accord. In May of 1697 the plenipotentiaries of the Allies and of France met in the château of Ryswick, and began their discussions.

There were endless details to be ruled upon before the talks for peace could begin. Charles the Eleventh of Sweden was dead in April of that year, and all the world knew it, but it was the middle of June before the Swedish moderator, having put his retinue, his carriages, his horses and all into black trappings, felt able to announce formally to the assemblage the death of his sovereign. Upon that, the discussions were further postponed until the representatives of the Allied Powers and of France could order suitable mourning for themselves and their retinues.

By late June nothing had been accomplished beyond the expenditure of much time and money in elaborate ceremonials.

But in the very last days of June, My Lord of Portland and the Maréschal de Boufflers met as old friends in an orchard near the town of Hal, not far from Brussels, and in the course of five conversations between the fruit trees and the parsley beds they worked out the essentials of an accord between France and England. In September the plenipotentiaries at Ryswick incorporated the substance of these conversations in a treaty, and peace was at last declared.

After the news of the treaty had been announced i.. Paris, Marianne Larcher, for the first time since her flight, r.. ..rned to the quarter where she had so long lived and worked. She came at dusk through a fine drizzle, to call upon Jacques Têtu.

She did not recognize the woman who opened the door, nor did the woman seem to recognize Marianne. She explained that there was a lady with the abbé; when the lady left, she would announce Marianne, and she had no doubt but that the abbé would find a moment for her.

"He's kind, the poor man, like no one in this world."

"I know," said Marianne humbly.

"Come in from the wet," said the housekeeper. "You can sit there."

Marianne took the chair indicated, and the housekeeper went about her business. She was an old woman with a broad face. She must at one time have suffered a light stroke, for the left corner of her mouth sagged a little, and a thin trickle of saliva ran from it constantly, which she wiped away from time to time with the hem of her apron. Marianne wondered if she could be the same woman who had once before ushered her into the abbé's presence, and who had told her on that disastrous November day almost three years ago that she could not see the abbé, that he had gone on a journey. She did not think she could have forgotten a face so completely, yet it was possible. She had each time come in such distress that she had no thought of anyone else. She did not ask, "Have you been long with the abbé?" She was content not to be recognized.

There were three small children in the kitchen, all girls, who divided their attention between the old woman and the stranger.

The old woman took three eggs from a pan of hot water on the hearth, and broke them one by one into a bowl. Then she tore a piece of bread in pieces and mixed it with the egg. She took a spoon in one hand, the bowl in the other, and sat down upon a stool near the hearth. The three children crowded about her knees, and the youngest, clad only in a smock which left bare to the firelight her little round buttocks and short fat legs, leaned her elbows on the old woman's lap and tipped back her head. She smiled with half-closed eyes and closed lips, altogether innocent in a pose of pure seduction. The chestnut curls fell back from the round smooth brow, the light flickered on the point of the lifted chin and on the round neck with the circlets of Venus creasing the infantine flesh. The old woman filled the spoon with bread and egg and thrust it into the mouth of the eldest child, and then, refilled, into the mouth of the next. The youngest opened her mouth and waited, her eyes still half closed. Before the fire a small spitted fowl turned slowly, with a counterweight; and on the hearth a row of apples set to roast. The skin of an apple burst with a hiss of hot juice. The fowl dripped into the pan set beneath it.

"These are my daughter's children," said the old woman. "She works elsewhere now. She's femme de chambre chez les Pomponne. There's more money that way. And more work here for me. After all, I'm only one woman."

That was it, thought Marianne. The woman who would recognize her was with the Pomponnes. The old woman went the rounds again with her spoon and paused, waiting for the children to empty their mouths. She said:

"So the King has made an end to his war. And about time. Can you observe that life is more gay since the peace? Not I. It comes too late."

When the bowl was empty she set it on the floor and began to undress the children, spinning them this way and that. A flare of torches passed the window. The housekeeper went to the door and looked out, the corner of her apron at her mouth.

"The linkboys with the lady's chair. She'll be leaving now. I'll announce you. Wait with the children, and don't let them touch the apples. Those are for Monsieur l'abbé."

Life had changed but little for Jacques Têtu during the last three years. He was, if anything, in better health, although he did not know the reason for it. He had suffered a great loss in the death of Madame de Sévigné. The companionship of Madame de Coulanges had been restored to him by the absence of the Italian doctor. They consoled each other for the loss of the incomparable Marquise as best they might by speaking of her often. He made his retreats with Monsieur de la Trappe. He worked at his verses. He "received" a great deal. His little salon was still fragrant from the presence of his last visitor when his housekeeper entered. There was a fire; the candles were lighted, curtains drawn against the inclement evening. On a table stood a silver tray with a carafe in crystal and two tall fragile glasses. The housekeeper looked about the room and asked if the abbé had need of anything before she mentioned the woman who was waiting in her kitchen. She said that his dinner would be ready in another thirty minutes. Then she said:

"There is a Veuve Larcher who asks a moment with you. When she told me her name I said to myself, 'Can it be the woman whose husband was hanged three years ago, just as the cold weather began that fall?' I told her I thought you would see her."

"Three years!" said the abbé. "Is it three years since then! Yes, I will see her." And when the housekeeper had gone, he said again to himself. "Three years. I never wrote my letter. She has come to reproach me." He tried to remember why he had not kept his promise; there had been some assurance that Larcher, if innocent, would receive justice. If he had been hanged, they must have found him guilty. "Nevertheless," he said to himself, "I should have done something. I should have asked for a mitigation of the penalty. But now I remember. I was at La Trappe when it took place. I didn't know about it until too late."

The explanation was not enough to clear him of reproach in his own mind. The charm of his evening had vanished. He put his hand to his face, feeling a warning of the tic, and when Marianne appeared he did not rise to greet her, but remained huddled in his chair. Her first thought was that he was not well, and then that he was not pleased to see her. She made the speech which she had prepared.

"Monsieur l'abbé, I have brought you back the money which you so kindly lent me."

She held out the coin, and since he made no motion to accept it, she laid it on the table beside the silver tray and, stepping back, folded her hands beneath her apron. The abbé waited to be reproached. She was not shabbily dressed, nor was she in mourning. He wondered if she had married again.

"I came to speak of my son," she said.

He frowned in an effort to remember.

"The young man who bound my book?" he asked.

"That was my husband's assistant. My son has been traveling. I don't know where he is, but now that peace is declared I think that he may come back to Paris."

"He has been abroad?" said the abbé.

"I don't know. I only think that he may come home very soon. If he comes to see you, Monsieur l'abbé, will you give him a message?"

"Why should he come to see me?" said the abbé.

She bowed her head at that, as if the question were too difficult to answer, and then, looking at him almost with a smile, she answered:

"For the same reason that I have come to you now. Monsieur l'abbé is known for his goodness."

The abbé dropped his hand from his face. "The message?" he said.

"That Paul Damas, who was his father's assistant, is working for Villery at the Sign of the Star, rue de la Vieille Bouclerie."

Out of gratitude that she had not mentioned the letter, the abbé reached for pen and paper and at once made a note. He would not fail her in this. Besides, it was useful to know where to find a good workman.

Marianne took her way across the islands toward the quarter on the left bank where she lived with Paul in one room no larger nor more light than the room in the rue des Deux Boules. They rented the privilege of cooking their meals in a kitchen in another building.

They had come back to Paris when the money ran low. Work in the provinces had been hard to find. Paul had been so ridden by the fear that the police still searched for him that he had never mustered courage to buy his master's papers and set up his own shop. The shop would have been foredoomed to failure in all events because of the hard times. He had never been able to persuade Marianne that they should leave France. She thought of difficulties, of danger. Who would help them across the border? What would they do in a country where they could not speak the language? The money would not last forever. The truth was that she could not give up every hope of seeing Nicolas again, and she could not hope to see him unless in Paris.

Word came to them that the police had closed the case. Two men hanged, two men sentenced to the galleys, something had been done about the insult to the King. Even the fear that Jean might have informed upon them at the last moment of his life grew so small that it was of no importance. After he had worked in the rue de la Vieille Bouclerie for a few months, Paul felt as secure as he had ever felt in his life. There were things which he did not care to remember, certainly.

Between Ile Notre Dame and the Ile de la Cité there was a footbridge which led to the cloisters behind the cathedral. It had been destroyed many times by the floods, and many times rebuilt, always of wood. On this bridge, midway between the quarter in which she had lived as Larcher's wife and the quarter in which she now lived, Marianne stopped to collect her thoughts. The light drizzle touched her face, and her hands, as she rested them on the wooden rail; she looked down upon the moving water. The rain was so fine that it did not mark the surface of the water. The currents which flowed beneath did not ruffle it either, but where they met, after their division by the Ile Notre Dame, the surface seemed to have a double texture, like certain kinds of doubly woven silk.

From this bridge during the years of the famine and the war a great many people had thrown themselves into the water. The deep current had carried them past the Ile de la Cité, under the Pont Neuf, past the Louvre to where the river curved at Chaillot, and there upon the beach of Chaillot had unburdened itself of their bodies, and gone on. The police had collected the dead and had disposed of them. Suicide was a great sin. Marianne had seen the body of a suicide bound to a hurdle and dragged behind a horse's hooves through the streets of the city as an example and a warning. The bodies found at Chaillot, however, were not treated as suicides. The drownings were considered accidents, and the corpses were disposed of quietly like any other refuse of the city. The water was a temptation, the temptation of oblivion, but, remembering the body on the hurdle, she shuddered, and became aware again of the rain on her face, and of the wet wood beneath her fingers. She was not yet ready for death. She had first to make her peace with life.

She had not married Paul. A sacrament required confession, and she had never made her confession. She loved Paul still, but with a bitterness which she could not have believed possible; the bitterness should have destroyed the love, or the love destroyed the bitterness, but they existed together. Paul had felt the bitterness, she knew. He had left her sometimes for other women; she had not needed to be told where he went; and he had always returned. He was bound to her as finally as she was bound to him, not only by their passion, but by their mutual knowledge of their guilt. If Paul were dead, she thought, she could make her confession; she might be able to repent. But what kind of repentance would that be in the eyes of God? A remission of sins, and a hope of heaven, however distant, after the long pains of purgatory? God would never let Himself be cheated so, when she had done what she wished to do, when she had surrendered only when the surrender had no price.

Very long ago, between the wars, when people traveled freely about the continent of Europe, a strange German priest had come to the shop in the rue des Lions. He had belonged to no order that she knew. He had come without introduction, happening to see the books in the window, as the abbé had seen Paul's *Phèdre*. She could not remember what he wished to buy, but when she had sold him what he asked for, he took up a missal which was lying on the table, and had leafed through it, and laid it down with the remark that the doctrine of indulgence was all very well for a few peccadilloes, but for true sin, sin that blackened the soul, there was for cleansing only the sacrificial atonement. Without the shedding of blood, he said, in the words of Saint Paul, there can be no remission of sins. He had drawn from his robe his own battered copy of the Holy Scriptures, and had shown her the words, incontrovertible. He had shown her other passages besides. She had replied that she had been taught that the blood of Christ had been shed for all sinners, and he had answered with scorn that Saint Paul advised men to atone for their own sins. He was heretical, she was sure of that. She had made an effort to forget him, but now she could hear his voice, with its heavy accent, and see plainly through the dusk his face, coarse-featured, badly shaven, with pale blue eyes lit by a conviction that was frightening. He had spoken of flagellations, of sacrificial deaths. He had reminded her of the martyrdoms. Then he had gone his way. She wished that she had not remembered him.

Chapter Thirty-two

*T*HE FRENCH COAST appeared toward evening as the clouds lifted. It appeared with the colors of a pearl, pinkish, white, faintly green and flecked with pale gold, as if all the colors might be the effect of the late sunlight. It was the Norman coast above Le Havre, and the pink, Nicolas knew, was the cliffs. The sight moved him beyond his expectations.

"You can go back to France," said the old clockmaker, "but you won't like it." That was on the night when London celebrated the news of the peace with bonfires and uproarious gatherings in the alehouses and in the streets. Later, in the coffeehouse near St.-Paul's Churchyard, Nicolas had met Monsieur Bouquet, and the question of his returning to Paris came up once more in their conversation.

"You have become accustomed to another climate," said Monsieur Bouquet, "and I do not speak of the English rains and fogs. You have acquired new habits of speech, and again, I do not speak of your careful English. No, you say what is in your

mind without first looking over your shoulder. You read what
you like. We saw what happened when the old Licensing Act
expired, unwept. Within a month, nay less, within ten days,
newspapers of all sorts and sizes appeared as quickly as weeds
after a rain."

"I still miss my family."

"As I have told you, found a family."

Nicolas colored, and shook his head. The old man screwed up
his eye, clenching the invisible glass, and smiled his tight-lipped
smile, malign and friendly.

"Go then, but wait until spring. The crossing will be more
pleasant. You may even, by then, contrive to go with an em-
bassy, and so remain under the protection of the British, not a
small advantage in your case. There will be gentlemen going
abroad. We shall have no more traffic through St.-Germain and
the Romney Marshes, but there will be men of learning wishing
to travel, as well as representatives of King William. There
exists a great curiosity in England to learn what has been accomplished in France in the sciences during the last seven years. I
am possessed by a great curiosity myself. Not all our compatriots have been employed with cannons and petards."

"Come with me," said Nicolas, teasing.

"Ah, if I could manage it—to travel as an Englishman and visit
the laboratories of Paris! What a temptation! But I have responsibilities here, my daughter and my daughter's children . . .
Even so——" He broke off and a light came into his eyes, flicker-
ing about his face like summer lightning, before he turned, smiling with transparent guile upon his young friend. "Wait a few
months, and I'll go with you."

Of course he had not meant it. He had burned his bridges long
ago, and all that he wished to know of the new theories of the
motions of the stars would have to reach him through the news
letters of the learned societies. However, for a few hours, Nicolas had been persuaded to wait until spring. Then with no
warning, a few days after the great celebration, Monsieur

Bouquet had contracted a cold which became a fever, and within the week he was dead.

His death had stricken Nicolas like a warning. If death could seize his friend so suddenly it could also seize upon his father or his mother. Panic invaded him. He was suddenly afraid that his father might die before he could see him again. He had not kept his promise to his father; he would be punished.

He went directly to his master and asked for his release. There were a few delays in London, and again at the coast, where he waited for the same fisherman who had brought him to England. But before the end of October he saw from the same ketch in which he had left Le Havre the shores of France. It was a great reassurance. What he remembered still existed.

At Rouen he inquired for his friends. He learned without surprise, although with regret, that La Veuve Cailloué was dead. She had been failing when he met her. The host of the bistro on the waterfront leaned his thick bare arms on the table and said with a curious expression:

"As for the daughter, she's in the Convent of the New Catholics." He made no comment, and his expression did not encourage inquiry. "Jean Dumesnil runs the shop, together with his brother Jacques."

"I'd like to see Jean."

"That you can't do unless you stay in Rouen for some weeks, for he's traveling." He straightened and turned his back on Nicolas.

The warnings of Monsieur Bouquet rang in his head, nevertheless, "Tell him I inquired for him," the young man said, and left a coin by his glass.

As the coach brought him closer to Paris on the day following, he thought more about his parents, and speculated less on the friends in Rouen. He was delighted to recognize certain turns in the road, certain clumps of trees. The country pleased him with its tawny woods, its freshly harrowed fields, its rushy ponds under the soft grey sky. The air seemed lighter to breathe than the air of England. He remembered all sorts of little things about the shop and the Quartier St.-Paul, of which he had not thought in several years. He remembered Paul Damas, whose image as a friend had been quite obscured by the more profound friendship of Jean Dumesnil. He wondered if Damas was still working for his father. He had spoken more freely with Paul than with anyone else in Paris, but there had been a skepticism, a lack of conviction in Paul, which had put him off before any real devotion between them had had time to develop. Still, he thought, Paul was not a bad fellow. He hoped that he would find him in the shop.

As for the change of climate of which Monsieur Bouquet had warned him, he did not think he would find it difficult to live with now that he had been away, and that he had established his own stature within himself. He would be able to agree now with his father that there were dangerous heresies in the work of Pascal. He had with him some of the new English coins. He thought his father would be interested as well as pleased to see them, and the thought held no shade of rancor against his father's love of money. Money was a good thing and hard to get. He had no gift for his mother, but he would take her to a good shop in the Palais and buy her what touched her fancy. He stepped from the coach into the courtyard of Le Cerf, and then into the rue St.-Denis with his portmanteau on his shoulder, exhilarated by the sight and sound and smell of Paris. It was good to hear his own language spoken all about him, good not to need to ask his way, and the smells of Paris, varying street by street, were perfume to his nostrils. The day was Sunday. The bells were ringing for vespers all over the city. There were more bells than in London. The rue St.-Denis, dirty as it had ever been, was as nothing to the filth of the streets of London. He set off for the rue des Lions, and as he went he observed as never before the beauty of the doorways of the great hôtels, the walls of grey stone, the spires which rose everywhere.

The rue des Lions was unchanged. The windows of the shop

were closed, but the big doorway to the court stood open, and above it the carved head of a child with hair spreading from it like the rays of the sun looked down from the lintel, smiling. He stepped into the tunnel, and pounded on the door of the shop with his bare knuckles. No sound came from behind the door. But this was Sunday. His parents were upstairs, or at the Harrow. He rapped again for luck, and as he waited a boy of ten or eleven years emerged from the stables, dragging a broom. He looked with curiosity at the young man with the portmanteau still balanced on his shoulder, and volunteered the information:

"Those folks've gone to the country."

"When will they be back?"

"They didn't say. Likely by nightfall."

Nicolas stood irresolute. He did not know the boy, nor like the looks of him very much. The face was slack, the eyes unsteady.

"I'll come back later," he said.

"Keep your trunk for you?" said the boy.

"No, thanks."

"Give 'em a message?"

Nicolas shook his head. He had no intention of spoiling his surprise. He set off for the Harrow, where he could wait in comfort, and where he could also get a bite to eat. He was famished. He reached the corner of the rue du Petit-Musc and of St.-Antoine, as it seemed to him, in two steps. Distances had become smaller since he had been away. But the sign hung just as he remembered it, and the wide door to the cellar, the stone ramp sloping down into darkness, the small courtyard were also unchanged. He entered the innroom confidently, dropped his portmanteau beside a table, and seated himself. The hostess gave him a casual glance as she took his order, and then a second glance, puzzled and unbelieving. He waited to be recognized.

The host himself brought the pasty, steaming hot, and the carafe of wine. His wife was close behind him. He arranged the

food before Nicolas, deliberate and careful, before he stepped
back and declared to his wife, as much as to Nicolas:

"I couldn't believe it, but it's true. It's the boy himself. You've
been gone a long time, my young friend."

"He's a man entirely," said his wife. "That's why I wasn't
sure."

There was a reserve in their manner, a certain lack of welcome, it seemed to him, which he did not understand. He
had not known these people very well. They had been the
owners of the Harrow, and as such they had made more of an
impression on him than he, as one of the small boys in the neighborhood, could have made on them. But he had expected more
from them. They had recognized him, however, and they continued to hover over him as if there were more to say than had
been said.

He explained. "My parents don't expect me. The shop is
closed. So with your permission I'll wait here till they come
home."

"You're welcome to wait as long as you like," said the host,
"but," and he turned to his wife with a very troubled look before he finished his question, "is it possible you don't know
what happened that winter after you left?"

They did their best, the host and his wife, to comfort Nicolas when they had told him the story. The wife poured him a
brandy, the man sat down beside Nicolas and put an arm across
the bowed shoulders, and declared that he had been his father's
friend and wished to be his. Neither one had any word of blame
for Larcher. His crime, for them, was not a crime but a misfor-
tune. The story of the theft, which had once run wild about
the Quartier, was quite forgotten. It had been discredited; it
was too improbable that Larcher had possessed so great a sum
of money to be robbed of. It had become merely one of those
rumors that spring up after any disaster.

Nicolas could not grasp the full extent of his loss. He insisted
that his mother could not have disappeared without leaving some

message for him. Surely at the building in the rue des Lions someone would be holding a message for him.

The hostess shook her head.

"We should have known it. The whole Quartier talked of nothing else for a month. It's my own opinion, although I don't like to say it, that the affair was too much for her." Nicolas lifted his head and looked her in the eyes. "Yes," she concluded in answer to that look, "the river. What else?"

But Nicolas was young. He would not accept it. He remembered Paul. What had become of his father's assistant?

"As we told you, he went back to his province before it all began. He could tell you no more than we do, even if I could remember the name of his village."

"And my father," said the boy. "He must have left a message for me."

"That's possible," said the host, welcoming this shred of consolation. "If you could find the priest who confessed him——"

"The Jesuit Fathers confess the prisoners of the Bastille," said his wife.

"But was Larcher in the Bastille?" said the man. "No matter. Inquire of the Jesuits, who confessed at the Châtelet that night."

Nicolas needed no urging. He was on his feet and out the door almost in the same moment.

"He frightens me, that boy," said the host. "It was too sudden. Imagine his not knowing! Well, we can keep his portmanteau for him till he comes back."

The distance to the Jesuits, straight down the rue St.-Antoine, was as nothing. Nicolas arrived breathless. In the cloisters behind the magnificent church he put his question and told his story, somewhat incoherently. The Fathers conferred quietly. Nicolas caught phrases. "Father Bourdaloue is conducting service. What of Father Broussemin? I don't know where he is at this hour. Did Father Broussemin confess for the Bastille in '94? But was the man a prisoner at the Bastille? Or at Vincennes? Or at the Châtelet?" Then: "We will have to inquire. Meanwhile, would it not be sensible to ask of Sanson? We can tell you where to find him."

"Who is Sanson?" asked Nicolas.

"The executioner."

Sanson was at dinner with his wife and children when Nicolas was announced. After one look at the face of the young man he said to his wife:

"Take the children away," and to Nicolas, "Sit down."

The room was more than comfortable, hung with tapestries, warm with firelight. The high-backed chairs were upholstered in red, with red fringes below the brass nailheads. The table was spread with a huge white damask cloth which reached to the floor and showed everywhere the neat rectangular creases in which it had been laid in press. Sanson himself was bluff and hearty in appearance, red-faced, with calm grey eyes. He did not look like a hangman. But there was a promptness in his conduct, a sureness in his commands, which left Nicolas with no doubt. This was the man he needed.

As the boy told his story, Sanson folded his large napkin deliberately, methodically, and placed it on the table beside his plate. He then folded his hands on his stomach and sat quite still for a while after Nicolas had ceased speaking, casting back through his memories to an event which for him had been silted over by a long series of events of greater moment. After a time he nodded his head, a squarish head, very heavy, the skull covered with grey hair, short and brushlike.

"I can't remember who confessed your father, but I remember your father well, and for a reason. When the priest had left him, and while I was preparing the rope, he took from his neck a scapular. I had remarked on the trip from the Châtelet, which was not long, but slow, because of the crowd, that he had his hand upon it, and that even when he spoke with the priest he seemed agitated, and filled with indecision. I said to myself, 'There's a guilty man who cannot bring himself to confess his sin, even in his extreme hour.'

"I don't think so badly of him now. All men are guilty, more or less. Many of them die for something other than their deepest guilt, but when your father died, guilty or not—and for me, you must understand, he was guilty or he would not have been condemned—when he died, he was thinking not of himself but of his son; he must have had a fund of goodness in him to have risked death without his scapular." He lifted a hand to forbid Nicolas to interrupt him.

"The scapular your father wore—it was his belief as it is mine; I wear one like it—could have assured him that his soul would not be lost eternally." He undid the top button of his shirt and reached his fingers inside to touch the precious thing he spoke of. "No one," he said with great earnestness, "no one asks to escape the pains of purgatory, but it is something to feel certain of ultimate salvation. Your father took this scapular from his neck, and gave it to me, and begged me to give it to his son if I should ever have the chance. For that, you see, he sticks in my mind. Well, I had thought you'd never come to claim it."

He pulled himself from his chair, throwing himself forward in a lurching movement, as if the weight of his great shoulders unbalanced him, and went beyond Nicolas to a bureau, which he unlocked. From an inner drawer he took a small packet wrapped in a single sheet of paper, which he unfolded; he lifted from it, dangling on the stained linen cord, the two small squares of brown cloth which Nicolas knew so well. Sanson placed the relic in the boy's trembling hands.

"You would do well to talk to a priest," he said.

In the street Nicolas stopped and kissed the scapular, the folded squares of wool embroidered with the name of the Mother of God. The street was empty. Dusk had thickened; the street lanterns had not yet been lighted. In this solitude, beneath the windows of the executioner, he might have wept in peace; but he was not ready for tears. He began to walk, because a man does not stand still indefinitely in a street. By habit, he moved toward his own neighborhood, reciting his Hail Mary as he went, holding the scapular as if it were a chaplet. Later he put it about his own neck and buttoned his shirt over it.

Sanson had counseled him to find a priest. He had been to the Jesuits, who had sent him to Sanson. He felt no inclination to return to them, nor any desire to enter the church where he had made the confessions of his childhood. He did not need to confess. He needed to be advised. Passing before St.-Paul, he remembered in a great flash of memory the abbé Têtu. He went to the old address, to which Paul's work for the abbé had been delivered, and was told that the abbé had moved. He returned to the rue Neuve St.-Paul and found the abbé's lodging. To his astonishment the abbé said, before the boy could open his mouth:

"I expected you."

Nicolas' first thought was that Sanson had warned the abbé of his coming, Sanson, who had advised him to visit a priest. Then the absurdity of such an idea struck him, but he still could not think who could have told the abbé that he was back in Paris. The abbé began very gently, seeing the distressed face:

"Your mother——"

The words seemed a shock to the young man, and the abbé waited, unwilling to proceed while it seemed quite possible that the young man would not understand what he was saying.

"They told me she was dead," said the young man. "She drowned herself."

The abbé was shocked.

"My poor young man," he said, "what a grief for you, what a sad welcome home! I am inexpressibly sorry. Had you come only a few weeks earlier, this might have been spared you. Only a few weeks ago——" He stopped, trying to remember the date of Marianne's visit, and could remember only that it had taken place well before the Feast of Saint Francis. "I am sure it was not more than four weeks ago," he said. "She came to me full of solicitude for you."

"She was alive four weeks ago?" said Nicolas.

"Alive and in this very room," said the abbé. "She is a good woman."

"But then they were wrong!" cried the boy. "They thought she drowned herself when my father was hanged."

The abbé shook his head sadly.

"A great pity, that affair," he said. "A great pity that your father should have been involved in such a business."

"My father was hanged for a crime which he did not commit," said Nicolas fiercely.

The abbé lifted his tufted, sandy eyebrows.

"You have proof?" he said.

"I know my father," said Nicolas. "Oh, I understand. He was tried, he was found guilty, otherwise he would not have been hanged. That's what Sanson told me. But I know that he wasn't guilty. He should be pitied for his death, but not for his crime."

The abbé was not prepared for such frank speech from the son of an artisan. From the boy's manner anyone would have judged that he was speaking to an equal. To his credit, he remembered that here was a boy whose world had fallen to pieces around him, and he checked the reprimand on his tongue. He remembered, too, that he had not written a letter.

"Your mother came to me with a message for you. I wrote it down. What can I have done with it?"

He turned his back on Nicolas and began to search through his desk. He could feel the tic pulling at his mouth. He tried, as always, to hold the muscles still, without success. He could not find the scrap of paper with the address of the bookbinder. He faced Nicolas again, his face distorted, and said:

"I remember this much. Your father's assistant, who bound the poems of Madame Deshoulières at my request, is working with a certain Villery, near the rue St.-Jacques."

"Villery?" said Nicolas. "But his partner, Moette, was put in the Bastille while I was still a prentice."

"Perhaps it's not the same Villery," suggested Têtu, very kindly.

"He was arrested for handling proscribed publications," said Nicolas. "He was sent to the galleys. I didn't know it then. I know it now."

"It's Villery you must look for," the abbé persisted. "Perhaps there is more than one Villery. Your friend works for him."

"I can find him," said Nicolas, and, without a word of either thanks or apology, ran from the room. The abbé had thought to say, "Come back when you have found your mother. Perhaps I can be of aid," but there was no time for it. He sighed, and turned again to his desk. He was sorry that he had not been able to lay his hand on the address.

The years in England, the climate of which Monsieur Bouquet had spoken, had done their work with Nicolas. There was no resignation in him for his father's death. There was fury that his father should have died maligned. He must find his mother. She would be able to tell him what had really happened. He made a great resolve to clear his father's name. But first he must find Damas. He knew the Sign of the Star in the rue de la Vieille Bouclerie. It might be the right shop, or it might not. There had once been a Villery on the Quai des Augustins, he thought. In either case, he must cross the islands. He arrived almost on the run at the Quai from which the rue de Vieille Bouclerie opened. He could see the Pont Neuf, the lights upon it and the reflections of the lights in the river. The rue de la Vieille Bouclerie was dark, all the windows shuttered, all the shops closed. He found the Sign of the Star, and pounded on the door. There was no answer. He pounded again, violently. He could not let himself be balked by a mere closed door.

He struck again and again with his knuckles; then he took off a shoe and pounded with the heel. He shouted. A window overhead on the opposite side of the street was pushed open by an exasperated neighbor, but before the neighbor spoke, Nicolas, with his head against the door, heard a stirring within the Star, ceased his pounding, and put on his shoe. The door was opened by an apprentice. Nicolas explained that he must see the master of the shop; his errand was urgent.

He followed the apprentice through the shop, past tables piled with books, covered with sheets to protect them from the dust and damp over Sunday, into a living room behind the shop where a small company sat at cards. There were an elderly woman, a young woman, and several men. He addressed himself to the oldest man. His tremendous need made him abrupt. He said:

"Where is Paul Damas?"

The man smiled just a trifle.

"Is it for that you make a noise to wake the dead?"

"Where is he?" demanded Nicolas.

"How should I know?"

"I must find him."

"Come in the morning," said the man.

"He works here?"

"But not on a Sunday evening." The man motioned to the apprentice. "Show this madman out."

Nicolas refused to move.

"I must find him tonight. He knows where my mother lives. Where does he lodge? It's a matter"— he drew a deep breath and spoke what was to him the simple truth—" a matter of life and death."

The women at the table began to take an interest in him. A drama was unfolding. The older man, whom Nicolas took to be Villery, looked regretfully down at his cards, laid them face down on the table, and folded his hands on top of them.

"It's not my affair where Damas lodges," he said, "nor do I know the whereabouts of your mother, whoever she is."

"She's the Widow Larcher," said Nicolas. The words as he pronounced them chilled his heart, but they brought no response from Villery. The young woman, however, spoke up.

"You know her. She lives with Damas."

"He didn't ask for the wife of Damas."

"It's the same—I guess."

"No," said Nicolas, going white with anger. "It's not the same."

"But yes, but yes."

"Impossible," said the boy.

"What's impossible?" said the young woman lazily. "That your mother should marry again? You called her a widow, didn't you? What ails you? Can't you keep up with your mother?"

"I haven't seen her in three years," said Nicolas. He looked at the expectant faces; some of them waited to be amused. He pulled himself together, and said with courtesy and pleading: "All I ask is that you tell me where I can find Damas tonight."

"Perhaps she's not his mother," said the older woman tartly. "Is it our affair?" To Nicolas she said: "Do you know the Quartier? Come here. I'll show you where he lives." She drew with her finger on the table. "Here is the rue de Seine, the rue Dauphine. Here is a side street. Here is the house. On the top floor, he lodges. And don't break your neck in getting there. If he's in bed, he'll wait for you. If he's not at home, you'll find him here in the morning."

Nicolas thanked her. He apologized for his intrusion, and turned to leave. Villery sighed, picked up his cards, and made the play which he had contemplated.

Nicolas went back to the river, and from there up the rue Dauphine. He was as horrified at the thought that his mother might have married Damas as he had been at the thought of her death. The one had not been true; the other could as well prove to be a lie; a lie to torment him because he had interrupted a game of cards. The sooner he found his mother, the sooner he would have the truth, and from her own lips. But the lie was full of poison. If his mother had in fact married Damas, he wished never to see her again. She would no longer be his mother.

It was fortunate that he knew the quarter well. He found the house that had been described to him. He pushed open a door, and went up, clinging to a shaky handrail. He passed a landing where the stairway forked, and then another landing. He came to a last flight of stairs as steep as a ladder, and had begun to mount when a door opened below and a head appeared. It was a head in a nightcap, and it spoke:

"There's no one up there."

Nicolas halted.

"I tell you a fact," declared the head, and disappeared.

Nicolas climbed the rest of the way and struck upon the door, hard, and heard the echo of his knock in the room beyond. He shook the door by its catch; it would not give. He struck and called, and struck and called again, and then groped his way down, step by step, to the corridor below. His steps echoed on the bare planking, and as he passed the door where he had seen the head, it opened again, and the head popped out grotesquely.

"You could have saved yourself the trouble, as I told you."

"Who lives there?" said Nicolas.

"You should know."

"Is it Paul Damas?" he insisted, determined to have some assurance.

"You should know," the head repeated mockingly. "Would you climb all those steps without knowing?"

Chapter Thirty-three

ALL THAT NICOLAS was certain of, as he stood once more in the street, was that the head had not denied that Damas lodged there, behind that closed door. A succession of closed doors, a succession of postponements, of disappointments, of being sent from one person to another, acquiring from each person a new hope and a new reason for grief, for uncertainty—the day which had begun with such high anticipation had become a waking nightmare.

What should he do now? Must he wait until morning to find Paul, to speak to his mother, to free himself of this last torturing uncertainty? He began to walk with no sense of any objective, a mere stirring of the limbs to keep from going numb. He was aware irrelevantly of touches of dampness on his face and about his temples. His head was bare. He did not know where he had left his hat, whether at the Golden Harrow, or at the executioner's, or at the abbé's, or even at the shop in the rue de la Vieille Bouclerie. He summoned a distinct recollection of taking off his hat before entering the room where Sanson sat at table. His mind went blank when he tried to remember his leaving the abbé. If he had broken in on the cardplayers hatless and breathless, he must have seemed sufficiently ill mannered to provoke hostility. Why else should the young woman have wanted to fling his mother's shame at him in such malice? Plunging ahead half blindly down one street after another, he realized with horror that he had already accepted all her implications as the truth. He struggled against this acceptance, but it was too late. The image had become fixed in his mind. His revulsion was no less, but his desire to see his mother was stronger than ever. If only to reproach her, he must see her.

He had gone by habit toward the river and then along the quais in the direction of the Quartier St.-Paul. When he reached the Pont de la Tournelle, he awoke from his daze, and knew where he was but had no memory of how he got there. At that moment he decided that he could not wait until morning to see his mother; he would return to the house where she lodged in infamy with Paul, and he would sit upon the step outside their door until they returned from wherever it was that they were spending their evening. He wondered then what the hour was. It was past curfew.

Beneath the windows of houses which were barred and shuttered at the street level he heard the tones of a viol and a flute in a gay and strongly measured music. The cabarets were closed officially, but behind their darkened fronts business went on as usual to a much later hour. In some bistro Paul and his mother sat drinking, perhaps. He searched his memory for the haunts of the journeymen of the rue St.-Jacques in the days when he had been a prentice. He remembered the coffeehouse near St.-Paul's Churchyard, and the memory brought him a renewal of his loss in the death of Monsieur Bouquet. The sense of guilt at his long absence from home, the superstitious sense that the death of his friend foreshadowed the death of his father, confirmed now, merged with his resentment at the betrayal of his father by his mother and by that journeyman assistant whom he had himself brought to the rue des Lions. He did not debate whether his mother had the right to marry again. She had not the right to marry Paul.

He crossed to the Cité, having remembered a cabaret which had been most popular. He found the place and stood outside the door, trying to think how the two people he sought might be behind that door, and how he would confront them. But there would be other people, also. He could not bear the thought of other faces, other queries and explanations, if by chance the two people he sought should not be there.

He turned away, guarding his solitude. At the entrance to the rue Dauphine he did not again turn to seek Paul's lodging. He held to the Quai, postponing the encounter which he sought, telling himself that he needed more time in which to decide what he should say to his mother, pretending that Paul and his mother could not yet have returned. He went as far as the Pont Neuf, and mingled there for a while in the late traffic, where no one spoke to him, where no one, he thought, observed him. But eventually he returned to the Quai before the Grands Augustins. He approached the portals of the convent church.

The inevitable river mist settled about him and chilled him. The violence in his heart which had demanded instant action, instant decision, had receded a little with all this walking. When he stopped before the church doors, it had become more grief than violence. Had the doors been unlocked, he might have gone inside, and on his knees sobbed out a part of his accumulating shock and pain. But the doors were solid, he knew. He did not even try them. He thrust his hands to warm them inside his coat, inside his shirt, crossed them beneath his throat, dropping his chin upon them. It was the posture of the naked shivering candidates for baptism in the old pictures of Christ and Saint John. He felt ill. He thought, "The soul is the shape of the body; my soul is ill." His fingers touched the square of the scapular, which he had placed about his neck hours ago. He felt, as he caressed it with his fingertips, a roughness at one edge which he had not noticed before. He drew it from beneath his shirt, the better to examine it. His curiosity was not strong. He was moved chiefly by a wish to feel the nearness of his father, to invoke his presence and, in a way, to communicate with him, as if touching the stuff which had lain so many years above his father's heart might counsel him and give him strength. But as he examined the brown woolen square under the dim light he saw that one edge had become unsewn. The stitches were broken; the thread might have been bitten. The break permitted him to insert the tip of his finger, and, doing so, he felt a bit of paper folded within. Excitement filled him. The idea of a message from his father was so strong, and the need of a message so great, that he was convinced before he succeeded in extricating the little scrap of paper, that here was the message he had asked for.

He unfolded it, and saw five letters firmly marked in black ink. DAMAS. He saw in imagination his father left alone with pen and ink to write the names of his supposed confederates. He had written instead the name of his betrayer; and then he had lacked courage to send the message to the only person he could trust. He had lacked courage until that moment in Sanson's cart.

Nicolas stood shaking from cold and excitement, and yet his forehead and his cheeks seemed on fire.

He had reconstructed, before he reached Paul's lodging, a story which was very near the truth. Before he reached the head of the stairs he had made a plan.

He had to wait while Paul struck a light and pulled on his britches over his nightshirt. Through the door he heard the astonishment in Paul's voice, and then expressions of welcome, and rejoicing. The tone seemed false to him, but there was no admitted reason yet that Paul, opening the door at last, should not stand smiling, candle in hand. The smile faded when he could see the expression on the boy's face.

Paul made an exclamation of alarm. Nicolas looked beyond him into the corners beneath the sloping roof, at a curtain hung from a shelf to make a wardrobe, at a bed, also curtained, and having the curtains drawn. There was no fire. The room was as cold as the stairway. He could not see behind the bed whether there was a chair or table or any indication of a woman's presence. He felt a sudden hope that it was only Paul he had to deal with, after all, but he could not trust it. Paul was asking questions—where had he sprung from, where had he been all these years? Nicolas brushed them aside.

"My mother," he said, "where is she?"

His mother answered him, speaking his name. He passed Damas, reached the bedside, and pushed back the curtains. The rings sang on the bar as he did so, stridently, and the sound continued to vibrate in the silence which followed. Marianne sat up in bed, her knees drawn up, her arms clasped about them, over the dark coverlet, expectancy in her face, and no trace of shame. But her hair was loosed about her shoulders. She looked at Nicolas with joy, and he retreated one step.

"Colas," she repeated, using his childhood name, "how did you find us? Did you see the abbé?"

"How did I find you?" he echoed her. "All the rue St.-Jacques knows that you live with my father's murderer." He turned to Paul, thrusting upon him the scapular, which he still held in his hand. "Do you deny it? Look at this. My father sends me to you."

Paul stared at the scapular, then at the boy, uncomprehending and unbelieving. He disregarded the scapular, but, before he had time to consider what he did, said to the boy:

"Your father accused no one. No one, do you understand?"

"Look," said Nicolas. "Can you read? Can you read your name?"

Marianne put out her hand then.

"Let me see, Nicolas. Where did you get this?"

"From Sanson."

He would not let her take it from his hand; he let her read the word, and, having read it, she repeated his "From Sanson" in a whisper of despair.

Paul spoke, his voice, to Nicolas, inexplicably icy, contemptuous and triumphant.

"And so, he wasn't so generous after all."

"What do you mean?" said Nicolas.

Paul addressed himself solely to Marianne.

"And he did not protect us to the very end."

Nicolas saw his mother drop her head upon her knees, hiding her face. Paul said to Nicolas, his voice as sharp and cold, still:

"What do you mean to do with that?"

"Hang you."

Paul laughed.

"It's too late. A scapular, with a name, is not a confession."

"You'll write me a confession then," said Nicolas.

"Do you take me for a fool?" said Paul. His free hand lashed out to seize the scapular, but Nicolas was more quick. He withdrew it beyond Paul's reach and shook it, his fist closed tight about it. He had grown in three years, and besides that, he was filled with a tremendous avenging energy. He commanded Paul, and Paul recognized that he was no match for him. He chose compliance and delay.

"Put down the candle. Fetch a paper and pen."

There was a table by the bed. Paul did as he was told. He found ink and a pen. The point was broken.

"Find another," said Nicolas. "You will write as I tell you."

But Paul could not find another pen.

"Let me tell you what happened, exactly what happened," he pleaded. "After that, you'll understand. It wasn't our fault. You won't judge us so severely."

If he had said, "It wasn't my fault," he might have stood a chance for further argument, but he had, like Marianne, once before, unconsciously included his accomplice.

"Sharpen the pen," said Nicolas, with a face of stone. He offered Paul his knife. Marianne, lifting her head, recognized it, the handle of carved ivory, the crocodile with its tail curled under its belly. She had last seen it when she had talked with Nicolas, trying to explain to him a man she did not well understand herself, his father. Paul, obedient as a schoolboy, took the knife, sharpened the pen, laid down the knife, dipped the pen in ink, and waited. Nicolas kept him waiting. .

"It's sharp," he said nervously, indicating the knife.

Nicolas answered calmly:

"My father and I kept our tools in order." Then, "Write," he said, in absolute authority, "I, Paul Damas, do hereby confess——"

"This will do us no good," said Marianne.

"It's all I need," said Nicolas. "I shall take it to Sanson, who will know what to do with it. It will clear my father's name. It will give me back my patrimony. It will rid you of your shame."

"You can't understand," said his mother. "I'm as much to blame as Paul."

Nicolas had taken up his knife. He stood with it in his fingers, absently; he had been about to put it away in its sheath. Now he stood without moving, and stared at his mother.

"You married Paul," he said at length, in a choking voice, "but you didn't murder my father."

"Yes, no," she said desperately, pushing her hair back from her face with both hands. "I didn't marry Paul. It happened this way." And she told him from the beginning of the first betrayal, which had seemed so harmless, the silly plot, still with no intention of great wrong, and Paul's mistake in planting the pamphlets, her long confusion while she waited, wondering what had become of Paul, what Jean would do, what she ought to do herself. Paul listened, hanging his head, the pen in his hand, the ink drying on the point. Nicolas listened, still without moving, until she spoke of her uncertainty as to what Jean would do when put to the question. Then he said, incredulous, his voice filled with horror:

"You let him be tortured?"

"What else could I do? They would have hanged Paul."

At this Nicolas cried out suddenly, a cry, no word, and struck at his mother. His knife was in his hand. He struck at her directly, and the knife would have entered her breast, but she turned, seeing the lifted hand, and the blade struck her throat close under the ear. A great spurt of blood broke across his hand before he could withdraw it, bright scarlet in the candlelight, pouring, in floods, across the white gown. He dropped the knife, and caught his mother in his arms, as astonished as she had been in his last glimpse of her face.

He tried to stop the blood, pressing his hand against her throat. When he was a child he had one day rescued a kitten from a dog, and had held it in his hands, searching for the harm which must have been done it by the dog's teeth, but he could find no injury to the skin beneath the soft yellow fur. He had held it, thinking it must recover, while it struggled in his hands, twisting, and arching its bony little spine. Then, as he tried to quiet it, caressing it, it had pushed out its curved pink tongue and had all at once gone limp in his hands. The complete resignation, the complete vanishing of the small individual will, had opened for him an abyss of finality. It was his first encounter with death. As he held his mother, she twisted once, like the little cat, then stretched herself, arching away from him, and then went limp in his arms.

He let her body fall to the bed, and turned, all bloodied as he was, toward Paul. His face was blank. Paul read there his own death, and made a motion to retrieve the knife, which lay upon the stained and crumpled sheets. Nicolas reacted to the motion. They both fell upon the knife at once, then straightening, stood beside the bed, their hands locked in a struggle for possession of the blade. There was no question which would win. Nicolas had every advantage of youth, and the overwhelming advantage of his fury. He left Paul, stabbed many times, lying across Marianne's knees. Then he walked out of the room.

The candle burned until it guttered in a pool of tallow, and the tallow solidified in the cold.

Nicolas descended the stairs very slowly, very carefully. He let himself out into the street. The lantern at the intersection still burned, haloed with mist. He walked unsteadily and slowly beneath the lantern, turned the corner, and made his way, still deliberately, to the river.

His hands were sticky with blood, his cheek was stiff where the blood was drying. His lips were stiff. He moistened them with his tongue, and tasted blood. He had but one idea in mind, and that was to wash his hands and his face. There was an *abreuvoir*, he remembered, beyond the Pont Neuf, where horses and cattle were led down to the river to drink. He moved along the Quai des Augustins past the bridge until he came to the stone ramp, and went down that, beneath the stone archway, still walking very slowly, until he came to the river.

It would be delicious to wash his face in the coldest possible water. His face was very hot beneath the stiffening blood. He heard the water lapping in the darkness. He knelt on the wet gravel, and plunged his hands into the water. It was cold as he had imagined, and the night was cold, and even when he had washed his face, in all that coldness, he still burned, as if he were afire. There were no gleams of firelight or of starlight on the water. It flowed, beyond the shallows where he knelt, in steady undulations. There was a breeze upon the water. It was perhaps the breeze of morning, for the Cité rose up to the east of him a solid mass against a less dark sky. He could see the two blunt towers of the cathedral above the roofs and spires.

He was found there at the water's edge by lackeys who brought their horses down to drink, after returning the carriage to its coach house. They came down with flambeaux in the very early hours of the morning, with a great clattering of hooves, talking and laughing, and singing snatches of ribald song, and it seemed to them odd that he should take no notice at all of them, until they pulled him to his feet and turned him about.

Then they saw the blood on his garments, dampened also with mud and water and stained with the black ooze that drifted through the river gravel where he had knelt.

He could not tell them how he came to be stained. He could not remember.

In St.-Lazare he lay ill of a brain fever for a few weeks. Once, during a few hours, he did remember enough to speak of Sanson, and of the room where he had found Paul and his mother, but he died before he could be arraigned for any crime.